PRAISE FOR
SHAILA'S DANCE

"A meditation on belonging, family, and the transformative power of art. Tender and fierce."

—Seattle Book Review

"India's culture, and its world of dance, comes to life under Mohini Dasari's hand."

—Midwest Book Review

"Mohini Dasari's *Shaila's Dance* is a luminous debut—a story that pulses with longing, memory, and the redemptive power of art. With lyrical prose and striking tenderness, Dasari carries us from small-town Idaho to the temples of South India, inviting us into the messy, beautiful work of finding one's roots. Innocence is balanced with emotional maturity, and mythology is woven seamlessly into the human and the divine, creating hypnotic moments where magic feels inevitable. This is more than a novel about dance; it is a meditation on belonging, resilience, and the ties to our mothers and motherlands that stretch across oceans and generations. A deeply moving, unforgettable read."

—Somia Sadiq, author of *Gajarah*

"In the fascinating coming-of-age novel *Shaila's Dance*, an adopted woman explores her birth country and finds renewed strength through friendships and love."

—*Foreword* Clarion Reviews

"*Shaila's Dance* is well-written fiction presenting a heartfelt devotion to dance and creativity. Mohini has woven concepts of Bharatanatyam into a captivating story reflecting her mastery of this art. For me, as her teacher, this book is a precious gift of our shared lessons transformed into something uniquely her own. It is a proud moment to see her dance training take on a powerful new life through her words."

—Smt. Veena Teli, director, Tarangini Creations School of Dance

SHAILA'S
DANCE

SHAILA'S DANCE

A NOVEL

MOHINI DASARI

Published by GFB™, Seattle
www.girlfridayproductions.com

Produced by Girl Friday Productions

Cover design: Emily Weigel
Development & editorial: Gail Kretchmer
Project management: Kristin Duran
Production editorial: Reshma Kooner

Image credits: cover © Shutterstock/Bariskina, Shutterstock/Pikoso.kz, Shutterstock/Sagar Kurhade

ISBN (paperback): 978-1-967510-02-3
ISBN (ebook): 978-1-967510-03-0

Library of Congress Control Number: 2025915747

First edition

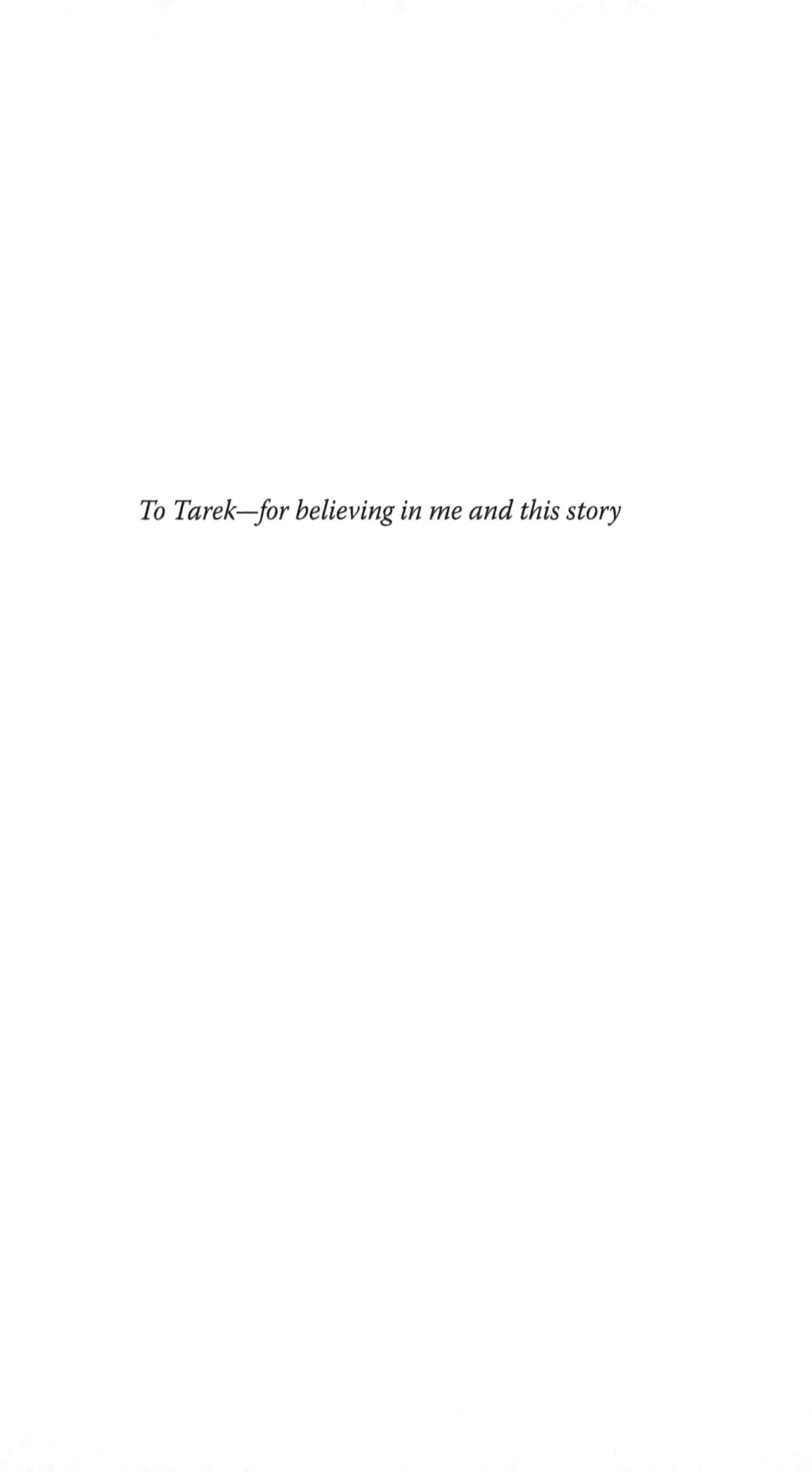

To Tarek—for believing in me and this story

INDIA: ANOKHI'S ROUTE

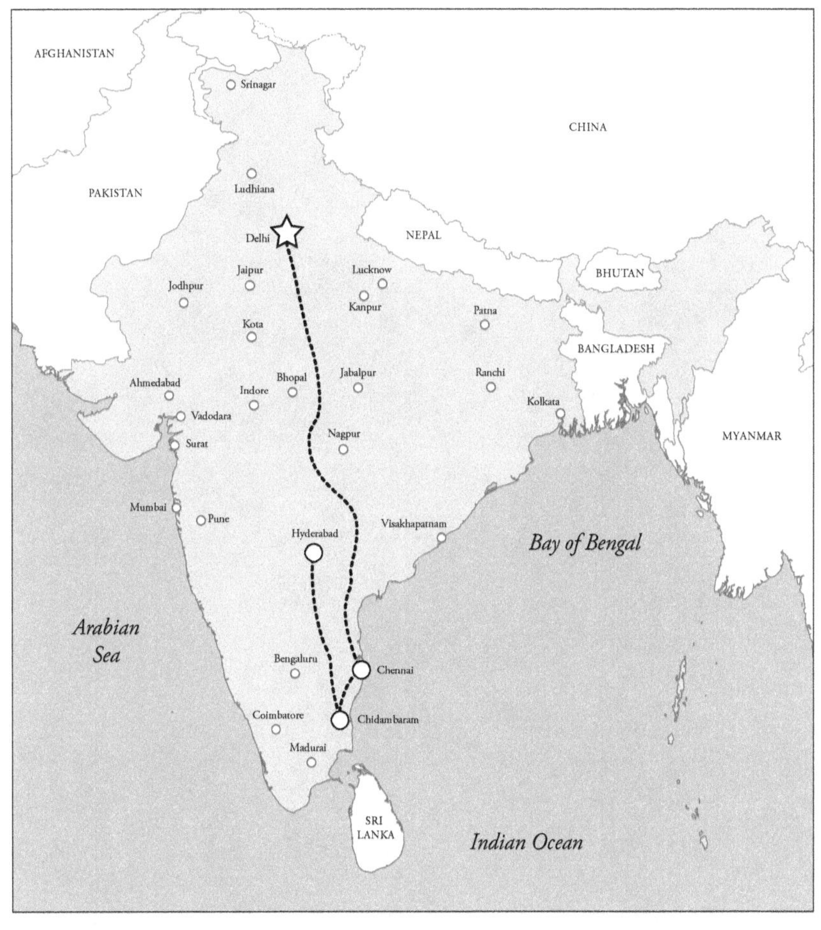

The earth dances in circles.
Idaho, USA

The ghungroos *on Shaila's ankles reverberated forebodingly with each of her movements. Tonight, Shaila's dance was full of anger: Her usually delicate footwork was harsh and exaggerated as she pounded her feet. Her typical buoyant grace was replaced by a fiery passion that pervaded all her movements. With hands pressed together in prayer position, she dropped to her knees, gazing up at the figure with the beating stick. Her wide eyes pleaded for forgiveness.*

Shaila stood one more time and began spinning in slow circles. As she moved across the stage, she glanced in all four directions, miming as if stuck in a cage, desperately looking for a door. She clearly wanted to escape. Eventually, she stopped at the center of the stage, and her dance became focused inward. Her footwork gradually picked up momentum again. The drums beat louder and faster. She began to cry; rivulets of black kajal *swirled down her cheeks. As she returned to spinning, her pleated skirt whirled with her. Faster, faster, faster, signifying the climax of the dance was approaching.*

And then she collapsed into a still heap, the color fading from her, until she became invisible. All that was left was the blood-red ground onto which she had fallen.

CHAPTER 1

My head throbbed and my ears rang like the bells on Shaila's feet. I could no longer pretend to myself that I was asleep. I slid out of bed and walked over to my faded blue window-seat cushion. Tucking my feet beneath my legs, I pressed my forehead against the fogged window. The cold glass felt medicinal against my pounding head.

After finishing a dance, Shaila always disappeared, and I was left to ponder the mysterious silence that she left behind. But I didn't typically feel such intense physical pain as I did tonight. I held my head in my hands and closed my eyes again, trying to squeeze out the incessant hammering that was rapidly taking over me. Impossible, of course. I contemplated going downstairs to get some ibuprofen and water but did not want to risk waking my mother, Sasha. My bedroom door creaked every time it was opened, and she was a light sleeper, just in the room next door.

Why had Shaila been so upset tonight? The pain in her dark eyes seared my heart. Her portrayal of someone large and roguish with a stick threatening to beat her, and the way Shaila collapsed on the floor afterward, had me convinced that she was describing herself in danger. This had been the scariest dance I had ever seen of Shaila's. I could have emerged from it by opening my eyes sooner, but curiosity had outweighed my fear. And it didn't feel fair for me to shut Shaila out of my mind. Her pain had to find its way out, and I had to witness it.

I didn't bother trying to go back to sleep immediately after Shaila's dance; I never did. I would first get up out of bed and go sit by my window or at my desk and write details about her dance in my journal, which I dedicated to all of Shaila's appearances. I began keeping *The Chronicles of Shaila* when I was eight. Now, *The Chronicles* were composed of twenty-one completed notebooks, and I was in the middle of the twenty-second one. When I started them, I'd thought that if I meticulously noted all the details of her dances, I might be able to notice patterns, understand why these dreams were happening, and discover who Shaila was. She didn't scare me, but it did often puzzle me that I had these vivid visions of a woman whom I had never met but felt like I had known my whole life.

Shaila always appeared in the twilight zone between wakefulness and slumber, while I was falling asleep. I learned this at a young age, when I was six—that was the first time I saw Shaila dancing in my mind. I didn't just see her; I *felt* her dancing up there. It was always beautiful, often poignant. She often told stories of animals, spirits, or humans. I came to associate different movements and hand gestures with different creatures and emotions. When she hooked her thumbs together and gently wiggled her fingers, she was a butterfly. When she held her skirt out and put her other hand close to her chest, she was a young woman on an adventurous quest. When she widened her eyes and drew her hands apart, with one arm straight in front of her and the other bent by her side, she was a hunter with a bow and arrow, poised to strike his prey.

I didn't always immediately understand the meanings behind her dances, but journaling often helped. For the first two years that I saw Shaila, I was still too young and overcome by the strange experience of having these visits from this mysterious woman to think about writing them down.

But when I turned eight, and Sasha gifted me a cloth-bound cerulean notebook for my birthday, I took that as a sign that I should start writing about Shaila's dances. Sasha didn't know about Shaila at that time because I hadn't told her yet. I was too worried that seeing these visions might mean there was something wrong with me. So I began confiding in the pages. I had loved writing and reading from a young age, and Sasha's very first notebook gift became the beginning of *The Chronicles*.

As time went on, I found that when I was going through my own struggles—whether feeling lonely at school, recovering from a fight with Sasha, or wondering what I would do with my life—Shaila's dances would often reflect my mood or give me insight into what I should do in each situation. Despite Sasha's kindness and love, I didn't always feel like I could tell her about everything I was experiencing, particularly these mysterious visions. Sasha was always busy, running the restaurant and dealing with her own relationship issues, and I felt bad adding to her stress. My journals gave me an outlet—a space to reflect, doubt, and dream.

Sometimes Shaila's dances seemed to have no apparent meaning, but I was convinced there were hidden messages, and if only I could uncover them, I would be able to learn something insightful about myself or the world around me. Through her deep brown eyes and her body movements, both brimming with expression, I felt I could know anything. Her stories always moved me, leaving me inspired or wiser afterward, often helping me navigate my own life and relationships with more clarity.

Now at the age of sixteen, after close to a decade of chronicling and analyzing Shaila's dances, I had come no closer to cracking the code of why she appeared to me. I was sure there was a reason, something divinely clever I was meant to decode. I wanted an *aha!* moment so badly. More than the moment itself, I wanted the peace that would fill my being after I finally figured out who Shaila was and why she had haunted me for all these years.

Some of Shaila's dances were sad; some were joyful. I had watched her portray fear, devotion, humor, and confusion. I even witnessed seemingly meaningless dances in which her movements floated in the sea of music created by the powerful drum and the lyrical flute.

Tonight's dance, however, with her depiction of a fearful figure about to attack her with a stick, was the first time I had ever seen Shaila so ablaze with anger and fear. She was not a dancer narrating a story; she was a woman in a fit of rage, then terror, her body possessed by a madness that unnerved me. I once saw a movie about a woman who was supposedly possessed by the devil. Her body would periodically shake when the devil entered her and she would dance uncontrollably, laughing hysterically. But the movie wasn't funny at all. It scared me to the core, and I didn't sleep for three nights afterward.

Shaila's dance tonight reminded me of that movie, and if she hadn't been such a constant presence in my life—if tonight's episode had been the first time I saw her—I would have run to Sasha's room, screaming, and jumped right in next to her under the covers. But I *knew* Shaila. Yes, her dance tonight frightened me, but I was also deeply concerned about her. I wanted desperately to ask her what was wrong and why her dance was so full of distress. I wanted to know who had attacked her and why.

No matter how close I felt to Shaila, however, there was a gap: We weren't close enough for conversation. I often wished she would stay in my mind after her dances and speak to me.

But perhaps we were so close that words couldn't fit in the space between us, because there was none—she was of my mind and flesh, though I had no idea why.

The next morning, Sasha saw the sleeplessness in the space under my eyes. She always knew when I hadn't slept because she said little creatures of darkness would make camp in the skin there. Not like traditional dark circles, but more like shadows. Inevitably she'd tell me to go back to sleep so those little creatures of darkness could go make camp elsewhere, because my face was no place for shadows.

"Sleepless night?" She looked up briefly from the omelets she was frying. Her long brown hair was tied in a messy bun with escaped wavy strands framing her small round face. She smiled at me, taking off her red-rimmed glasses and wiping them on her apron, before shaking salt and pepper onto the omelets.

I nodded and inhaled deeply. Mushrooms, goat cheese, and scallions. I walked toward her, kissed her cheek, and pulled out bread to put in the toaster. The aroma in our kitchen was always soothing. Sasha's cooking had a way of comforting me beyond words and physical gestures. Food was a huge part of our life. My earliest memories of home revolved around the kitchen, and her restaurant, which was like a second home.

Cooking was Sasha's love language. As long as I could remember, she cooked for me to show her affection. My homemade lunches were always the envy of my classmates at school. And when I would eat lunch alone, which I often did, I would lose myself in the flavors and feel less lonely as I remembered my mother, who prepared the turkey-and-brie sandwiches, chicken-and-cranberry salads, and squash pastas with tremendous love.

I leaned against the kitchen counter, crossing my arms over my chest as I waited for the bread to finish toasting. She always kept the heater low toward the end of winter, to help save on energy bills.

She sighed as she put the omelets onto plates and handed one to me. We stood in the kitchen eating, as we often did. "Eric isn't coming to work today," she said between bites. "Jessi's sick, and he has to stay home and take care of the baby. Can you help out in the kitchen today?"

"Sure." I nodded. I didn't have much planned for the day. It was striking how time had suddenly opened up, maybe a little too much, after I abruptly dropped out of high school. Though we had talked about it, and she told me she was supportive of my decision to work odd jobs while I figured out what exactly I wanted to pursue outside of traditional schooling, I often wondered how much Sasha disapproved of my decision. I was still trying to figure out whether I wanted to become a writer, given my lifelong love for words, or study dance, inspired by Shaila's mysterious presence in my life.

Sasha, unlike me, had finished school and college before deciding to become an entrepreneur. Her parents had found her to be business savvy and drawn to the kitchen at a young age, and her talents morphed through different iterations of being both a chef and a hostess. She started with bake sales, moved to packing lunches for family and friends so she could practice new recipes, and eventually started her famous neighborhood dinners, where she would cook up three-course meals and raise money for charities while friends and family gathered for delicious suppers together.

Now Sasha owned and operated a small diner named Sweet Potato, the only restaurant in our little idyllic town. She had opened the diner when I was three years old, with her partner at the time, Roy. She named it with her flair for dry humor and irony, as sweet potatoes are incompatible with the Idahoan climate; they thrive in southern and tropical climates.

Throughout elementary and middle school, I would always go to Sweet Potato after school and do my homework in the corner of the diner at the countertop. Eric, one of Sasha's oldest friends and longtime employees, would often bring me a snack, usually a freshly made cheese dip and a pretzel, or a colorful fruit salad with banana bread. During those years, I had few friends. There were girls I walked to class with, boys I sat next to, and kids I did homework with. Yet, I never really spoke much to those kids. Words didn't come to my lips as easily as they came through the nib of my pen or the tip of my pencil. I was painfully timid, and as I entered my preteen years, my self-awareness about my shyness only made it worse.

It hadn't always been that way, though. I remembered laughing and playing with children on the playground in kindergarten. I also remembered going to playdates and having other children over to our own house to play. Sometimes, Sasha would take me to a local park where she would get together with a few moms from my class and we would have picnic lunches and playdates underneath the plentiful Idahoan sunshine.

But things started to change when I turned six and started having dreams of Shaila. I was so shaken by these mysterious visions that, at recess and lunchtime, instead of playing and talking to my friends, I started getting lost in my thoughts. I preferred sitting by myself on a swing, or eating alone at a table, so I could think about what was happening to me.

Kids love to pick on others to feel better about themselves, I soon learned. And nothing attracted bullies like someone who was different and withdrawn. Apparently, as I'd drifted away from friends, I had transformed into prey on the open savannah of our school's playground to some of the boys.

One day, seemingly out of the blue, a couple of fifth-grade

boys took interest in my escalating introversion despite the fact that I was a few years younger than them. Dylan and Max stormed up to my table, snatched my lunch, and threw everything onto the floor before I had a chance to eat a single bite. They jumped and stomped on my metallic flowery lunch box until it was irreversibly bent and damaged. All the while they shouted and heckled, calling me weirdo, loner, loser.

The cafeteria was silent; not a single kid said anything while this was happening. One of the teachers finally came running over and took the boys to the principal's office, but nothing could erase the memory of that day. My face was hot with shame as I felt the stares of all the children sitting there, watching me in silence, as I retrieved my squashed sandwich, crumbled cookie, and disfigured lunch box off the floor. Tears fell down my face, and I skulked out of the cafeteria. My teacher called Sasha to tell her what had happened, and she picked me up early that day, hugging me as I cried to her outside, shaking with sobs. She continued to pick me up for a while after the incident, believing it was better to show up in her creaky old station wagon than to have me face more bullying on the bus. But that made me feel even more embarrassed and singled out.

It was bad enough that Dylan and Max hated me even more after they were sent to the principal's office. Every time I walked by them in the hallways after that day, they made ghoulish faces at me, signed that they were going to cut my head off, and showed me the middle finger. Although I didn't know what that meant, I inferred it was bad. Then one day, as I waited for Sasha to pick me up, Dylan picked on me again.

"Where's your dad, Anokhi? Oh right, you don't have one. Weirdo." He spat on my old tennis shoes.

There were no other children in my class or neighborhood who had a single parent. All the other kids I knew had two parents. I looked down at my sneakers, not knowing what to say. I hoped that my lack of reply would bore Dylan, and he would leave me alone. But he didn't move.

By then, a few other kids on their way to the bus stopped to find out what was going on.

"You don't have a dad?" someone else asked.

"No," I said quietly. I looked ahead at the road, desperate for Sasha to come so I could be done with this conversation.

"Why don't you have a dad?" another kid asked. "How is that even possible?"

"I'm adopted," I said, my voice shaking. The word felt big in my mouth.

"What the heck does that mean?" Max jeered, putting his face close to mine.

"I . . ." My throat burned as I tried to take deep breaths and move away from Max. But he just stepped closer to me.

I felt suffocated by all the kids standing near me, listening to this conversation. Sasha had told me several times before that my birth parents had not been able to take care of me but loved me very much and wanted what was best for me. She had also told me she brought me to her home here, in the US, all the way from India, where some of her relatives are from. She always assured me that she loves being my mother and is proud that we are a family.

But in that moment, with Max and Dylan breathing in my face, everything felt blurred. I was afraid that Max was going to hurt me. But more than that, I felt like I didn't know who I was, or why I existed. The ground beneath me had seemed to shake when they asked me about my father, and I didn't know how to defend myself. It all made me feel sick to my stomach.

Finally, after what seemed like forever, Sasha pulled up in her station wagon.

On the car ride home that day, which is my earliest concrete memory of having a detailed conversation about my adoption with Sasha, I pleaded with her between sobs. "Mommy, why don't I have a daddy?"

"Oh, honey," Sasha said, looking at me thoughtfully in the rearview mirror. "You do have a dad. I just don't know where he is." Her eyes were big and serious, and I could tell she wanted to hug me but couldn't because she was driving.

"What do you mean you don't know where he is?!" I screamed, kicking the passenger seat in front of me so hard that Sasha hit the brakes in shock. There was no one in front of or behind us, and the tires screeched on the quiet country road.

We pulled over to the side of the road. The drive home from my elementary school was quite rural, the back roads lined by quiet farms and sprawling fields. Dark storm clouds loomed above us, and I heard a crackle of thunder in the distance, but rain did not fall—yet.

"Anokhi," she said quietly, staring at the road ahead, before turning around to look at me. "You are my daughter. I love you more than anything in this world. I know it's hard to not have a family that looks like most other families. But just because you don't have a dad who lives with us doesn't mean you are not loved, or that you don't have one. It also doesn't make our family any less whole. You—"

I kicked the seat again, and this time, my shoe smashed through the fraying cloth lining, leaving a large hole. "I don't care!" I screamed. "I want a daddy like the other kids. I don't want to just have you! It's not fair!"

Sasha gasped. Her hand flew to her mouth. She stared at me for a few moments, and we both were silent. I knew I had crossed a line, though I could hardly make sense of the fear and anger that was racking my body. I saw a tear fall from her eye, but she quickly brushed it away. She reached her hand back to touch my knee, but I jerked my leg back, hugged my knees to my chest, and glared out the window, refusing to look at her.

I don't remember any words being said after that. We drove home in silence, and rain began to fall heavily in sheets, pattering on the car windows.

I looked at Sasha once through the rearview mirror and saw that both of us had tears streaming down our faces.

CHAPTER 2

We ate dinner quietly that evening, which was unusual because typically Sasha and I would chat animatedly during meals. I would tell her about what happened at school with my teachers, or she would tell me stories from work. Our town was situated off a major highway, so we would get lots of folks passing through from different states, often truck drivers but also people taking a scenic road trip across the country. This made for interesting characters who stopped at the diner, which I always enjoyed hearing about.

But that evening, it was as if neither of us knew how to speak in the aftermath of the car ride. The next morning, a Saturday, Sasha rapped on my door. It was around eleven, the sun lazily high in the sky and looking exhausted, as if she were about to drop down to the earth at any moment. I hadn't gone downstairs for breakfast; I was feeling too terrible. I had never yelled at Sasha like that before.

I was sitting at the window seat in my room, staring outside. The ground was now covered in white—a calming, soft layer of snow after the rough rainstorm the previous afternoon. The trees, the road, the fields—all white. My room was filled with white too, like a snow haven in itself—white walls, comforter, pillows, and furniture. Each of the other rooms in our one-story home had ostensible color themes: the lilac bathroom, the marigold kitchen, the pea green sitting room. Secretly, Sasha could not bear the idea of choices, which inevitably meant saying yes to one thing and no to a multiplicity of other possibilities. So white, for me and my room, was perfect; the presence of all colors, it encompassed everything and betrayed nothing.

Her eyes twinkled as she pushed open the thick wooden door. Her face, soft and kind, didn't harbor any evidence of anger from yesterday's incident, but I could see sadness in the soft set of her brows and the curl of her pale pink lips.

I stared at my mother's face, as if for the first time. Even without touching her cheeks, I knew Sasha's olive skin was as soft as a baby's. Her hair fell in unplanned, picturesque dark brown curls upon her small delicate shoulders.

Too beautiful to be my mother.

I had never thought this thought before, but for a moment, it flashed in my young mind: the unshakable and unsettling feeling of doubt. I tried to dismiss it.

But really, we resembled one another less than a fork does a spoon. We were both composed of flesh and bones, just as a fork and spoon in a set may be composed of the same material. Yet many of our features were contrasting. My hair was wild and frizzy, always pleading but never yielding to being tamed; Sasha's was as calm and soft as silk. Sasha's eyes were warm and light like almonds; mine were dark brown, deep and, according to some people, mysterious.

There was nothing externally extraordinary about that Saturday morning. November had wrapped her arms around the slender northern tip of Idaho where we lived, her embrace chock-full of snow and something akin to love, smelling of burnt wood and stories waiting to be told around a fire.

Yet this morning, for some unknown reason, while letting my eyes brush over the beautiful countenance of Sasha, I was filled with unease.

Too beautiful to be my mother.

It was as if, incited by the incident the day before with Dylan and Max and the other children asking me about my lack of a father, the ground had been pulled out from underneath me. I suddenly doubted everything I knew about my safe little home, loving mother, and small hometown. I felt my heartbeat in my throat, sharp and acidic.

It hurt—this undeniable feeling of displacement that only needed substantiation. I knew I was adopted—or I thought I knew what that meant. But suddenly, after yesterday's events, I was questioning my very existence in this house.

Sasha, who had a quick eye for my ill-disguised changes in demeanor, saw the lump forming in my throat. I think she even felt the pain I felt. Her face grew tense with concern.

"What is it, Anokhi?" she said, coming to sit beside me on the window seat, putting her arm around me.

I never lied to Sasha. Yet I didn't always tell her everything. Though I had been having dreams about Shaila for over two years now, I hadn't told her about them yet. It felt too embarrassing, and I was scared that she would think something was wrong with me.

Now, as I looked at my mother sitting beside me, I felt so incredibly far away from this woman who had been raising me with such love and devotion since I was little. The distance felt like betrayal. I wanted to pull my hair out and make the feeling go away.

Sasha had told me before that my birth parents could not take care of me, and that she had adopted me as a baby, so I could live with her and she could raise me and love me. She told me she was also my mother, and I her daughter, and we were a family. But until recently, this all felt like a vague part of my backstory. Now, in the aftermath of our fight yesterday, it was as if pieces were falling into place that I had not understood before. The other kids asking me about my lack of a father had me wondering about what my birth parents looked like. Did they look like me? Where exactly was India anyway? Is that where my home was, rather than here?

It had always felt enough to know that Sasha and I were a family, albeit small. Sasha's parents had died when she was in college, and she didn't have any siblings. She had moved to Idaho with Roy and opened up the diner, and by then she had adopted me. When their relationship ended, she and I just had each other. Committed to the diner, she decided we would stay here and, with her meager savings, she bought the small house that we still live in today.

There had been men who had come and gone in Sasha's life since Roy, but she was always fiercely protective of the two of us as a family unit. Our atypical family didn't really bother me much until now. I felt loved and cared for and didn't understand how life could be any different. But things changed when the kids started calling out these differences and mocking me. Suddenly I felt incomplete, revealed, and insecure. I felt confused about Sasha too. I knew she loved me. But why was our family different? Why was no one else that I knew like us?

In that moment, sitting with Sasha in the aftermath of my dramatic outburst in the car, confusion filled my little body, and I did not know what to say. I did not know how to ask Sasha to tell me more about my birth parents. It felt rude, especially after how I had yelled at her and kicked a hole in the seat of her car.

Instead, I felt the urge to tell her about Shaila. The previous night, after the somber afternoon and evening, I had a spooky vision of Shaila dancing a tale about two ghosts. It was a man and a woman who loved each other, but they were sad for some reason, and I couldn't understand why. In the dance they moved toward and away from each other, back and forth, until ultimately, they drifted away from each other and the dance ended on a lonely note. I had a strange feeling Shaila might have been telling me about my birth parents through that dance.

"Mommy," I said finally, breaking the silence. I could feel the tension in her grip around my shoulder relax once I uttered the word. "Sometimes at night I see a woman dancing in my dreams. And . . . sometimes I can't sleep because of it."

Even as I said the words I knew it was a gross understatement, only a fraction of the complexity that was Shaila and her enigma, whose feet had been rooted firmly in the ground of my mind for the past couple of years. But my eight-year-old brain did not have the capacity to articulate the complex feelings that Shaila brought up within me.

Sasha brushed the hair out of my face, and I scooted closer to her. She stroked my hair. She wasn't smiling or frowning, and I knew she was trying not to show distress and confusion. She was trying to have as open an expression as possible. I loved her so much for her earnestness and the pink color that enveloped her ears when she felt stressed but wanted everyone else to be at peace.

"Tell me more, sweetie. What is the woman like?" she asked softly.

I began to talk to her about Shaila and her dancing. I told her about the stories of animals, spirits, people, and feelings in her dances. I recalled the first time I saw her—or the first time I remembered seeing her. I didn't tell her that I was scared of Shaila, because I wasn't. I told her that Shaila was beautiful and that her hair flowed down her shoulders and looked blacker than ink, often woven into tight, thick braids. I told her about the bells on her ankles, the white flowers in her hair. Her strong, expressive, storytelling eyes, her graceful dancing body.

Sasha nodded as she listened. Suddenly, my heart leaped.

"Do you know her too?!" I asked. Was it possible Sasha saw Shaila in her dreams too? For a moment, my world brightened; I felt a little less alone and a little less unsettled than I had been feeling for so long. I also felt relief at finally telling Sasha about Shaila. I hadn't realized how much keeping this secret from her had been weighing me down.

"No." She shook her head. "But I think I can picture her, in my mind, from what you are describing."

I hung my head. I was filled with hope, however brief, that Sasha would be able to validate my visions of Shaila with some knowledge or insight that would make me feel more rooted to reality.

"Anokhi, I know this has been a tough last few weeks for you with what has been going on at school," Sasha said. Her eyes momentarily flitted to the window, and she gazed outside with a lost look in her eyes.

I nodded. I wasn't sure if she wanted me to speak, and I didn't want to interrupt whatever she was about to say. I craved comfort from her words, in whatever shape it would come.

Finally, she continued. "I know it is hard not having a dad. And we have talked about this before, but as you are growing up it is totally normal that you will have more questions about where you came from. And"—she paused, raising her eyebrows slightly—"I think perhaps your dreams—or visions—of Shaila may be related to some of your memories from your past. Your past before me."

"My past?" I asked. I didn't understand what she meant.

"I adopted you from India when you were a little baby. I brought you back to Idaho with me so I could take care of you and we could be a family," she explained.

"I know," I said. She had told me all this before. She had even shown me India on the globe in my room, its triangular tip pointing down into the Indian Ocean.

"But maybe I didn't do a good job explaining things to you," she said, shaking her head and putting it in her hands for a moment. I wondered if she was going to cry. Sasha was a very strong woman. Yesterday in the car was one of the first times I had seen her cry. I waited, too scared to say anything that might provoke more tears.

"You are my daughter, and I am your mother. But you also had—have—another mother. And a father. Even though I do not know them or know who they are. You did have—and might still have—two other parents in this world," she said softly.

I felt a sinking feeling of dread in my chest. I could remember having these conversations when I was younger, but somehow it never hit the way it did today. It felt like an abstraction before. But sitting here, hearing her say this, in the aftermath of our fight yesterday, I felt out of place beside her. My hair was frizzy, hers was smooth. Her skin was olive, mine was dark brown. We didn't look alike. And now that I was hearing, as if for the first time, that I didn't have a father here, and I had a different set of parents somewhere else, across the world, I felt torn, as if I had nothing to anchor me to this white bedroom, the walls around us, or the snowy world outside. I felt sick.

Sasha put her arm around me. "You are my daughter, Anokhi, and I love you. That will never change, okay?" she said calmly but firmly. "I did not give birth to you—meaning you did not come out of my tummy. But you are my daughter. There was a mommy and a daddy that also loved you, but they could not take care of you in India. And I am so sorry that I do not know more about them. If I knew them, and if it was possible, I would love for you to meet them—for us to know them."

"Why could they not take care of me?" I asked, my voice quivering, on the verge of tears. I felt sad as I wondered if they did not like me, or what I had done for them to want to give me away.

"Oh sweetheart," Sasha said softly. "It's nothing you did wrong. They may have been sick. Or something else happened. I don't know, unfortunately," she said, shaking her head.

"Do you know what they looked like?" I asked. I had a feeling she would say no, but my mind yearned to conjure a picture of these two mysterious people.

"I don't," she said quietly. "But I am sure they wanted what was best for you."

I threw off the blanket that was draped over us and threw my arms around her neck. I cried into her soft off-white sweater.

Finally, when I felt I could speak again, I asked, "So you think Shaila is related to my past? From where I was born? From . . . India?" The word felt far away on my tongue.

Sasha sighed and tucked a stray piece of hair behind my ear. "I don't know, sweetheart. But it does make me wonder," she said, looking out the window pensively. "I think dreams have meanings, even if we don't always know them right away. And I wonder if, perhaps, there is some deeper meaning to Shaila. Perhaps time will tell."

"Maybe." I nodded, wiping my tears with the back of my hand.

"I'm sorry, Anokhi, that I don't have more details about your birth parents. If you'd like, we can look at the pictures from my trip to India, when I went there to adopt you," she offered.

"That's okay," I said. I had seen the pictures before. She kept an album underneath our coffee table in the living room. It was dark red with softened corners. Inside there were large plastic sheets filled with photos from that trip she took in 1990 to India to adopt me. I had taken my favorite photo from that album out and put it on my nightstand, and she had framed it for my fifth birthday. It was a picture of Sasha, her hair loose, wearing a light flowery *kurta*, holding me in her arms. My eyes were dark, and my lips curved into an O, with one little hand grabbing the collar of her shirt, and the other pointing at the camera.

I don't recall either of us saying much more on that snowy Saturday morning that changed our lives forever. I believed Sasha when she said she didn't know more about my birth parents. But the emptiness inside me started to grow after that. It hurt to have more questions than answers about my past.

And just like that—not because I loved her any less after that day or because she had become less of a mother to me, but because the universe had taken the word "mom" out of my mouth—I began calling her Sasha.

I could tell Sasha was hurt when I stopped calling her Mom, but she never directly said so. I could also tell she felt bad about the bullying I had faced at school for not having a father. She began checking in with me regularly about my dreams of Shaila. I knew she was concerned and cared, but I found myself getting irritated with her questions. I felt a defiant streak rise within me, though I knew I was not being completely fair to her. As she couldn't give me more details about my birth parents, I began to rationalize to myself that it wasn't my duty to give her more details about Shaila—especially because I didn't fully understand her myself.

Her mention of how Shaila might be connected to my past from India haunted me, but I didn't know what to do with that thought. So, I tucked it deep into a corner of my mind, but I didn't forget it.

A few weeks after we had that conversation in my bedroom, Sasha made an appointment for us with a family counselor. We drove almost two hours to the nearest big city to meet with them. I didn't fully understand why we were going and didn't really want to go. I didn't want to talk to anyone about my being adopted if they couldn't give me answers.

It was an hour-long session. To my surprise, the counselor, a serious thin woman named Laura, asked me how I would like to be addressed and what I would like to call Sasha.

I looked at Sasha in panic, but she simply nodded calmly at me.

"I . . . I'm Anokhi," I said. "And . . . I like to call her Sasha." It sent a surge of guilt through me to say that out loud, though I had already been calling her Sasha instead of Mom for a few weeks now.

"Okay," Laura said. "Sasha, is there anything you would like to share with Anokhi about that?"

Sasha looked down at the floor and was quiet for a moment. We were both sitting next to each other on an old red couch. The counselor was sitting in an armchair adjacent to us. The room had a bunch of books on a bookshelf but no windows. There was a vase of fake flowers on the coffee table. The office made me feel sadder about everything between Sasha and me.

"Well, Anokhi," Sasha said, turning to look at me. "I am sad that you don't want to call me Mommy anymore. I wonder if you are angry with me."

I looked at the counselor. Her face didn't show much expression. I looked at Sasha, who looked thoughtful but hurt.

"I don't know," I said. I felt hot and stressed. I didn't feel like making eye contact with either of them.

"It's okay, Anokhi," Laura said, patting my knee. "We can also talk without Sasha in the room, if that would help you get your feelings out."

I looked at Sasha, who had a brief look of surprise on her face before she smoothed it out. I felt confused, not wanting to hurt her more, but feeling like me saying more or less would hurt her in different ways.

Finally, I said, "I'm sorry, Sasha. I'm not angry. I love you. But I don't know what I am supposed to say right now. Ever since those kids teased me about not having a dad, I have been feeling very confused."

They were both quiet, and I wondered for a moment if I had said too much. But Sasha smiled and squeezed my hand.

"Thank you, Anokhi, for telling us how you feel," Laura said.

"Yes, thank you, Anokhi," Sasha said, smiling, though it wasn't her typical smile. Her lips were closed, and she still looked hurt. "I cannot imagine how hard this is for you. I just want you to know I love you no matter what."

We sat there in silence for a couple of moments. I gazed longingly at the wall, imagining there was a window through which I could escape the quiet discomfort of the room.

Finally, Laura cleared her throat and spoke. "Anokhi, do you want to tell us more about what happened at school that brought on a lot of these recent feelings?"

I found it funny that she was asking me if I wanted to tell them more, knowing that was the whole reason we were here. Resigned, I began telling her about Dylan and Max and the questioning that prompted my outburst in the car and the conversation with Sasha the next morning. The windowless room suddenly felt even smaller. But I kept talking. I kept my gaze focused on Laura. It felt too hard to look at Sasha.

Strangely enough, the more I talked, the easier it felt. After I had spoken for a while and answered some of Laura's follow-up questions, Laura asked Sasha how she felt after hearing me tell her about all this.

With tears in her eyes, she replied quietly, "Horrible. I feel horrible knowing that my daughter is going through all this at school. But . . . I'm grateful she is willing to talk to me about it, even though it's hard."

We looked at each other for a moment. I blinked back tears

too, though whether they were for me, or Sasha, or the strange turn in our relationship, I didn't know.

"I think this is a good spot to stop for today. Thank you, Sasha and Anokhi, for both having these hard conversations. It is normal to have many complicated feelings when talking about adoption. I am here to help you both with these conversations. I can tell you both love each other very much."

And of course, I did. But somehow, each conversation we had about this recently just made me feel worse. We walked out of Laura's office, and I had a feeling wash through me that I never wanted to come back.

As we left the city, we stopped at a McDonald's on our way to the highway. Sasha and I ate our burgers and fries parked in the parking lot, not saying much.

"Anokhi," she finally said, crushing the wrappers into the brown paper bag and wiping her lips with the back of her hand. "I love you very much. I'm sorry if I have hurt you in any way by not talking about your adoption with you more clearly. I've tried to bring it up with you since you were little . . . but I guess it wasn't enough."

I looked at her. I noticed wrinkles under her eyes and some shadows on her face I had never seen before. It struck me in that moment that, as hard as this was for me, it was hard for her too.

I decided to try my best to let go of the heaviness I had been holding in my heart for the last few weeks.

"I know, Mom . . . Sasha. I love you too. You did talk to me about it. I just don't think I really understood what it meant—that I could have other parents somewhere else, far away—until now," I sighed.

She winced when I said Sasha but did not say anything. She squeezed my shoulder as she turned the car back on to pull out of the parking lot and start our long drive home.

I promised myself that day I would try to love her as

though nothing had changed within me. But I felt a distance grow between us after that visit to Laura. I knew Sasha had taken me there because of what had happened over the last few weeks. I was eight years old, old enough to start to really grasp the things she had told me when I was younger about being adopted. And now, the details were starting to mean different things to me. India had previously felt like an abstraction. In the context of my strange visions of Shaila, and these recent hard conversations with Sasha, I wondered more and more about the place I was from. I stared at Sasha with a new curiosity, whereas previously I had only felt familiarity with my mother.

I think she wanted to bridge the distance and didn't know how, and that's why we went to Laura. But as we drove home, we both knew we weren't going to go back there, though I don't think we had any idea of how to close the expanding gap of once-imperceptible space between us.

Sasha brought me up with a velvety appreciation for literature, culture, and art, but social skills fell to the wayside after the bullying incidents early in elementary school. After my two formative memories of being bullied, in the cafeteria and as I waited outside school to be picked up, nothing quite as bad happened afterward. But I felt an unmistakable wall crop up between me and the other children. I found myself veering away from other kids, seeking solitude and occasionally talking to a librarian or a teacher. I still liked listening to conversations, particularly between grown-ups, but became much quieter than I had ever been.

My childhood wasn't all sad, though. My happiest memories were during evenings and weekends, when I wasn't at school. Though I loved the learning aspect of my education,

I looked forward to weekends and days off, mostly because of the anxiety I developed about being around other children and the fear of being teased or bullied again. Sasha and I spent weekends reading, cooking, and making bead jewelry on the front porch. I found peace in our quiet routines and simple comforts.

By the time I reached seventh grade, my school experiences had improved, and I had begun to develop some true friendships. Better yet, that was the year that Sasha was with Jay, a carpenter who built just about everything within a fifty-mile radius of our town: houses, stores, barns—everything. He had a trim dark brown beard, which I used to imagine would scrape Sasha's soft cheeks when they kissed. Not that I ever saw them kiss, but I was sure they did—their love for each other was hard to miss.

Sasha belonged to the class of people who liberally dole out smiles to the world. I never thought it could be possible for anyone to smile more than she did, and when Jay came into her life, her smile grew even bigger and brighter, enveloping her face with a sweet radiance that lifted those around her.

Jay was a fantastic cook—secretly, I thought he was even better than Sasha. He used to pack the best lunches for me and prepare our meals at home, giving Sasha more time to work and manage Sweet Potato. Although he never moved in with us during that year they were together, he was at our house frequently, from morning until night, and it felt as if our small house had stretched its sides to allow him to fit in there with us. I have happy memories of that year, the three of us sitting together and enjoying meals, laughing on the couch over silly jokes, and watching sitcoms before bedtime.

I hardly knew what to say when I came home one day and Jay wasn't there. Sasha was sitting, bleary-eyed, on the couch. I hugged her and she cried into my shoulder for almost half an hour without saying a word. Over the next few weeks, her smile seemed to be on permanent leave. She even closed the diner for a few days so she could sit on our sofa and stare into her lap, then a book, then out the window. She didn't ask me how school was every afternoon like she had usually done. We didn't do any arts and crafts or reading in our spare time. It was awful. She was quiet, and so was our home—cold and incomplete without Jay's hearty, infectious laughter and deep, husky voice. Emptiness is only tangible when you know the potential for something to exist there—when something *did* exist there and then is gone. I suppose that is how Sasha felt about the space in her life where Jay used to stand, smiling and laughing and loving her.

I never asked Sasha why they broke up, and she never told me. In the weeks and months that followed their breakup, I found myself missing Jay more than I realized I would. He had filled a void in my life that I never knew existed, because it had never been occupied before. He was almost like a father to me, though I didn't realize it until after he left our lives. I especially cherished the times he took me driving in his pickup truck on weekends to do errands for his construction jobs; we'd chat about everything from music to books to school. And boys. He would sometimes tease me about not having a boyfriend, telling me he would come to school and help me pick out someone suitable. One warm, fall afternoon, we were driving home from the closest Home Depot—which was about thirty miles away.

"Anokhi," he said, rolling down his window, breathing in the fresh air and running his hand through his curly brown hair. "When are you gonna let me come to school with you? We gotta find you a boyfriend before your school dance in a few weeks!"

I laughed, shaking my head, and rolled down my window to stick my hand out. The breeze beat against my palm as the truck sped up on the highway. Jay was a fast driver but somehow never got a speeding ticket.

"I don't want a boyfriend, Jay," I said, uncomfortable even talking about boys. I had never had a boyfriend, though there was a boy in my class, Cooper, whom I did have a crush on. He was nerdy, quiet, and loved books. I usually saw him in the library, and I didn't know how he felt about me because we had never spoken. Both of us were shy, and I assumed we would probably never speak to one another. But I admired him nonetheless.

"Oh come on," Jay said. "Having a boyfriend isn't bad. Look at Sasha, she doesn't seem too unhappy having one, eh?" He glanced over at me from the road, a twinkle in his eye.

I laughed. "Good point. But what you and Sasha have is special. I don't know if a lot of people have relationships like that."

He was quiet for a moment. Usually, he was quick to respond with wit and sarcasm, and I was unaccustomed to hearing him pause like this. Finally, he said, "Yes. It's hard to find a good relationship. With anyone—not just a boyfriend or girlfriend. Even with a parent, a sibling, or a friend. It takes work. And some magic."

"Magic?" I asked.

"Yeah, magic." He nodded, sipping his iced coffee with one hand, the other draped over the steering wheel. "There's gotta be a spark—a connection. And then the two people have to build on that spark. Put in some work. But magic, or love, carries the flame a long way, in addition to the work two people put in."

I nodded. It was a good point. I had felt since Jay came into our lives that some of the magic that had been missing between me and Sasha had come back too. Having him around was good not just for us individually, but for our relationship as mother and daughter, it seemed. It provided more balance, another perspective in the house, and more variety to our conversations. It felt like he was the missing piece of our puzzle.

"Anyway," he said. "You just let me know when you get over your shy thing. I'll be at your school in a snap of your fingers, and we'll find you the best boyfriend there is at that school of yours."

"Okay, Jay," I said, rolling my eyes. "I'll let you know."

"You're a smart young lady, Anokhi," he said, looking at me thoughtfully. "You deserve nothing but the best. Just remember that."

I was surprised by his serious comment. I smiled, unsure of what to say. But it filled me with a vague warmth—having him care about me, being protective of me, and wanting the best for me. I didn't know it at the time, but I would realize later—it was the warmth of feeling loved and looked after by someone akin to a father.

CHAPTER 3

Somehow, I made it through the next few years of my awkward adolescence without Jay—and that notion that he would find a boyfriend for me never came to fruition. Then, in the middle of my junior year, I fell out of high school. The term "dropped out" didn't feel accurate; my decision had been a long time coming, though not one that I had been consciously anticipating. I fell as one might fall out of a chair or out of the sky. The gravity of my approaching adulthood and uncertain future, combined with my even more uncertain past, pulled me down.

One Wednesday, in the middle of precalculus, I was staring out the dirty classroom window at the gravel parking lot and saw various people coming and going. And laughing. I then pivoted my gaze to the chalkboard, where I saw nothing but white lines and scribbles. My teacher's voice, as he droned on about equations and variables, became a background hum. A crushing emptiness came over me as I felt the utter meaninglessness of everything around me. I wondered how I had come this far and saw no future for myself within the walls of this building.

So, I got up and walked out.

It was like there was a string at the top of my head, and an invisible force gently picked it up and pulled me out of the brick building, down the street, and walked me the four miles home. Sasha was still at work at the diner, so I sat on the couch and waited for her, composing and recomposing in my head my explanation about why I had left. And why I could never go back.

Sasha opened the front door a little past three o'clock, home at her usual time after closing the diner after lunch.

"Anokhi?" she called. I knew she had seen my backpack by the front door. I usually wasn't home until four.

"I'm in the living room," I called meekly as a quiet panic rose in my chest. Now the gravity of my decision weighed even more heavily on me, knowing I had to confess the decision I'd made aloud. And why.

I sat on the couch, facing the fireplace, and didn't turn around to look at her when I heard her walk in. I still had no idea what I was going to say.

"Everything okay?" she asked as she sat down beside me, raising her eyebrows and placing her hand on my shoulder. The twinkle in her eyes had finally returned now—it had been absent for several years after Jay had left. Which meant she was in a place where she could hear some difficult news.

"Not really," I said, drawing my knees to my chest but still unable to look her in the eye. "I walked out of math class today."

She was quiet for a moment. I finally managed to look at her face. Her expression was concerned.

"Are you planning on going back?" she asked quietly.

I sighed. She knew me too well—I could tell she already knew the answer without me saying it.

"No," I whispered.

We sat there for a few moments in silence. I couldn't read what was going on beneath her calm demeanor. Finally, she spoke.

"Okay, Anokhi. We can talk about this when you're ready. I can't know exactly what you're thinking, but I can imagine this is not an easy day for you." She put her hand on my cheek for a moment, then got up, leaving me to the solitude she knew I needed as I wrestled with my fading sense of self.

I didn't talk to Sasha much that day at dinner; I felt too horrible to speak. She could tell I was feeling embarrassed, and she unfolded a newspaper to read as she ate, graciously leaving me with my thoughts. I got up and went to my room and lay in bed, feeling as though my life was over. I knew I hadn't made the wrong decision, but I also didn't know what decision could come after this one.

Around nine o'clock, the time we usually stopped watching TV or reading on the couch and made our way up to our bedrooms, Sasha knocked on my door.

"Come in," I said, uncertain whether I had the energy to talk with her.

Sitting on my window seat, she regarded me for a moment and then looked out at the dark night sky.

"Anokhi, this is a big decision you have made today," she said, turning her gaze back to me. "You may not have all the answers, and that's okay. But as your mother, who is responsible for taking care of you, it's important to me that we talk about this. Even though it's uncomfortable."

For the first time ever, I sensed a bit of steeliness in her usually soft gaze. I sat up and hugged my knees to my chest.

"Please don't be mad at me, Sasha," I pleaded.

"I'm not, Anokhi. But I am confused. And concerned. I need you to talk to me and help me understand why you have chosen to not go to school anymore."

I paused for a moment, drew a deep breath, and closed my

eyes. It somehow felt easier to talk about this with my vision shut to the outside world and, specifically, to her countenance, which betrayed some understandable frustration.

"I have felt out of place at school for a while," I said. "You know how after I was bullied in elementary school, I felt anxious about going to school for years? Even though I always enjoyed subjects like English and history, and I made some friends by the time I got to middle school, I still found being in the classroom overwhelming, and I couldn't wait for the day to end so I could go to the diner or come home and do my homework. I don't mind doing reading, writing, or assignments—that was never the issue."

I opened my eyes. She was nodding, and she looked curious about what I was going to say next. She didn't look mad.

Feeling encouraged by this, I closed my eyes again and continued. "I did well in a lot of subjects. But when I met Kale when we started high school, I began to think about the world differently. I began to ask myself questions about what's next—and realized that maybe I don't have to go to college just because it's what everyone else does. That maybe I should listen to the voice inside me that has always told me that I don't feel quite right at school, and that my calling is somewhere outside the walls of the classroom."

I opened my eyes and found that Sasha had an eyebrow raised. A shadow crossed over her face. "So this is all about Kale?" Her tone was a bit sharp.

Kale had been my best friend since freshman year. His parents moved to Washington State from Hawai'i when he was ten, and then later to Idaho just before he started high school. Kale was warm, confident, and kind, and his smile was broad and effusive. Like mine, his hair was untamed and unruly, and he wore it in long, free-flowing curls to his shoulders that would often fall over one of his eyes. Perhaps what initially drew me to him was that he was the only other kid at my school who looked somewhat like me—brown skin and frizzy dark hair. The first time we saw each other, we instinctively smiled—the knowing smile that comes from recognizing another person who knows what it feels like to stand out in a crowd.

Although I had begun to emerge from my shell in middle school, I was still somewhat shy, especially around boys. But Kale drew me out completely with his candid, easygoing manner and persistent attempts to be my friend—sitting next to me in classes when there was a free seat and finding me in the hallway to walk to the cafeteria together. It didn't take long for his warm, unusual yet strikingly familiar personality to make me feel at ease.

I was devastated when he dropped out at the end of sophomore year, but I understood that he needed to work in his dad's convenience store to help his family. Now, I couldn't honestly say how much my own decision had been influenced by his departure from traditional education the previous spring. But I didn't want Sasha to drag Kale into this and look critically upon our friendship.

"No."

"Then tell me, Anokhi," Sasha said, a small sigh escaping her. "What are your thoughts? What do you want to do with your life?"

"I . . . I want to study dance," I confessed. It was the first time I had said it aloud to anyone.

The truth was, for years, as Shaila had made countless appearances to me, I had become fascinated with the interpretive and storytelling power of dance as an art form. I felt a calling to learn dance so I could be closer to Shaila. Admitting this to Sasha made it feel a bit frivolous that this was the reason why I wanted to drop out of school. But it wasn't the only reason. There was still the anxiety, the feeling of not belonging, the general sense that traditional schooling wasn't my path. But dance was a tangible reason that I could name for Sasha, as outlandish as it might sound.

"But why can't you go to school *and* study dance?" Sasha pressed.

"I just can't go to school anymore, Sasha." I sighed. "I am sick of feeling dread in my stomach every morning when I get up to go there. I don't want to go to college. I just don't see the point anymore."

She was quiet, looked at me for a moment before looking down at her hands in her lap.

"I have felt anxious about going to school for years," I confessed. "From the moment I get on the bus to the moment the last bell of the day rings, I feel on edge. I don't know why. But I just have never felt like I belong there, or that what I am learning is helping me get closer to what I want to do with my life."

She was quiet for a moment. "Okay, sweetheart," she finally said. "I may not completely understand. But I am trying to. I'm sorry that . . . I didn't know school has made you so anxious over these years. Or to this degree. I wish I had known. Maybe there would have been something I could have done . . ." She shook her head. "It's okay. I am not going to start talking about the past."

"Thank you," I said. I knew I was disappointing her but had no desire to go back on my decision.

She kissed my forehead, let out a small sigh, and walked outside my room, closing the door behind her. I slumped against my headboard and picked up my phone.

Are you awake? I texted Kale.

Less than a minute later, my phone rang.

"Anokhs! You're up late, old lady," Kale teased, his voice cheerful and loud, jarring compared to the internal bleakness I felt. I held the phone a little away from my ear, squeezing my eyes shut. He didn't know yet.

"Hey," I said, after taking a deep breath.

"What's wrong?"

I wasn't embarrassed to tell him, but I knew he was going to be surprised. Since he had left school last year, I had felt more alone than ever. Previously, I would look forward to seeing him at lunch, going to the library after school, or sometimes, when the weather was nice, walking back to my home or to his parents' house together. Now that he was out of school, he had been working a lot, and we barely saw each other compared to our previous almost-daily pattern. Now it was no more than once a week. I missed him more than I'd ever admitted, to him or to Sasha.

"I quit school today."

I could hear him breathing on the other end of the line, but he didn't say anything for a moment.

"Wow," he finally said. "That's . . . a big move. Are you doing all right?"

"I don't know," I admitted. "I feel like it's been a long time coming. But I think Sasha is really upset. Understandably. I just feel very lost."

"Oh, Anokhs," he said, his voice soft. If he was in front of me, he would throw his arm around my shoulder, squeezing me in toward him for a hug. He always had a way of making me feel better, even without words. I wished I could see him in person right now. "It's a big decision," he said. "Obviously you know I get that. I'll come see you this week, when I can get away from the store. I'm here for you, okay?"

I started to cry. Tears rolled down my cheeks, but I held in the sobs. I didn't want him to hear me, but I knew he knew I was crying, because he was silent on the other end. As if he was just giving me the silent space to cry because he knew I needed to, and needed to not be alone.

"Okay. Thanks, Kale," I finally said. "I'll talk to you later."

"Good night, Anokhs. Take care of yourself."

Several days later, Sasha made an appointment for me with my doctor in town. I had barely been touching my food and had been spending the days sitting quietly on the couch, occasionally going on walks. She had asked me to go with her to the diner to work and get out of the house, but I dreaded the thought of seeing other people.

"I think we should get you checked out," she said, as we drove together to the clinic.

"I don't know why," I said. "I'm not sick. I feel fine."

She gave me a quizzical look from the driver's seat. "You feel fine? Really?"

I laughed a little, because of how silly it sounded. Of course I didn't feel fine. I felt unmoored. Like I barely belonged in civilization. The weightlessness made me feel almost unreal, as if I were just walking through my life like a ghost rather than living it.

I had no doubt in my mind that leaving precalculus class, and leaving my school, was the best decision for me. What troubled me was that I had no idea what was next. And I felt too oppressed by the fact that my decision to drop out just further alienated me from society. As I walked into the doctor's office, I felt nauseous, like being at the peak of a roller coaster before the plummet. But this was my life hanging in the balance, not a ride at an amusement park.

Dr. James was a thin man with thick spectacles and a bald patch between two islands of wispy brown hair. He smiled at me and Sasha when he came into the exam room.

"Anokhi," he said. "It's nice to see you." He had been my pediatrician since I was a baby. He was a nice man, professional and calm, but with a veneer that made me feel like I didn't really know him, even though I had been seeing him for the last fifteen years.

"Thanks, Dr. James," I said, readjusting my seat and inevitably tearing some of the exam table's crinkly paper as I shifted my body weight.

"Sasha, I'll ask you to step out, please. Since Anokhi is a teenager, and now also sixteen, I usually perform parts of these interviews alone. I will let you know when you can come back," he said, opening the door for her.

I looked at Sasha, surprised. But she just smiled and nodded, as if it were no big deal, and walked out. The door closed.

"Anokhi, you can come down off that table. You're getting a little too old for that," Dr. James said, gesturing to a seat where Sasha usually sat. I got down and slumped into the chair. He sat on a stool a few feet away from me, his hands in his lap.

"How have you been feeling, Anokhi?" he asked, placing his pen on his clipboard and looking at me intently.

"I . . . I don't know." I had barely known what to say to Sasha. How could I know what to say to him?

"Your mother called our office yesterday. She booked this appointment because she said you have had a major change in your life recently and you have not been doing so well at home."

"Well, yeah," I sighed, relieved in a way that he was just cutting to the chase. "I dropped out of school last week." I looked up at him. His eyes were soft and concerned.

"How are you feeling about that?"

"Lost," I said, looking down at my feet. "Like I don't know what I am meant to do. I mean I thought I knew what I wanted to do . . . but I don't know, I can't seem to do anything right now. It feels like I'm stuck in mud."

He nodded and didn't say anything.

"All I know is that I don't want to go back. But I feel like I am not really living my life," I continued.

"I see," he said. He picked up his pen and jotted down a couple of notes. His face was open, patient, and kind, and somehow—perhaps because I didn't know him well enough to worry about disappointing him—I felt the urge to tell him more. To get the weight off my chest.

I told him about how I had felt anxious about going to school ever since I was seven and got bullied by Dylan and Max. I told him how, despite enjoying certain subjects, like English and history, I was always waiting for the day to be over so I could get out of the school building.

"It sounds like school has caused a lot of anxiety for you for many years."

"Yes." I nodded. "A lot."

"If school didn't make you feel so anxious, do you think you'd like to return?"

I sighed. I didn't think he was trying to get me to change my mind, and the question was a fair one. But the truth was, I had no idea. It was complicated. Could we predict if our future could be different if our past had taken a different course? Did the question even matter, given that we can't go back and change the past? When Kale dropped out of school last year, I had felt a pulse of hope flicker within me because I saw a potential to end the misery I had silently endured for years. Maybe I was traumatized from my childhood, which is why I never really cared much to make friends or engage in after-school activities. Sasha, despite all her goodness and love toward me, never really understood what I was going through. She was always busy with the diner and paying our bills, and she had a very practical view of the world. I had hidden a large portion of my anxiety from her well, I suppose. So it wasn't her fault.

I struggled to know what I was to do with all these tangled feelings. Especially now that I had already made this big decision.

"I am going to ask you some questions, Anokhi. Try

your best to answer them without overthinking. Just answer honestly."

"Okay," I said.

He pulled a piece of paper out from his clipboard and proceeded to ask me nine questions about my mood, my sleep, my appetite, and my feelings about myself. The questions made me feel incredibly depressed. So, it was a bit ironic at the end when he said, "Well, Anokhi, you are moderately depressed." I felt more than moderately depressed and didn't know why he had to ask me a bunch of questions to prove it.

"Okay." I was unsure of what I was supposed to say next.

He then asked me seven questions about anxiety—about feeling nervous, worried, or irritable. "You score very high for anxiety," he commented.

I wasn't exactly surprised—the questions seemed to have been handpicked for me, encompassing just about everything I felt, especially toward school and my uncertain future. But, in some ways, I *was* taken aback because I'd thought—or maybe I'd just been convincing myself—that things were getting better. I'd made friends in middle school. Kale was a game changer in high school. So, on the outside, it may have appeared that I had no reason to be depressed or anxious. But childhood bullies, whether in human form or in the form of circumstances that life plagues us with, apparently leave deep bruises. And now here I was in the doctor's examination room, looking into an unwelcome mirror.

"My job is not to change your mind about school, Anokhi," Dr. James said as he slipped the papers back into his clipboard and then wiped his brow. "But my job *is* to try to see how I can help you feel better. I am sorry you have been struggling with these feelings about school for so long."

"Thank you," I said, still unsure exactly how he was going to make me feel better.

"I think you would benefit from some medication and also therapy, for your depression and anxiety. You don't need to suffer like this alone."

I blinked. Although kind, his words sounded very serious. And I wasn't sure I wanted any of it.

"I'm going to call your mom—Sasha—back in now. Is that okay? Unless you have anything else you would like to share with me—"

"No, that's fine," I replied. I was ready to leave. I didn't like spending this much time talking out loud with someone else about the feelings and emotions I usually kept close to me.

"Before I bring Sasha in—is it okay if I talk to her about what we have discussed?" He rested his hand on the doorknob, waiting for my reply before opening the door.

I shrugged. "That's fine." What difference would it make if he talked to her? I already felt like a failure in her eyes for dropping out.

Within moments, Sasha walked back in and placed her hand on my shoulder.

"Well," Dr. James said as he shut the door. "Anokhi has scored moderate on the depression scale and very high for anxiety. I think a lot of the anxiety she had brewing for years about school may have contributed to this recent decision to leave school entirely."

Sasha nodded, but I could tell she was surprised by his assessments. I had shared some of my feelings about school with her, and bringing me here *was* her idea after all. So I know she suspected there was something going on. But I don't think she expected a diagnosis this serious.

"And, after such a major life change last week, it's not surprising that some of these symptoms, particularly the ones related to depression, may be worse than usual," he mused, looking at us both carefully. We both stared at him, finding that easier than making eye contact with one another. I had not spoken to Sasha in much depth about my feelings, largely because I had not understood them myself.

"In addition to some medication, I suggest she start therapy; my office can give a referral to a counseling office for young adults in town," Dr. James continued.

Sasha squeezed my shoulder and kissed my head. "Thank you, doctor."

"I'd like to see her back in my office in two weeks."

We both nodded. I felt like a specimen outside myself, as if he were talking about someone else.

The drive home was quiet. As we pulled into our driveway, Sasha said, "I'm sorry if that was hard for you, sweetie. I have been really worried about you not eating, not speaking much. I didn't know what else I could do to help you, which is why I wanted Dr. James to see you." She turned off the car. "I'm also sorry I didn't really know just how anxious you felt all these years about going to school. Perhaps if I had gotten you to see someone sooner—" Her voice trailed off.

I got out of the car and walked around to her side. When she climbed out of the driver's seat, I gave her a big hug. "I love you," I said, squeezing her close to me. "I will be okay. You didn't do anything wrong. You're a great mom."

She pulled back when I said this and smiled. "Thank you, Anokhi. That means a lot."

I really didn't know if I would be okay, but I knew I wanted to try to be. For Sasha's sake. Even though the visit to Dr. James was strange and in some ways made me feel weirder about myself and my decision, getting out of the house and going and speaking to another human being about where I was in my life felt like something that could help anchor me back in reality. So, I took the medication he prescribed, and I went to see the therapist. Step by step, I promised myself I would somehow emerge from this strange uncharted territory I found myself in. Dropping out of high school was the first step. Now, apparently, I had to heal from years of untreated anxiety. I could either keep going up, or I could go down. But I knew I had to keep going. So I did.

CHAPTER 4

A few weeks after the visit with Dr. James, and after the follow-up I begrudgingly agreed to, I was beginning to feel noticeably better. Eating three meals a day didn't feel as hard, nor did getting out of bed in the morning. The choking sense of doom didn't seem to wrap its fingers around my throat, enveloping my first breath of the day when I woke up in the morning. I was now working regular shifts at the diner to have something to do during the daytime.

Also, I was taking steps toward a potential future. I was researching more about dance schools that I could apply to. Part of this research was eye opening, especially when I learned that some programs didn't require a high school diploma while others were geared toward more of a traditional college-education track—like a bachelor of fine arts in dance. I was annoyed with myself for not thinking through the plans more concretely before dropping out. But I also knew that, given how I'd been aimlessly wandering, depressed and disengaged, I would not have been able to finish high school or succeed in college. That path wasn't in my heart, and my mind wasn't up for talking my heart into it.

One evening at dinner, Sasha surprised me by putting an envelope in my hand.

"What's this?" I asked.

"Open it."

The letterhead was from our local bank, and the letter contained instructions about accessing my college savings account. When I read the word college, my heart dropped.

"Since I opened the diner, ever since you were a young child, I've been saving for your college fund. I didn't know what you would want to do with your life, but I assumed—now I realize, perhaps closed-mindedly—that college would be part of your plans." She looked at me and smiled, before softly adding, "You've always been so good at school."

I sighed. I felt horrible. "Why are you giving this to me, then?"

She took my hand in hers. "I want you to know this fund exists. It's yours. If you want to enroll in a dance school, or take a trip somewhere to decide what exactly is next for you, there is money here for you—even though it may not be used for what it was initially intended for. But it's still yours, and I want it to go toward whatever is next for you."

I felt nauseous for disappointing her, on the heels of finding out about this money in my name. She was right—I had always been good at school. I had seemed like the student who would flourish in college, academically. Which probably made my decision to leave school even more bizarre.

"It doesn't feel right for me to have this, then," I said. "If this was for me to go to college, and I'm not—"

"This is an uncertain time for you," Sasha interrupted, resting her chin in her hands. "I don't expect you to know what you want to do. You're still figuring it out. But maybe using a bit of this money to kick-start something—whether that is enrolling in a dance program or taking a trip somewhere— maybe that is just the inspiration you need in this moment."

Words like this from Sasha's sweet, sensible mouth made me want to cry. I looked past her, out the window in our dining room. The stars that night were cluttering the sky, squeezing out blackness from the dome above as if unwilling to let the darkness reign. But that contrast between the bright stars and the night sky just made the blackness within me, the uncertainty and guilt I felt, all the bolder.

"My darling, please don't look so upset. It's yours." Sasha got up from her chair, walked over to where I sat, and embraced me. I let my arms fold around her waist.

Was it wayward to not know what my life's calling was at age sixteen? I had expressed this fear to Sasha before, and she brushed it away, telling me I was too young to have all the answers; I would figure it out eventually. I still had no answers, and it felt worse now that I had fallen off the traditional education train tracks. I knew it grieved Sasha, and yet, here she was, giving me access to my college education fund, for deciding not to go to college. The irony hurt.

"Thanks, Sasha," I said, putting the envelope down on the table. "I'll think about it. I don't . . . I don't really know what to say. I don't feel deserving."

"Well, I hope you do feel deserving one day," she said. "I trust that you will figure things out. But you do need to feel better and believe in yourself first. That's a must."

I took the envelope up to my room after dinner and placed it on my desk. It felt like her giving me access to this college fund was a sign. If I wasn't going to finish school and go to college, then I had better come up with a plan for how to put this money to good use. To honor all the hard work Sasha had put into saving this for me over all these years.

I spent my free time before and after my waitress shifts at the diner thinking about what to do. I spent time researching different dance academies, focusing on those located in Seattle and California. But both those places felt so far and inaccessible. I had a tough time imagining moving to another place to embark on a new adventure without having traveled much in my life.

Sasha and I would take trips occasionally while I was growing up, but it was infrequent. As the owner of the restaurant, she seldom felt comfortable leaving the diner alone for long periods of time. Plus, it wasn't financially feasible to close it for an extended length of time either. So, we would take shorter trips around our part of the country, often by car. We took road trips to Glacier, Yellowstone, and Crater Lake. I have beautiful memories of traveling with Sasha, and in recent years, even Kale, who had joined us on a trip last summer to Mount Rushmore after he had dropped out of school.

One day during that trip, on our daylong drive home, he asked what I was thinking about. I usually let him sit in the front seat, next to Sasha, when the three of us traveled together; he was tall, nearly six feet, and that way he had more room to stretch his legs. I would sit behind Sasha so he could push the passenger seat back as far as it would go. But I secretly liked sitting in the back seat of Sasha's station wagon, because there I still felt like a little kid, looking out the window at the beautiful landscapes.

"Nothing," I mumbled, pushing my cheek against the window. It was approaching evening, and it was too cold in the mountains to leave the window down.

"You know how she is," Sasha said, winking at me in the rearview mirror. "She likes to be with her thoughts."

"Mm-hmm." Kale nodded, looking back and poking at my knee teasingly. "She's a big thinker, that one."

I smiled and rolled my eyes. I didn't mind being the butt of their jokes as they teased me about my moody, dreamy personality. I knew they both loved me and cared about me. They were also both practical, optimistic people who got along quite well, and this made me happy because they were the two most important people in my life. Sometimes I even felt envious of their relationship and their similarities of character, but only in passing.

Now, as I sat on my bed, recovering from the shock of the college fund, that trip seemed so long ago. I was still a kid then, and over the course of less than a year I'd become an adult with access to funds I didn't feel the right to use. And yet this gift allowed me to smile again for the first time in days, reflecting on happy memories and discovering that I had a lot to be grateful for—including these people in my life who loved me and wanted the best for me. Even if I didn't quite know what the best might be.

Within moments of closing my eyes, Shaila appeared. She was dressed in a brilliant peacock blue dress, her eyes sparkling, a calm smile on her red lips. She moved her arms in undulating waves, circling around the perimeter of the stage, reminding me of the ocean. She put her hand to her forehead and squinted her eyes, standing on her tiptoes, as if looking out at a scenic view. The music was soft tonight, the flute melodic and light, and she seemed like she was on an adventure. She went on dancing, and images of mountains, various animals, and long winding paths magically manifested.

I got out of bed to journal once she had left me and I had woken up. Unlike some nights when I was left to puzzle over the meaning of her dance, tonight's meaning felt markedly clear.

She's telling me to travel, I wrote in my journal. *I need a change of scenery.*

The next morning, when I went downstairs, I smiled at Sasha, who was sitting at the table with her coffee, reading the newspaper.

"Hi, sweetheart," she said, looking a bit surprised.

I guessed that my change in countenance for the first time since my leaving school was unexpected to her.

"I've been thinking," I said, sitting down at the table. "Maybe I should go somewhere. Like on a road trip. I think that would be good for me. To have a change of scenery, as I figure out exactly what I want to do next."

Sasha hesitated as she set down her cup. "That's a lovely idea. Where are you thinking of going?"

"Maybe Seattle?" I said. "Especially if I'm thinking of enrolling in a dance school, it would be helpful to go to a big city and get a feel for it. I'd probably have to move anyway, if that's what I ended up doing . . ." My voice trailed off. I had never really thought about leaving Sasha before. Of course, I knew one day, when I grew up, I would move away from home at some point. But that was an abstraction in my mind still. This *was* home, despite the fact that sometimes I wondered where else I might belong. I had never ventured out of the comfort of her love to seek any other place of belonging—because I hadn't needed to.

She folded her newspaper and brought her cup to the sink. "That's a great idea," Sasha said as she turned to face me. "Were you thinking of going alone?"

Part of me wanted to ask Kale to go, but we hadn't done a road trip together just the two of us yet, and I also didn't want to exclude Sasha.

As if she was reading my face while I contemplated my reply, she said, "You know, you might consider asking Kale if he wants to go with you. I think he has some family in Seattle, right?"

"Yeah, that's true," I said, trying to remember more about whoever that relative was. "But . . . do you want to come too?"

She smiled and shook her head. "No, Anokhi. I think it's important that you start to figure out who you are and what you want to do on your own. It might help to *not* have your mother hovering over you."

Her wink said it all, and I couldn't help but laugh. Sasha was anything *but* a hovering parent. "You know you're not like that. But thank you. I'll talk to Kale."

Later that day, after I finished waitressing around 3:00 p.m., I took Sasha's car and drove to Kale's dad's convenience store. It was just five miles away, but I was still getting used to driving by myself. I got my driver's permit when I turned 15, and after completing the necessary driving hours with Sasha supervising me in the car, I had just recently taken and passed my written and road-skills tests so I could finally drive alone.

I parked in the gravel lot and walked toward the door beneath the brown wooden sign reading **K's GENERAL STORE** in white capital letters. Inside, Mr. Kealoha stood behind the counter, rearranging the cigarettes in the glass display.

"Hello, Anokhi!" he said warmly, coming around the side of the counter to give me a hug. I loved Mr. Kealoha. He always smelled like tobacco and peppermint, because after he smoked, he would chew some mint gum before coming back into the store.

"Hi, Mr. Kealoha! How are you?"

"Oh, good, good," he said. "How are *you* doing, dear? How's the time off treating you?"

I hadn't seen him since I left school, but I inferred that Kale had filled him in, which I didn't mind. It felt less stressful to talk to Mr. Kealoha about quitting school than it did Sasha. I knew Sasha and I were not on the same page about my decision, though she was trying hard to be supportive and was generally being very kind about it. But it still hung in the air between us, some sticky awkwardness we couldn't name and thus couldn't dispel.

"It's good," I said quickly, before deciding to be more honest. "I'm not sure what exactly is next. I've been working at the diner with Sasha to keep myself busy. But I came over to talk to Kale. I was thinking of taking a trip to Seattle."

"Ah," Mr. Kealoha said, nodding his head pensively. "Traveling is always a good idea. Clears up your head. It'll be good for you."

Suddenly Kale came walking toward the front of the store through one of the aisles. His arms were filled with two large cardboard boxes, which looked heavy. He was wearing a tight T-shirt, and his biceps bulged beneath the sleeves, the veins coral green underneath his bronzed skin. I forced my eyes away from his toned arms and up to his face as he set the boxes down next to the counter.

"Anokhs!" he said, wiping his brow with the back of his hand before giving me a quick, strong hug. "You made it here in one piece in the car?"

He knew I was still getting used to driving alone. He had been driving a bit longer than me and had felt comfortable much earlier on.

"Ha ha, very funny."

He glanced out the window. It was clear outside and still sunny, although cold.

"Pa, is it okay if I go on a quick walk with Anokhi?" I thought their relationship was so sweet—and always marveled at how respectful and deferential Kale was to his father.

"Of course." Mr. Kealoha nodded. "Just as long as you get all the boxes unloaded by the end of the day, you can do whatever you want."

We walked out the back entrance of the store toward a winding path that led past the dumpsters to a plot of rural land on which their home was built. We wove through the trees on their property.

"What's up?" Kale asked, pulling a piece of gum out of his pocket. He motioned to offer me a piece, but I shook my head.

"Well, I'm thinking of going to Seattle. I had a dream about Shaila last night. It felt like she was telling me to travel."

"That's amazing!" he gasped. "I'm coming too, right?"

"Well . . . yeah, that's what I came to ask you," I said, trying to stifle my grin. "I mean . . . I don't really think Sasha wants me to go by myself."

"Not with your newfound driving skills." He laughed.

"I'm trying to figure out exactly what I want to do next. I think a change of scenery might help. And plus, it would be fun for the two of us to go together." I was sincere in wanting him to join me, but the thought of traveling alone with him did make my heart bounce a little.

"Anokhs, we can totally do Seattle. But someday, we gotta go on a road trip all over the country. Down the West Coast, hit the Grand Canyon, weave through Texas, go down Florida and come back up, and see all of the East Coast. There's so much so see." He picked a leaf off a nearby branch and peeled it along its spine.

I knew Kale meant every word; he always did. The only reason he hadn't gone on some sort of grand road trip yet was because money was too much of an issue. After his mother was diagnosed with cancer, he and his father had been working extra hard to run the store at a profit to pay her medical bills. This meant they had let go of a couple of the employees, and the two of them were working a lot more instead. In addition to helping his dad with the store, Kale was also working occasional night shifts at a larger grocery store in one of the adjacent towns.

I felt a twinge of guilt that I was making plans to travel but didn't have the weight of having to care for a sick family member to tether me back to reality, like he did. I also felt guilty at the generous college fund from Sasha, which I hadn't told Kale about yet. He didn't have any such savings to fall back upon.

"This trip feels like a reasonable next step," I said. "Seattle isn't somewhere far and crazy, and I could use what I've saved from working at the diner over the years. Or . . . I could use some other funds."

I figured I couldn't keep the college fund a secret from him for much longer, so I told him about the envelope Sasha had given me. "I don't know what to do with that money. I almost want to give it back to her. I don't feel like I've earned it."

"You're her daughter," Kale said. His light brown eyes were caught in the setting late-evening sun, and they sparkled. "She loves you. Even if you're not going to college like she thought you were going to. That doesn't make you undeserving. Okay?"

I wanted to believe him, but I didn't feel it in my heart. As my guilt threatened to derail our conversation, Kale came to the rescue.

"Remember that trip we took to Seattle with my family?"

His family had invited me to join them one summer, and other than Chicago, where Sasha and I had gone to see a musical for her fortieth birthday, Seattle was the biggest city I'd ever been to. We all had a great time trying out different restaurants, sightseeing, and spending time with his extended family.

I told him I absolutely remembered it. And then I hit him with another surprise. "Wanna go to Seattle tomorrow? Maybe we could stay with your cousin."

"Tomorrow?" Kale asked, surprised. "That's . . . really soon, Anokhs." He laughed. "I can't just leave tomorrow without giving Dad enough advance warning. He needs help with the store. I need to make sure he'll be all right without me."

"Oh yeah, of course," I said, feeling foolish for my impulsive suggestion. Kale was such a devoted, responsible son. In the time since he quit school, he had been helping full-time with his father's store and driving his mother to all her specialized medical appointments in Boise, which was almost a half-day trip just to drive there one way.

When I asked him last summer what he wanted to do with his life, he laughed. "For now, my path is laid out for me. I need to help my parents."

"I know. Of course," I said. "That is who you are. And they are so lucky to have you as their son. But . . . what else do you want to do?"

I could feel a gust of sadness sweep over his being when I asked him that. "I don't know, Anokhs. I don't think I've had the time or space to think about that deeply. All I know is I want to travel. But the traveling I want to do feels like a distant dream. I want to travel the world. I want to see exotic places, meet different people. I want to eat new foods, experience new cultures, and learn about lives very different from my own. But that can't happen right now. Not with Mom sick, dad getting older, and the store being more and more work for him, especially with money being so tight."

I never asked him again, though I often wondered. Kale was smart and excellent with people. I could see him doing almost anything he set his mind to. He was practical and patient—quite the opposite of me.

"Okay," I finally said, as we ended our walk and got back to the store parking lot. He was standing next to me by the front door of my car—it was getting close to dark, and as I was still on a partially restricted license, I had to drive home before it got completely dark. "Just let me know when you think you can go."

"Of course," he said, grinning and opening the door for me, making a dramatic sweeping bow with his hand. I laughed, got in the car, and waved as I drove away.

I felt a little stir of something fluttering within me that I eventually recognized was the only thing that could ever get me out of the hole of uncertainty I had fallen into: hope. Hope that whatever lay ahead, though I didn't know exactly what, was perhaps exactly what I needed.

CHAPTER 5

Just two weeks later, we found ourselves on the road to Seattle. Kale insisted that I drive, because he knew how much I enjoyed driving in the absence of traffic.

And I did. I loved how the open road felt like it was paved for me and me alone. I told him this once, when Sasha had let me drive part of the way home from Yellowstone last summer. I loved how my heart felt as free as a field when I looked in the rearview mirror and saw nothing but asphalt and green and gold and blue. Kale didn't ask for particulars, but from the smile on my face that would not leave once I was behind the wheel, he knew it gave me peace.

Our bond was simple and unspoken, as I always imagined a great friendship would be. Kale was the only true best friend I had ever had. We loved to laugh and talk about books and movies, tease each other about various idiosyncrasies—the way I scratched my ear mindlessly when I was lost in thought, the way he would rather keep incessantly pushing curls out of his eyes every few moments than tie his curly locks up. But we equally enjoyed our silences, and this made me feel even more comfortable with him. The way space didn't always need to be filled with words, and in fact, the space without words was revered and treasured equally, if not more, because we were still together.

The drive to Seattle, which per GPS was supposed to take about five and a half hours, only took us four hours and forty-five minutes. I guess I was feeling especially charged with adrenaline in the wake of my recent departure from school, and the absence of a concrete plan filled me with restless energy. I didn't have the sense of bounded duty that Kale had to stay with his family, working alongside his father in the convenience store and seeing his mother through her cancer treatment. Sasha, though I knew she loved me, did not expect me to stay—and in some ways, I felt she was silently but surely waiting for me to make a decision about what I was actually going to do, now that I was off the beaten path. My life seemed reckless, as open as the road itself, and the freedom was more terrifying than it was liberating to my young self, who had seen so little of the world.

Our plan was to visit Seattle for the weekend only; Kale couldn't leave his father for more than two days. They didn't have consistent help at the store, so he was really the only employee Mr. Kealoha could rely on. Both he and his dad were busy around the clock, between keeping the store open and running to pay bills and caring for his mother, who was getting weaker with her recent chemo sessions. I started spending a few mornings with her each week, before I had to go work the lunch shift at Sweet Potato. I would help make her lunch and keep her company. She was often too weak for conversation but held my hand gratefully as I sat next to her on their worn, taupe sofa and watched reality TV shows with her—her not-so-guilty pleasure.

I had looked up potential dance schools to visit during my trip to Seattle but, feeling overwhelmed by decision paralysis and feelings of inadequacy about my candidacy as a potential dance student at any serious institution, having never formally studied dance before, I ultimately decided to hold off on investigating dance schools seriously on this trip. In my mind, this trip was more to just reacquaint myself with the feel of a big city—to see if I felt ready to leave the small town where I had grown up—and also to try to figure out if I was ready to leave Sasha just yet.

Our plan was to stay with Kale's cousin Rob and his girlfriend, who was a student at the University of Washington, also known as UW. Rob, who worked in an electronics store in Seattle and had recently moved in with Tanya, was more than happy to welcome us. So, Kale and I found ourselves at the door to a brick apartment building, nudging each other to press the off-white doorbell button next to 3A.

"Hello?" A chirpy voice emerged from the speaker.

"Hi! It's Kale and Anokhs," Kale said, putting his face unnecessarily close to the speaker. I suppressed a giggle.

"Oh, hey, guys! Come on in," the woman's voice replied, and the door beeped. Kale and I pushed it open and walked into the foyer. I pressed the elevator button and we ascended to the third floor. When the doors opened, Tanya was standing right there, ready to greet us. She was a tall woman with dark brown hair tied up in a high bun on her head, wearing sweatpants and a royal purple T-shirt that read "University of Washington."

"Hey! How are you guys?!" She gave us both a hug and ushered us toward their apartment door, which was already ajar. Fragrant, spicy smells were wafting into the hallway, and they intensified once we stepped across the threshold.

"Kale! Anokhs!" Rob called out from the kitchen. "We've got quite a grand feast cooked up for you guys. Have a seat. You must be tired from the drive!" I peered past the doorway to the kitchen and smiled at Rob, who was standing at the stove, a dish towel over one of his broad shoulders, stirring various items in pans and pots that covered the cooktop. His hair was like Kale's—dark brown, curly—but pulled back in a bun. He waved at me with his free hand.

Kale and I sat at their wooden kitchen table. As Tanya, a chatty and friendly young woman, started answering Kale's questions about what she was studying at UW and how she liked Seattle after moving here from California, Rob walked into the dining area and set the dishes down on the table. He gave Tanya a kiss on the forehead before sitting down next to her.

Rob and Tanya were a really cute couple. They had been dating for four months before moving in together. As I looked around their apartment—the beige sofa set, the flowers on the kitchen table, the slightly comforting clutter on the kitchen counter—I felt myself inwardly approving of them. How strangely we sketch our judgments of people, based on sofa colors and flowers and the messes they leave behind.

The next day we went to a cultural show some of Tanya's friends at UW were involved in. Prior to our visit, Kale had mentioned to Rob that one of the reasons for our visit was for me to get a sense of what life in the city would be like, as I was considering moving to a bigger city to pursue study in dance. When Rob mentioned this to Tanya, she had suggested we go to this performance where there would be a lot of dances being showcased.

After parking in a visitors' lot, we walked across the grassy, tree-laden campus to the auditorium where the show was taking place. I felt weird seeing so many people close to my age at university. It was the first college campus I had ever set foot upon. I was filled with admiration for the old cement and brick buildings, envy toward the students who were walking on the sidewalks and into the dorms and buildings with a sense of belonging, and sadness for my own displacement. Kale and I had decisively opted out of this path. But amid the fountains, the nature, and the buildings whose mysteries I wanted to know immediately, I felt confused and uncomfortable. I wanted to get into the auditorium quickly so that I didn't have to confront the surprising possibility that I might have liked going to a place like this next year—if I hadn't dropped out of school.

Rob and Tanya had bought tickets in advance, but Kale and I had to dish out ten dollars each. I had never been to a cultural show; I didn't even know what to expect. Posters affixed to the auditorium's main glass doors depicted students—mostly women—dressed in brightly-colored ethnic attire, frozen in the middle of dances.

I stopped in front of one of the posters and my mouth fell slightly open. Six women were dressed in pristine white outfits with pleats in the front of the skirts. They wore heavy gold earrings and necklaces, and white flowers in their hair, which was tied back in buns. It reminded me so much of Shaila, I was taken aback. The possibility of seeing dancers like her hadn't even crossed my mind.

"Pictures from last year's show," Tanya noted when she saw me gawking at the poster.

As we moved through the crowd of people, I was struck by the appearance of others in the crowd. I saw several other girls who looked like me, much to my surprise. Several women and men with skin as dark as or even darker than mine. People with all different shades and textures of hair—straight, curly, wavy, frizzy, thick. It was the first time in my life that I didn't stand out in a crowd. It filled me with a strange feeling that I had never had before. I didn't feel self-conscious about my appearance. My shoulders relaxed and I even took the hair tie out of my hair, let down my ponytail, and let the frizzy black waves on my head hang down and frame my face. It felt liberating.

The show started shortly after we took our seats. Two of the ten acts absolutely blew my mind. The first was a drum performance by a young man, a soloist. He wore a simple cotton uniform composed of a long-sleeved, long white shirt, almost like a dress, and loose white pants. The announcer said he would be performing on his Indian drums called the tabla. When the curtains opened and I saw him sitting, cross-legged, all alone on the front right corner of the stage with two asymmetric drums in front of him, I was confused as to what to expect.

All my thoughts were replaced by shock when the sound emerged boldly at the behest of his nimble fingertips. For the next fifteen minutes I sat in complete rapture. How could two pieces of an instrument, side by side, produce such fine vibrations—such a soulful, earthy timbre—that I felt them move all the way across the rows in the hall into my very being?

He kept closing and opening his eyes intermittently while he was playing. I could tell he was absorbed in concentration, and it was impossible for me to take my eyes away from him. He was so focused on what he was doing that the rest of the world—all of us in the auditorium, the lights, the venue— seemed nonexistent to him. His intense devotion to his art mesmerized me.

His music also moved me deeply because I recognized the drumbeat although I had never actually seen the physical instrument before. It was the beat to which Shaila danced.

The other performance that floored me was the final one. The announcer said it was a Bharatanatyam piece, a classical dance form from South India. It was listed as a Thillana in the program and was performed by eight girls wearing matching red costumes. They wore bands studded with golden bells on their ankles, and their thick hair was braided neatly down their backs. They stood in the plié stance, which seemed to be their default position, with beautiful pleated fans unfolded, which were attached to the two pant legs of their costumes. Their movements were utterly synchronized, flawless in my perception, with their feet striking the stage only when the beat in their music told them to. Their dramatic eyes, outlined in heavy black eyeliner, moved with elastic exactness, shifting alertly from left to right, up to down. They sculpted crisp shapes with their hands with such fluidity that I could not tell where one gesture ended and another began. Altogether, their formations shifted from a single line to multiple staggered lines to a rotating circle—all performed effortlessly, it seemed. They were dancing to a slow song filled with ripeness and yearning for spring to come, according to the printed program. As their piece flowed to a finish, and I emerged from what felt like a captivating trance, I realized what had beguiled me most of all: It was as if I were seeing eight Shailas dancing at once.

I had watched videos of Indian classical dance over the years as part of my efforts to research and learn more about Shaila's style of dancing. I never knew for a fact that she was Indian—how could I know anything absolute about her, as she only existed in my mind? But Sasha's suggestion early in my childhood that Shaila might have had something to do with my past origins never completely left me. I had come across Bharatanatyam previously during my research but had never seen it performed live. Now, after the piece ended, a part of me knew, in the place that exists beyond words and rational logic, that I was witnessing an art form that was deeply intertwined with the very fabric of my being.

When the performances were over, Kale nudged me as I was frozen in my seat, processing everything I had just seen. When we left the auditorium, it was already dark, and rain was falling like pebbles from an invisible palm above our heads. Meanwhile, the tabla's beat was still rapping on the inside of my skull. I had felt so intensely energized while hearing it that it had brought tears to my eyes, and now I knew what I wanted: to dance, to play the tabla, to sing—all at the same time. I started thrumming my fingers on my thigh, almost without realizing it.

"Amazing, wasn't it?" Kale smiled, glancing at me, as we walked in tandem behind Tanya and Rob back toward the car.

"Yes!" I said. "And I want to learn. All of it. It sounded so amazing. The music, it sounds like the music . . ."

That Shaila dances to, I wanted to say, but I didn't. Not while we were with Rob or Tanya, at least. I wanted to wait until we were sitting somewhere alone and outside so I could tell him about the parallels I saw and felt while I was in that auditorium. I wanted to tell him about the chill that went through me when I was watching the group of girls in red costumes performing the Thillana, when I realized that I saw Shaila's familiar mannerisms and grace embodied in each of their dancing, living, and breathing forms.

After we all climbed into the car, Tanya turned it on and started blasting the heat. I hugged my arms. It was cold.

I looked at Kale, who was sitting next to me in the back. "I really need to start looking seriously into taking dance classes."

"You should move to Seattle and take classes here!" Tanya chimed in.

"Yeah, there probably are a lot of Indian dance and music teachers here, for sure," Rob said. I wondered at the authority with which he made his statements—I didn't doubt that he was right, but from where did that certainty come in people's voices when they talked about things they weren't familiar with yet felt that they were anyway?

I felt conflicted—I really did want to start taking dance classes right away. But using Sasha's college-fund money, which would be the only way I could afford to move here currently, didn't feel right. I still carried too much guilt about dropping out and not pursuing college, which I had come to

realize would remain an unspoken but palpable divide between us, despite her best efforts to mask her disappointment
and be supportive.

"Maybe." I deflected, leaning my head against the window
and watching the raindrops fall against the glass. "I'll need to
make sure Sasha is okay with it."

"Sasha would probably be happy if you made concrete
plans to start learning dance. I know you've been thinking
about it for a while, and we don't really have the opportuni-
ties back home. I'm sure she would be supportive," Kale said,
glancing over at me.

"I'll talk to her about it." I relented, more because I wanted
the conversation to be over than because I had any intention
of bringing it up with Sasha. Of course, she had raised me to
do what felt right in my heart—if I didn't hurt anyone and
kept myself safe. But I didn't want my next big move, such as
moving to a new city, far away from her, to be financially de-
pendent on her. Even though she had told me clearly that the
college fund was my money to use toward my future.

But the thought of learning dance—Shaila's dance—and
being surrounded by new yet deeply familiar music and words
with bells adorning my ankles made my heart skip a beat.
That thought had never felt real in my mind until I saw those
girls dancing on the stage. Now that the thought had a form, a
shape, a sound, and a feel, I couldn't let it go.

"So, do you think you'll move to Seattle to learn dance?" Sasha
asked me over dinner. I had returned from Seattle earlier that
afternoon and told her about the cultural performance right
away. Visiting Pike Place Market and exploring the different
Seattle neighborhoods had been fun too, but the performance
had undoubtedly been the highlight of the weekend for me.

"I need to start researching different options. I got a bit overwhelmed before the trip, but I feel more motivated now. I think the two Indian dance styles that are most popular, in terms of finding a place to learn, are Kathak and Bharatanatyam," I said, enunciating the word slowly, syllable by syllable. *Bah-ruh-tha-naa-tyum.* "That's what I saw the group of girls perform on stage. They looked just like Shaila. Their dance and costumes, I mean."

"Well, I'm glad you took the trip, sweetheart. And maybe you will need to take another trip or two before you figure out exactly what you are going to do. That's okay. It's a big decision, I know," Sasha said, getting up and taking my empty plate from me.

I stood up and started putting our leftover chicken and rice away. I thought, for the first time since dropping out, which was nearly a month ago, that things might be happening for a reason. I never subscribed to fatalistic thoughts before, unlike Kale, who believed a lot in fate and destiny. But, if I hadn't dropped out of high school, I wouldn't have gone to Seattle with Kale. We wouldn't have stayed with Rob and Tanya. We wouldn't have gone to the cultural performance at UW. And now it seemed that night was about to change my life by renewing in me the yearslong but quiescent, and still unrealized, desire to reconnect more with Shaila and my Indian heritage through dance.

I spent a long time on my computer that night reading about the different Indian classical dance styles. Bharatanatyam and Kathak were the two I had come across before, but there were others—Odissi, Mohiniyattam, Kathakali—that I hadn't previously read much about. The more I searched, the more deeply overwhelmed I became. How had I not been more proactive about learning dance before? Maybe if I had started learning sooner, I would have been able to understand more about Shaila's origins by now. Over the years, I had been so obsessed with noting minuscule details about her—the red stains on her fingertips, the different hand gestures she made with her graceful fingers, the melancholy flute and commanding drum to which she danced—that I had almost forgotten that there was a world out there with possible answers. That I didn't have to come up with them all myself and that I could look outward, instead of inward, to learn more about her.

Most of the dance videos I watched were beautiful but lacked some essential spark. It was probably nothing but my individual bias toward Shaila's dancing, for it was all I had ever known for the longest time, and thus the only true point of comparison for me. It was unfair but inevitable. But then goose bumps broke out on my arms and legs the more I listened to the music and discovered how powerful it could be—and how critical it was to the spark I searched for. I began looking up Indian classical instruments and styles: veena, mridangam, sitar, tabla, Carnatic, Hindustani. My head swirled with the desire to absorb everything.

I found a link to a sitar piece by Ravi Shankar, the most famous sitar player in the world, an influential musician and virtuoso who helped popularize appreciation of Indian classical music around the globe in the second half of the twentieth century. The heartfelt shrill pluck of the first strings compelled me to close my eyes. Sasha came to say good night and, seeing my silent tears shining on my cheeks, sat on my bed and closed her eyes, joining in on the listening. When I opened my eyes, I saw tears falling gently from hers too. We both sat there, perfectly and wholly entranced, allowing our minds and hearts to be plucked clear with each of the cries of the strings. Fast, slow, single strings, many in unison, crescendos. I had no idea what was going on technically, yet intuitively I felt myself swimming in the sea of notes he was weaving—expertly, tactically—to drown me in a sense of understanding. Shaila's face alone appeared in my head, her eyes closed. She was not dancing, but

I could see her breathing lightly in sync with the music, her nostrils flaring gently. I was so calm I could not even analyze her presence. The three of us sat and listened together, eyes closed in reverence.

What would Shaila's bells feel like on my own feet? I wrote in my journal that evening, after losing myself in the heart-wrenching music of the sitar. Sometimes I wrote questions in place of descriptions in *The Chronicles*; it felt freeing to have a place to put down my endless questions about her, as if the pages would magically somehow, someday, start writing answers back to me.

Sometimes when Shaila danced, I tapped my feet, trying to keep time with her dexterous movements. The dozens of golden bells lining the cloth bands that covered her ankles jingled like coins. I wondered if they were heavy.

When I was in elementary school, I tried drawing Shaila. But in the night, Shaila would look agitated as she danced, as if she knew I was trying to outline her in colored pencils and fill her in with crayons. Something about my attempting to draw her disturbed her greatly. She did not want me to restrict her to two dimensions. I did not want to insult her, so I stopped, somewhat. I still drew because that was the best way I could process my confusion about her appearances without telling anyone, but then I tore up the drawings into tiny square pieces the size of my pinky nail and threw them away.

I could never make her bells look quite right. I used the crayon labeled gold in the Crayola sixty-four pack Sasha gave me for my seventh birthday. But the glimmer was never there. Sometimes I tried to use goldenrod to accentuate the slight changes in color that occurred depending on which way her feet were pointed. I tried to capture subtleties in light that my young eyes could barely fathom, but the bells just looked like a golden mess by the end.

If I knew her story—if I knew anything other than her name—I might know what those bells would feel like and how to draw them perfectly. I would know whether her costume felt starched or smooth and thus know where to draw wrinkles or pleats. There must be meaning behind each of her movements, I reminded myself when I felt confused and anxious about dances I didn't immediately understand. Otherwise, how could it feel like every movement was trying to tell me something? When she pointed off into the distance, I could not look at what she was pointing to because I was not standing next to her. She stood in my head, danced in my head, vanished in my head, but returned always. I tried to see everything from her perspective, thinking that if I did, I would eventually know who she was. But the gap between us persisted, despite my efforts to decipher everything about her.

"So, what did you decide?" Kale asked. We were walking along the road behind my house. Rain clouds gathered in the sky like old friends hugging each other—faces heavy with memories and an aged sort of contentedness.

"About what?" I asked, turning my gaze away from the clouds, which had been capturing my attention with their dense grayness, and toward him.

"Seattle. Dance classes. Obviously," he said.

The night before, when Sasha and I had listened to Ravi Shankar, and Shaila had appeared in my mind, and I had drowned in the soulful melody of the sitar, I knew that I had a duty to stay home, at least for a while. My heart was ready to leave, but my insecurities and sense of obligation were not, and I had to see that through for myself. I knew Sasha was having a hard time with the restaurant—one of her best employees had just left, and she needed to reevaluate the state of her accounts. "*Our* accounts," as she said, though I didn't feel entitled to them. The college fund still hung over my head as a possibility to dip into, though the word "college" attached to it made me wince with guilt every time I considered it or it was brought up in conversation.

"I'm going to get a job in town first. Until I have enough money to rent a place in Seattle and enroll in classes. The restaurant isn't doing so well, and I can't take that much money from Sasha. Even though she said she set it aside for my college savings, I don't feel right tapping into it, especially right now."

"Ah." Kale nodded, understanding. Of course money would come between us and our dreams. Something so simple and logistic and far away from anything that dreams are made of—but that was the background of our lives. Sasha for me, and Kale's father for him, were both hardworking business owners whose very real ebbing and flowing issues with money were present realities for us early on in our lives as their children. We couldn't turn a blind eye to it, and in fact, in some ways the fear of money troubles kept both of us from taking the leap and doing what we wanted.

"What are *you* going to do?" I asked. His mother had recently completed her chemotherapy, and her cancer had been successfully treated. His father had also started a partnership with a gas supplier, and they were going to start selling gas at the store; this was going to help with business and revenue. It seemed like a good time for Kale to possibly branch away. I was anxious to hear his answer. I wanted to know his plans. And secretly, in a part of my heart I wasn't accustomed to acknowledging, I was hoping his plans included me.

"Looks like it's going to rain," Kale said, looking up at the sky and then turning around so we could walk back to my house. I stole a glance at him. He was now several inches taller than me. Little tufts of black hair had begun to peek through the opening of his black V-neck shirt. And he had become even more muscular recently from helping his father with more of the manual work at the store. But his usually sparkling light brown eyes were clouded over today.

He did this sometimes. He would pretend that he didn't hear me and switch the topic. Did he really think I didn't notice? Maybe there was nothing to be said. Maybe it didn't matter if he was going to work at the convenience store for the rest of his life. Out of obligation to his father or out of fear of actually taking the plunge and pursuing all the grand plans of traveling the world and starting his own travel and food show, which he used to describe elaborately on the long walks we took before either of us had dropped out of school.

I would never call Kale a coward. But there was something holding him back. As close as we were, I could not confront him about this, because I knew he would just pretend that I had never spoken, haunted and silenced by his own demons or thoughts that, despite our treasured friendship, he couldn't seem to share with me, or anyone in the world. I wanted to take his lonely longing away and replace it with freedom, but I knew that I couldn't do that for him—only he could do it for himself.

CHAPTER 6

As Sasha's financial issues with the diner improved slowly and she found a new full-time employee to hire in place of the one she had lost, she encouraged me to go to Seattle. I still wasn't emotionally ready to leave her until I knew that the diner and she were doing better—or that was what I told myself as my excuse anyway.

About three months after I left school, I began working as a salesclerk at a bookstore called Dusty Pages two towns away. One of Sasha's customers at the diner had told me about the opportunity during one of my waitressing shifts, and I decided to apply. I was just putting off the decision of when I would leave home and start taking dance classes. My guilt about leaving Sasha and using the college-fund money hadn't lessened, despite time passing and my steadily saving money from working.

The sign above the bookstore entrance was written in black cursive lettering on a white board. It looked like there were little black dust marks underneath "Pages," but they were just tiny holes in the board that had been there since Melanie, the owner, bought it. The bookstore was the only one within a

fifty-mile radius of our region in northern Idaho, so the business was steady. Not everyone wanted to drive all the way to
Spokane to go to the Barnes & Noble there. To Melanie's satisfaction, there was still a robust community, mostly of middle-
aged and older women in the nearby counties, who preferred
to go to bookstores in person rather than ordering online.
Shopping for books online hadn't been an option for me when
I was a young teen in the early 2000s, but it was becoming
an increasingly popular option among kids my age and some
younger adults.

It was an exciting new job for me, the first job I had ever
had outside of Sweet Potato. Somehow, working away from
Sasha made me feel more legitimate, as though I were really
going out to earn my wages and contribute to my future. She
had always paid me for my shifts, but I had always felt a twinge
of unease that, because I was helping my mother, I shouldn't
be paid for them. Of course, she told me that was nonsense.

At Dusty Pages, I did many different jobs. I helped re-
stock shelves, process book orders, and recommend titles to
curious shoppers, who were usually older folks but sometimes
shy, introverted teenagers like me from surrounding towns. I
began to observe a lot about people from the types of books
they purchased—and even more from the books I caught them
lingering over at the shelves but never actually bringing to the
register.

I borrowed books regularly from the store—bringing
them back in impeccable condition as much as I could—
with Melanie's lenient permission. Working at the bookstore
opened my world to new genres and authors. Melanie and her
sister were avid readers, and she loved to share her vast knowledge about new and old books with anyone willing to listen.
Although I had always considered myself a bookworm, I was
surprised by how much more I was reading than I had ever

before. I couldn't get enough, and I started reading two books at a time: one nonfiction, to keep me rooted, and one fiction, to allow myself to be carried away.

After working there for a couple of months, I shared my idea with Melanie to start hosting a monthly book club at the store. She was elated, and we managed to get it running by July, nearly half a year after I dropped out of school. There was a good mix of elderly folks and younger people, some even my age, who came to the book club. I was impressed that a few high school students were willing to give up a Friday night to read and discuss books. Then I realized that it was probably no different from what they would have done—reading in their beds—except that here, they were together, next to other bodies, hearing words spoken aloud, not simply writing quiet notes that might never be shared. Reading together and being able to discuss the stories together was a powerful and fun process. Something I would have liked when I was growing up, that may have drawn me out of my introverted shell. I was grateful for the opportunity now, and I found myself finally, after years, getting over my hesitancy to talk to strangers and make new friends. The book club was the most unassuming, stress-free way to make new friends, both young and old. And my mind was rapidly expanding, both from the new books I was reading, at a rate of three or four a month, and, perhaps more importantly, from the conversations I was having about books with others.

I had read plenty of books throughout elementary and middle school, but I did it slowly and alone. Under trees, on the porch, in the sunshine, and on rainy days in bed. But this collective setting for discussing books was new to me. Pretentious as it felt sometimes when they all came trudging in quietly, the bell ringing with each one who pushed open the door, our book club always settled into a flow of words about words that felt so natural. The members of the group came to life in a way they never allowed themselves to anywhere else. That made everyone feel special, including me.

The days ran like tap water. For the next year, I continued to live with Sasha but spent most of my time—six days a week—at the bookstore. Words sifted in and out of my consciousness. I came to worship the divine power of language to conjure the feelings of eternity and bounty through typed words on a page. I also felt the blackest holes of emptiness breathe upon my mind. "You are what you read" became the truth of my existence. My mood and outlook fluctuated with whatever I was reading. I had never felt so simultaneously impressionable and opinionated. No feeling unfelt, no thought unexplored—I was utterly in love with it all. Finally, with the community of the book club to grow with, being surrounded by books and ideas, I felt like I had found a place where I fit in.

When I wasn't working or reading, Kale and I would go on long walks. He and Sasha were the only two people on whom I depended outside of my world of books and book club friends. And those book club friends weren't even as much friends as accomplices in the world of books, companions in the caves of words we found ourselves exploring and trying to make sense of. I loved chatting with them at our monthly meetings, and we often texted about new book suggestions on the side, but I rarely hung out with them otherwise. The free time I had away from work, I wanted to spend with Sasha or Kale. As much as some of my painful shyness was healed by working at Dusty Pages, the essence of being an introvert could never truly leave my being.

Sasha and I spent time together whenever she wasn't running the restaurant and before I headed to the bookstore, which was usually in the early mornings. Kale and I hung out a few times a week, spontaneously. I would often stop by the convenience store on my way home from work, leaning on the counter and munching on whatever snack he was willing to give me for free: a bag of salted peanuts, gummy bears, licorice. Sometimes we drove to Coeur d'Alene for a day trip, usually on a Sunday, if he could get away from work. We both worked six days a week, not so much because we absolutely had to, but because we feared what would happen if we didn't push ourselves to the limit. When you fall out of the boundaries, as we fell out of school, the fear of losing oneself in the vastness multiplies greatly.

And no one can understand how much bigger that sea of blackness gets until you personally dip a toe into it. As high school dropouts, as the world harshly termed us, we'd both joke that we were simply taking the unbeaten path—Frost's "road not taken." The truth was that our path had no streetlights, no footprints, and no encouraging signs, only imagined consolations that we had to derive for our own self-comfort. We found our grounding through our friendship and the jobs that we poured our energy into, and we were desperate for that grounding because of the fear of what might happen to us— and the disappointment we'd bring upon our families—if we deviated.

One evening, after leaving the bookstore, I drove to Kale's family's store. He was outside speaking to someone by the gas station pumps. I parked my car and leaned against it, texting Sasha that I would be home late as I had stopped by to see him.

"Hey," Kale said, walking toward me. He had the easygoing grin on his face that he often had when I saw him. As usual, while at work, he wore his hair tied up in a bun. Beads of sweat glistened on his forehead, and a rag had been slung over one of his shoulders, which were bare in his white tank top. I glanced back down at my phone, careful not to stare at him for too long. It had become increasingly hard to deny to myself, over the last year, that I had feelings for him. But I was scared these feelings would ruin our perfect friendship, which gave me so much solace and comfort. I didn't want to lose him, so I suppressed these thoughts deep inside me. Though they seemed to be getting more difficult to ignore lately.

"How was your day?" he asked, leaning against my car beside me. I detected the same cologne he'd recently started wearing the last few times I saw him. Its deep, musky scent reminded me of a beautiful forest with tall oak trees.

"Good. It's been a bit busier the last couple of weeks. I guess because it's summer; people seem to like to read more when the weather gets better."

"Yeah, that makes sense."

"What's on your mind?" I asked. I could tell he was thinking about something. He usually made jokes or, being chattier than me, carried the conversation if I didn't have much to say. Early on in our friendship, his talkativeness soothed me and put me at ease, and I still found comfort in hearing his detailed, animated stories about day-to-day things. Somehow, whatever Kale said was interesting to me. He could be talking about restocking shelves or dealing with store bills, but I always found it fascinating enough to listen. Though that probably had more to do with him being the one speaking—his slow, yet energetic drawl, his hand gestures, and his expressive, quick-to-smile countenance.

"Oh, Anokhs," he said. "I just have been wondering. When the hell am I gonna put my money where my mouth is? When am I going to do it?"

I was confused. "Do what?"

"Travel," he said. "I know I have to do it. I've been telling you this since I met you, that my dream is to take a trip around the world. Ma and Pa are doing okay. I mean, Pa is getting old and he needs to sell the store—or find someone younger to manage it. And that someone could be me . . . but I don't want it to be me." He sighed. "I just don't know when I am going to be *done* being the good son I feel like I need to be."

"Oh, Kale," I said, putting my hand on his shoulder. His eyes darted to my hand and then to me, and I felt self-conscious and drew it back. I was trying to comfort him but my skin upon his bare shoulder had felt more electric—maybe to both of us—than I had intended, especially in that moment.

"You are a good son," I went on. "You always will be one. But if you want to do something for yourself, for your life, outside of doing what you feel obligated to do for your parents . . . that doesn't change that. That doesn't make you a bad son." As I finished, I looked straight ahead. It felt too weird to look at him after that unexpectedly intimate touch on his shoulder.

He sighed and shook his head. "I don't know, Anokhs. I tell myself that. I tell myself Pa wouldn't be sad with me if I told him I had to leave for a while and travel or do something for myself. But I can't imagine going through with it. If something happened to him, or Ma, while I was gone . . . I wouldn't be able to live with myself."

I was quiet. I really didn't know what to say. The love and devotion that Kale felt toward his parents had always floored me. I loved Sasha, yes, but I don't think I had ever felt that degree of filial obligation and duty toward her that he felt toward his parents. Though I did use it as my excuse to stay here at home in Idaho, instead of taking the risk of going to learn dance somewhere and leaving the safety net that Sasha raised me in.

Or perhaps I did feel guilty about leaving her. Perhaps I felt guilty that, knowing I was adopted, my leaving Sasha would make her feel like I was abandoning her, like I no longer needed the love and care she had provided to me so abundantly over the years. Perhaps I feared she would feel that I wouldn't come back.

Perhaps I wasn't sure I would come back.

I was about to open my mouth to say something to Kale, to comfort him, but he clapped his hand on my back, almost in a bro-ey way, and stood up straight.

"Come on. Ma's going to make stew for dinner. It's your favorite. Please stay?"

I could never say no to her stew, and more importantly, I could never say no to an offer to spend more time with Kale.

During that period when I was working so much, I didn't see Shaila as often. The renewed energy I had felt after that trip to Seattle, shortly after dropping out of school, had somehow faded away, replaced by the sense of purpose I felt in my new job and the time spent keeping Sasha company. Instead of journaling and daydreaming about Shaila, my sleeping and waking moments were filled now with plots or imaginings or analyses from my books. I even lapsed into thinking that perhaps all those apparitions of Shaila were just delusions that I'd had as a lost, confused young girl. Maybe I didn't need Shaila anymore.

The tides of my past came crashing back down on me unexpectedly one day, however, when Melanie presented me with a book on world dance, as a gift for all my efforts in starting and running the book club. I had mentioned to her, when I'd first started working at the bookstore, that my eventual goal, though vague, was to move away from Idaho to a bigger city where I could learn Indian dance. I guess she never forgot that detail, though we'd hardly spoken of it again and I had thrown myself into my new job.

Now, as I flipped through the book's pages, filled with detailed text and large photographs, one dancer caught my attention. A lone dancer, dressed in all white with a magnificent silver headpiece that resembled a crown, posed with a confident smile, almost a smirk. Her body was curved in numerous places, like a stick bent in zigzags. Her head was tilted to the right, her left arm bent at the elbow, her right hip jutting out to the other side and her left thigh opened so the left knee was splayed out to the left. I marveled at how she stood up with her body bent in so many different directions, yet her face looked serene and comfortable. She was beautiful and strange in this angled, complex pose.

"Odissi is an Indian classical dance originating from the state of Orissa," the bolded caption read, before a much longer paragraph followed.

I thanked Melanie for the unexpected gift and took the book home with me that evening, eager to pore more over it. I guiltily thought of the plan I had made and then abandoned, over a year ago, about going to Seattle to learn Indian dance. I had told myself, when I first took the bookstore job, that I would make the move once I had saved enough money and Sasha's diner was doing better. The problem was I never had defined to myself what "enough" and "better" was. And now, it seemed, it was too scary, or the energy required was too great, to go past my comfort zone, leave the love of Sasha and Kale behind—as well as my cozy corner in the world and my now stable, satisfying job—for a new adventure. I wasn't sure I wanted that anymore.

That night, as I was falling asleep, Shaila entered my mind. She was dressed like the woman in white, her body bent in graceful yet jarring angles, from the world dance book. She danced to music I had not heard before. From the sad hopefulness in her eyes and the ginger movements, putting her hand to her brow and scanning an invisible horizon, I could tell she was looking for someone. She twirled and then showed herself as a mother, miming a draped cloth over her head and around her bosom. She was rocking a baby close to her chest. The music changed into light flute music, almost like a lullaby.

Shaila danced softly across the stage, all the while not letting go of the child in her arms.

But when she twirled again, the child was gone, if it had even been there. Her palms were pressed together in prayer. She prostrated herself, reaching her fingertips just past the edge of a stage, as if there was someone there. She closed her eyes, then slowly fluttered them open and came back to a standing position. And as demurely as she had entered, scanning the horizon, then finding some child and losing it again, she was now devoutly leaving the dance, standing tall, but her eyes were black and emotionless. It was the dance of someone forgotten.

After this dance, which was one of the most vivid I had seen in months, I was baffled. I did not journal. I simply lay there in bed, in the dark, blinking through possible explanations for the dance.

It was not until the next morning that it became clear the meaning was very much intended for me. I *had* forgotten Shaila. I had also forgotten about dance, about India. In getting wrapped up with the bookstore, I forgot what I had originally turned down when deciding to take the bookstore job: learning dance.

And although it had always been true that learning dance might be a way for me to connect more with Shaila, through her art form, I wondered if it was the correct way to get closer to her. Or could it be that Shaila, whoever she was and whatever she represented, embodied so much more than the physical dances that she performed? What other history did she embody through these dance forms that had originated over two millennia ago on the other side of the world? And how could dance feel so real and near to my heart, so rich and vi-brant, when I had no single memory of experiencing it myself?

It dawned on me that I might have been thinking about it all wrong.

Instead of moving to Seattle to learn dance, maybe I needed to go further back. Maybe I needed to understand more about the roots of this dance form that had somehow taken such a strong hold in my life. Maybe I needed to go to the country where all this originated from.

The country of *my* origin.

The country of Shaila.

India.

Now I had money—as well as newfound guilt, which is al-ways the strongest because it rushes in like oxygen after hold-ing one's breath for too long. I would have to take control of my breathing again; I would have to push myself to explore the world. Which meant learning more about where I came from.

I decided then that there was no better way to be closer to Shaila, and more importantly, no better way to be closer to understanding or knowing myself, than to go to India. I didn't know how I had evaded this option for so long, but the rest-lessness and questions I had about where I was going with my life suddenly seemed to have no other antidote than looking back to my past. Yes, I would have to go to India.

CHAPTER 7

I was sitting in the living room, observing the clouds congregating in the sky outside the window. I had been meditating on the decision, or the urge, growing inside me to travel to India. But I hadn't brought it up with Sasha yet—I didn't know how. How could I tell her I wanted to go to India when I couldn't even manage to move to Seattle? I felt like she would call me out on my ridiculous plan to travel across the world without proving I could move to the next state.

"Where did you adopt me from?" I asked her as she watered her plants in the corner of the room.

Sasha, glued together by serenity as always, stopped watering and turned around. "Delhi, sweetie."

"I know it was Delhi, Sasha," I pressed on. "But which orphanage?"

She walked over, sat beside me on the couch, brushed her hands through her hair, and sighed. "I'm sorry, Anokhi. These are answers I should have given you a long time ago." Her eyes were soft and sad, and now that my mother's face was getting older, she had light wrinkles that crinkled at the corners of her eyes when she smiled. Gray wisps had also begun to poke out between the brown curls that she kept tied back in a messy bun while working.

"You did, Sasha," I said gently, putting my hand on hers. "You told me you adopted me from India when I was about a year old. You told me all that when I was younger." I didn't want her to feel bad that I was bringing this up after so many years. But she seemed to be feeling guilty.

"I know, baby," she said, but she still shook her head and then wiped a small but unmistakable tear from the side of her eye with the back of her palm. "I know. But I have never known how or when to talk to you about this more." At this, she squeezed my hands into hers and looked at my face, her eyes glistening.

"It's okay," I said. I rested my head on her shoulder. "I'm just asking because . . . I want to know now. I never asked for more details before because I was scared. Or I just didn't want to know. And your love, this life here, has always been enough for me that I didn't want or need explanations that would bring more questions than answers."

She looked at me curiously. "What questions do you have?" Her almond brown eyes grew large. "Of course, it's understandable to have questions. And there's no right time for you to ask. I just hope I have answers for you. I don't have a lot, which is why I haven't been able to share more with you over the years."

"Oh, I don't even know. I've just been thinking about India more lately." I shrugged.

She stared at me, looking slightly confused, but mostly just fatigued. I paused, trying to clear the clouds that had accumulated in my mind over the past few days, after I had picked up the book on Indian dance and had a vivid dream about Shaila for the first time in many months.

"I've started wondering more about where I'm from. Like in India. It feels like a big part of my identity that I have never really understood or had a reason to investigate more. But now that I'm at this crossroads, out of school and still unable to decide exactly what I want to do next, it feels like this is a good time to go and find out." There. I'd said it out loud.

"Of course you want to know more . . . That makes sense." She nodded. "As I've told you before, unfortunately I don't know anything about your birth parents. The orphanage didn't give me any of that information when I adopted you. And believe me, I tried, but I got conflicting messages. First, they said that information wasn't available, and later, when I asked more, they said they were not able to disclose anything to me."

I nodded, waiting for her to continue.

"After my parents died in the crash during my second year of college, I went to India in the summer for an exchange student program," Sasha began. "Losing them both so suddenly was incredibly hard. I didn't know how to process my emotions. And without my parents, I didn't know what home even meant anymore. I had an urge to go somewhere far away. Perhaps it was a form of escaping or trying to heal myself with distance. So, on a whim, I applied and got into this program through my university."

"I can't imagine," I said. The thought of losing Sasha suddenly to a medical tragedy or an accident sent goose bumps through me. Though the closeness of our relationship often ebbed and flowed, and was never truly the same since I stopped calling her Mom, she was still the oldest and most predictable constant in my life.

I had never known my adoptive grandparents, although Sasha kept a photo of them on her nightstand—a black-and-white picture of a young, attractive couple at the beach. Their faces were a bit too blurred and pixelated to decipher, but Sasha totally had her mother's lovely curly hair. And her father's smile was so big and unreserved that I could almost hear laughter emanating from the frame.

"Why did you choose to go to India for the exchange program?" I asked.

"My mother's mother, your great grandmother, was Indian, and her father was British. He lived in India during the time of the British rule. I had always been fascinated by my mother's Indian heritage, and the stories she would tell me about her early childhood in India, before she moved to England as a little girl." She paused and laughed softly. "Anyway, I'm very mixed, and that's why I have so many different physical features represented in me—my dark but tight curls, my olive skin, my freckles. I suppose that's why we don't get more questions about whether you are my biological daughter or not. Because we don't look too different, do we?" She smiled at me and tucked a loose strand behind my ear.

I laughed, nodding, though I knew, and I think she did too, that we had always looked quite different. As a young child I don't remember thinking much about our different features— her light eyes and olive skin, my dark eyes and brown skin, her tame curls, my frizzy waves. Even after I found out about being adopted and it sank in fully, a few years later, that she did not give birth to me, I never paid much ongoing attention to our different physical features.

"Anyway, the university's exchange program was in Delhi. I stayed there for two months and took a couple of history courses there. I shared an apartment with a few students from across the US who were staying for the summer too. This was back in the early eighties, so the whole study-abroad thing wasn't as huge as it is now. But if you wanted to go, there were ways. And I found one," she said, smiling and looking out the window. "Getting away, back to the country of my mother's birth, helped me process some of that shock and grief I first felt when I heard of my parents' death. I hadn't even been in the same state as them, and their bodies were so disfigured from the car crash I never really got a chance to say goodbye to them physically," she added.

I closed my eyes. The loss of Sasha's parents had been so traumatic and sudden. I could not relate to that but could relate to the vague feelings of loss and grief in not being able to say goodbye to a set of parents—in my case, the birth parents I had no memory of, though they were very much a part of my flesh and blood.

A streak of lightning flashed outside, followed by a loud growl of thunder. I looked out the living room window instinctively. The thin trees lining the sidewalk along our quiet street swayed in the wind, and rain fell silently from the clouds.

Sasha paused and took a sip of water, perhaps grateful for nature's timely interruption during this heavy conversation.

"The thing that bothered me the most, above everything, wasn't the pollution or the traffic or the many, many gawking boys and men. I was okay with all that. Who was I to find fault with any of it—I was there as a visitor, an observer. But the children, begging on the street . . . I hated seeing that. Coming from here and going there and seeing all those street kids, left and right, in rags, hungry, hair yellowed and reddened from dust and grime and I don't know what else, malnourished bodies barely surviving under their worn-out skin . . . Whenever they begged, I had to give, Anokhi—I couldn't refuse even one. I would keep a huge bag of change with me whenever I went out because I knew I would see at least twenty children.

"Anyway, when I left India to come home that summer, I decided I would adopt one of those children, if not more, in the future. It wasn't just something I wanted; it was a vow I made to myself. I had never felt so sure about a promise. So, yes, I came back to the US. I graduated and started working in management at different restaurants. I knew I wanted my own restaurant someday, but of course, I had to get experience first. You know that part of my story already."

She had told me about her path after college, before opening the restaurant here in Idaho with Roy, when I was just a toddler. But I wanted to go back to her story of India. I wanted to hear more about the time around my adoption, before she met me. My memories were blurring, and I was sure she had told me some details about this before, but it had been years since we had talked about it. "Can you tell me more about the orphanage?" I asked.

"Yes, I will. But before that, I need to tell you a bit more about Tim."

I had heard about Tim in the past; there were even pictures of him in old photo albums that I used to flip through as a kid. Sasha was always very open with me about her past relationships—and she had had many of them. Tim had been the longest, though. They had dated for seven years, starting at the end of college, and they broke up when they were both approaching thirty.

"I never told you why we broke up, did I?" There was a glint in her eyes. Not a happy one, but a mysterious one.

No, she hadn't.

"We both started feeling like we might want kids. We felt ready. We didn't feel the need for a wedding; it just seemed like a formality we could do without. We knew we loved each other." She fiddled with her tiny gold hoop earring. She never changed those earrings except for special occasions.

"Gosh, it sounds so funny to say that. We *knew*. Ha! What does anyone ever really know, especially when they're young?" She laughed without a trace of humor. Then she sighed. "Sorry. I'm being cynical. I shouldn't be. We really were in love. But . . . big decisions came, opinions came, and an ending came. Neither of us wanted to budge. We both knew what we wanted, and bending wasn't an option for either of us. So, we broke up."

I waited for her to continue, not knowing precisely what

she was referring to but vaguely sensing that it had something to do with me coming into her life.

"My internal oath from when I went to India never left my mind," she went on. "And when I felt that I was ready to be a mom, I didn't even question whether I would have my own child biologically or adopt. I knew I wanted to adopt. That was it. I had seen too many children on the streets while I was in India that summer, so I could never think of doing anything else other than adopting. Too many children who, through no fault of their own, didn't have a stable home. I couldn't see how I could do anything but help, in some small way, address that issue.

"But Tim . . . Well, Tim wanted to have a child of our own, biologically. At the time I was furious. I called him all sorts of things, my words tumbling out like fire. Selfish. Heartless. It was only after I'd moved out and gone as far away from him as I could that I realized how wrong I'd been. We each have our own dreams for our future and principles that we live by; who was I to criticize him for his?" Her gaze went far beyond the walls of the room. "And yet, his were incompatible with my beliefs. I couldn't change my mind."

"Hmm." I nodded. "That makes sense." I didn't really know what to say. I had never had a boyfriend, nor could I imagine being at a point where I wanted to have or adopt a child with someone. But I could tell from Sasha's impassioned speech how much this breakup had affected her. She had really loved Tim and envisioned a future with him.

"Anyway, we split. Our differing views on adoption were the deciding factor. I told him I was going to adopt a child from India, and that was it. I was not going to have a biological child as long as I knew there were so many children who needed a home. I just could not do it." She sighed, tracing the outline of her water glass wistfully.

I knew this was hard for her to tell me. But I did not want

her to stop. I was soaking in her words, eager for more, waiting patiently for her to tell me about my part of the story. I wanted every detail.

The incessant stream of rain droplets sliding down the smooth glass was creating a gentle swooshing sound like a brook. I pictured cold pebbles playfully poking underneath my toes, my jeans rolled up to my knees—a memory I had in the recess of my mind from a day trip I had taken with Kale to a nearby lake. I had no idea why that was coming to mind now, but I was grateful for the happy interlude before returning to the somberness of the present moment.

It pained me to hear Sasha recount her breakup with Tim. I knew she had dated other men, including Jay and Roy, but Tim was her longest relationship. Deep in my heart, I often felt sorry for Sasha being single. I knew she wouldn't want me to feel that way for her, but I also wondered, behind her strong, resilient exterior, if she ever regretted that she never married or had a consistent life partner. I had never found the words to ask her, but I imagined that sadness about being single creeped into her from time to time, though she never explicitly told me.

"When we split, I moved to Coeur d'Alene—there was a new restaurant, part of a chain, that had opened and they hired me as the manager. That was where I met Roy. He was also in the food business, and we both wanted to open a place together, and he had local ties to this area. I also realized I was sick of cities. So, I came here, to Pineville, with him. And even after he left, and Sweet Potato was already opened, I stayed. And I've never left."

"So, you adopted me right after you moved here?" I asked. As interesting as the other parts of her story were, I needed to get her back on track.

"Well, I began the process in Coeur d'Alene. I had a second cousin from my mom's side who lived in Delhi, and I contacted her to get details about how to go about it. Of course, there were adoption agencies and such, but I wanted some insight from someone local about which orphanages might be good to approach. It wasn't easy. So many rules, so many procedures, and each step took several months. I understood, of course, why it was like that. But it was a long process. By the time I found an adoption agency that seemed like a good mutual fit and was going to possibly work out, six months had passed. Many of them had strange specifications, and most rejected my application because I was single. They said they wanted traditional, stable homes for children to be adopted into, meaning two parents. Finally, though, I found a place, and I went to Delhi. I stayed there for about a month with my cousin—that's how long it took for all the paperwork to be sorted through."

"Did you . . . choose me? Or did they assign me to you?" I asked uncertainly. It sounded like a transaction, and I felt awkward even phrasing it. The words of my questions left my lips feeling dry.

"I told them I really wanted to adopt a girl—a baby or toddler, if possible. They didn't seem surprised by this—many people who adopt prefer to adopt young children because they've spent less time in the orphanage. I felt bad for having this in my mind, but I did, and I had to admit it.

"I still remember the orphanage so clearly: the tame yellow walls, the window overlooking the quiet side street with mango trees. Heat with bursts of a stale breeze from outside, silence with bursts of a cry or a coo. There must have been about ten toys in that room for twenty or thirty little kids—some in cribs, others just on the floor, crawling or lying down or trying to walk, even. I wanted to take every one home. I'm sure I'm not the only one who felt such an overwhelming sensation. Can you imagine walking into a room of so many little abandoned kids, knowing you can only help one? Which one?"

"*Abandoned.*" The word felt harsh. Sasha had told me my parents had loved me, had wanted the best for me. Calling me, among my other small playmates, "abandoned" felt like a punch in the chest. I knew she didn't mean it, but it hurt all the same. To imagine my birth parents abandoning me. I had never blamed them before, because I didn't know them. But when she said it, I winced. I wondered again, as I had over a decade ago, whether they had left me because they hadn't loved me.

I couldn't help but also feel transported to where she was at the time, in this old yellow-walled orphanage, facing this impossibly hard decision of which child to bring back to her home. I closed my eyes and tried to imagine myself there.

Oh wait, I was there.

I shifted uncomfortably in my seat. Even though I knew the story had a happy ending as far as I was concerned—being adopted, becoming Sasha's daughter—I felt nauseous. How would my life have been different if Sasha hadn't chosen me? Where would I be? Who would I be now?

Sasha noted my unease. She put her hand on my arm and gave me a little squeeze.

"I'm sorry if this is too much detail, Anokhi. This must be a lot for you to hear. I'm speaking to you now as an adult, but you are still my child and always will be. Is this too much for today?" she asked gently.

"No." I shook my head. "Please keep going." I had to hear the rest—this story that somehow, though I had heard pieces of it over the years, had never manifested itself into a full beginning, middle, and end with vivid details. Or perhaps I had never asked for the details, and that was my fault. How could we say, over the years that had elapsed, if someone hadn't asked enough or had said too little? Did it matter anyway, now that I felt a new sense of urgency to find out about my past, what had happened all those years ago?

"I saw a small girl sitting in the corner of the room. She looked about a year old," she continued. "Her eyes were dark and expressive, and even at her young age, her brows were furrowed, full of concentration. She was playing with a small steel tumbler. First, she put it face down on the ground and moved it around in circles in front of her. Then she smiled at the tumbler and followed it with her big eyes, as if she knew some hilarious secret that was only hers to enjoy. She picked it up and held it very close to her face, almost covering her nose and mouth like she was going to drink from it, and she looked at it so closely she was almost crossing her eyes. I walked over to her and bent down. She put the cup down and gazed at me, her lovely eyelashes blinking like wings on a butterfly.

"'What's her name?' I asked.

"'Anokhi,' the staff member replied.

"'What does that mean?'

"'It means "different." Or . . . how would you say . . . like, unique, special. From the day she came here, she has always been a little different from the other children. She never cries. She can get along with the other children, but she also loves to be alone and play her own games. We never know what exactly she is thinking, but she can entertain herself for hours with the simplest things.'"

I couldn't help but smile. She sounded like such a sweet little girl. Innocent, mysterious, independent. I almost forgot for a moment she was talking about me.

Sasha smiled too. "And I just knew. Simple as that, I wanted you. You and all your differentness, your uniqueness. I knew each child was special in her own way, of course. But your name even called out to me. I liked the way the syllables sounded in my mouth, like honey and possibility and a dash of mystery. I loved you from the moment I met you."

The rain was pounding harder now and the light in the room made space for the darkness that was spreading outside.

I smiled and closed my eyes. How could I have not asked

her to tell me this whole story, in all its beautiful, though painful, details before now?

Bits and pieces always shone through, of course, over the years. I knew I was born in India. I also knew Sasha's mother was part Indian, which meant Sasha had some Indian heritage too. Sasha had no living family, none that she ever talked about anyway, so it was always just me and her, islands in a sea full of people unrelated to us.

And now, I had the age and maturity to investigate a past that I could more fully understand. The details were now making more sense, scraps I had heard of Sasha's past brought to life through our conversation today: Tim, their breakup story, her parents dying abruptly when she was in college, and her decision to go to India for an exchange program that changed her life in more ways than one. Which ultimately led her to me.

When I was a child, my sense of family and identity crumbled on that day when I was seven years old and I realized Sasha and I weren't made of the same swirls of genes. For the last eleven years, I had tried to convince myself that it didn't matter.

But it did matter. I realized I had feared asking her these details because I thought it would break us, just as I had stopped calling her Mom once I truly understood what being adopted meant.

The truth was the opposite. Now that I knew this part of the story, of our story, I felt closer to Sasha.

"Anyway," she said, looking at me thoughtfully. "Did that answer your questions? And can I ask—why today? Why did you choose today to ask me all this?"

I smiled. "Yes. It did. And . . . it's because I would like to travel to India. To see the place where I am from. Where I was born."

Sasha nodded, not looking in the least bit surprised. "I always thought you should, at some point. I never wanted to push you or influence you. I thought of taking you before when you were younger, but as you know, money has always been a bit tight, and I also wasn't sure when the right time would be. But I think it would be good for you. And perhaps there could not be a more perfect time, as you are at this crossroads in your life."

I nodded, the idea of traveling to India suddenly taking shape in my mind. There were so many unknowns. I had never traveled outside the country before. And I had never taken a trip so far by myself. Would Sasha come with me? Did I want her to come with me? I wasn't sure. Part of me felt like I had to make this trip alone, but I didn't know exactly why.

"Do you think you'd want to go to the orphanage?" she asked, interrupting my reverie.

"I . . . Probably," I said. "I really haven't thought about the details yet. But yes, I think I would want to go there. If I could."

The potential plans rolled out so easily. But was there anything easy about this? I had a vague feeling I was underestimating the enormity of this trip, even in the nascency of planning it.

"Even if you don't want to go to the orphanage, I understand. I didn't mean to push that idea on you. You should do whatever you want," Sasha said. "I'm just glad you're thinking of going back. I have wanted this for you for a long time. I think now that you are older, it is a good time," she said, squeezing me tightly in a hug. Then, she added, "I've been waiting for this day when you would, of your own will, feel your heart being pulled back across the years, before we flew over the oceans to come here together."

I hugged her back deeply. I loved her for her support, her openness, and her honesty.

She pulled away from me and stroked my cheek affectionately. "A trip back to India may be exactly what you need in this moment in your life. I don't think umbilical cords, to mothers or motherlands, are ever fully cut."

The next morning, after I had slept on my decision, I felt it more fully in my heart that I wanted to make this trip alone. It was nothing against Sasha—she had been wholly supportive yesterday. But I felt that as I discovered my roots, saw the place from where I was adopted, and immersed myself in the country of my birth, I would want to be alone. I would want to take in all the sights, sounds, and feelings by myself, and form my own opinions. I didn't want to be swayed by Sasha's memories of India, from her time in college or when she went back to adopt me. As I was figuring out what to do next—whether that was really moving to Seattle or another big city to learn dance, or something else yet undiscovered—I felt like I was on a path of self-discovery that I needed to travel alone.

"Good morning, sweetie," Sasha said, pouring herself a cup of black coffee from the coffeepot. "I was looking into some flight options this morning. I know you don't have a date set, but I was looking at tickets for us . . ."

My heart sank. I had hoped she would intuit that I might want to take this trip alone. I didn't want to have this conversation with her and hurt her feelings.

"Sasha," I said, taking a deep breath and sitting down at the countertop stool. "I was sort of thinking that I would go to India alone."

She put down her mug slowly, reshuffling her newspaper neatly into a folded pile before looking up at me. "You want to go to India alone?" she echoed, her voice quiet.

"I . . . yeah. I think so. I mean, I think it would be great to go together. But . . . I sort of feel like I need to take this trip on my own." I paused, unsure of what to say to bolster my case. "To prove to myself that I can do it."

Sasha looked at her coffee for a moment, then looked back at me. "Anokhi," she said slowly. "You've never traveled so far by yourself before. India is . . . a big country. It's not the safest." She let her words settle in the air between us. Her face exhibited her concern.

"Yeah . . ." I said, my voice trailing off. Sasha had been to India twice. I had left the country when I was an infant. What could I say to argue with her? She was right.

Yet I wasn't ready to let it go. It felt important to me that I take this trip by myself. For the past almost two years, since I left high school and settled into my comfortable routine working at Dusty Pages, after initially feeling a lot of motivation to leave Pineville and move to a big city to learn dance, my life had been devoid of any real adventure or marked self-growth. Of course I had grown, physically and mentally, as I entered early adulthood. But I had not left for college. I had not even left. It felt like I had to prove something to myself through taking this trip.

"I'm not saying no," Sasha said, looking at me unsmilingly. "But . . . it's a big decision. And ultimately, you *are* eighteen," she said, factually but without any trace of encouragement. "You can do what you want. But . . . I'm surprised, that's all."

I didn't know what to say, so I didn't say anything. I didn't expect her to understand; I didn't even fully understand myself. I knew I had hurt her feelings. I got the sense that she may have been envisioning, since our conversation yesterday, a trip with us together, rediscovering my roots, and her roots too, through new eyes as a mother-daughter pair, with me now grown up.

We left the conversation at that. I felt terrible, but I also felt that I just had to keep making plans and go. Nothing else would quell the deep desire in my heart to unearth answers to who I was meant to be. Answers that I increasingly felt could only be found by looking back at who I was and where I came from.

Kale and I were walking around his huge backyard, enjoying the late afternoon. Earlier, we had been lying on the knotted-rope hammock his dad had put up between two pine trees when they first moved.

It was a beautiful winter day, the sun bright and the sky cloudless. I didn't say much the whole afternoon, and Kale didn't seem to care. He smiled serenely as the December breeze kissed his face, his cheekbones bronzed and prominent.

"I'm going to India, Kale," I announced abruptly. I'd had no idea how to broach the topic with him, so it came out bluntly.

He dropped the twig he had been peeling the bark from.

"You *what*?"

"I'm going to India," I repeated.

He didn't say anything and just stared at me, his mouth slightly agape.

I cleared my throat and continued, uncomfortable by his reaction. "Remember the college fund Sasha gave me when I dropped out? I never used it, and she refused to take it back, even when the diner was doing badly. Now thankfully it's doing better. Plus, I've been saving all my money since I started working at Dusty Pages. So, I'm going to buy my ticket tonight. I've decided I need to go back and learn more about where I am from. I think I'll buy a one-way ticket for now, because I'm not sure how long it's going to take."

I don't know why I started babbling about money and logistics; obviously, Kale didn't care about how I was going to go as much as *why*. I looked at him and his expression was still one of shock.

"How long *what's* going to take?" he asked, confusion lining his thick brows. He looked upset.

"The trip. I've decided I'm going to go back not just to see the country. But I'm also going to try to find my birth parents," I replied, exhaling slowly. I had previously told him about the conversation with Sasha about the orphanage. But I didn't, at that time, have the courage to tell him about my going. I had already hurt Sasha by telling her I wanted to go alone.

"India . . ." he said. As he studied the trees we strolled beneath, he appeared lost in thought. Or maybe just lost. It was Kale who had always been the one who talked about his grand plans of traveling the country and the world, not me. Sadly, he hadn't been able to do that yet because he was so loyal to his parents. First it was his mother and her cancer treatments. Then it was his father's financial strains with running the convenience store. Now Mr. Kealoha had also, over the summer, been diagnosed with a progressive neurological condition that was causing weakness in his arms and legs. But, as a proud family man, small-business owner, and main breadwinner for their home, he did not want to stop working even though Kale offered many times to take over managing the store. He said he would die sooner than stop working.

And that was what appeared to be happening: a slow but certain death sentence with this new diagnosis. I knew Kale would never desert him, despite having saved enough money to finance his traveling dreams, and this fact alone caused a pang of guilt and sadness in my chest. I didn't bother asking Kale to come with me because I knew he was tied to his father now more than ever. It saddened me to see him—young and full of life, curiosity, and energy—tethered to this small corner of the world out of filial obligation. His sense of duty to his family was unshakable, admirable, and not something I could challenge.

But Kale's ability to take advantage of all that life had to offer was also admirable. It was as if he consumed the world through one big inhalation—deep, slow, and clear—no matter where he was and what curveballs were thrown at him. It amazed me how much he made of our small town and our pocket of life in the Pacific Northwest, with all the day trips, hikes, adventures, and road trips he managed to plan and go on, often dragging me along, which I loved. My worldview was that much bigger because of his adventurous spirit.

Yet here I was going farther than he had ever been. I knew it would hurt him, but I also knew he'd want me to go. Still, it hit me like an icy wave that none of us exists as an independent string; we're all tied together. Tied in knots. And when two ends of a knot are pulled apart, the knot only gets tighter.

I put my arm around Kale's shoulder. His silence was painful, and my heart was beating faster, anxious for him to tell me that it was okay, I could go, and he would forgive me for leaving him. "I want to ask you to come with me. But I know you can't."

He gently brushed my arm off his shoulder and continued walking. "Yeah, it may be easy for you to get up and leave home, go across the world. But it's not so simple for me."

His words stung. There was nothing easy about my decision, but it hurt to hear him say this. I knew I was privileged in a way, not being tied to an obligation like helping an aging parent run a business or care for a sick parent. And I had the funds to take this trip too. Yet the disdain in his voice, as I heard it, made me feel ashamed and hurt, which turned to anger.

As we walked on, he veered slightly away from me. It was probably only three inches, but I could not ignore what he'd done. He knew that distance would twist my heart more than walking away from me completely would have. I suspected his unspoken message was the idea that inches of space can hurt more than miles. That sometimes you can feel the most pain when you are close and that pain might be the inverse of distance when you love someone.

"I can't just come, Anokhi," he said, after our shared silence. "My dad. The store. You know I can't."

My eyes burned and my throat followed suit. I wouldn't cry, not here, not now. He hadn't called me Anokhi since the first day we talked in ninth grade, when we sat next to each other in algebra.

"What's your name?" he had asked, brushing a lock of thick, curly brown hair away from his forehead, a gesture I would come to see so many times over the course of our friendship and tease him about mercilessly.

"Anokhi. What's yours?" I whispered. From a young age, I had always feared speaking during class, afraid the teacher would notice and call me out. I hated drawing attention to myself.

"Kah-LEH-ah."

"Kah-LEH-ah?" I repeated uncertainly. Growing up in Idaho, I wasn't used to encountering names sounding foreign like my own.

"Yep." He nodded.

"How do you spell that?" Understanding how to say and spell this mysterious boy's name became more important to me than paying attention to the algebra teacher, which was very uncharacteristic for me, a self-proclaimed nerd.

"*K-A-L-E*," he replied.

"As in the vegetable?"

"Yeah. Well, it's actually spelled *K-A-L-E*-apostrophe-*A*. But I've shortened it to Kale."

"So . . . what should I call you?"

"Just call me Kale, like everyone else does."

And just like that, I could never forget his name. Usually when you meet people, you ask them their name and then immediately go on to the how-are-yous and the chitchat, migrating further and further from the introduction so fast that most of the time you can't remember their name at the end. But I never liked that. A name is a name, and it matters. And once I learned Kale's name, I wanted to know more about him.

Soon after that first meeting, he began calling me Anokhs. Initially it annoyed me; no one had ever shortened my name before. They had mispronounced it, sure—AY-no-key, Uh-NO-kai. (Close, but not quite: It's Uh-no-KHEE.) Why did Kale have to shorten it? I liked my name and how it meant "different, unique." Sometimes, I imagined that my name meant something deeper. That it was an assurance that things would be all right and that I would find unique sparks throughout life that would shape me. And I knew I had already found one important spark—Kale.

Why are you calling me Anokhi? I wondered.

I stopped. He kept going for a few steps, then stopped and turned around. Our eyes locked. I didn't want to look away first, at the risk of coming across as coy and demure—why in the world would I be coy and demure anyway? This was Kale, my best friend. Yet for some reason, I was overcome by a feeling that bordered on shyness.

Look away, Kale, I thought. *I'm getting tired of staring into your deep beautiful eyes. The longer I stare, the less I know how to feel sure of this decision. I really don't want to leave you.*

As he held my gaze, a myriad of emotions and memories hit me, like the acorns that fell on our heads one afternoon last fall when we sat under the trees in his backyard and read Shakespeare, laughing until we cried at the dramatic parts that bore so little resemblance to our own lives.

Now our lives felt dramatic. But not in a good way. A foreboding feeling threatened to break open my heart. I'd never known I could feel this type of pain.

"You will have a wonderful time. What an adventure for you, Anokhs," said Kale softly. "Be safe. I hope you find them."

What was he saying? He sounded too old. He sounded far away, like something he was not.

Stop, Kale, I thought. My vision blurred as tears filled my eyes. I felt a desire to run into his arms, to tug him back to the space we used to fill with our childlike closeness. The deep friendship—or was it love?—seemed to have rapidly changed just during this conversation. It was as if our four years of knowing each other had been lit on fire.

I was only going to India. I would be back. Why were these inches between us so searing?

Please, make this moment stop, I thought to myself. *I just want to bask in our youth and endearing ways, our silly jokes, and our long, silent, peaceful drives.*

"Kale'a," I said, a desperation lining my voice. I didn't know how to express what I felt. He had called me Anokhi; now I had to call him by his full name. Maybe it would invoke visions from his childhood that might flood his mind: his father's fishing dock, the creaky wooden planks upon which he played as a toddler, the taste of home-cooked mahi-mahi flaking gently on his tongue, his young tastebuds awakened by their reverie. Maybe the palm trees of his homeland would blow in his mind and trigger a heartache for Hawai'i that would help him understand how I had begun to feel about India. And maybe, with that understanding, he could forgive me a little for leaving him behind.

I thought I saw his eyes glistening for a moment, but then the opacity returned. "Anokhs, I have to get back to the store. It's almost five. Dad's going to need help unloading and restocking since it's Friday. Let me know when you're leaving. I'll come see you before you go, if you want me to."

If you want. The nonchalance and indifference of his words seared into me.

Shakespeare was right about the world being a stage. We have to act like we *are* feeling what we are not and like we are *not* feeling what we actually do feel. And I had to play my part. I shrugged, trying to match Kale's indifferent tone with my actions. And with that shrug, I lost what I wanted the most: to spend as much time with my best friend, whom I loved beyond my ability to articulate it to him, as I could before I left.

CHAPTER 8

Sasha drove me to the airport in Spokane, Washington, a few months after I had conceptualized my plan for India. The drive there was mostly quiet; she had never outright told me she was upset with me for wanting to go without her, but the weight of my decision hung in the air between us. She did give me a lot of tips about traveling solo—I could tell she was worried. She told me to keep my backpack in front of me in crowds, to not walk outside in the dark, to not take public transportation without being with someone trusted who was a local, and to stay near groups of women and children rather than wandering alone or in areas where there were only men. I was too excited and naive to feel her concern, but I did listen to her advice. She had been to India, after all, and I hadn't.

She made me buy a prepaid international plan for my cell phone. She also, after I had told her I wanted to go to Delhi, reached out to her second cousin, Jasmine, who she had stayed with in Delhi all those years ago, before adopting me. She hadn't spoken to Jasmine in many years but was able to find her on Facebook and connect with her. Jasmine was very happy to hear from Sasha and told her I could absolutely stay with her.

When Sasha parked the car at the terminal, she got out and took my luggage out for me from the trunk of her station wagon. I wanted to travel light, so I was just taking a backpack and a small rolling suitcase.

"Please text me as soon as you land in LA," she said, shutting the trunk and extending the suitcase handle for me. She pushed a strand of hair away from her face and removed her sunglasses so she could look at me better.

"I will, I promise," I said, nodding. It felt like a goodbye that I never thought I'd be saying to her. Pangs of guilt and nervousness hit me unexpectedly. I would be traveling so far away.

"I love you, sweetheart," she said, her voice cracking. She wrapped me up in a tight hug, and I let myself breathe in the scent of her simple and ever-changing perfume—the aroma from whatever she had last cooked. Today it was spaghetti and meatballs—my childhood favorite, which she had cooked for me as an early goodbye lunch.

"I love you too, Sasha."

I headed toward the terminal's glass doors. When I turned around to wave bye, she had already climbed into the car, but she was still parked there, slowly waving at me through the passenger window. Her face was red, and she held a tissue in her hands.

On the flight from Los Angeles to Delhi, I sat in a window seat, grateful to be nestled in the corner so I could gaze out at the sea or darkness or whatever was passing above, below, and around us. I hadn't flown much, and flying felt so strange to me. I felt a little nauseous with the takeoff but quickly grew to love the view from so high up in the sky. I felt like a trespasser up there, yet I enjoyed every minute.

I was struck, as I boarded and found my seat, by how I did not stand out at all on this plane—almost everyone was brown skinned and dark haired, like me. I had never been around so many people who looked like me. I was sitting next to a young woman in her mid-thirties who also appeared to be Indian. She was quite pregnant and slept most of the trip. She had the sweetest, most content smile on her face as she slept, which I could not help but notice and admire. I don't like to think that it was the fact that she was pregnant that made me more appreciative of her smile—as if it were a great accomplishment that she was smiling so serenely in the height of her pregnancy. But in some way or another, if a nonpregnant woman had been sitting next to me and had been beaming that same peaceful smile, I don't think I would have thought as much of it.

A succession of Hindi movies was played over the course of the eighteen-hour flight. I watched bits and pieces without wearing headphones. I found the viewing more interesting without sound, but I didn't want to endure the headache of squinting at the subtitles either.

I had bought the Hindi version of Rosetta Stone a few days after deciding to go on this trip and had spent the last few weeks diligently going through the videos in the evening. It felt futile, trying to learn an entire language in such proximity to my arrival in India, but I knew I had to try to at least get basics down. My anxiety had been somewhat quelled after I had read that a lot of people spoke English in major cities in India.

I had reviewed the videos and silently practiced some of the more basic conversational exercises again on my laptop during the flight to LA:

"Aap kaise ho?" (How are you?)

"Mera naam Anokhi hai." (My name is Anokhi.)

I felt fake, perfunctory. I wanted to just know how to get to the meat of conversation—though of course I had no idea what exact conversations I'd be having there. The only language I knew other than English was French—which was limited to basic skills learned in a classroom setting, and I had never actually been anywhere where native French speakers lived. I had hated how we had spent so much time on introductions and greetings every year in French class. Of course they were important, but I never felt like I was learning the crux of what I needed to know. And then suddenly the focus would shift to fruits and vegetables and verb conjugations. Without ever using my French outside of the classroom, I never knew how I might fare in Paris.

Sasha had always loved watching foreign films. When I started high school, we often watched Bollywood movies together on weekend nights after dinner. We usually watched older films that Sasha had been introduced to by her own mother, from the sixties. The songs were a bit kitschy, and the acting was often overly dramatic. They were most always love stories, interspersed with family drama and catastrophic plot twists between friends and foes. I found the stories unrelatable as well as the characters; the actresses were all too picture-perfect and the actors too suave and cheesy. But I loved the music, which was always accompanied by elaborate dance routines, and used to listen to some of it when Sasha wasn't around. The fact that I couldn't understand the words made me feel like the lyrics rained into me like poetry read into the wind.

The movie I now watched on the plane was more recent—the info tab said it was filmed in 2005. Eventually, the scenes of couples dancing in the mountains and having intense discussions in household entryways, and of families crying together, began to blur on the small screen in front of me, and I drifted off to sleep.

As we made our descent into the sparkling darkness of Delhi, I relished my last few moments in the air before we officially touched the ground. India: the land in which I was born, the earth that nourished my first days, weeks, and months of life. I felt intimidated. The trip did not feel like a homecoming as much as a test. I wanted to see if I could find my roots and learn to love them naturally. And I craved to see if my roots would love me back.

The pregnant woman woke up suddenly, as if she did not want to miss the landing.

"Oh great, we're almost here!" she said, grinning and peering past me to look at the darkness sprinkled with city lights that were slowly becoming clearer.

I smiled back, tried not to look at her tummy and failed, and then looked quickly out the window again. I felt that she would be a great mother. She was so smiley; how could she not be? For a moment, I wondered if all her smiles and joy would melt quickly with the stress she would experience as a mother or during the birthing process. Or would she always smile—through pain, through laughter, through silence once her child grew up and left her?

As I considered the inner musings of this unsuspecting woman next to me, I was suddenly shaken out of my dreamy wonderings with a disturbing thought. What had my own birth mother looked like when she was pregnant with me? Did she smile—was she happy to be pregnant? Or was her pregnancy distressing, either because of health issues or external circumstances? I wondered under what conditions I had been in her womb and how that may have unknowingly affected me now, as a birthed human who had grown eighteen years in the world, outside her, whoever she was.

I also was struck as we approached the ground—India, the land of my ancestors, the land of my birth—by the sobering thought that I may never see or know her, my birth mother.

That was one of my goals of my trip—to find out more from the orphanage about my birth parents and to try to meet them, if I could. Booking tickets, getting Rosetta Stone, and boarding the plane had all been relatively easy, even though leaving Sasha and Kale certainly wasn't. But now, I realized with a wave of dread, came the hard part. Who would this woman, my birth mother, be? Would she even want to see me? Could I even see her?

THUD. The landing was impressive and ended my internal monologue abruptly, which was just as well as I was starting to panic from the spiraling of my unanswerable questions. I stared out at the runway, half-expecting to see some great big sign that said **INDIA!** This felt like such a huge moment: I was here, I was home! But was this really home? Several people began clapping and cheering—for the landing, I assumed. I wondered if the safe landing wasn't a given and that was why they were appreciative. I clasped my hands together in muted thanks.

"Namaste and welcome to Delhi," announced a flight attendant on the overhead speakers. "The outside temperature is thirty-two degrees Celsius. The local time is 4:55 a.m. Please remain in your seats until we reach the gate. Thank you for flying with us on Air India, and we hope to serve you again in the future. Namaste." She then repeated the entire text in Hindi. Her speech was melodious and sounded very formal and clear. Like the slightly stilted, crisply enunciated speech of the woman on the Rosetta Stone videos. I wondered how this would compare to the more colloquial Hindi I assumed I'd hear among people in Delhi—I suspected it would not be the same at all.

The moment she stopped speaking, about half the passengers were already out of their seats and bustling about, opening overhead bins and picking up bags off the floor. I looked around confusedly, and the lady next to me laughed at my incredulous expression.

"First time flying to India, hmm," she half asked, half stated.

I nodded.

"People don't usually wait until the plane stops before getting up. It's merely a suggestion, no?"

I shrugged. It was funny if I thought about it. I had been so annoyed in LA when we were getting ready to board and no one paid any attention to the zone numbers for boarding. People had shoved past one another, flocking together in a disorganized cluster of bodies, totally disregarding the instruction of forming a line and instead forming a clump that hovered around the gate entrance. I understood if adults with small children or elderly people wanted to try to get ahead of the line, but *everyone* seemed to want to board first. Everyone was important, everyone had to get on the plane first, and everyone was going to try.

Sasha had mentioned to me some cultural differences I might notice when I traveled to India—the tendency to take off shoes before entering people's homes, the habit of eating food with hands, the way people nodded their heads side to side in a slightly wavy way to signify saying yes. She hadn't mentioned this cultural phenomenon pertaining to boarding and disembarking practices. Perhaps this wasn't something she'd noticed before. Perhaps it didn't matter—for, after all, what did it matter how people got on and off planes? Weren't we all just travelers trying to get to our destination?

I knew I had to chill out if I was going to make it through this trip and what it had in store for me. So I took a deep breath, made my choice to wait for the seat belt light to turn off, and got up to leave.

Dance breathes life into our story.
Delhi, India

Shaila's dance thrummed with vitality, her movements sweeping across the stage like gusts of wind in concert with the violin, sitar, and tabla. Her poses were magnificent representations of strength as she balanced on one leg or squatted down with one leg extended out so that the pleats between her pants spread like a shimmering fan. She often held her palms joined together before they blossomed out into elaborate hand gestures. She was like a blooming flower depicting the potential for life, renewal, and celebration.

With her red lips curved into a big smile and her dark, mystical eyes shining brightly, she radiated excitement and happiness. She danced in broad, sweeping movements, like a young woman exploring a new land. She seemed excited, curious, and full of life. Her enthusiasm was infectious, and the music accompanying her was playful and youthful.

But after a while, the music began to slow down. The violin and sitar took on melancholic notes, and Shaila began to center herself on the stage, taking up less space. Her exuberant energy was replaced by a calm concentration that seemed to focus inward. She twirled gently in the middle of the stage before taking up an impressive meditative posture, standing on one leg, holding her arms up above her like an unshakable tree. It seemed that her energy had found its focus, after an initial dazzling display of excitement and chaos. Through the undeniable concentration required from her balancing pose, the center of her energy was rooted in her own unwavering sense of self.

CHAPTER 9

After getting off the plane and walking long, dimly lit corridors that matched my jet-lagged, awestruck state of mind, I went to the bathroom. The first stall I opened surprised me; there was just a toilet built straight into the ground with a metallic small hose attached to the wall. I had never seen anything like it.

I opened the next two stalls until I found a stall with a full toilet. It was only after I used the bathroom and was leaving that I saw, in small thin letters on the stall doors, **Western Toilet** and **Indian Toilet**. I smiled to myself. I had never been somewhere where there were different types of toilets.

I turned on my phone. It took a few moments for the signal to come through, and for a second, I panicked that my phone, despite the international prepaid plan, wouldn't work here. I got a string of three text notifications all at once—from Jasmine, Sasha, and Kale.

Jasmine's text read, Hello Anokhi! I'm here at the airport waiting with the driver. Call me as you are walking out of the airport, we will come pick you up at Arrivals.

Sasha and Kale's separate texts were both checking to see if I had reached India. Bleary-eyed and scrambling to walk out of the airport to get some fresh air, I texted them in our group thread, which we had set up long ago for logistics, like to coordinate Kale coming over to our house for dinner. But they also used it if neither of them could get in touch with me when I was at the bookstore—because I wasn't replying to texts. Now I used it to let them both know I was fine and waiting to meet Jasmine.

The jet lag started to hit me as I navigated through the airport, which made sense after I spotted a clock indicating that it was just a few minutes past 5:20 a.m. local time. Because I hadn't checked my bag, my exit from the airport was pretty quick once I made it through immigration and customs, and I called Jasmine as I followed signs toward the exit.

"Hello!" She answered her phone brightly, as if it weren't such an early hour, and told me where we should meet. "I'm wearing a bright orange top, and I'll be waving outside the car. Don't get into anyone else's car!" she said, laughing.

The hot, early-morning air greeted me when I left the terminal. I took a deep breath in—humid and heavy, not particularly refreshing. The sky was still a dark blue, with just a whisper of an impending sunrise. As I waited for Jasmine, I glimpsed a sign for prepaid taxis with the English translation directly below the curly, intricate Hindi letters. I was pleased to see that the language of the colonizer was below the native language, though I then wondered why I cared. Who was I to have an opinion on which language should go where on the signs in the Delhi airport? It was as though a vague bicultural cloud existed within me, but I was too tired to explore it now. I had a headache, my eyes felt tired, and my whole body longed for a shower after traveling for over twenty-four hours. I would investigate my conflicted cultural feelings later.

The humidity was already soaking through my long-sleeved cotton shirt, and my backpack was sticking to my back with sweat. I recalled Sasha's advice that I keep my bag in front of me, though, looking around, I didn't see any particular reason why I should be worried—everyone seemed too wrapped up with getting into taxis, cars of family members, and so on. Rows of rounded black taxis with bright yellow tops lined the curbsides. Porters in dark blue and taxi drivers in white helped weary, stumbling travelers load their belongings into trunks. There was a long line to acquire a prepaid taxi.

Far ahead, I spotted a woman in a bright orange long shirt standing outside a car. She was waving at me with both arms above her head. I smiled and waved back and walked toward her, weaving around a bleary-eyed couple trying to pacify their howling toddler. Just as I neared Jasmine, I noticed an old woman crouched on the ground near the wall who made me stop. The sight of her protruding collarbone, peeking out from her tattered red blouse, pierced my heart. Collarbones, I had always thought, were a symbol of youthful beauty. Their frailty was not apparent to me until I saw hers, which conveyed nothing as prominently as hunger. So much bone should not be visible through the skin, I thought. I wished I had some change to give her, but I was going to exchange currency later with Jasmine and didn't have any rupees yet. I forced myself to walk on, though it was hard to stop looking at her.

"Anokhi! You have made it! Welcome to India!" Jasmine cried with a huge smile on her face. When she threw her arms around me in a big warm hug, I detected the fragrances of cardamom and freshly washed cotton. She hugged me tightly, as if she had known me forever, and this caught me off guard. I wasn't used to hugging people I barely knew with such deep affection. But I accepted her comforting embrace all the same.

When I pulled back, I finally was better able to see her features. She was a short, middle-aged Indian woman, with dark brown skin similar to my own, and she wore a bright orange kurta over cotton pants with a red paisley pattern. Large gold earrings dangled from her ears, and a small black purse hung from one shoulder. When she smiled, I noticed a little gap between her front teeth. Her thick black hair, gray at the roots, was pulled back into a bun with a large clip.

"Thank you," I said, smiling, holding onto my luggage handle and the strap of my backpack. She was so friendly and welcoming, but I felt shy and didn't know what exactly to say to her, though she was a relative. "I'm glad to be here."

"Yes, baby! I am so glad you made it safely! You must be exhausted," she said. As we talked, a thin dark-skinned man emerged from the driver's seat on the right side of the car. He took my suitcase from me wordlessly and loaded it into the trunk.

"Sasha didn't tell me you were so beautiful! Or so grown up!" she went on, taking me by the arm and leading me into the back seat of the car. Before she shut the door behind herself, she said something in Hindi to the thin man who had taken my bag.

"Yes, madam," he said, bobbling his head faster than I had ever seen anyone do. I couldn't tell if he was shaking his head or nodding. Then I remembered about the head nod that Sasha had told me about.

"Oh, and you can call me Jasmine Aunty, dear," Jasmine said, smiling at me and patting my arm. "We are family after all!"

I smiled. I didn't grow up having any aunts or uncles because Sasha had been an only child. I had never called anyone Aunty. I knew it was going to take some getting used to, but her warmth was contagious.

Small brightly colored figurines, who I assumed were Hindu gods, lined the dashboard, and a small orange garland hung from the rearview mirror. Jasmine and I both sat in the back, which I thought was a bit strange, but it became clear to me quite quickly, though Jasmine didn't explicitly say it, that the man in the front was the driver. I wanted to address him, to acknowledge him—it felt rude to me not to say something to the person driving me away from the airport. But I froze, uncertain of what I would even say. I didn't even know if he spoke English, and I was not prepared to try my Hindi just yet.

Jasmine and I chatted for a couple of minutes about what I had eaten on the plane, my impressions of the airport—I told her the story of my encounter with the different types of toilets, and she laughed. But she knew I was tired and told me to sleep, as it was going to be about an hour in the car. I was grateful for her invitation to take time to rest, though instead of sleeping I fell into a daze, staring out the window and watching this old city, although it was new to me, wake up and start its day.

Now close to seven in the morning, the streets teemed with honking cars and motorcycles. I had never seen such traffic, and what made it even more striking was that there didn't seem to be any lanes. Cars didn't follow one another in a straight line—it seemed like vehicles just fit in wherever they could, like a giant jigsaw puzzle on the road with motorcycles weaving into any gaps. We also were driving on the left side of the road, with a short meridian in the middle and oncoming traffic to our right. It was both fun and disorienting to observe the seemingly trivial but very visually noticeable difference in traffic patterns here.

People were everywhere too. They lined the sides of the streets and the sidewalks, where those things existed, but in many places it just looked like large patches of dirt between the road and the buildings or gates protecting the buildings. There was no way I could sleep; instead, I drank in all the new sights, like wooden carts heaped with colorful orange, green, and yellow fruit or brown and black cows shuffling slowly and carelessly along the sides of the road, seemingly oblivious or indifferent to all the cars and people around them. I also noticed, more than once, individuals sitting or standing on the sidewalk who were missing one or more limbs. The first man I saw was sitting on what looked like a small skateboard, his arms thinner than a baseball bat, and I saw that he had no legs; his torso just seemed to dissolve into the board. We were not going very fast in the car, so there was a lot of time to observe these sights. I felt an immediate pang of horror when I saw him, and felt terrible for him—but I was barely able to process seeing him before I saw another woman, hobbling on the side of the road, swinging her body back and forth in exaggerated motions, and I saw that one of her legs was markedly shorter than the other and she was missing one arm. Her existing arm was holding a cane. My heart felt heavy; I had of course seen people with different bodies, a few in wheelchairs, back home. But to see these people, absorbed in the hustle and bustle of the street's commotion, but also with such striking physical irregularities in their bodies, filled me with a sadness I could not place. I wanted to do something for them but also felt naive for this impulse. *What could I possibly do?*

There was so much visible suffering on these streets, beyond anything I had ever seen in my life. I had read about some of the poverty statistics in India before my trip, but seeing it with my own eyes was completely different. The magnitude and complexity of this country of over one billion people was pressing into me slowly, the way the rising tide presses into your feet when you stand at the edge of an expanding ocean.

After almost an hour of driving on busy main roads, we turned onto a smaller, quieter street. There were still pedestrians everywhere, but fewer than before, and there were also fewer carts and people sitting on the side of the road. Instead, I noticed more tall, residential buildings with iron gates.

Finally, we pulled up to a white concrete building with a black iron gate. A stout man with a thick black mustache, wearing a gray uniform, came out of a little concrete house adjacent to the gate. He waved at the driver, and the gate opened. We climbed out of the car, and by the time I walked to the trunk to get my luggage, it was already on the ground. I looked around for the driver, wanting to thank him, but he had already walked away to talk to the security man.

Jasmine Aunty led me up a narrow stairwell to the second floor. Modest and clean, her apartment had two bedrooms, two bathrooms, and an open living and dining area. She left the front door and the door to the balcony open, so a gentle, albeit warm, breeze floated through the main sitting area as we sat at the table together, drinking chai. Sasha had made chai at home a few times when I was younger, though she mostly preferred coffee. The times she made it she boiled loose black tea in a pot with milk and spices, like cardamom, cloves, and cinnamon. This chai was different, though—it had a bit of a sharp spicy taste that hit my nostrils when I took the first hot sip. It was sweet and delicious but had more zing than I was expecting. I must have made a face because Jasmine Aunty laughed.

"It's masala chai! Do you like it?" she said, pouring me more before I had time to reply.

"Yes." I smiled. "I do! It's delicious." I drank two cups slowly as we talked, though I did ask her for water on the side.

"So, Sasha tells me you're very much interested in Indian dance!" Jasmine Aunty said, brushing invisible crumbs off the kitchen table, which was covered in a white-and-red checkered tablecloth in protective plastic.

I paused, wondering whether I should tell her about Shaila, but then thought it was too much for having just met her. I could be interested in dance even without all that detailed backstory, I reminded myself. "Yes, I really would like to learn more about it and take classes formally one day. There wasn't much opportunity to do so back home. All the teachers live quite far away from where we live," I said.

I found myself putting on some strange accent without even intending to. I was slowing my speech and enunciating my syllables, mirroring the way Jasmine spoke. I knew I sounded weird, like some confused hybrid between Indian and

American. The truth was that, until I sat in Jasmine Aunty's flat, seeing the light, yawning blues of morning peeping into the house through the open entrance to the balcony, I had never felt at all Indian. But something was shifting, even if only because of the slightly sweet smell of biscuits, or the aroma of meticulous newspaper packaging guarding something holy and earthy, like crushed spice powders and a hint of ash. And sitting here in her flat, as she called it, while drinking chai with her, just put my feelings of nostalgia over the top. I wondered how I had *not* grown up drinking chai more regularly.

"Well, you must go to one of Nikita's Kathak classes! Then at least you will be able to say you have seen one style of dance in Delhi, *na*?"

I didn't bother to ask who Nikita was just yet because I was sure she was about to tell me.

"Nikita is my sister's daughter," she continued. A silly smugness, from being right, settled into my cheeks. "I'll give her a call and see if you can go with her one of these evenings to her Kathak class."

I recalled Kathak from the videos I had watched before—with its rapid spins, intricate and fast footwork, and beautiful dresses that fanned outward from the waist. It looked different from Bharatanatyam, the style I had watched at the cultural show in Seattle which seemed to most closely resemble Shaila's style of dancing. Kathak originated from northern India, where Delhi was situated, whereas Bharatanatyam was from the south.

"But you came here to go to the orphanage mainly, isn't it?" Jasmine Aunty added. Her face became sympathetic, and she leaned toward me. "I'm so sorry, *beti*. It must be difficult."

She gave me a sad, forlorn look, but her eyes were kind. I smiled, not knowing what to say. I appreciated her thoughtfulness but was a little confused why she was feeling sad for me.

As if she read my thoughts, she went on. "Sasha told me

about your plan to visit the orphanage where she adopted you from. To see if you can find out more about your birth mother and father."

My heart sank a bit. I had been so wrapped up in thoughts of dance, enjoying the intoxicatingly sweet and spicy chai, and getting to know Jasmine Aunty. It had been a while since I had reflected on the more serious side to my trip, with outcomes still very much unknown.

"Anyway, it will all be all right," she said, bobbling her head. "I am sure you will enjoy your trip and find what you have come here for." She rearranged the snack bowls on the table. I had tried one of the hard cracker-like snacks, and it was way too spicy for me, so I hadn't bothered to try the mysterious contents from the other bowl that looked like hard fried onion rings.

"Thank you," I said, tracing abstract shapes on the table with my finger. "Sasha has been a great mother. She *is* a great mother. I guess I just felt that now, since I'm older, I should learn more about where I am from—where I was born. And part of that means finding out who my birth parents are."

"Yes, yes, yes, of course." She nodded, reminding me of a woodpecker. "Sasha told me the name of the orphanage, and I have already asked the driver to go and have a look at the location today. So he will know exactly where to take you tomorrow." She paused, looking up at the clock, which had just chimed nine o'clock. "*Arre*, it's already nine! What will you have? Coffee? More tea? Biscuits? I have some tasty biscuits my husband brought me from Pune. He is on a business trip there this week again, you know. He goes there quite a lot, maybe once every two or three weeks. So, what will you have?"

"Aunty, I'm not really hungry . . ." It felt nice to call her Aunty. She could be anyone, any woman older than me, but somehow, through that relational word, she felt familiar.

There had been just one other Indian girl at my school,

a couple of grades ahead of me, and the few times I saw her parents I remembered calling them Aunty and Uncle. I don't remember who told me to do that, or if by inherited instinct I just knew. That's how it was done. Simple and universal: Everyone became family by those two words. You could sweep middle-aged women and men away from the stranger category and make them your own, dispelling potential awkwardness and ensuring not just amiability, but warmth, compassion, and care from them—simply by using those words.

"Nonsense," she said. "What is this, you must have had nothing to eat since you left America!"

I really didn't feel like eating; the chai had made me quite full. I did, however, really want to shower and then sleep. The noises outside—particularly the crows and horns—were in full throttle, and I knew the morning was not turning back. The thought of staying awake the whole day was too much. On top of that, there was going to the orphanage—which suddenly didn't feel like it could wait until tomorrow. Once Jasmine Aunty had brought it up, and knowing it was still so early in the day, I wanted to go *today*.

"I think I just really need to sleep for a couple of hours, Aunty. And I would like to try to go to the orphanage later today instead of tomorrow, if I can," I confessed.

"Oh! Today? Are you sure? Won't you be tired?"

"I think I'll be fine if I nap. Can we ask the driver if I can go today?" I asked hesitantly, feeling weird calling him "the driver" without a name.

"Oh of course, beti, you can do whatever you like. I'll tell him. But yes, for now, you must get some rest after your long journey." She nodded while getting up, her golden bangles jingling. "Okay, I've made the cot for you in the other room; you can sleep there nicely. We'll close the curtains, and you can switch on the fan." She gestured for me to follow her down the hallway to the bedrooms.

I left the door open, plopped onto the cot, and shut my eyes. I didn't need to think of anything to fall asleep. The continuous *click click* of the fan as it blew cool air upon me was my lullaby.

I awoke to a cacophony of car horns mixed with people's voices shouting and birds chirping loudly. If it had come on suddenly, it would have been jarring, but it was the same mélange of noises I had drifted off to sleep to, so somehow the blend of all these disparate sounds felt oddly soothing and natural. They were also somewhat muffled, as they were coming from outside, although the walls were thin—so the noise could never really be completely shut out.

I felt as if I had been sleeping for hours and feared I had slept through the day and night into the next day. As I walked out of the bedroom and into the hall, feeling the cool marble tile beneath my bare feet was the loveliest sensation. Jasmine Aunty was in the kitchen, humming. I glanced at the clock on her wall and then blinked in disbelief. To my dismay, it read 4:30. I had slept for hours! I was upset, wondering if I could still go to the orphanage this late but knowing, with a sinking feeling in my heart, that I had probably lost the chance for today.

"Hi, Aunty," I said. She was at the stove, boiling milk and spices for more chai—the same familiar sweet, warm milky smell from the morning greeting me once again.

"Hello! Did you have a nice rest?" she asked, straining the tea leaves from the concoction and pouring the chai into a large steel bowl.

"Yes. I can't believe how much I slept. Do you think I can still go to the orphanage today?"

"Oh dear, it's quite late in the afternoon. And you have just arrived from such a long journey. It will be better if you just take rest today and go tomorrow morning, once you are feeling relaxed and fresh."

I frowned, but I knew she was right. After waking up from my nap I felt more tired now, and the thought of going out was exhausting.

"It's still quite early in the States," Jasmine Aunty said, handing me a steel tumbler filled with chai. "But in a few hours, you can call your mother. She'll be happy to hear from you." She patted me on the shoulder and led me out to the living room.

I immediately felt a pull at my heart. *Sasha.* I had texted her and Kale when I first landed in Delhi, which felt like days ago, though it was just earlier today. I missed her—and I envisioned her sitting in this simple yet cozy room, drinking chai, with Jasmine Aunty and me. Again came that wave of guilt from insisting I needed to make this trip on my own, effectively excluding her from the experience of coming back here together.

I called her later that evening, around 8:00 p.m. The ringing of her phone sounded different here in India, with the rings muffled and higher pitched than back home.

"Anokhi? Hi, sweetheart!" she said when she picked up. I could picture her sitting at the kitchen table with her morning coffee, reading the newspaper in her pajama bottoms and oversize T-shirt. I wished I could hug her.

"Hi, Sasha," I said. I felt a lump in my throat and blinked back tears.

"How are you doing? How is it there? How is Jasmine?" she asked animatedly, though I could hear a soft restraint in her voice, which I interpreted as sadness.

"She's wonderful," I said, smiling. I shared how Jasmine Aunty had welcomed me into her home seamlessly, as if we had seen each other regularly over the years. Despite my reticence and the fact that we had never met before, I didn't feel weird about staying in her house. "The chai, the conversation, the simple comforts have all made me feel at ease rather quickly." I also told her about the drive home from the airport and how the sights on the streets had been unlike anything I could have imagined. I told her about seeing so many people, cows, and traffic that did not seem to follow any rhyme or reason yet somehow flowed on.

She laughed. "Yes, sounds familiar. I feel like I was just there yesterday when you describe it . . ."

We were both silent. I think she was lost in her reverie, thinking of Delhi as she remembered it from nearly two decades ago. But I also worried that she was still hurt and mad at me.

"Sasha," I finally said. "I'm sorry I wanted to go on this trip alone. I didn't mean to hurt your feelings."

"Oh, sweetie." She paused and I wasn't sure if I needed to say something. But then she continued. "Please don't worry. I mean, I won't lie, of course I wanted to come with you. But I also understand why you wanted to go alone. If I were in your place—at your age, with your recent life changes, and wanting to know more about your past—I think I may have wanted the same for myself."

I heaved a sigh of relief. Sasha could be so pragmatic with feelings in a way I couldn't. And even if she felt things more complexly, somehow she was always able to see the straight path through the mess of emotions. I admired her for that.

"Thank you. I love you," I said. Closing my eyes, I imagined myself back at home, sitting next to her at the table, eating breakfast together before I left for the bookstore and she went to the diner.

"I love you too," she said. "Nothing will ever change that."

CHAPTER 10

I fell asleep on my bed again shortly after my phone call with Sasha. I woke up sometime around two in the morning but drifted back to sleep again. I could not believe how much I had slept by the next morning. But I felt much better—my headache was gone and the tired ache had left my muscles. I was ready for the day.

"Ah, you're awake!" Jasmine Aunty said when I came into the kitchen. "Come, sit. I was about to have my breakfast and then wake you up. Let's eat and then you should go with the driver, Raju. He came about thirty minutes back and will be ready to take you whenever you are ready."

Raju, I thought to myself. *Well at least now I know his name.* I sat at the table, looking forward to eating—my stomach was growling.

We ate *idlis,* round spongy rice cakes that reminded me of moons. Dipping them in the *sambhar* was mesmerizing, the sponges soaking up the thin brown lentil liquid. It was spicy, and I ate only two plain idlis, barely letting them touch the sambhar, to tame the fire in my unaccustomed mouth.

"Come now, let's go downstairs, and Raju will take you to

the orphanage. I can't come because I've got an appointment at two thirty, but I'll take an auto there. Don't worry, your work is more important today. Come," she said, and I followed her. I wondered to myself what an "auto" was, but then my mind darted to the image of hundreds of little yellow minicars with no doors or windows that I saw on the drive home from the airport, and I put two and two together.

The elevator door consisted of two rickety black metal gates. As long as one of them remained open, even slightly, the elevator, or lift, as she called it, emitted a shrill continuous beep that was impossible to ignore. She banged the inner door shut before we descended to the ground level.

As soon as we stepped out of the lift, Jasmine began calling out loudly, "Raju! O Raju! Raju!" The driver from yesterday, which felt like a lifetime ago—the lean man with short hair and a mustache—was wearing gray slacks and a blue long-sleeved button-up shirt and was once again talking to the security guard.

Raju came running in our direction, slowing to a brisk walk as he approached. "Yes, madam," he said, nodding.

I smiled awkwardly, wishing I could introduce myself. In addition to Rosetta Stone, I had tried studying Hindi before leaving with the help of a book I had found in the storage room at Dusty Pages. It was one thing to read and pronounce under my breath, another thing to remember for later, and yet another thing to find the courage to pull up the words in real life. *Teach Yourself Hindi in a Week* definitely hadn't taught that courage.

Raju opened the door to the back seat of the white car, which was parked a few feet from us. I stepped in, feeling weird about still not really having said a word to this person who picked me up from the airport and was now about to drive me on such an important mission. I also found myself intensely despising the social constructions and constrictions of this situation. I slid across and sat behind the driver's seat so I would not have to confront my qualms with the status quo and could reflect on my own discomfort with these social differences that were new to me instead.

I realized I would need to get over myself and eventually speak Hindi, to the best of my ability, if push came to shove. I felt somewhat ready—the hours and hours I had spent listening to the videos had instilled *some* confidence within me, though my own insecurity about sounding dumb was still getting in the way. I had also wondered whether they would speak English at the orphanage, but both Sasha and Jasmine Aunty reassured me that English was quite widely spoken in major cities in India, and I shouldn't have too much of an issue. I also had Jasmine Aunty's number to call if I got into any situation I couldn't handle, though I hoped I wouldn't need to.

We drove past streets whose names I did not know and probably no one else did either because they seemed not to officially exist. I didn't see street signs anywhere. My brain was grabbing images and sounds in fistfuls, pieces falling from my grasp as I latched onto the next sensation. Horns fell to background noise as I listened to children's voices clamoring for change through the closed car window at busy intersections. Meanwhile, Hindi music echoed from the speakers in our air-conditioned car as we moved along like a spider on her web.

I wondered for a moment where else my trip in India might take me. I wanted to sightsee in Delhi, and I also had vague plans to visit the cities of Agra and Jaipur with Jasmine Aunty, though we had not made any specific arrangements yet. I was waiting to see, first and foremost, how the trip to the orphanage went.

I also felt conflicted about the concept of "sightseeing" and being a tourist. I felt like this was supposed to be a homecoming, though I hadn't been here for almost seventeen years and really felt like a foreigner in every sense—language, customs, culture, familiarity. Despite that this was my birthplace, I struggled to know how I could begin to understand this complex, beautiful, and diverse country I found myself in.

When the car came to a halt outside a large gray building with a big black iron gate on a quieter side street, Raju announced our arrival. *"Aa gaye,* madam."

The building was wide, with many windows, though they all seemed tinted, because I could not see anything on the inside. Thin trees had been planted in clusters, and the black iron fence seemed to encircle the entire property, as far as I could see. The orphanage was located in a small colony, or neighborhood, and the rest of the street was relatively quiet, with some office buildings and gated homes. There were no children playing outside, but I could hear shouts and laughter coming from farther away, perhaps behind the building. I wondered if there was a playground in the back.

I took a deep breath, imagining myself as a little baby inside the walls of the building in front of me. I also imagined Sasha walking up the wide, marbled steps to the main front entrance, which had quite fancy-appearing sliding glass doors. The building must have undergone a renovation recently, I thought. I struggled to imagine that it looked like this years ago when she was here to adopt me, back in 1990.

We had parked in the semicircle driveway after being allowed in by the security guard at the gate, who waved at us as he opened the entrance. I was surprised he didn't ask us for identification, but he waved at me as we drove by him.

Raju came around the side and opened my car door in the back. "Thank you, Raju . . . *Main . . . undar jaoongi,"* I said. *I'm going inside*—an obvious statement, but I smiled and felt proud of myself, and a bit shy, for trying to communicate in Hindi. Perhaps the sentences would get easier the more I tried. I was surprised the words came out at all.

As I walked into the building, I discovered a lobby which

appeared strikingly new, with marbled floors and ceiling fans. Gold-colored frames encompassing smiling faces of cute children—some portraits, some candid shots—lined the walls. A middle-aged man sat typing at a desk at the end of the hallway, and he glanced up at me for a moment before returning to his computer work. The atmosphere was slightly odd with so many pictures of children on the white walls and no one in the room except the man at his desk—and now me.

I walked down the expansive hallway, which was also lined with empty plastic white chairs, to his desk. He looked up again, surprised, as if just now noticing me.

"Yes, madam? Good morning. How can I help you?" His English was polished yet slightly stretched, like a sweater that fits too tightly over an ample body frame. His Indian accent bulged in small bursts between his words, just as Jasmine's did when she spoke English. I wondered what it would be like to go to school and learn English here.

"Hi," I said. "My name is Anokhi. Anokhi Marna. I was adopted here in 1990, and I'm eighteen years old now. I have my adoption papers here, and I was wondering—"

"Is everything all right, madam? With your adoptive family? Why is it that you've come here?" he asked, raising his eyebrows, genuine concern lining his neatly shaven face.

"Oh, no, yes, everything is fine. I . . ." I paused, surprised that he was so surprised I was here. Didn't other people come back asking questions about their past? "I came because I want to find out who my birth parents are. I have brought all the paperwork that my mother—my adoptive mother—received when she went through the process, and I was hoping I could get information about my birth parents. I really would like to meet them, now that I'm older," I explained, the words tumbling out anxiously.

I felt flustered and hot. Panic started to build inside me. Taking the leap to decide to come to India and surviving the longest plane ride I had ever taken—I had felt such relief once that was done. I had not conceptualized what would happen when I walked into the orphanage. I realized now how naive I had been to assume I could just waltz into a place and demand answers without anticipating that there would be barriers. My excitement and confidence in my quest had taken up space in my mind where perhaps there should have been more reservation and doubt.

It sobered me now, standing in front of this stranger, that I may not be able to get what I so desperately wanted— the names of my birth parents. I straightened my shoulders, tucked a piece of hair behind my ear, and stared at the man, offering a small smile. He didn't smile back.

"I see," he finally said, shifting his eyes uneasily across the room to a door at the far right, near the main door, and back. "That is not in my hands, madam. You will have to speak with the supervisor, Mr. Rajgopal. He is very busy, however, so I do not know when he will be able to—"

"Please," I interrupted. "I've come all the way from America." Jasmine Aunty had told me, before I had gone with Raju in the car, to be persistent. Oftentimes it took a little prodding to get things done here, she had said. Or a lot of prodding.

"Oho, America, is it?" he echoed with a smirk. I wondered if he was mocking me. "Well, that is quite far away."

"Yes . . ." I didn't know what else to say. I didn't want to banter with him about how far I had traveled; I wanted information. Was I entitled to think I could just barge into a place and get what I wanted? And yet, there was such simplicity in my request. Didn't the request of a child looking for her parents warrant universal compassion?

Just then, the door at the far-right end of the room opened, and a tall hefty man in a pinkish button-down shirt and black pants walked out. He looked as if he were about to exit the building.

"That is Mr. Rajgopal," the man at the desk said to me, nodding his head in that direction.

I looked at him and then looked at Mr. Rajgopal's back as he walked toward the glass doors. I found my legs deciding for me while my mind couldn't, as I raced across the hall to catch up with him. He must have heard my flip-flops clapping on the tiled floor; he turned around and looked at me, eyes widening.

"Yes, madam? Is something wrong?" he asked, his voice carrying a thick somewhat-British accent, more formal and crisper than Jasmine Aunty's English or that of the man at the desk. He slowed down, and so did I.

"Hi, sir. My name is Anokhi Marna. I was adopted from this orphanage almost seventeen years ago. I'm looking for information about my birth parents. I would like to meet them, and I have all my paperwork from my adoptive mother," I stated, pushing my shoulders back and holding my folder of papers toward him.

He looked at my face, then the papers, and paused for a moment. "I see," he said, his eyebrows furrowed slightly. "Well, Anokhi, madam, that is a very complicated process, and it will take time to locate the records, release confidentiality, et cetera."

"That's okay," I said quickly. "I came all the way from the US for this information. I can go through the process."

He stared at my face, then my outfit—straight jeans with a loose white cotton button-down shirt—then back at my face. I hated the way his eyes fixed on my eyes, then my hair, then my lips; it felt invasive and impolite. But I forced myself to maintain eye contact.

Perhaps I was being annoying, but I didn't care. After what felt like a very long time, he spoke.

"Yes, well, I am about to step out for some work. When I come back, I will investigate your case. If you leave your name, case number, and contact number here in Delhi, I will contact you later this afternoon." He peered down at me over the tip of his long nose.

"Thank you very much," I replied, somewhat satisfied with his response. It didn't feel like a no, which is what it was sounding like earlier. I felt temporarily appeased.

He gave a curt nod and left. I went back to the desk to give my information to the other man. I sensed him watching me as I was writing the requested information down. I also glimpsed a smirk on his face from the corner of my eye, and I wondered if it was my handwriting or my persona that he found amusing. I guessed it was the latter, so when I was done, I quickly muttered thank you and saw myself out.

I was silent on the drive home, just as I had been on the way there, but I supposed the difference was palpable to Raju, even though we'd barely spoken at all. The silence of anticipation had been replaced by the silence of irritation. I met his gaze in the rearview mirror a couple of times from where I was sitting in the back, diagonally across from him this time, behind the passenger seat. Each time our eyes met, he quickly shifted his away, as did I. From where did this strange aversion come from? I tried to imagine doing this when taking a taxi in the US—something I had only done once, with Sasha, when we were in Chicago years ago. Neither the taxi driver nor I would feel any shame in our eyes meeting. Maybe even a perfunctory smile would appear, the slight, polite curling upwards of lips. So, what was this?

I intuited a strange, cultural gender dynamic at play. Here I was, essentially a foreigner, being driven around by him and therefore, as much as I hated to think it, I was deemed to be of a higher social position. Plus, I was a young woman. I did not feel threatened; that was the farthest thing from my mind. What I felt was more complicated than fear. It was a bizarre twisting of the soul—the feeling of being restricted from having a simple conversation with this other human being, the invisible threads of social status and personhood making the distance between us seem uncrossable.

Finally, after much premeditation, I slowly addressed Raju. *"Kal shaayad waapis aana padega."* I hoped I had correctly communicated that I might have to come back again tomorrow.

"Teek hai, madam," he replied, glancing at me in the mirror ever so briefly before looking back at the road.

I fumbled for what else to say. There was nothing to say, of course. But in this moment, it felt necessary to respond to him, to keep the conversation going. To try to prove to myself that all these constricting social forces I knew existed didn't have to exist. That we were not caught in some crazy cobweb of social hierarchy, intercultural and gender dynamics at play—that these were simply overanalyzed observations in my mind.

But I knew that he felt them too. The thing was that here such distinctions in culture, class, and gender seemed to be unquestioned threads in the fabric of society. I'd already seen examples of it in the few limited interactions I had witnessed since coming here—between Jasmine Aunty and Raju earlier in the morning, for example. The way she hadn't introduced me to him by name, hadn't even acknowledged his bodily presence, though he was clearly someone she knew and was driving us home from the airport. And he didn't seem bothered by it—in fact, the times I had tried to make eye contact and acknowledge him as a human seemed to feel more awkward than just ignoring him. I also felt like Jasmine Aunty was not particularly bothered by any of this. I struggled to think of parallel unspoken but clearly divided class dynamics back home, and I wondered, if I had grown up here, if I too would not think twice about these interactions.

I sank into the back seat of the car, feeling overwhelmed by my realization that I was not only in a very different country but a vastly different culture, where the bridges that connected people were built of very different components. My naive conviction that we were all human and therefore all should be able to relate to one another felt childish and meaningless in the face of these social constructs and customs that I struggled to understand but also felt I had no right to question. I felt out of place, and it hit me, with a wave of nausea and sadness, that I missed home, the familiarity and customs that only became apparent now that I was thousands of miles away. I also missed Sasha. If she were here sitting next to me in the car, I could have talked to her about these thoughts. I am sure she would have noticed it all too.

As much as I wanted to believe this was my home too, because I was born here, it really did not feel like home. India felt enigmatic, like a mystery I was just beginning to try to solve, unsure if I would ever really be able to.

CHAPTER 11

After I got back to Jasmine Aunty's flat, I spent the rest of the afternoon waiting by the telephone. Three o'clock turned to four o'clock, which crawled to five o'clock. When five thirty struck, Jasmine Aunty thumped her hand on the kitchen table, stunning me out of my daze.

"Anokhi, that man is not going to call today, I'm telling you. I called Nikita, and she is coming here to pick you up before she goes for her Kathak class at six o'clock. It is only a ten-minute walk from here, so you can walk together. It will be good for you to go outside of the house. Poor thing, you've been sitting like a stone statue next to the phone all afternoon," she chided gently, making a sucking *tsk tsk* sound with her tongue.

I frowned. My heart sank. With each passing minute, I had truly believed the phone call would come. He had said he would call back this afternoon, and I believed him to the word. Why would he say it otherwise? My own naivete felt like a slap in the face now that I looked at the clock and heard Jasmine Aunty's words.

"Come now. She'll be here soon. Change into a *salwar kameez*. Her guru may not like it if you come to the class in Western clothes," she said, eyeing my jeans with slight disapproval.

Reluctant to leave the phone, but eager to get out of the jeans, which admittedly were not very comfortable, I followed her down the hallway to the bedroom.

"I don't have a salwar," I admitted.

"Oh! You should have told me," Jasmine Aunty said. "We could have gone to the market in the afternoon. It's okay. You can take one from me. It might be too big for you, but it will be nice and loose. It's good not to wear it very tight in the heat. Girls nowadays buy such tight clothes, I wonder how they don't melt or suffocate . . . I like to wear loose clothes, personally, in this weather especially," she related, searching through her armoire.

I changed into the plain, light blue salwar she handed me. It was very loose, and I tied the pant string tightly, high on my waist. The top came down to my knees, and the bunched-up cotton and knot at my waist, beneath the top, bulged awkwardly. But once she handed me a long scarf that matched the outfit, called a *dupatta*, it all came together. At first, I just stared at it, and she laughed when she recognized my confusion as to what to do next. She draped it across my neck so that the ends of the scarf hung down my back, and she adjusted it so it hung high on my chest. She smiled approvingly and patted my shoulders before leaving the room. As soon as I moved, however, the dupatta slipped off my right shoulder. I took it off and hung it around my neck instead—the way I had seen some of the men wearing it in the Bollywood movies I had watched with Sasha.

"Hi, Aunty, I'm here!" a high-pitched voice called from the front entrance of the flat.

I stepped out of my room, walked down the hallway, and peered around the corner toward the front door. A girl about my height, with a slightly younger face, was slipping off her sandals just outside the doorway. She wore red cotton pants that bunched up at her ankles, a long, light pink tunic, and a red dupatta tied artfully across her torso in a triangle.

"Hello!" She greeted me as she crossed the threshold into the flat. Her eyes were bright and friendly, and her hair was braided in a thick black rope that hung all the way down to her low back. What most attracted my attention were her golden earrings and the small black dot on her forehead.

"Hi," I said, walking toward her. "I'm Anokhi."

"Yes, Anokhi! I'm Nikita, Jasmine Aunty's niece. Aunty has told me all about you, and I have been waiting for your visit." She gave me a quick but strong hug. "She mentioned you are interested in dance, so I thought I could take you to my dance class tonight!"

"Oh, Nikita, you've come already!" Jasmine Aunty exclaimed as she came into the front hallway. "This is Anokhi, beti—"

"Yes, we've just met!" Nikita said excitedly, and I nodded.

"Okay then, girls, have a good time. Anokhi, Nikita will take care of you. If you get tired and want to leave, just call me and I'll send Raju to pick you up."

Nikita and I slipped our sandals on and took the stairs down to the ground level.

"Aunty said you dance Kathak?" I asked, by way of starting a conversation.

"Yes, I've been learning Kathak for a long time. It has influences from Persian and Mughal cultures," she explained as we walked through the front gate and onto the dusty side road, heading toward the main road, which was just as full and bustling as at any other time of day. "Did you know the name comes from '*kathaa*,' which means 'story' in Sanskrit? Kathak is all about telling stories," Nikita said. "Actually, most dance is about telling stories, I think."

As we turned the corner onto another side street off the

main road, my thoughts drifted to Shaila. Storytelling was a perfect description to encapsulate those dances I had known for most of my life. They had never felt random—they always seemed to have a purpose: to convey beauty, fear, love, anger, or longing. Those emotions were portrayed through movements representing people, animals, or places, and it astounded me how a single person could transform their body to communicate so many different meanings.

"What about American dance?" she asked, pulling my arm gently to prevent me from stepping in a puddle on the side of the road.

"Oh, I don't know much about American dance," I confessed. "There are a lot of different types—jazz, ballet, tap, hip-hop. But I have never really explored any of those." The truth was, I was primarily interested in Indian dance because of Shaila. But I couldn't tell Nikita that. This seemed to be a pattern for me—I simply found it too personal and weird to disclose my dreams to someone I had just met.

"Oh, I see," she said. "Well, today in class you'll see Kathak. It's my personal favorite, of course. Kathak is the only one of the eight Indian classical dance forms that originates from the north."

I counted in my head the other dance forms I knew. I had already concluded that Bharatanatyam, from South India, most closely resembled Shaila's dance, based on the mind-blowingly similar performance I saw at UW. And I'd also been studying Kuchipudi, also from the south, which was similar but not quite the same—it was less rigid and more curvaceous in its movements.

"What are the others?" I asked. I remembered reading about some others from the book Melanie gave me for my birthday, but I wanted to hear more from Nikita rather than embarrass myself by sharing my incomplete knowledge.

"Aside from Kathak there's Bharatanatyam, Kuchipudi,

Kathakali, Mohiniyattam—those are all from South India. Then there's Odissi, Manipuri and Sattriya," Nikita said, her voice lyrical as she counted each dance on her fingers. The names sounded beautiful as she listed them in a string, like petals of a single flower unfurling together.

Odissi, of course. I recalled the picture of the woman in white. Her angled posture and Shaila's dance that night, which had been the impetus for me to come to India. I hadn't come across many of the other styles. I wanted to ask more but held back for fear of sounding more ignorant than I already felt.

"In Kathak, we wear *churidar*-style pants and long, flowing tops that are tight on top and then fan out from the waist when we spin. There is lots of spinning," she continued, laughing. "In the beginning when you start learning, it can be very dizzying."

"How old were you when you started learning?" I asked.

"Mm, perhaps six years old."

"Six?" That seemed so young to be learning something so complex.

"Yes, but it is quite common for girls to start learning from that young age. Teachers prefer that actually, because the younger you are, the better learner you are. Once you get older you have already become more set in your ways, and you're less flexible, and all that."

We turned into a quiet cul-de-sac with white and cream-colored buildings.

"Here we are," she said, taking off her shoes at the gate, adding them to a neat pile of sandals and flip-flops. "Take off your *chappals* here."

I followed her lead and kicked off my flip-flops before going through the gate into the small courtyard.

"This is my dance teacher's—my guru's—home, but it is also where we have our classes. She has a big room that we learn in," she explained. She bent and touched the threshold of the front door with her fingertips, then put her fingers to her head, and then pressed her hands together in prayer form.

Past the open threshold was a huge open room with marble flooring. Nine teenage girls stood in two staggered lines. The guru, whose gray-black hair was pulled into a tight bun, sat cross-legged. Nikita walked in, touched her guru's feet, and then put her hands to her closed eyes and bowed to her. I pressed my hands together in namaste, mimicking Nikita, not wanting to disrespect her, yet feeling out of place doing this. I then did the same series of gestures Nikita had done; I wasn't going to, but Nikita looked at me expectantly after she had done it. The guru was the first person whose feet I had ever touched. I wasn't exactly sure why we were touching her feet, but the silent and solemn nature of the gesture seemed anchored in respect.

"*Yeh kaun hai?*" she asked Nikita.

"Anokhi, *meri cousin sister. America se aayi,*" she said by way of an introduction. "Anokhi, this is my *guruji.*"

"Namaste," I said. It came more naturally this time. I wanted to say something else in Hindi, thanking her for allowing me to observe the class, but was too intimidated by her stern appearance to try my unconfident Hindi with her.

"Welcome, Anokhi," she replied in English, giving me a curt smile and nodding, before turning her attention back to the class. The group of girls had all paused and were watching me intently. I looked at them and gave them a closed-lip smile, feeling very self-conscious and out of place, wondering if I should have come with Nikita at all. As Nikita walked to join the back of the line of girls, she signaled for me to sit along one of the side walls of the room to watch.

"*Dha dhin dhin dha, dha dhin dhin dha,*" the guru said lyrically, each syllable as crisp and clear as the next.

The girls began their warm-up. Their legs were straight, their elbows raised and bent. Their hands were in front of their torsos, each index finger and thumb touching. Their feet moved quickly with her syllables. Heel-flat-flat-heel-heel-flat-flat-heel.

"You also try," the guru said, looking at me and then nodding toward the lines of girls. "Go stand in the back and try, if you can." Her English was crisp and clear, though accented.

I walked around the girls and stood at the back as instructed, suddenly conscious of my bare ankles, while the other twenty ankles were covered by thick cloth bands studded with bells. I was grateful though; I didn't want the asynchrony of my footwork to be captured and amplified by bells on my ankles.

"Dha dhin dhin dha, dha dhin dhin dha. Dhin dha dha dhin, dhin dha dha dhin."

The rhythmic chant took flight from the teacher's lips with impressive precision, given the speed at which she was saying it. Even though it was the same few monosyllables being repeated, the complex combinations seemed endless.

The girls moved their arms, seeming to fly, and I glanced repeatedly at my feet, trying to keep in time. I watched the girl's feet in front of my own, then looked at mine, back and forth, trying to touch my heel when she did and stomp flat when she did. My mind was so consumed with the effort, I didn't even notice how hard I was frowning until the guru said, *"Arre,* Anokhi, smile! This isn't meant to be punishment!" The other girls giggled, and I smiled at my own novice struggle.

Once they were done with the drills, they started practicing fully composed dance pieces, and the guru motioned for me to sit down and watch on the floor at the side of the room again. Their hands moved seamlessly into *mudras,* reminding me of the many graceful contortions that Shaila's fingers made during her dances, communicating entire stories through hand gestures and facial expressions.

I recalled what Nikita told me about Kathak's name coming from the Sanskrit word "kathaa," which meant "story." As

I watched, with fascination, the girls cycling through sleek, emotive sequences, I longed to understand exactly what story they were telling. From their expressive eye movements and the changes in their countenance, I could follow along with some of the emotions—longing, sadness, joy. But it did not feel familiar to me, as it did when Shaila danced. I could not guess the exact meaning of their dance, so I contented myself with watching the beauty of their movements.

I watched one girl's face, then another girl's hands, then another girl's feet. There was no single girl or single aspect of the dance I could focus on for too long. The dancers embodied holism—they moved as one fluid wave. The beauty of the group was rooted in each individual dancer and intensified by the grace of many bodies moving in unison to a rhythm greater than themselves. No matter who I looked at, I found myself admiring how a sum is so much greater than its individual unique parts.

I said goodbye to Nikita after the class ended at eight o'clock, insisting I would be fine walking back to Jasmine Aunty's flat by myself. I heard Sasha's voice in my head telling me not to walk anywhere after dark, but I rationalized that it was only a short way. Nikita had offered to escort me, but I was so robbed of speech after witnessing the beautiful dances that I preferred to walk alone and be with my thoughts. Plus, she mentioned she had to go home and get some studying done before going to college tomorrow, and I didn't want to keep her from that.

She walked me to the main road and told me to go straight down to the right until I reached Café Coffee Day—which had a bright red sign that I couldn't miss. And once I saw that, I just had to turn right and then take the first left and I would be back at the cul-de-sac where Jasmine Aunty lived.

As I walked the main road, this time without Nikita, I felt more acutely aware of everything, including myself. I noticed the dust that kicked up repeatedly on top of my exposed feet with each step I took. I saw other women walking past me, mostly wearing similar outfits to mine, and men selling fruit and drinks from small stands, and motorcycles weaving in and out of the cars, sometimes coming too close for comfort to my side of the road.

I tried to make eye contact with several people, but whether it was just in my head or was actual reality, I seemed so out of place walking there. I was dressed in Indian clothes. I had similar skin color to many people on the street. But I felt they could see right through me to know that I was not from here. It filled me with a vague sadness and self-consciousness, and I wondered how I would feel if I had walked these streets my whole life. I couldn't imagine it. It felt too foreign to feel like home; as much as I wanted nostalgia to flood my being, it didn't.

As I walked, I came across several people who appeared homeless. One older woman was wearing a dirty old sari, had a limp as she walked along with a cane, and held her hand out, mumbling something which I inferred was a request for money. I took a five-rupee note from my inner backpack zipper and gave it to her. Her eyes widened and she nodded her head aggressively. I nodded and walked on.

A set of two little kids, a boy and a girl who appeared less than ten years old, came up to me, their eyes lined with dirt and their hair grimy and disheveled. *"Didi, didi,"* they both called. The girl ran up to pull at the edge of my kameez. I gave each of them a five-rupee note. They scurried away before I could even look at their faces. My heart ached, seeing all these people whom I could never help sufficiently, whose suffering I could never completely understand. Giving money felt like a drop in a bucket, and I didn't know what a solution looked like. But I also couldn't look away.

I kept walking the main road for almost twenty minutes when I was finally compelled to stop and scratch a small red mosquito bite on my ankle. As I looked around, I panicked, realizing I had been so absorbed in my thoughts that I had failed to look for the one thing I needed to have been looking out for—the red sign for Café Coffee Day.

I turned around in my place and almost bumped right into a man walking behind me. He swerved around me and gave me a bit of an angry look up and down before walking on.

I started walking back in the other direction, on the same side of the street, checking the many billboards and shop signs. I didn't see any red signs. When I walked by one stall where a bunch of men were sitting and drinking chai, I heard one of them shouting and whistling. I glanced over at them and saw them all staring at me. I began to walk faster, backtracking, my heart beating hard in my chest and my ears.

I was about to call Jasmine Aunty in a fit of panic but finally saw the huge, bright red fluorescent sign that read "Café Coffee Day" a few yards ahead. I glanced over my shoulder, and there was no one except a man and a woman walking a few feet behind me. I turned down the side street and walked quickly, took the first left, and nearly ran all the way to the black iron gate. I was safe.

"So, how did you like it?" Jasmine Aunty called out from the living room, where she had been watching a show on her small television. I watched the screen for a moment as I thought about how to respond—the show reminded me of a telenovela with the actors' dramatized expressions and gestures—and I decided it would be better not to tell her about my stupid walk home. I felt embarrassed but also sobered. I should not have turned Nikita down to walk me home my second day in this new city and country, especially at night.

"It was wonderful," I said. "I'm so glad I went. It was so sweet of Nikita to take me along."

I felt unqualified to have more of an opinion on something so ancient and sacred as a dance form that had existed for more than two millennia. I could only silently acknowledge and respect that the beauties of the world's art forms were far grander than I had ever imagined. I couldn't wait to see more during my trip.

But in the back of my mind, my primary motivation for my trip was like an itch I couldn't fully scratch. I didn't think I could immerse myself in learning everything I wanted to about Indian dance, or India overall, while I was still unsure where the search for my birth parents would take me.

That night, Shaila appeared to me again, as I was drifting off to sleep. She was dressed in the traditional Kathak attire that Nikita had described to me: A pale yellow churidar adorned her legs, and a well-fitted matching yellow top flew out from her waist like a billowing golden fan. Thick sets of bells were tied around her ankles, and big lustrous gold earrings hung from her ears. She spun and leaped nimbly, her fingers delicately motioning as always.

For a moment, her expression reminded me of how I had felt earlier that evening as I tried to find a place for my feet in response to the quick syllables that emanated from the guru's lips. Of course, I was no match for Shaila's grace. But our shared appreciation for beauty and dance, our feet trying to keep time with rhythms old and new, made me feel closer to her. I longed for that closeness to morph into some new knowledge of her. But even here in India, she was consistent; she remained elusive as she had always been to me since I was a child, slipping out of my mind as gracefully as she entered, never with a word of explanation.

CHAPTER 12

The next morning after breakfast, I went with Raju to the orphanage again. The supervisor, Mr. Rajgopal, had never called back. I didn't bother going to the front desk; I walked straight to the office door near the front and knocked. The man sitting at the front desk furrowed his brows and glared at me, though it was too late—I had already knocked, and I think he also was curious what would happen now that I went straight to the supervisor's door. I didn't care what he thought. I wanted to speak to Mr. Rajgopal directly without wasting time.

"Who is it?" called a voice from inside.

I pushed the door open. He was sitting at his desk, sipping from a small teacup, and holding the saucer with his other hand. When he saw me, he set them down.

"Ah, it is you again. Come in," he said flatly.

I stepped past the door but didn't fully enter the office. I didn't like the way he was staring at me, irritably it seemed. I clung onto the distance between us, my ally.

"You said you would call yesterday afternoon. I waited for your call for hours," I said bluntly. I hadn't intended to be rude, but *his* manners were not bringing out the best in me.

"*Haan*, well you know, Miss . . ."

"Anokhi," I filled in.

"Haan, Miss Anokhi," he said, popping the first button of his collar. He seemed uncomfortable and shifted his eyes away for a moment and dabbed at a bead of sweat above his brow with a white handkerchief, before looking back at me. "You see, Miss Anokhi, we have a lot of work to do around here. Many children to look after. So, you will understand, of course, that it is not possible to keep up to date with everyone and their requests."

I didn't care to hear his excuses, and I didn't want him saying my name anymore. It made me uncomfortable. But I also didn't want to leave without getting what I had gone there for.

"Well, what happened?" I asked. "Were you able to track down my case?"

"As a matter of fact, yes," he replied coolly, turning on a switch behind him. The ceiling fan began to noisily start spinning.

I waited. I hated that he was making me beg for the information. His behavior was so immature, it aggravated me. And I knew he knew it.

I cleared my throat.

"Yours is quite an interesting case," he said. "Why don't you sit down?"

"I'm fine," I said, resolved to stay put.

"Hmm, as you wish." He shrugged. "Anyway, as it turns out, you were a transfer case from Chennai."

Chennai? I racked my brain for a moment, then realized with a sinking heart that I had remembered seeing that name on the map of India I had studied while on the plane ride here. That was at the other end—the south—of the country. I waited for more, hoping he would clarify.

He read my confusion and threw his hands in the air. "I do not have access to the reason why you were transferred here.

This was done when you were only a few months old, and sub-sequently, you were adopted less than a year later. So, you really were not with us for very long."

I stared at him. "So, my birth parents transferred me from Chennai," I repeated.

"Yes," he said. "I can give you the name of the orphanage, if you want to go there and see what you can find. But that is all we have here about you in this file," he said, pointing to a manila folder on the corner of his desk.

I walked closer and traced the edge of the folder pensively. "Can I read the file?"

He shifted his eyes to the side. "I suppose," he said. "There isn't much inside. But you can read it—please have a seat there," he said, pointing at a chair against the wall in his office, near the door.

I took the folder. It was light and very plain looking. My fingers trembled as I opened it. The first page had a standard-appearing document with prefilled lines and sections. I read the lines but struggled to read the flowy cursive writing, even though I could tell it was English. Next to "Given Name," I could see the letter *A*, followed by a few cursive letters—it looked like Anokhi. Next to "Surname," the line had been left blank. Next to "Date of Birth," it simply said June 1989. There was no specific date.

Sasha had told me when I was little that my birthday was June 15, and that's when we always celebrated it. My eyes blurred as I saw this written here. She had later told me, when I was a bit older and able to comprehend more of the nuances of my adoption, that when she adopted me the orphanage hadn't known my exact birth date. It had felt weird when she first told me that, but I didn't make much of it, especially since Sasha always threw such lovely birthday parties for me with the most delicious and beautiful homemade cakes and thoughtful themes. June 15 had always been my day, and it still would be, as far as our family was concerned. However, reading it now, on this old, slightly stained piece of white paper, it hit me differently. I scanned the rest of the page but there was only a short paragraph in cursive, which I could not decipher at all, and then two fading official inked stamps at the bottom. There was no picture of me.

"What does this say?" I asked, walking up to the desk and then putting the folder in front of him, pointing at the paragraph.

He took the folder from me, took off his rimmed glasses, and held the paper closer to his face. He scrunched his nose in concentration. After a moment he put it down and said, "It is too difficult to read. I cannot make it out."

As I struggled to process the disappointment that filled my chest, I also felt bad for assuming he was being evasive and weird a few moments ago. Then I felt bad for feeling guilty—he *was* being evasive and weird. He was very cagey before giving me the answer to my question, and he didn't call me yesterday as he said he would. So why was it that now, after he had given me the information, I was trying to forgive him for his strange demeanor? My own complex feelings toward this man and his odd behavior left me puzzled. But I was more distraught that my search for answers here had just resulted in more uncertainty.

"If you could give me the name and contact information of that orphanage in Chennai, that would be great," I finally managed.

He took a sheet of unlined paper from one of the drawers and scribbled on it. He extended his hand, not getting out of his chair. Grudgingly, I took the paper from him. I felt a slight resistance on his end as I took it, which I knew I wasn't imagining.

"Thanks," I said curtly. I turned on my heel and walked out the door, closing it firmly behind me. I had seen his mouth open to speak before I turned around, but I'd rushed out with as much dignity as I could without having to hear what he had to say. I was done dealing with him and hoped I didn't have to deal with another person like him again on this trip.

"Apparently I was placed for adoption in Chennai, then transferred to the orphanage here," I said quietly to Jasmine Aunty as I walked back into the flat from my outing with Raju. She was sitting on the sofa reading a book. I wanted to call Sasha or Kale, but it was two or three in the morning at home, and I couldn't wake them up for this. But I also couldn't keep it inside me. I felt like I was about to break down crying at any moment.

"*Arre*, what?" she said, her eyes growing wide. "Oh, beti. Come sit here," she said, patting the cushion.

I slumped next to her. It was hard reconciling this new information with the old information in my head, which still didn't feel all that old in the grand scheme of my life and my limited knowledge of my early childhood.

I told Jasmine Aunty what happened at the orphanage— the manila folder with largely undecipherable writing, the frustrating conversation with Mr. Rajgopal. "I need to go to Chennai now. Maybe I will just leave tonight," I mused aloud.

"But you've just come to Delhi! It's only your third day here!" Jasmine Aunty gasped. "What will Sasha say if she finds out how horrible I have been, not even showing you the major sights! Qutb Minar, Chandni Chowk, Rashtrapati Bhavan . . . You haven't seen anything! And I haven't even taken you shopping for Indian clothes."

"Aunty, honestly, it's okay. I really appreciate being able to stay here. But I need to go and continue this search for my parents—that is the main reason I came to India."

I did want to see the sights in Delhi and Agra too; it was a mere four hours by car to see the Taj Mahal. How could I come all the way here and not see that historical, architectural masterpiece? Yet, it all felt trivial compared to finding my parents. Of course, learning more about dance, inspired by the ghungroos jingling on Shaila's agile feet, was another thing I wanted to do while here. But even that was secondary.

"Okay," Jasmine Aunty said, sitting upright and turning her body toward me. "Listen to me, dear. You can go to Chennai. Of course you can. But please, let us spend a couple of days together. And it's nearing evening anyway, so there is no way you are going to be able to leave for Chennai today."

Again, just like when I'd wanted to immediately head to the orphanage the same day that I had landed, I had to relent. Jasmine Aunty's logic was sound, and I did not have the emotional strength or reason to argue with her. It also occurred to me I had no idea how I was going to get to Chennai. Plane? Train? I would need to research tickets and costs. I also didn't know anyone in Chennai.

"Let's do this," she said, putting her hand on my shoulder kindly. "You take rest today. Maybe we can go out in the evening for some dinner if you are feeling up to it. Tomorrow, I will take you around Delhi to see some sights. And," she said with a glimmer in her eye, "some shopping! And you take your time to figure out when you want to go to Chennai. But please, you are family. Spend at least a few more days with me here."

"Okay," I said, smiling at her and giving her a hug. "I will."

I had waited my whole life to find answers about my past, my birth parents. Surely a few more days wouldn't hurt.

That night I called Kale.

"Anokhs?!" he said, his voice deeper than I remembered. I smiled as I heard it. I hadn't spoken to him since I had arrived here, and typically we would talk every day, if not in person, then by phone, back home—at least up until that hard conversation we had when I told him I was going to India. He texted a few times after that, but our last in-person conversation left us both hurting in different ways.

"Hi, stranger," I said.

"What's up? How are you? How are things going over there?" he asked.

"Oh Kale," I said, flopping onto my bed. "There's so much to tell you about. I went to a dance class—it was incredible. I went to the orphanage where Sasha adopted me. But I found out, after two visits, that apparently I was a transfer case from Chennai—a city at the opposite end of the country. So, it doesn't look like I am going to find any more information about my birth parents without traveling there."

"Wow," he said. "That is incredible, Anokhs."

"What is?" I asked. I was confused. How was it incredible that my search for my parents was going like a wild-goose chase?

"That you're there. In India," he said, his voice pensive and distant. "You were there, at the very building where Sasha adopted you as a baby. You are walking the streets, smelling the smells, and seeing the sights of your motherland."

Of course, Kale always saw the good, the magical, the beautiful in everything. I found myself transiently annoyed— why didn't he share my frustration that now I had to go to Chennai?

Yet he was right. Just being here was amazing in so many ways. I closed my eyes and inhaled deeply. Somehow, Kale managed to school me and teach me a life lesson even though he was thousands of miles away. In his classic fashion, he was inspiring me to live more in the present and to appreciate the goodness of a given moment or situation, rather than focusing on the negative or what is lacking.

"You still there, Anokhs?" he asked.

"Yes," I said, laughing. "I was just reflecting on your wise words. You're right. It is amazing that I'm even here. I need to be grateful."

He chuckled at this. "Hey, I'm glad I'm good for something." Then he added, a bit more seriously, "But I am sorry. That does sound defeating to have to go somewhere else now to find answers."

We chatted a bit more about his work—nothing terribly exciting was happening at the store, and his parents were both doing okay health-wise, so he was relieved. I sensed some of the vague sadness I had heard in Sasha's voice too. I felt guilty for leaving him behind too, though it was less clear to me whether he would have ever truly considered joining me, unlike Sasha, who I knew was more than ready to accompany me.

"All right, I gotta go to the store now. Pa's gonna be waiting for me. Keep me updated on your trip, okay?"

"Of course. I will. Say hi to your parents from me," I said, sad to be ending the conversation.

"It's nice to hear your voice, Anokhs," he added. His voice was husky still but softened when he said that last bit.

I had tears in my eyes. I missed him so much. But I didn't have the courage to tell him this. "You too, Kale."

I spent the next two days with Jasmine Aunty in Delhi. She took me to see the Qutb Minar, a beautiful minaret tower in the historic old part of the city. She also took me to some of her favorite places to eat. I enjoyed spending time with her and tried my best to live in the moment, but still I felt internally distracted by what awaited me, potentially, in Chennai.

My research about travel options found that the train, though it was notably longer—over twenty-four hours compared to under three hours by plane—was the financially viable option for me. I had been saving money by staying with

Jasmine Aunty in Delhi but knew I would have to stay in a hotel in Chennai. Jasmine Aunty didn't know anyone there whom I could stay with.

I felt a bit nervous about leaving the comfort of her home, but my passion for uncovering the next clue to my past motivated me to move past my fear. Sasha was also worried about me traveling alone to Chennai and didn't really approve, but she didn't outright tell me not to go. And I wouldn't have listened anyway. I was determined to get to the orphanage, to get the information I wanted, at all costs.

A dancer holds back nothing.
Chennai and Chidambaram, Tamil Nadu

The neat circles of red that always covered Shaila's fingertips and toes, and the center of her palms and soles of her feet, pulsed in time with her dance movements. Energy flowed from the glowing red ink, and her skin appeared translucent. She was unmistakably alive.

As she danced, the light surrounding her intensified, until she became intolerably bright. A border of vermillion red appeared at the fringes of the pure white light, and soon Shaila was no longer visible. But her feet still pounded, thud thud thud, *flawlessly keeping time with the drum.*

Eventually, the blinding white light faded, and Shaila reappeared. She was still dancing, almost in a frenzy, shaking her body back and forth, dancing faster and faster. As she jumped and leaped through the air, her movements were wild yet poised, and the red ink on her hands and feet served as focal points.

The red light, the white light, they were all part of Shaila. Her light was her energy—always dancing onward, never maintaining a single set composition.

CHAPTER 13

When I got off the unimaginably long train ride and stepped down onto the platform in Chennai, I was lost in reflection about the dream I'd had along the way and how Shaila's energy felt inseparable from mine. Her footsteps still pounded in my brain, and I still felt the heat of her gaze looking deep into my core. In my vision, it had been tough to know where her light ended and my light began.

But then Tamil bounced me out of my reverie, the language hitting my ears like chili flakes landing on my tongue: spiced and loud and unintelligible. I let the sound of words settle in my ears and flow to the place in my mind where I made assessments and comparisons. Except I had nothing to compare Tamil to; it was unlike anything I had ever heard. In Delhi, everyone I met spoke either English or Hindi, which had been at least somewhat familiar from my Rosetta Stone lessons and limited viewing of Bollywood movies. It didn't feel as foreign as Tamil did. Here, it seemed the people themselves were talking more and louder than what I'd experienced in Delhi. Screeching, laughing, shouting, rambling—their voices covered all variations of sound.

I struggled to keep myself oriented on the busy train platform. The ground beneath me was cement, though I could hardly see a stretch of free space. There were people—feet, saris, pants, shoes—seemingly covering every inch of ground. The platforms were covered by metallic awnings, but the tracks where the trains were parked were exposed to the hot, midday air. The sky was a smoky white—there was indirect sunlight, but it was as if the heat was so strong that the sky could not bear to stay blue anymore and, overcome with the heat, faded into a grayish white. And even the sun seemed hotter here, like it was closer, hugging the earth. I imagined it was because I was over a thousand miles closer to the equator than I was in Delhi.

The train ride had lasted just over an entire day and night. I had brought with me two novels from Dusty Pages and got through both on the ride. Jasmine Aunty had offered to buy me a plane ticket to Chennai, horrified when I told her my transportation plans. But I was insistent; there was no way I was going to take money from her, and buying a plane ticket would have dipped into the money I had brought with me significantly, which I wasn't willing to do without knowing how much longer—and more expensive—my trip could potentially be.

On the train, I had been in an all-female cabin and slept on the berth where we all sat during the daytime, before it converted into a bed in the evening. My other five cabinmates slept on the other bunks within our cabin. The other women had been a range of ages—there was another girl about my age, with two thick braids that reached down her back. There was a middle-aged woman who looked like Jasmine Aunty and a much older woman with her, with gray hair and a hunched back, both of whom wore saris. Then there was another set of two middle-aged women, also both wearing saris and thick gold bangles that clinked whenever they reached for their bags. They were all polite, and we smiled at one another, but I didn't talk to any of them. From the conversations they were having with one another, I did not recognize the language and figured it might be Tamil, since we were traveling to Chennai. It was definitely not Hindi.

I drifted in and out of sleep but didn't sleep for any long stretch of time. Our cabin was at the end of our train car, and the noise from the wheels on the tracks and the door to our cabin opening and closing every time someone entered or exited the cabin to use the adjacent restroom kept me up for most of the night.

My sleep-deprived haze made me feel like I was floating within this sea of strangers now that I was at the Chennai station, this mass of shared humanity. I followed the hordes of people out of the station onto the main road. At first, when I stepped outside into the open air, a gust of wind in my face felt refreshing after the suffocating heat of the crowded train station.

After a few seconds, though, the breeze dissipated. The humidity was stifling, and in some ways worse than the heat inside the station, where I had at least been able to rationalize the suffocation as being the result of so many people crammed together. Outside, although the sky stretched above us like a pale white scarf, I felt even more smothered by the heat, which seemed to expand to fill any available space.

I found myself coexisting in this oppressively hot environment with total strangers, in a foreign city. Delhi, now that I had left it, felt somewhat familiar in retrospect, maybe because in my mind I knew I was adopted from there. And of course, I had had Jasmine Aunty.

Here, I knew absolutely no one.

I found a spot at the bottom of a staircase where I wouldn't get trampled by people and turned back toward the train station, which was a beautiful and impressive building. It was wide and brick red, with a white awning, and it stretched out in either direction from a large, thin tower in the center. I stood on the steps for a brief while, appreciating the reprieve from chaos.

An auto driver laughed as he pulled up to the curb where I stood, lost in my thoughts. He shouted something at me in Tamil. I turned my gaze from the train station to him blankly and walked farther down the sidewalk in confusion. Something about the language and the sun and the dozens of autos milling about, along with the bustling saris and porters hauling luggage all around, was rapidly disarming me of the confidence I had built up over the last twenty-nine hours on the train. Would my weak Hindi get me anywhere here?

I walked along the sidewalk, trying to spot an approachable person, preferably a woman, who I could approach and ask for help with finding the orphanage. I spotted a young couple, the man in formal slacks and a white button-down shirt, the woman wearing a bright teal sari with flowers in her hair, standing against a wall, chatting with one another. The man had a briefcase and the woman was holding a large duffel bag.

"Excuse me," I said, walking up to them and waving. They both raised their eyebrows at me.

"No English," the man said, shaking his head.

I nodded. "Okay . . . *Aap Hindi bolte hain?*" I ventured, asking if they spoke Hindi.

The woman furrowed her brows and pulled at her husband's arm. They walked away from me a few feet and stood further down on the sidewalk.

My cheeks hot with shame, I looked up the staircase to assess the possibility of heading back into the train station and trying to find a help desk. In the mass confusion of trying to exit the building and get some fresh air, it hadn't felt possible to even think about looking for an information booth. I glanced at the wide staircase, which was impossibly cluttered with people walking up and down. I didn't consider myself claustrophobic, but the thought of trying to navigate my way up those stairs and into the station again brought on a wave of nausea.

I tried walking in the other direction on the sidewalk, and a few more auto drivers shouted at me in Tamil. I assumed they were offering me their driving services, and I shook my head, walking on. How could I tell them where I wanted to go when I couldn't even communicate with them?

As my eyes started to tear, from exhaustion and stress, a girl about my age was looking at me curiously from beneath an overhang, where she stood with her luggage and what looked like her large family. I wandered over, desperate and clinging to the hope that filled me upon seeing someone of my own age and sex.

"Are you all right?" she asked me in very crisp English. Internally I thanked some unknown stars deeply.

"Well, I just got here on the train from Delhi." I heard my voice amplified and became acutely aware of my accent, its sharp drawl colliding with the air between us where her words hung.

"Where are you trying to go?" she asked kindly.

I paused, trying to formulate a response that wouldn't reveal the craziness of my actual plans. I don't know why I felt embarrassed to tell this girl—this kind stranger I ran into with a safe demeanor—that I came to Chennai all the way from Delhi to go to the orphanage where I was placed for adoption.

As her eyes grew wider, presumably at seeing the worried, harried expression on my tired face, I felt stark truth tumble out of me.

"I'm looking for my birth parents. I came from Delhi, but before that I came from the US," I said. "I was adopted as a baby from Delhi. But the orphanage there told me I was placed for adoption here, in Chennai, before being transferred there. So, I came here to find out more information."

"Oh, wow. You have traveled so far," she said softly, as her little brother or cousin began tugging at her sleeve. How was she even wearing long sleeves in this heat?

She swatted him away gently. "Well, what is the name of the orphanage you are looking for?"

"I have an address here," I said, removing the piece of paper from my backpack and showing it to her. I felt giddy with anticipation that this girl might be able to help me feel less lost. It was also refreshing to be able to talk to someone, after spending the last thirty minutes since disembarking the train feeling escalating levels of anxiety. Running into her temporarily made the unbearable heat less sticky and lonely. Temperature clings to the skin more readily when things like worries and uncertainties are already stuck there.

"Janaki Colony," she read. "Lot 52. Rainbows of Hope. Hmm, I've never heard of this place." She extended her long slender arm toward a shorter woman nearby wearing a starched purple sari and called out. "Amma?" She followed that with some rapid Tamil and handed my paper to the woman, who I assumed was her mother. She grasped her glasses, which had been hanging on a chain around her neck, and slowly positioned them on the middle of her narrow nose bridge.

"*Ille*, Geetu," she said, shaking her head, after scrutinizing it. She glanced at me, and curiosity brought sharp color to her round face. I felt shy and didn't know where to look as she stared me up and down.

"I'm sorry," Geetu said, handing it back to me. "My mother doesn't know it either. But I can help call an auto for you. You don't speak Tamil, I take it?"

"No, I don't. Only a bit of Hindi," I added to redeem myself.

"Okay. I wish I could help you more, but we are waiting for my uncle to join us, and then we'll be going on a train to Bangalore."

"Oh, that's okay," I said. "You've helped me so much already. Thank you."

She smiled and walked over to an auto that was parked at the curb a few yards from where we stood. I followed slowly with my bag.

I had not yet ridden in an auto since coming to India, having either walked wherever I went or been chauffeured by Raju. I had of course seen these autos, as they were called, everywhere on the teeming streets in Delhi, and now Chennai. Like little yellow bees, with black hoods and open space in place of doors and windows, they were quite cute. The driver sat in the front, and the back row was for passengers. I had been amazed at how many people I saw cramming into the backs of some of the autos. In Delhi I observed a family of six crammed into the back of one. It looked terrifying to me, but as we had driven by them, the parents and all the children had broad smiles on their faces, their hair softly blowing in the heated wind.

Geetu seemed to be talking to the driver for longer than necessary to simply give him the address. Was she ascertaining his character and making sure he was a good sort of person? How could we know? I felt a flush of shame as I realized how I was borderline irresponsible, coming all the way to Chennai in a rush, not more carefully considering what would happen when I got off the train. At least it wasn't nighttime. But I could hear Sasha's foreboding words in my head, initially warning me about being safe in India, and later cautioning me about my plan to travel to Chennai alone. I felt foolish for not worrying about these things more, as I stood here in Chennai, totally alone, unaware of the language and customs, beholden to this kind girl, Geetu, who, like an angel, was trying to help me.

"Okay," Geetu said, stepping away from the auto and turning toward me. I tried to ignore that it bothered me that I didn't know what they had just talked about for so long. "He'll take you directly there, no problem. Where will you stay?"

Of course, I hadn't figured out exactly where I was going to stay. My plan had been to get off the plane and go straight to the orphanage. And then, depending on where that was located, to find a nearby hotel. The plan, which had sounded adequate in my head in Delhi, felt like a farce now that I was here. It felt like I had come to India in some kind of fever dream of my own, with totally unrealistic expectations of what was to happen, when, and how.

I kept believing I would find my birth parents once I was in the correct city. I now realized, with a growing feeling of unease, that the reason I hadn't reserved a hotel ahead of time was because I'd had a bit of hope in my heart that, after finding them, they would welcome me with exuberant joy and everything would naturally lead to a happy ending. As doubts now threatened to surface, I forced myself to at least cling to the belief that my birth parents had to be in Chennai, although a sinking feeling in my chest contradicted that belief.

"Oh, I'm not sure," I confessed. "Depending on how it goes, I'll either stay with my birth parents, if I can find them, or I'll find a hotel near the orphanage."

I saw a flash of concern in her dark eyes, quickly masked with an earnest, warm smile. "Okay, then," she said. "All the best. Take care of yourself." She patted my shoulder gently. "My name is Geetu, by the way."

"I'm Anokhi. Thank you so much, Geetu. I hope you have a good trip to Bangalore," I replied, feeling wistful at saying goodbye to her. Selfishly, I wished she could stay and help me navigate whatever mysteries lay ahead in this city. And so I could thank her properly, buy her a coffee, and talk to her.

She smiled, waving, as she watched me step into the auto. The auto driver had been watching our entire exchange in apparent fascination.

For a moment, I imagined myself as him. I was amused by the prospect of watching two strangers talk in a language I couldn't understand. Even without knowing what they were saying, would their body language and facial expressions betray that they had just met? I wondered, peering at the driver through the small rearview mirror that was bedecked with multiple chains of different deities and a garland of flowers.

A statue of a god was also situated at the base of his steering wheel. To all the gods I did not know but wanted to know, and all the gods who existed and would continue to exist, I did a silent prayer in my head as I clasped my hands in my lap and looked out at the dusty side roads we whirred by in the little open auto. The auto going to Rainbows of Hope, I hoped.

The visit to the orphanage in Delhi flashed through my mind. The cold marble floors, the unhelpful man at the front desk, and Mr. Rajgopal—who eventually did give me information but was as slippery as molasses and difficult to read. I hoped that Rainbows of Hope would be different, though in my heart I knew I had no right to believe that anything would come easily. Just because I wished with all my heart did not mean that my dream of finding my birth parents would come true.

And yet, I still felt the sliver of hope in my being, as I gripped the edge of the auto seat and stared out at the sights—hordes of people, carts of bananas and coconuts, cows, and the occasional cluster of palm trees. I took a deep breath.

Please, gods. Help me find my parents. And help me stay safe, despite my naive, impulsive nature.

CHAPTER 14

When the auto pulled up to a plain-looking, white concrete building down a quieter side street off one of the main roads, it took me a moment to register that I needed to get out. I paid the fare, which showed up on the meter in numbers, so I didn't have to say a word to the driver, which was just as well since we didn't share a language in common.

The security guard sitting outside the front door nodded at me lazily. Inside, the entryway was sparsely furnished. A trim woman in a forest green sari sat behind the desk with stacks of files before her and an archaic '90s-era block-style off-white computer. The ceiling fan whistled, the mosquitoes hummed from some undetermined corner of the room, and the off-white color of the walls echoed whispers of age.

"Yes, can I help you?" she said, as I walked toward her. There was no one else in the waiting area.

"Hello, my name is Anokhi Marna." I stepped up to the counter. "I was adopted in Delhi, but the orphanage there told me I was a transfer case from Chennai—from here, Rainbows of Hope. I was hoping I would be able to find information about my birth parents here."

"In what year were you adopted?" she asked, peering at me from behind her thick glasses with thin wiry frames.

"1990," I replied. The roof of my mouth tingled with excitement and hope. This was already going better than my first experience, at the orphanage in Delhi. I held my breath, watching the woman's austere face.

"Madam, all the records before 1995 were burned in a fire. We have changed physical location since the original building was destroyed in that fire. That old building was rebuilt only many years later and is now a government archives building," she explained, her lips drawn into a thin, pursed expression.

My mouth dropped open. In my periphery, I spotted a plastic white chair next to her desk and slumped into it.

I refused to believe it at first; this felt like a movie. This could not be real life. Was she telling me that the only evidence of my real identity, my birth parents, was irrevocably lost in a fire?

"But . . . I came from Delhi, and they told me to come here." Gazing blankly at her ancient-appearing computer, I felt untethered from the present moment.

"I'm sorry, madam," she said, with little emotion in her voice. She reminded me of my teacher from fourth grade, Ms. Witter: not unkind, but unyielding. "I cannot help you any more with your case, as your adoption occurred before 1995."

I sat on the plastic chair for a few more moments, in silence. A mosquito buzzed by my left ear and I absently swatted at it. When I felt like I could finally take some deep breaths, I stood up, trudged to the entrance, and walked outside the building. The warm, humid late-afternoon air slapped my face. I made it down the front steps but could go no farther, so I sat on the lowest step and slipped off my flip-flops.

The staff at the Delhi orphanage had told me to come to Chennai because information about my birth supposedly was here, at Rainbows of Hope. I had not even bothered to question why I had been shipped, as a baby, across the country. But now that I sat here, crushed and exhausted, it did seem strange. It seemed uneconomical and time consuming; I was just one child in a country of millions of orphans. What could have been so important or dangerous about me or my parents that would have warranted sending me all the way across the subcontinent?

I was now angry with myself for my impulsivity and poor planning. What had felt like the first time in my life that I was being daring and brave and following my heart, when I'd first decided to make this trip to India, now felt like immature decision-making culminating in failure. Why didn't I think to call Rainbows of Hope from Delhi, before embarking on the bone-achingly long train ride all the way here? Why didn't I agree to borrow money from Jasmine Aunty for a plane ride to Chennai? Where did this dire need to do everything by myself at all costs, and without help, come from?

I had enough of my thoughts and my failures. Suddenly, I couldn't bear to sit there, outside the orphanage, and be reminded of it any longer.

I passed through the black iron gates and headed back down the alley toward the main road. I almost got hit by a bullock cart with a man sitting on it as I turned onto the main street, having forgotten about looking both ways before turning and also about traffic being on the left side.

The main road felt similar to Delhi's busy streets, though significantly hotter. My cotton kurta clung to my armpits and lower back from sweat. I walked into a Café Coffee Day, bought a bottle of water, and sat in a corner.

It was approaching early evening, about five o'clock. I was on the verge of crying, and my throat burned with the pressure of tears held back. I wanted desperately, more than anything, to be hugged and comforted by someone I loved. My mind drifted immediately to Sasha and Kale. I hadn't spoken to either of them since I left Delhi.

It was early morning back home in Idaho. I knew Kale often got up early to go running in the morning before work, so I gave him a call first. But after a few rings it went to voicemail. My heart sank. Hearing his voicemail recording—"Hey, it's Kale. I can't answer the phone right now. Please leave me a message, and I'll get back to you. Mahalo!"—made me miss him even more.

I then called Sasha. I knew she was probably still asleep; she didn't usually wake up until after six. For a moment, I considered not calling, not wanting to interrupt her sleep—I knew how hard it was for her to sleep, especially after she broke up with Jay years ago. She never was quite the same after that.

But I needed her. I dialed the number and listened blankly to the scratchy ringing of the dial tone.

"Hello?" she said. She hadn't been asleep, I could tell from her voice. I sighed in relief.

"Sasha," I said. "Hi, it's me. Anokhi."

"Anokhi! How are you, baby?" she asked, excitement rushing into her voice. "Where are you calling from? Are you okay?"

I swallowed the painful lump in my throat. Tears began to spill out in huge, undisguised sobs. I was so tired, so frustrated, and so alone. I turned my back toward the rest of the café and hunched in the little swivel armchair I was sitting in, my head against my knees.

She let me cry without saying anything for a few seconds. "It's okay, sweetheart," she then said softly, a few times. But she didn't ask more; she understood how hard it was to talk amid tears. I was grateful for her silent presence, which comforted me, across all the miles between us. I didn't feel quite as alone.

"I'm okay. I'm in Chennai. I got off the train and went to Rainbows of Hope. But the woman there said there had been a fire at the orphanage in 1995. They don't have any documents from before the fire." I couldn't hold back a few more sobs after I told her the truth.

"Oh, Anokhi," she whispered. "Anokhi. I am so sorry."

We were both silent. What was there to say?

"Do you want to come back home?" she finally asked, interrupting the background humming static of the phone connection.

I thought for a moment. As disappointed as I was, I didn't feel ready to go home. I couldn't bear the thought of going back to Idaho, leaving everything here behind. At least while I was here, the possibility of finding answers kept me going. Though now, admittedly, I was at a very convincing dead end.

What do you do when you go somewhere far away from home with a determined purpose and your plan fails? Can you just adopt an attitude of nonchalance, sweep it away with an accepting smile, and see sights and embrace the novelty of new surroundings?

"I don't know what to do," I confessed.

"I can't imagine how disappointing this is for you," she said. "They had never told me you were a transfer case from Chennai. I had asked for details about your birth parents and history when I adopted you," she said, her voice sounding distant, as though she was lost in memories. "But they had told me that your case was not authorized to share that information, for safety reasons. That's just what it was. I couldn't ask anything else."

I was silent as I listened to her. It made sense. Though now, it felt like knowing that ahead of time would have potentially saved me some of this colossal disappointment. I reconsidered my decision to come to India alone without Sasha. I wondered if it would have been more comforting to have her with me as I faced these crushing roadblocks in my search for my past.

"It's okay," I finally said. "I don't want to even talk about this anymore. I don't know what to do, though. I don't know anyone here. I should have listened to you and Jasmine Aunty. It was silly of me to come here, all the way across the country, alone and without a firm plan."

She was silent on the other end. I wondered if she got some maternal satisfaction from hearing me say she was right—and I wouldn't blame her if she did. I knew I had been a handful recently, ever since dropping out of school and then with my insistence that I come to India all alone.

Finally she said, "Maybe you should switch gears for a bit. I was in your room last night, looking to borrow one of your sweaters, and I saw that book that Melanie gave you about world dance on your bed. It made me miss you a lot, seeing it lying there, as if you had just been reading it and walked out of your room only recently."

Dance. I had forgotten about dance. That had been the other reason I came to India—to get more exposure to dance and connect with that part of myself, inspired by Shaila, that was always deeply drawn toward Indian dance. Despite feeling so disconnected from my heritage and feeling like a foreigner in the country of my birth, I still felt kinship with dance. I had felt the simmering of that deep connection light up during the Kathak class I attended with Nikita.

Sasha continued, as I was silently lost in my thoughts. "I know this has been such a frustrating trip so far. You must be exhausted after traveling all the way to Chennai, only to get this news. But maybe this is the universe giving you a sign. Maybe you should look into dance classes now. Or at least get more exposure to dance while you're there."

I was quiet as I listened to her suggestion. Of course, it was a totally logical alternative. I wasn't ready to go home, but Sasha's gentle reasoning, which always felt like a guiding hand—when I could put my stubbornness aside and listen— was reminding me that there was still more I could get out of this trip.

"You're right," I agreed. I gazed out the pane-glass window. A couple was getting off their motorcycle, parked on the side of the road. The man held out his hand as the woman stepped down. I found myself smiling, watching this simple gesture of intimacy amid the busyness of the street.

"Do you want to learn . . . Bharatanatyam?" she asked slowly, enunciating every syllable and trying not to mispronounce it—only it didn't sound like a word by the time she finished as much as a string of carefully uttered syllables. Her effort made me smile, as she normally spoke in quick, confident speech patterns.

"Yes, I would love that," I said. "But I don't know if I'm ready to just join classes. I don't even know anyone here. And now I'm in Chennai, which was basically for nothing. It's pretty overwhelming."

"Well, sweetheart," she said, chuckling. "This *is* your first trip by yourself. And all the way to India! You couldn't have gone farther from home. You're learning how to travel, how to plan, all on the spot. It's all right. Don't be so tough on yourself."

I relished her words, encouraging me to forgive myself for my rash decisions. She was such a good mother to me, always. The guilt of leaving our home to come so far away to find my birth parents was still strong and saddened me.

I could hear something rustling—it sounded like crisp paper being turned. "What are you doing?" I asked.

"I'm sitting on your bed, looking through the dance book. It's such a beautiful book, such lovely pictures," she said. The rustling stopped.

"What are you reading?" I wished I was beside her on the bed in my cozy bedroom, reading the book together.

"I'm looking at the Bharatanatyam section. 'There are three elements in the name itself,'" Sasha read. "'*Bha* stands for "*bhaava*," or "expression"; *ra* stands for "*raga*," or "melody";

and *ta* stands for "*taalam,*" or "rhythm." "*Natyam*" means "dance." The word is derived from Sanskrit.'"

"I remember reading that." I nodded. These descriptions of dance in the book still felt like an abstraction, so foreign and unfamiliar from the intimacy I always felt whenever Shaila danced. But maybe that was because I felt unfamiliar with her dance as an *art form*, despite my familiarity with her as a being. I had to learn more about dance before I could truly understand more about her.

"It says here that 'the rules of Bharatanatyam were formulated in an ancient treatise on performing arts called Natyashastra, formulated sometime between 200 BCE and 200 CE. Many of the poses in Bharatanatyam were derived from and inspired by the one hundred eight sculptures of dance poses in the Nataraja Temple at Chi . . . Chidam . . . Chidambaram.'" She had conquered "Bharatanatyam" but now struggled to get that last word out.

"What?" I asked.

She took a breath. "Chidambaram." Sasha laughed. "Phew, that was less of a mouthful than I thought it would be, since I just said each syllable slowly."

I began to imagine dozens of sculptures of poses of Shaila dancing. I had seen her do a myriad of hand gestures and postures, so it wasn't hard to imagine that there could be 108 poses. But that there was actually a place where they all were depicted, in stone . . . "A hundred and eight poses?" I asked again.

"Yes, that's what it says."

"Wow. That would be so interesting to see. You said there's a temple with all those sculptures?" My curiosity was piqued.

"Yes, it says in this place called Chidambaram. Let me see where that is. Hold on a second." I heard the squeaky door to my bedroom and closed my eyes, relishing the distant sounds of home. I then could hear Sasha typing in the background, presumably on her laptop in her room. "Let me see where this place is . . . Oh, it's just about four hours by train from Chennai! Maybe you should go pay that temple a visit? Perhaps visiting this place, this birthplace of dance, will give you some inspiration and guidance?" The excitement in her voice was palpable.

A place to go. Something concrete to do. Purpose renewed.

"That sounds . . . like a wonderful idea," I agreed. "Thank you, Sasha. For talking me through this and helping me feel less alone. I'm going to go find a hotel to stay at and a place to eat dinner, before it gets too dark."

A soft sniffle on the other end surprised me. "You're my daughter, Anokhi. As long as I'm in this world, you are never alone. Okay?"

I closed my eyes and felt such gratitude for Sasha, and everything she encompassed—love, support, hope, and kindness. We said our goodbyes. I opened up my laptop to look up trains to Chidambaram. As I'd suspected, it was too late in the day to get on one today. So I would stay the night in Chennai and leave the next morning.

I found a small, decent hotel close to the train station. The sign for the Sri Ramanathan Hotel was white with red letters and depicted a colorful image of a blue-skinned god with a golden halo of light fanning out from behind his head. I found him strangely comforting. After checking in and putting my bags in my room, I wandered the street outside the hotel to find dinner. The outside air was still hot and the sky still bright, but I made a mental note not to walk too far and to be back in my room before it got too late.

The street outside the hotel was bustling with life. I felt safe walking the streets—there were lots of couples walking, and I saw several young women who appeared my age walking around too. There were many restaurants with brightly lit signs and lots of people milling about outside, finishing *thalis*—huge steel plates with at least five different brightly colored *sabjis* portioned out neatly, separated by divisions in the plate. The food smelled delicious, but I walked past these restaurants, many of which were called "hotels" on the sign-boards, looking for something else but not really knowing what. I wanted to try all these authentic foods, but I was afraid of getting sick. Sasha had warned me several times before leaving not to eat street food because my immune system would not be able to tolerate it—she had learned this the hard way when she traveled to Delhi.

I calculated that the experience of eating truly local cuisine was not worth the risk of falling sick and not being able to go to Chidambaram tomorrow, which is what I had set my heart on. I was too annoyed with the failed trip to the orphanage to stay in Chennai much longer. It seemed like a warm, lively city but it also felt too big and foreign to navigate by myself. There was also less English on the signs here than in Delhi, and more of the beautiful curlicue script of Tamil, which was lovely to look at but completely unintelligible to me.

As I walked the streets, searching for a place to eat that was indoors—and that had a name I could at least read—I felt a panic building up inside me that was similar to what I had felt as I walked home from the dance class, after declining Nikita's offer to walk me home, in Delhi. That had been less than a week ago but felt like a lifetime away. It seemed like the part of the city I was in had a lot more Tamil and a lot less English, both on the signs and among the people talking. Near the train station I had heard some people speaking English, but now as I walked here, I realized I hadn't heard anyone speak English for over twenty minutes. I glanced at my watch, and it was already nearing seven thirty.

I finally walked by a Pizza Hut situated at the corner of a busy intersection that I had no interest in trying to cross. A set of stairs led up to the restaurant, which was situated in a shopping complex with billboards of women wearing beautiful pastel saris and heavy gold jewelry. Two teenage boys stood at the edge of the stairs, lanky and wide eyed as I walked past them. They started saying something loudly in Tamil as I walked by, and when I looked back, I saw them pointing at me. I felt stressed about being followed and acutely aware of my position as a young woman traveling in a foreign city where I knew no one and didn't speak the language. In my haste to make it up to the glass doors of the Pizza Hut quickly, I tripped on the last step and fell flat on my face at the top of the marbled stairs.

I could hear the boys laughing but didn't want to look back at their faces. A security guard standing outside the Pizza Hut saw me fall and looked at me with some kindness in his eyes, but he did not say anything or help me. I stood up, dusted off the front of my kurta, and walked inside the restaurant, the air-conditioning hitting me like an icy blast in the face.

I ordered a personal-size veggie pizza and sat by the window looking out at the street. I suddenly missed Jasmine Aunty, not realizing how comforting it had been to be welcomed into her home and have a companion in that new city. I thought traveling alone would be wonderful, and I did enjoy the train rides and the walks. But when I felt hungry and unsure, and borderline unsafe as evening approached, as I did now, the loneliness was amplified.

I ate quickly so I could walk back to the hotel—a faster walk now that my belly was full and I knew where I was going—before it got dark. I set my alarm for 6:00 a.m. so I could get to the train station with plenty of time for the nine o'clock train.

In my dreams that night, Shaila danced with a gold halo twinkling from behind her deep black tresses. I was sure her skin was tinged with a blueness that looked holy and reminded me of cool, distant waters on a shore I hadn't yet reached but had seen before.

CHAPTER 15

The train ride to Chidambaram was considerably shorter than the ride I had taken from Delhi to Chennai. After we left the busy metropolitan area of Chennai, filled with cars, motorcycles, buildings, and dusty humidity, we entered the lush, verdant landscape of rural South India. As we headed south, I leaned my head against the window, facing the eastern morning sun, and gazed at the coastal landscape, which was mostly flat but occasionally hilly. Our route ran parallel to the coast, and every now and then the train would course along a tributary or river before snaking away from the water deeper into the green plains. We stopped at a few small villages and towns along the way, which all seemed quaint and quiet compared to the hectic chaos of Delhi and Chennai.

When I got off the train, the relative lack of commotion compared to the train station in Chennai felt much more manageable. It was still crowded but not nearly as much. I stepped out of the station into the bright sunlight, gauging where I could find an auto.

I heard someone shouting animatedly in Tamil somewhere behind me, but I didn't turn around. The screaming intensified until suddenly, "Watch where you're going; you'll get hit!" a voice cried out right behind me.

Before I knew what happened, a girl my height in a mint green outfit was gripping my arm and pulling me in another direction. I stumbled with the sudden change in movement and my luggage handle fell from my hand.

"You were standing right in the way of the cars! They won't stop for you! You want to get hurt or what?" the girl exclaimed.

Her face's brilliant expression illuminated her features as she spoke. I was struck by how an emotion like concern, which was just her exasperated frustration with my aloofness at my surroundings, could evoke such beauty and intensity of feeling on a countenance.

"Thank you," I said, smiling. I liked her already.

"Please be careful. The drivers here are not merciful," she warned, letting go of my hand and smoothing her hair, which was braided in one thick long braid down to the middle of her back and was almost three times the thickness of my own hair.

"I will," I promised. "Thanks again for saving me."

She grinned. "Of course! I could tell from the way you were walking uncertainly that you aren't from here. And also because you weren't turning around when I was yelling at you in Tamil that you were about to get hit by a car!"

I laughed. "Yes, I just got here. From Chennai. But visiting from the US."

"Wow! The States! What brings you to Chidambaram?" Then, before I could reply, "By the way, my name is Nalini. And yours?"

"I'm Anokhi," I said, extending my hand to shake hers. She pulled me into a hug instead, laughing.

"What? A handshake?" she said. "I just saved your life, na?"

I laughed too and relaxed at her friendly teasing. Her demeanor reminded me of Geetu at the train station in Chennai. Neither of them seemed to be capable of withholding kindness from a stranger; they wore their compassion on their faces. It shone in their eyes and in the tone of their words. Yes, they had both helped me, but I felt that was beside the point. That was only an avenue for me to see their kindness in action.

"I'm here to visit Nataraja Temple," I explained, answering her earlier question.

"Oh my god! You have seriously come at such a good time. I am a dance student here! And Natyanjali Dance Festival is starting tomorrow!" I stared at her, absorbing her words. "Did you not know that?" Her expressive dark eyes widened.

She's a dancer? Seriously? I struggled to wrap my head around the fact that this girl who had just saved my life was also a dancer. "No," I finally said. "What is that?"

"Ayo," she said, shaking her head. "Come with me, Anokhi. I have some time now. Let me take you to the temple! It's one of my favorite places. But, did you have plans to meet someone else here?"

I laughed at her reasonable question. "No," I said, shaking my head. "I am terrible at planning. I was just about to take an auto there by myself. Or, I guess, get hit by an auto first."

We both laughed. She picked up my luggage handle and handed it to me, hailing an auto with her other hand.

I had never really believed in fate until this moment. I followed her into the back seat, gratitude and awe filling my heart for the strange turn this visit was taking in this new city as we whirred away from the station.

The Nataraja Temple loomed above us when we stepped out of the auto. It was the most beautiful structure I had ever beheld. I stared, squinting, and then stepped back, trying to get the best view. It was teeming with detail: Brightly colored pillars and figures stood out like bursts of rainbow on platforms of gold, arranged in numerous neat layers. A huge trapezoidal roof grew narrower toward the top. An archway was carved out in the middle for people to walk through. Statues were everywhere, with layers upon layers of intricate carvings—hundreds of figurines dancing and posing, each telling their own story. In that moment I wanted to know the meaning behind each and every one of them. Who put them there and why? I didn't want to miss a detail, yet that was like asking to see each drop in the ocean.

"It's not going anywhere." Nalini laughed, watching me stare in fascination. "You can look as long as you like. But let me tell you some things about it first. Only then will you appreciate its full meaning."

I nodded for her to continue.

"You must be knowing who Lord Shiva is, right?" she asked.

I nodded. Lord Shiva was the destroyer in the famous trinity of Hindu gods: Brahma, the creator, Vishnu, the preserver, and Shiva, the destroyer. I was aware that what I knew only tickled the surface of what there was to know, but I had read enough to know that much.

"He is also known as Lord Nataraja, the god of dance. It is said that he resides on Mount Kailash, in the Himalayas, where he dances his great cosmic dance, the Tandava," Nalini explained.

I tried to conjure in my mind an image of a mysterious, wild, powerful god living on the snowcapped peaks of the tallest mountains in the world, dancing. It seemed otherworldly.

"If you see his statue in dancing form, he is always dancing on top of a body—the demon of ignorance. When he dances, all the gods and sages—the *devas* and *munis*—watch him, spellbound. His dance is the dance of creation *and* destruction," she went on, taking my arm gently and steering me toward the main entrance to the temple.

I peered past the archway entrance to the temple, trying to visualize a statue inside who represented this intense description she was painting for me. I couldn't see much other than hordes of people milling about inside; bells chimed frequently, and smoky *agarbatti*, or incense, wafted toward us in the hot afternoon air.

"Lord Shiva is the father of Ganesha, the elephant god, and Murugan. His other half, his female counterpart, is Parvati, also known as Shakti. The holy river Ganga flows from his thick locks of hair, and that is why another name for him is Gangadhara. You're not getting bored, are you?"

"Not at all," I confessed. Listening to Nalini talk, with such passion and knowledge ensconced in her words and explanations, was a captivating experience. I could listen to her for hours. It was so much better than reading anything from a book or watching videos online. Her passion reminded me of Nikita's love for Kathak.

"Come, let's go inside. I will tell you more there. I don't want to make this into a lecture!" She laughed, taking my hand and leading me toward a small area to the side of the main entrance where people were taking off their shoes and placing them on racks. We did the same.

When I stepped past the threshold into the main entryway, I gasped. Pillars upon pillars adorned with carvings surrounded us while holding the temple upright. Intricacy upon intricacy melded together in a massive, stony mosaic of indestructible beauty. Just when I thought I could look up to relieve my eyes from the overwhelming grandeur that surrounded us at eye level, the golden ceiling commanded the attention of every atom of my being. On the wall facing us, the 108 sculptures of Lord Nataraja were carved into the stone, depicting the various poses of Bharatanatyam. I found myself trying to mimic one of the poses, without thinking. I bent my left knee and opened it to the side, bringing my right leg out in front of my body and pointed to the left, with my left arm pointing across my body and down and my right arm bent with the palm facing forward.

"Eh, what are you doing!" Nalini gasped, slapping me gently on my shoulder. I dropped the pose, embarrassed, and she laughed.

"I didn't realize you are so interested in dance! But you must start smaller, not with such grand poses. And perhaps not here." She giggled again.

We walked around the temple together quietly. The stone floor was cool against my bare feet. The temple was huge, with many different halls and foyers. There were *pujaris*, or priests, in front of the various *murthis*, or idols. Nalini pointed out worshippers doing *pradakshina* around the gods' altars, walking in circles with their hands in prayer, and then taking *prasadam*, the holy offering, at the end before prostrating on the floor in devout prayer in front of the deities. Most of the women wore saris, and the men wore either slacks and shirts or long white cotton cloth tied into a skirt around their waists—*dhotis*, Nalini later told me they were called. I watched the devotees closing their eyes and whispering prayers silently under their breath. I wondered for whom they prayed— themselves or their loved ones, alive or dead, past or present. It was the most dynamic, real-time expression of prayer I had ever seen.

Back home, Sasha never took me to church or temple. There was only one small church in Pineville, and people came from neighboring small towns to attend the church, but we had never gone, as neither of us felt a strong inclination to do so. We celebrated Christmas at home every year with presents and a tree, because we liked the lights and the reason to have a fancy dinner, not because we really had a personal connection to the holiday's origins, and certainly not the religious aspect. But lights and good food spread a special sort of happiness on the days before and after the holidays, and that was good enough for us.

"Are you all right?" Nalini asked.

I was staring into space between two small shrines. The deities inside were too far away for me to make out if they were male or female. I felt an amorphous awe for the white and orange flowers strewn at the base of the shrines, the intricate gold work, and the soft, curious respect that these displays engendered within me.

"Yeah, I'm fine," I said, snapping back to the present moment. "There is so much to see here. Where should we start?"

"I usually like to start at Lord Ganesha's murthi when I come," Nalini replied, taking me by the wrist and walking through one of the elaborate stone arches into a separate hall.

I liked Ganesha immediately. His head was unmistakably that of an elephant, but his hands and legs were humanlike. His round belly and his tusks, which helped curve his mouth into a deep smile, were endearing. I felt warmth exuding from his statue and could not help smiling as I gazed at his playful, mysterious form. As I found myself reacting so strongly to the statue, for the first time since setting foot in the temple I began to wonder if the spirits of the gods might partially live inside these stone statues. Until then, statues were only symbolic to me; I never considered they might be living and breathing embodiments of the divine for humans to access directly. Like pieces of heaven on earth.

Nalini did *namaskar*, putting her palms together and bowing deeply, in front of the murthi and circled it three times before stopping again. She was silently mouthing some prayer I couldn't hear. I followed her quietly and mimicked her actions as best as I could, but I was more consumed by wondering what she was doing than by focusing on the act of praying itself. I could not pray just yet, not authentically anyway. I had to discover my love and connection to these spirits before I could pray to them. To skip directly to prayer would be a farce.

"Why do you start with him?" I asked after she took ash that the pujari offered her. She pinched it between her right thumb and middle finger and applied it to her forehead. I had waited a few feet away, afraid I would mess up the steps and cause some offense unknowingly. The rituals seemed so specific and exact, and despite being welcomed into this world by Nalini's warmth and friendliness, I once again felt like an outsider.

"Whenever you begin anything, Lord Ganesha is the one who you must pray to first," she explained. "Whenever there is a dance performance, the first segment is usually dedicated to Lord Ganesha. He is the remover of obstacles. He is the auspicious one. When people move into new homes, they do a Ganesha *pooja*, or prayer, before anything else."

After visiting a few of the other shrines, we exited the temple down a series of stone steps and came into a beautiful open space. There was a large rectangular pool in one corner. The water's surface was glistening, the ripples laced in silver light dancing down from the late-afternoon sun.

"Sivaganga," Nalini said, pointing to the body of water. "There are several bodies of water on the temple grounds."

I watched two women dancing at one of the corners of the pool. Another woman was sitting on the ground near them, singing. The music was full of longing.

"They are portraying the love between Radha and Krishna," Nalini explained as we walked closer to them to watch.

I listened carefully to the singer's voice, which was melodious and clear, though I had no idea what she was saying. I felt small and removed from my life, transported by the magic of their devotional song and dance. For a moment, I felt like I was disintegrating and becoming part of the air, leaving my body and my day-to-day thoughts, and being transported into the greatness of the love story they were portraying. I felt my soul diffuse into the soles of the dancers' feet and into the holy lips of the singer, whose eyes were closed and whose facial expressions complemented her emotive singing. She was feeling every word she sang, letting the depth and meaning of her song sink like ink into the canvas of her skin. Watching her took me back to another time, reminding me of the tabla player I had seen at the cultural show at UW, seemingly in another lifetime. They both had the same devoted look of pure love on their faces as they performed their art form.

"Thank you for taking me here," I said quietly, turning to Nalini after the dance ended. "Are you sure I didn't distract you from something?" I asked. It had been a couple of hours since we had arrived at the temple. I had been lugging my suitcase and backpack around with me ever since, and I appreciated the rest we took at the edge of the water to put my bags down.

"Don't be silly," she said, swatting a mosquito away from where it hovered near my shoulder. "Actually, wait. It's not yet five o'clock, is it?"

I looked at my watch. "No, it's four thirty."

"Okay, good!" she said, wiping her brow with her wrist. "I told my guru I would come at five to help."

"Help with what?"

"Remember how I was telling you, when we first met, that your timing could not have been better? Tomorrow the Natyanjali Dance Festival will begin. It's one of the biggest dance festivals in all of India, right here in Chidambaram, and will take place for five days. The best Bharatanatyam dancers come from all over India to perform their dances of dedication to Lord Nataraja."

Lord Nataraja . . . That's Shiva, I reminded myself. I was soaking up every bit of information that Nalini shared with me over the course of the day, but keeping all the new names and stories of gods and deities straight in my head was challenging.

"I need to help my guru prepare some of the outfits for the girls from our school who are performing at the festival. Tomorrow is Shivratri, the anniversary of Lord Shiva's birth, which marks the beginning of the festival. Dance performances will take place on a big stage in the temple, and many rituals and poojas will take place inside too. That is why it is more crowded here than usual. There are always so many people here for the festival. Many tourists come. That's why I thought you had come, initially!" she said, beaming at me and giving my arm a gentle squeeze.

"Wow," I said. My timing really was impeccable. I had to give it to Sasha for suggesting I come here to this temple. I felt it was more than pure coincidence that I had arrived right as this huge festival was about to begin. Fate radiates an unmistakable warmth whose heat only grows when you actively recognize its presence.

"Do you have anywhere to stay here?" Nalini asked, interrupting my reverie contemplating fate and good fortune.

"Um . . . no," I admitted. "I came here on a bit of an impulse, to see this temple. Which is kind of how my whole trip to India has been, honestly. I was planning to stay at a hotel. Do you have any recommendations?"

"Oh, Anokhi! Come now," she said, shaking her head. "Please, stay with me and my family. It will be much more comfortable for you. I live with my parents and my younger sister, Priya. She also studies dance."

She already felt like a friend, after the afternoon we had spent together. I was grateful for not needing to find lodging and for the company. The time I had spent with her so far had been the happiest hours I'd spent yet in India.

Nalini took me to her home on the way to her guru's house. I didn't want to inconvenience her, but I also felt hot and gross, desperately in need of a shower, and tired. Her house was a modest single-story pale yellow house at the end of a small alley. The iron gates at the front were short, about three feet in height, with green vines laced around them. There was a small garden in the front, leading up to the veranda, where a beautiful wooden swing hung from the ceiling of the porch with heavy metal chains.

The door to her house was open, with a hand drawn, decorative pattern at the doorstep. It appeared to be outlined with white chalk, with bright pink and orange flower petals neatly placed in between the white lines.

"*Kolam*," Nalini said, smiling, as she saw me admiring the ornate pattern. "My mother usually does it before festivals. It's called *rangoli* in the north."

There was a small pile of sandals outside the entrance, and I took my shoes off instinctively. I had learned quickly enough after staying at Jasmine Aunty's house in Delhi that this is a nonnegotiable part of Indian culture: removing shoes before entering a home—or a temple, as I learned earlier today at Nataraja Temple. I really loved the gesture, as a symbol of respect and cleanliness, and was already planning to suggest we do the same at home with Sasha when I got back.

"Nalini!" a bright voice called from inside the doorway. Nalini led me inside the house. The front entry room had stone floors and modest wooden furniture—a sofa, two chairs, and a coffee table, as well as some floor cushions.

The aroma upon entering the house was arresting. It smelled of a myriad of spices—sweet, savory, and hot. My eyes teared up a little, and I wiped the corners of my eyes with my dupatta.

We walked past the living area to the kitchen. Steel pots and pans hung from a fixture above the stove. A middle-aged woman wearing a plain yellow cotton sari stood at the stove. It seemed she had six arms, like a goddess, as she stirred pots, dumped in spices, and chopped vegetables in a coordinated but mesmerizing frenzy.

"Amma, this is Anokhi," Nalini said. "She is a new friend I met in town. She is visiting from the States! She didn't have a place to stay, so I told her she can stay with us. She is interested in coming to the Natyanjali Festival with me." Nalini's accent was thicker and somewhat stilted as she spoke to her mother. I wondered whether they usually spoke English at home, or if she was doing it so that I could understand. I was grateful, since it was probably the latter.

"Oh, hello, dear. Welcome! I am Meena," her mother said, smiling, with a thick accent and crisp enunciation. Her teeth were slightly crooked, her smile sincere and warm. She put down what she was doing, wiped her hands on a towel, and gave me a hug. I was caught off guard by the hug but enjoyed it. She smelled wonderful, like spices and old newspapers.

"Thank you, Meena Aunty," I said. "Thank you for welcoming me into your home. I'm so glad I met Nalini. She saved my life earlier today!"

Meena Aunty laughed. "Well, you must tell me all about it, and your visit here. But you must be tired. Where are you coming from?"

"I just came from Chennai," I said, a hint of sadness entering my voice. I hadn't thought about the failed trip to the orphanage or my strange trip to India all afternoon. Meeting Nalini had been such an exciting and much needed distraction.

"Poor thing," she said, making a *tsk* sound with her tongue. "Come, you can take rest in Nalini's room. She can sleep with Priya while you are here," Meena Aunty said, taking my arm and leading me down a dark corridor past the kitchen and dining room. We turned into the first doorway on the right, which opened into a cool room with the shades drawn and thin, light blue cotton curtains fluttering in the air that was quietly circulating from the ceiling fan overhead.

"I'll go now to my guru's house, Anokhi. You stay here and rest. Amma will take care of you. Priya will be home soon too. I'll come back and meet you for dinner," Nalini said, waving to me as she walked out the door.

Nalini's room was small and clean. She had a dark brown wooden armoire in the corner, a thin tall mirror in another corner, and a low bed on a simple frame. She had some pictures on her nightstand but otherwise there was minimal decoration.

I looked at the pictures. One was of her with a group of other young women, all clad in bright ornate outfits with pleated fans between the legs, beautiful hoop earrings, and white flowers in the braided buns coiled on the back of their heads. They were smiling and posing in a variety of complex dance positions.

"Those are her friends from her dance school," Meena Aunty said, as she came over to stand next to me by the nightstand. "She has been learning dance since she was a small child."

"That's amazing," I replied.

"I learned dance too when I was a girl, and so did my mother. There is a big love for classical dance and music in our family," she explained.

"That is so beautiful. I am really looking forward to seeing more at the festival tomorrow," I said. I still couldn't believe how lucky I was with the timing of this trip to Chidambaram.

"Yes," Meena Aunty said, placing a towel on the bed. "But now you should rest. Nalini will keep you up late talking for a long time. She loves making new friends. She is a very social girl. And she will be very glad to have you to accompany her to the festival this year. Everything works out for a reason, as we say," she added.

"She told me some of the girls in her dance school are performing for the festival. Has she ever performed?" I asked.

Meena Aunty shifted a little in her stance and sighed. "Nalini has had some health problems this year. She had a seizure, quite severe, in dance class a few months ago. We had to take her to the hospital. Since then, she has been taking it easy. Her doctor advised it would probably be best for her to not perform at the festival this year. The bright lights, the vigorous physical activity, the excitement might bring on another seizure."

"Oh wow . . . I'm so sorry," I said, wishing I hadn't asked but also heartbroken to hear this about my new friend. Nalini was a radiant person, full of warmth and life. I could only imagine the sorrow she must have felt, or may still be feeling, at the prospect of not being able to perform this year. Clearly, dance was a huge part of her life.

"Oh, it's okay, dear. What is meant to be will be. God only knows why such things happen. But we are grateful she has not had any seizures for the past few weeks. She has another test she needs to get done in a month's time, but hopefully if that is all right, she can get back to dancing. She has been quite sad about the festival, of course, but she is happy to support her guruji and her friends. And perhaps meeting you was exactly what she needed. As a guest, she can introduce you to the festival, explain to you all the dances and stories and traditions. She has been going to this festival for years, since she was about five years old. It is such a big part of our lives here," Meena Aunty said, taking my backpack and bag from me, which I hadn't put down since arriving, and placing them at the end of the bed on a chair.

"For now, dear, take some rest. The washroom is just at the end of the hallway. We will come wake you up before dinner. Please, be comfortable. This is your home," she said, gently touching my cheek. She walked out and closed the door behind her.

I marveled at Meena Aunty, how she made me feel so welcome within only minutes of knowing me. Then again, her daughter had done the same thing. I sat down on the bed in stillness, in awe of what she had just told me about Nalini's recent health issues.

I never thought much about religion or God, but I certainly felt that I was meant to be here, in this warm, loving home, my path crossing with these kind souls. Even though they were strangers, I felt very much at home here. The disappointments of Chennai felt like a remote memory that didn't hurt as much as they had yesterday. I lay down on the bed, and my eyes quickly closed as sleep overtook me with little warning.

At dinner, I spoke with Nalini, Priya, and their parents. Her father was a tall, soft-spoken man with a thin mustache and kind eyes. He worked at the local bank. Priya was bubbly and energetic, like her sister, and fourteen years old. She wanted to be a dance teacher when she grew up. Her family asked me many questions about my life in Idaho, about Sasha, and about the days of my trip prior to arriving here. I found I was able to relate the details with little sadness because their friendly conversation; the delicious dinner of buttery rice, vegetable sabjis, and tangy yogurt; and their hospitality filled my heart and made being with them so easy.

After dinner, Nalini and I sat in the small courtyard behind her house. She lived in a residential part of the town, away from the clutter and commotion of the temple and the train station. Her backyard was very green. A few palm trees swayed gently in the wind. The sky was softening in preparation for nighttime, with streaks of periwinkle, pink, and orange smiling tenderly upon the earth. We were playing a game in which she showed me different poses in dance that signified different animals and deities, and I had to guess which animal she was portraying. It felt like a version of charades.

"*Mayuro,*" Nalini said. She touched her index fingers to her thumbs and spread her arms out, hopping nimbly on her toes in a circle and throwing her torso back and forth gracefully as she did.

"Umm," I said. "Some sort of bird?"

"A beautiful bird!" she offered, winking.

"A peacock?" I guessed.

"Yes!" She clapped, sitting back down. "So, you see," she said, wiggling her fingers, flexing and curling them as if stretching, "dancing is like acting too. To tell the stories there need to be meanings behind hand movements. Sometimes there is no meaning, of course, just decoration and show. But most of the time, there is meaning."

I flexed and curled my fingers too. She began sculpting her fingers into different mudras, and I followed her example. I was amazed by how versatile my hands felt, a vehicle of expression without words. I was excited for the festival, more so because I knew Nalini would be there with me, explaining the meanings and nuances behind things that otherwise I would have no insight into. I felt immense gratitude in my heart for having crossed paths with her.

"Tomorrow is the first day of the festival. It will be quite amazing for you to behold," Nalini said, looking up at the sky. I studied the stars overhead; it was easier to see them here, compared to Delhi or Chennai, where the smoke from the cities produced a gray atmospheric sheen, dulling the view of the stars.

"Have you lived here your entire life?" I asked her.

"I was born in Chennai, but we moved here when I was four years old because my parents started teaching here at the university. Priya was born here. It's a nice place, and I think growing up here made it inevitable that we would both become interested in dance. Amma and Appa never forced us, you know. Although dance does run in our family.

"From a young age, I remember going to the Nataraja Temple every week with Amma. It is huge, as you saw—there are five main halls. When I was a child it seemed like a never-ending enchanted palace to me."

She drew her knees to her chest and continued. "I remember so well the first time we went into Nrithya Sabha, the main dance hall in the temple. Amma and I sat in a corner, and she told me the story of how Shiva danced a duel with his female counterpart, Kali, the goddess of power, death, destruction, and salvation. Whichever one lost had to leave the Thillai Forest, which is Chidambaram. Lord Vishnu himself was the judge. After she told me that tale, that hall became so much bigger to my eyes. Still, every time I go in there, I feel the vibrations through the floor that Shiva and Kali must have caused when they danced. Those vibrations will resound forever, Amma says."

"I think I can relate," I mused aloud.

"Really? How?"

I drew in my breath. I felt so close to Nalini, after the day we had just had, that it didn't make sense for me to hold back. So I started to tell her about Shaila. I hadn't meant to bring it up, but now that I had started talking, I found I couldn't hold back from telling her the truth. "There is a woman, a dancer, who has appeared to me in my dreams for most of my life. I feel her mysterious ankle bells reverberating softly in my head even when I cannot see or feel her dancing. She haunts me in a beautiful way that I don't want to ever lose. She is like family to me."

I paused, closing my eyes. Other than Sasha and Kale, I had never told anyone about Shaila. And it had been a long time since I had spoken about her out loud to anyone. I had continued to write about my dreams in *The Chronicles*, which

I had brought with me to India. But otherwise I hadn't been thinking much about her actively, having been so distracted by all the unexpected traveling, disappointing orphanage visits, and now this magical trip to Chidambaram. My chest felt heavy with the weight of this mysterious truth that I had carried with me for so many years, but also lighter after saying these words aloud to my new friend.

"It also drains me," I went on, as she listened intently. "Because I cannot, after all these years, figure out the root of her presence. I have no idea who she is, though I know she is in my mind for a reason."

"Wow," Nalini said. "That is incredible, Anokhi. Is this why you are so interested in dance?"

"Ever since I found out what Indian classical dance was, I knew that was exactly the dance Shaila had been dancing in my mind. Of course, it also made more sense once I understood that I was adopted from India. But growing up, I never had an opportunity to take classes; the place where I live in the US is not very diverse. The closest place where I could learn dance would be almost six hours away. I have watched performances, mostly online, and read more about dance in books. That was one of the reasons for my trip to India—to learn more about this dance form and the culture, which feels so close to my heart, through Shaila's presence in my mind. The other reason was that I wanted to try to find my birth parents."

Nalini sat up straight and clasped her hands together decisively. "Wow. I can't begin to imagine how exciting, and frightening, it must feel to be searching for your birth parents. I really hope you find them, Anokhi. As for Shaila and learning more about dance, I would love to teach you everything I know about dance. It is my passion. And now that you're here for the festival, I will take you with me to all the dance performances within the next five days. Or as many as we can see; of course we can't be in two places at once."

Nalini hugged me tightly. She was so kind and thoughtful toward me, and I wanted to respond with something equally compassionate about her seizures, conveying how I was sorry that she couldn't dance this year. But it felt wrong to bring it up in this moment, when she was clearly so happy to be sharing this big part of her life, her culture and her community, with me. Plus, she hadn't brought up any of her health stuff with me; I had only heard about it from her mother, so I wanted to respect her privacy. I held my tongue, but my heart felt overwhelmed by how loving and supportive she was, despite her own suffering.

That night, I dreamed of Shaila dancing in Nrithya Sabha. She wasn't dueling anyone, but Kali and Shiva were standing off to the side, magnificent and still, watching her lovingly like a mother and a father beaming proudly at their daughter.

The first day of the festival was an explosion of Carnatic—South Indian classical—music like I'd never heard before. I had a preview of the immensely moving quality of the instruments from prior videos I had watched and during the performance I had attended in Seattle with Kale, but hearing it in the temple, in person, was a completely different experience. Three musicians and a singer sat cross-legged side by side on the stage, and the veena, flute, and mridangam blended together with the vocalist's impeccably trained voice. My day-to-day thoughts were blown away, my soul lifted into a place untouched by time. Being here in person with the music live was a different plane of sensory experience, something incomparable to anything I'd experienced before.

"What is this one about?" I asked, pointing to the stage from where we sat. I had been asking Nalini about the meanings of different pieces—which gods they were dedicated to and which stories they were telling.

The main stage was where the best dancers got to perform. This huge stage was in the performance hall and only open during festivals. It bore impressive lighting, plentiful strings of white flowers draped around the stage, and a large cylindrical stone, known as Shiva Lingam, devoted to Lord Shiva and adorned with flowers and ash markings at the back center. At the edge of the stage stood a solo dancer in a beautiful peacock blue, fixating on a calculated point in the distance, far beyond the audience's heads, as if staring into a face high above. The depth of her gaze illustrated an impenetrable connection between her and the invisible target of her attention.

"She is speaking to Krishna, her lover," said Nalini.

"Wow, everyone is in love with Krishna, huh?" So far, several pieces had been about lovers calling out to Krishna.

Nalini made a *tsk* sound and shook her head. "Oh Anokhi, it is not what you think. This is divine love. *Bhakti* love. Spiritual love. Do you understand?"

I shook my head. "I don't think so."

"In most performances, the dancer either portrays different characters while telling a story or she herself will be the heroine, the *nayika*. In the latter role, she is usually calling out to the lord in a sense of longing but not confined to the traditional human longing." She whispered, but the hall wasn't completely silent even though the performance was already underway. No one seemed to mind the crowd's murmurings, and the music was so loud that their conversations were drowned out.

I furrowed my brows, trying to understand. I thought about longing and love and tried to understand what the next step above that would be. All that kept coming to mind was Kale. I blushed. Even though Nalini didn't know my thoughts, I felt embarrassed for thinking about him while she was explaining something clearly so pure and divine to me. But the truth was, many of the dances that portrayed anything about love, especially between a male and a female character, always reminded me of Kale. The distance between us had been seared into me, and it became clearer to me, more than ever now that I was so far away from him, that I loved him. I didn't know when I would ever be able to tell him this, but I knew it now in a way I had never known back home, due to my own shyness and inexperience with romantic relationships.

"It is not just passion," Nalini continued, as if in response to my thoughts. "Her love is bhakti, devotion to the Supreme. It is the purest kind of love you can imagine. Think of totally selfless love. Love for the sake of love and respect, not for personal gain. Worship and adoration of Lord Krishna is the most cited form of love when it comes to bhakti love. The end goal of bhakti lovers is to reunite and merge their souls with Krishna, the essence of the supreme consciousness."

She was gesturing with her hands as she explained all this to me. As she did, she intermittently touched a small gold chain with a pendant on her neck. I could see it was a deity but was unsure who it was. Perhaps Krishna.

"Krishna loves anyone who shows him utmost devotion and selfless love. That is why he has many lovers. But really, he loves each individual bhakti lover as if she, or he, were the only one in the universe. In that sense, the bhakti relationship between Krishna and devotee is entirely singular. Each person feels special because they *are* to Krishna," Nalini concluded, clasping her hands in her lap.

The concept of reciprocated, divine love between a dancing devotee and Lord Krishna seemed beautiful but was tough to wrap my head around. "I thought dancers dedicate themselves to Nataraja, or Lord Shiva?"

Nalini paused and looked at me thoughtfully before replying. "There is no black and white. Dance is for the soul, for the

Supreme, for the self, for many things. What I say and what someone else says about dance may not be the same. It is experiential loving, learning, feeling. It is not contained in words, even. Some people love Krishna, some people love Shiva. But it is all in essence the same. It is about loving something bigger than yourself, a power that unites us all and represents the divine beauty in all that we experience."

I nodded, trying hard to understand. Though I didn't have the background to comprehend the intricacies of the polytheistic family of gods and goddesses, the feelings she was expressing sounded similar to how I felt about Shaila's dances. I could never convey how they stirred my emotions because they were just that—*my* emotions. They could not be contained in words adequately, even if I tried. And I did in my journals. But it was never quite the same.

Nalini continued, "See what I am trying to do here, putting such big concepts into neat little explanations? It will never do. You need to only watch some of these amazing dancers, see it in their eyes, in their movements, the divine love I am struggling to put into words."

She stood from her seat during a break between the performances and motioned for me to follow her. Crowds milled about the assembly hall and congregated by the exits. Like the day before, most women wore brightly colored saris and white flowers in their braids. Many also had red or white markings on their foreheads between their eyebrows—religious markings, Nalini had explained to me.

As we walked, Nalini kept talking while leaning in close to me to be heard over all the noise. "Hear it in the soulful cry of the flute, the fiercely passionate beat of the mridangam, the devoted calling of the singer. Then, watch all these elements reflected in the dancer's movements—through her body. Then you will know what it means to dance for something far greater than yourself."

The first day of performances ended at nearly five o'clock
the next morning. Shaila began dancing as soon as my head
touched the pillow and dawn was crawling into the sky. She
danced for a long time. Her dances combined elements of the
stories and performances I had seen the previous day and night,
her costume changes inspired by colors that had adorned the
dancers' bodies: fire orange, royal purple, sea green, all embel-
lished with golden seams and glistening jewelry.

Now that I was becoming more familiar with the meanings behind the dances, I could better understand what Shaila
was dancing about. When she posed majestically, she was not
merely extending limbs in every which way to display her flexibility. When she stood with her right leg bent and her left leg
lifted and crossed in front of her, bent at the knee, and held her
right hand in the blessing position and her left hand extended
under it and across her body, she was posing like Lord Nataraja
himself, the cosmic dancer. Each movement and pose were
tributes to the Divine or to beauty itself, which were arguably
one and the same.

CHAPTER 16

By the middle of the second day, I felt like I knew more about dance than I had known for all the years that I spent watching videos and trying to learn about it from a distance. Through Nalini's friendship and experienced eyes, and her eagerness to communicate and teach me, I was fully immersed in the Natyanjali Festival and felt like I was just one of many floating in a sea where we all tried to understand the beauty and chaos of the cosmic dance of life.

We had just finished watching a performance describing Lord Nataraja's great strengths and virtues, a haunting piece called "Bho Shambho" set to a foreboding raga called "Revathi." The performance was done by a single dancer, a woman wearing a dark blue dress with thick black makeup around her eyes and a daunting expression of power on her face. Throughout the dance, she did several impressive static, one-legged poses of Lord Shiva interspersed with crisply performed *jathis*—sets of complex technical steps set to fast rhythmic chanting by the vocalist. The melancholic melody of the song combined with the dancer's powerful awestruck facial expressions and intense performance sent chills through my being and left me longing for more. It was my favorite piece that I had seen so far.

We had somehow managed to find space to sit, despite arriving a bit later in the morning. Meena Aunty had prepared a special breakfast for me of *dosas* and idlis. I was overcome by the delicious savory pancakes and rice cakes, dipping them into lentil soup, chutney, and potatoes until I could eat no more. But we paid the price, arriving later to the hall, struggling more than we had the day before to find a place to sit. The room was packed, filled with the sounds of shuffling feet, side conversations, and breathing, a constant whir of movement from one place or another. It was hot and stuffy, but there were fans and at least some circulation of air, compared to the stifling humidity outside. And I also was developing a strange appreciation for being just one body amid hundreds in a room, crowded there for the unified purpose of partaking in the magic of Natyanjali. I was beginning to understand it was so much more than a festival—it was a community of artists, viewers, and devotees gathering to express love through art, directed to a cosmic power greater than any of us alone.

"As you can see, there are many more dances today dedicated to Lord Nataraja, or Shiva, the god of dance and destruction," Nalini explained. "Yesterday, many of the pieces we saw were devoted to Lord Krishna. Although this festival is primarily dedicated to Lord Shiva, there are many other gods who are honored through dances."

I nodded. The plurality of Hinduism was starting to make more sense to me. Worshipping one god didn't take away from another's importance or the devotion toward him or her. They all coexisted in a complex, interconnected web of divinity. *Not unlike humans.*

"I could tell you liked the Bho Shambho piece. It is one of my favorites too," Nalini said. "And, as you can see, anger is not always a bad thing. Shiva dances his Tandava, the dance of destruction, with a great display of his fierce power," Nalini continued. "But with destruction, there is also a beginning. There is also the creation of a new universe as the old one comes to an end."

I mulled over her words as the violin began to hum and the drums picked up the pace for the next performance, preparing to introduce the next two dancers, a young man and woman dressed in matching silk outfits. They were about to perform a Kathak duo, which I was excited to see, as I hadn't seen Kathak performed onstage yet. I thought about Nikita in Delhi and wondered if she had ever been to this festival. I wondered if, had I grown up here, I would have known about this festival and would have come. Now that I was here, I couldn't imagine how I hadn't known about this before. My life felt completely changed by the past two days.

The Kathak performance was captivating and playful. It was like a dance-off or a duel in which each dancer performed their part in response to the other one, their teasing expressions and agile movements set to melodious, fast-moving musical compositions. After it ended, my thoughts drifted back to Nalini's comments about Shiva's dance of destruction and anger. I tried to comprehend the magnitude of a god's anger that was powerful enough to both destroy and create universes. Like many concepts I had encountered over the last two days, it felt beyond reach. But it intrigued me nonetheless.

"What are you thinking so hard about?" Nalini asked.

"Just reflecting on what you were saying about Shiva's cosmic dance of anger and powerful energy," I said. I couldn't translate everything that was bubbling in my head as a result of being exposed to such a multitude of new inputs—sensory, spiritual, and artistic.

We stepped out of the hall a little past two o'clock, when there was an intermission in the afternoon programs. Nalini said there was a particular part of the temple she wanted to show me. We pushed our way, gently but persistently, past throngs of sweaty people. I was becoming used to the crowds. Initially I could only focus on my own condition amid all the people. I was hot, sweaty, and claustrophobic. I felt like I couldn't breathe at all, and this sent panic and frustration throughout my being. I could breathe, of course, but I was entirely convinced that if there were just one more person in my way I would surely suffocate.

I watched Nalini move adeptly through the masses, trying to pinpoint what was different between her technique and mine. Invariably, I ended up getting separated from her whenever we moved from one place to another. To avoid this, she had started grabbing me by the wrist from the beginning, before entering the sea of people, to get from point A to point B.

I soon gathered there was no difference in technique, only outlook. Where I saw others—sweaty, irritating multitudes of other people—she saw fellow devotees, lovers of dance, and the piece of the Divine that connected us all. I admired and envied her sincere, unfeigned loving acceptance of everyone that we found ourselves beside.

We came to a big gold-adorned idol. Not many people were in this wing of the temple at all. The sudden breakthrough into empty space was refreshing and startling.

"Which god is this?" I asked.

"This is Lord Vishnu," Nalini said. Thick red and yellow garlands were heaped around his neck, and it was hard for me to focus on the simple statue behind all the ornate flowers and jewelry that adorned him.

"I thought Nataraja Temple was a Shiva temple?"

Nalini smiled and nodded, as if she was waiting for me to come to this confused conclusion.

"Yes. This is the Thillai Nataraja Temple. But one of the things that makes it so special is this: The temple houses shrines to both Vishnu and Shiva."

It did seem quite remarkable. Nalini had mentioned there were well-defined lines between Vishnu and Shiva devotees, Vaishnavites and Shaivites, especially in South India. Their co-existence in one temple suddenly highlighted the importance of unity to me.

My head swirled among all the dances and murthis. So many gods, so many deities . . . yet there was room for so much warmth and storytelling, and space for all kinds of people to find at least one representation of the Divine that spoke to them. There was no single right way; there were many paths, and the temple conveyed this quite effectively by housing shrines to both Vishnu and Shiva. In another sense, all paths merged into some greater shared trajectory. Perhaps we were all going to the same place after all.

We stood together in the cool chamber, leaning against a pillar. I realized that this section of the temple was proba-bly empty because of the ongoing dance festival dedicated to Shiva. A few devotees were paying their respects to Vishnu here, but the distinction seemed firm. These days were set aside for celebrating Shiva. It felt nice, though, to have some reprieve from the crowds, the heat, and the noise.

"I like to think of Vishnu and Shiva as two best friends," Nalini said. "Two faces of one coin. Where Shiva is energetic and impassioned, Vishnu is a sea of calm. Where Shiva de-stroys, Vishnu protects. Yet without the context of one, the meaning of the other is . . . incomplete."

Nalini paused, smoothing the pleats of her cotton sari. "I try to remember that duality. And of course, there's more than that. There are all the shades in between the two, all the dif-ferent devas and munis and human beings—you and me. We all fit in somewhere, you see? All our emotions, our thoughts, they fit in somewhere too. One of the many things I've learned from studying dance, Anokhi, is that there is a place for every emotion, every feeling. Don't be afraid of expression, of bhaava:

It is the light that illuminates your soul. To be a skilled dancer, one must know when to use which form of bhaava, and for what purpose. It all has its place."

She made so much sense. I admired her gentle wisdom and her humility. I was in awe of her as a person and couldn't believe she was my age. It filled me with a translucent stream of contentedness, listening to her speak.

"That's enough of my talking. Shall we take a break for lunch? What do you want to eat?" Nalini asked.

"I don't know, maybe we can find something outside the temple?"

She laughed. "Oh yes, we'll find more than something. There will be lots of vendors, and if you want to go sit in a hotel and eat, we can." I had to remind myself that hotels often referred to restaurants here, not necessarily literal hotels where people stay overnight.

We wandered along the main road outside the temple and ended up sitting inside one of the many hotels nearby, teeming with people, though the crowd was steadily waning, as it was three o'clock. There was no English on the sign but now that I was with Nalini, I appreciated how the possibilities opened up, and I felt like I could go anywhere, thanks to her companionship. The table was covered in plastic, and the waiter hurriedly brought us two steel tumblers of water. The small menu in Tamil was printed on a laminated card on the table.

"Do you know if they have bottled water?" I asked Nalini.

"Ah, probably not . . . but don't drink that, I don't want you to fall sick. Shall I run to one of the shops and buy you a bottle?" she offered, about to get up.

"No, it's okay, I'll get some later. I'll just get tea instead," I replied.

I really wanted to try to drink the water and test my immune system. The longer I was here, the more I wanted to try to blend in, to prove that I was from this country. Ever since coming to Chidambaram, I could see parallels between me and Nalini. In some ways, I envied her—growing up here, with dance and culture and heritage such a central part of her life. It felt like this had been missing from my life for so long. But from the small things, such as water that I couldn't drink, to the larger gaping differences, like language barriers, I was being humbly reminded that belonging is not something to be neatly achieved.

On a more practical note, it didn't seem worth getting sick now, with three remaining days of the festival at hand and so much to enjoy. Would I feel a smug sense of pride if I fell sick and spent the next few days tossing and turning in illness, lying on a bed in her home, instead of coming to the temple? That at least I didn't cave and drink bottled water like a *pardesi*? At least I was authentic and drank the water in the tumblers, the water that everyone else from here drinks without thinking twice? *Of course not,* I chided myself, forcing myself to push the glass aside, putting my thirst and my pride aside too.

Without knowing it, I was automatically calling everyone here "local" in my mind, necessitating a distinction between me and those who surrounded me. Even around Nalini, I could not pretend I had a background anywhere close to hers. Even if our parents had similar childhoods—which I couldn't really know, only assume—that didn't mean anything culturally was transferred equally to us both.

Nalini ordered two dosas and chai for us, and the waiter brought them out so quickly that they must have been mass-producing them back in the kitchen. I didn't mind that we had eaten dosas for breakfast; I loved the savory, paper-thin texture and how it tasted whether plain or with potatoes or chutney. It was quite hot where we were sitting, and I couldn't imagine how hot it must be back in the kitchen, with the stoves on and the cooks busily producing meals for the people that never stopped coming. The ceiling fans above us whirred half-heartedly, but at least that made some difference in circulating the stagnant air in which we sat and ate in silence, lost in our thoughts.

Most of the dances at the festival looked incredibly complicated, requiring great agility, flexibility, and grace. The amount of maturity that even very young dancers exhibited in their facial expressions amazed me. The youngest ones must have been no more than eight years old, yet their dancing was so professional. Although I had never seen anything like it, I wasn't surprised. There was so much genuine love here for dance and art that only greatness could be born of it.

It occurred to me then that Shaila's age never changed in my dreams. She always looked like an adult in her thirties. Her outfits and hair changed, but her face always looked the same. She did not grow older with me. I had to remind myself that, unlike these girls and women who performed on the stage, Shaila was a phantom of my imagination—my version of an imaginary friend I had conjured, as many do in childhood, though not by any power or intention of my own, as far as I knew.

But that night, and the night before, after attending the days at the festival, I saw Shaila's dances more vividly than ever in my mind. Over the years her dance varied in intensity, but it was always clear to me that she really was dancing. Here, though, in India, and in Chidambaram in particular, her dances had taken on a liveliness that bordered on paranormal. When I saw her dancing, I felt a strange energy, almost like there was someone beside me. Of course, there was no one there. But I did not feel like I was alone—it felt like her essence lingered around me even after the dance finished. This had never been the case before. In the past, when I'd open my eyes, she would be gone, unmistakably. Now, even during the days spent at Natyanjali, I clearly felt her presence following me around, watching the dances with me—her body and calm, curious energy lingering in the corner of my mind. Dreams didn't feel like the right term anymore to describe her appearances. They felt like apparitions.

"Do you think Shaila is real?" I asked Nalini. It was something I wondered off and on as a child, but always pushed to the back of my mind. Now, again, the question was resurfacing for me.

"I don't know, Anokhi. You are the one who sees her, not me! What is real anyway? Does it matter, if she means something to you regardless?"

Yes and no, I thought. I didn't want to dwell on it too much aloud. Thinking about Shaila seemed safest in the sanctity of my own head. I could share it with Sasha or Kale and now Nalini, but was there a point if no one else could feel her or see her?

"Let me teach you a dance when we go home tonight," Nalini said. "Now that you have seen a couple of days of the festival, and since I've explained so many of the stories and details, I'm sure it will be more enjoyable for you. Of course, I am no guru at all—and my *guruji* should not know that I'm teaching you, or else she'll be upset! But I want to teach you. I want you to dance." She smiled.

I was excited and surprised when she suggested this. I had thought about asking her to teach me a little bit on the first day that we met, but I'd refrained, not wanting to put her in a strange spot or be disrespectful.

That evening we left the performances early and walked down a different road than the one we usually took from the temple to her home.

"Aren't we going home?" I asked.

"No," she said. "I'm taking you to a nice open area where

I can teach you. Dancing outside in the evenings is the best. I often come here to dance. For some reason, no one seems to know about it, and once the heat from the day disappears, it's the perfect place to be."

We came to a quiet enclosure encircled by tall, thin coconut trees. The ground was almost completely shaded at this time of day, with little slivers of sunlight making their final goodbyes to the ground. The dust was packed down and did not fly up with our footsteps. We were now at the perimeter of the small city. I heard the birds chirping louder, with the sounds of humans and vehicles muted.

"Take off your chappals," Nalini said, as she slipped off her own and placed them at the base of a tree.

I did, following her to the center of the open space.

"First things first," she said. "We must do namaskar."

I had seen many of the dancers do this already on the stage. Praying to the ground, saluting Mother Earth, apologizing for stomping on her while dancing, thanking her for allowing them to step on her for the sake of dance and life.

Nalini held her hands in front of her, bent at the elbows, and stomped once with each foot. She then made a big circular motion with her arms, spreading them out to the sides. She squatted down gracefully, balancing on her toes as she did so. She touched the ground reverently with the tips of her fingers, then pressed them to her closed eyes. Next, she put her hands together in namaskar above her head, then moved them to her forehead, and finally in front of her heart. She rose slowly.

I stood with my hands pressed together, watching her.

"Three times," she said, going through the namaskar again. "Above the head for God, at forehead level for guruji, and at heart for the audience and the world."

I did my own version, trying to mimic hers as best as I could. It struck me as very considerate that we were thanking the ground for allowing us to step on it. Never in my life had it even occurred to me to do such a thing.

"Okay," Nalini said. "I'm going to teach you a Pushpanjali, an introductory piece. Really, first we should only do footwork, the simple steps, and only then move to the full sequence. But I want to teach you a dance performance very much, so you can know what it feels like. It's a simple opening dance in which you offer flowers to a god, usually Ganesha or Shiva."

She spent about an hour teaching me. I knew I was far from graceful, but it gave me so much joy just to try, to feel my arms and legs and eyes moving in ways that could, with practice and time, become fluid and expressive, like her.

Once the sun had set and we could no longer see the ground clearly beneath us, we walked home, mostly in silence. I was trying to recall the few steps I had learned. Most of the movements felt foreign in my limbs, like words of a new language in the mouth. But rather than feeling like a stranger to the novelty of it all, I felt like I was *relearning* something I had known long ago. I understood that the currents of time, which had carried me away from this land so many years ago, were finally bringing me back home. I understood that I had to learn to trust myself, even if I did not know exactly where one dance would end and another begin.

The days of the festival were full. The performances were often long, yet I never once felt bored. There were many different combinations of performers: old and young, female and male, groups and soloists. I was falling fast and hard in love with the music. Even when the performances ended, the earthy, mystical beat of the mridangam or tabla would stir longingly underneath my skin, the vibrant notes of the sitar and veena buzzing in my ears.

Several of the dances at the festival illustrated details from the great Hindu epics of the Ramayana and Mahabharata, which Nalini described to me. She was somewhat mortified when I had told her that I had only a vague sense of what those stories were about.

"Stories?" she exclaimed. "Hardly mere stories, Anokhi— they are epics. They are the foundation of Hindu mythology!"

The Dasavatara dance was one of my favorite pieces that we saw at Natyanjali. All ten avatars were described in sequence with a futuristic projection of Kalki. Nalini had proceeded to tell me about the ten avatars of Vishnu, the preserver of the universe, the being in which everything and nothing was contained. Lord Rama was the seventh and Lord Krishna the eighth of his avatars. The tenth was apparently yet to come, and when he came, it would be the end of this age, this *yuga*, Kali Yuga. The cycle would start again with the Golden Age, the age in which Lord Rama had come. "Cycles and cycles," Nalini whispered as the dancer describing parts of the Ramayana danced in dramatic circles, playing out the epic battle scene between Rama and Ravana the demon.

Was there always a demon? Is there always a bad guy? All of Vishnu's avatars came to earth to rescue the world from evil or disaster. Matsya was the first avatar, a fish who came to take everything from an old to a new world in which we now live. He rescued creatures from an apocalyptic flood. He reminded me of Noah.

I didn't want to show disrespect by asking Nalini philosophical questions about the implications of all the mythological retellings we had watched. Everything was new and beautiful. Yet after the novelty of the stories, I found myself faced with a certain emptiness at the words I could only understand through Nalini's translation. After the glittering jewelry and movements of the dancers and the tantalizing music ceased to bewitch me, I was left to wonder about the deeper meanings behind the elaborate performances.

What did it all mean? Do we dance for a higher power? Is there anything vested in ourselves? Do we even dance, ourselves, or are we controlled by marionette strings?

Nalini hardly seemed bothered by any such musings. Her faith guided her, and she was secure in what she knew and did not know about life, as I gathered from our conversations together. Inspired by her, I abandoned my unanswerable questions after some time, preferring to enjoy the music and dance for what it was. My doubts glimmered like tempting shells on a shore far away, but I ignored them. I wanted to lose myself in the music, in the dance, and in the faith. I wanted to find peace in the unknown, manifested through the beauty all around me here at the festival.

By the fourth day of the festival, everything was starting to blur together. By then I had already seen dozens of dances. I felt I had exceeded my threshold for understanding, though I continued to appreciate the beauty and novelty of all the performances. Even Nalini admitted that it was a lot to take in all at once, for my first time.

"Some dances are better than others," she remarked, as we stood in the back of one of the shrine rooms as a Nataraja pooja, an offering, was being conducted on the last evening. Hordes of people gathered up close near the large murthi. We lingered toward the back to have a little more space to breathe and talked about which dances had been our favorites so far.

"Mm." I nodded. "You're doing a wonderful job explaining everything to me, by the way. I don't think I would have gotten even one percent of this experience if I wasn't here with you."

It would have been a beautiful experience regardless—the

costumes, the music, the dancers. But without the extensive background on the mythology behind the stories and the technical aspects of the pieces, everything would have blurred together. Even now it was commingling in my mind.

"Oh, Anokhi, come on," she said, lightly tugging at my hair. I had taken to braiding it into one tight braid, following her example. I'd also borrowed her clothes for the festival, since the clothes I'd bought with Jasmine Aunty in Delhi were not quite festive enough for this occasion. Nalini insisted I dress nicely, and I was enjoying wearing her slightly fancier salwars and churidars. She and her mother even helped me wear a sari one of the days. I had found it very difficult to walk in, and didn't really want to wear one again, but I had appreciated the experience.

"Tonight we should go watch the stars from my terrace," she said. "Do you mind missing a few of the performances tonight?"

"No, not at all," I replied earnestly. I did want to spend time with her. She was half, if not more, of the reason why the past five days had been so meaningful.

We took some Parle-G biscuits and chai up to her roof after we got home, and sat on the ground. Her terrace was not marble but a bumpy tile that was slightly rough to walk on barefoot.

"Hmm," she said, chewing on a biscuit. "So, tell me more about your home back in America. You've told me about Shaila. Tell me more about your mother, Sasha. And your best friend, Kale," she said, giving me a wink.

I rolled my eyes and laughed. Last night I had called Kale after we came home from the temple. It had been a quick call, because he was on his way to work, but it was still nice to hear his voice. I told him about the festival, and he listened, and then he asked thoughtful questions about where I was staying and what the town was like. Before Nalini went to bed, she came to my room to say good night, and when she asked me who I had been talking to, as my room door had been closed, I told her it was my friend Kale. She insisted that, when I said this, a coy smile came to my face, and she asked if he was my boyfriend. I protested that he wasn't, but now she was determined to keep teasing me about him.

I wondered what to tell her about Sasha. I had told her that coming to Chidambaram to visit the Nataraja Temple had been at the suggestion of my adoptive mother. I had never called her my adoptive mother out loud, so when I now did, it sounded so distant. It sounded as if I loved Sasha less, knowing I had another mother out there. This was not at all true, but it caused me pain to think about the complexities of having two mothers. And potentially hurting Sasha by coming here all the way to India without her, to look for my birth mother.

"Sasha is wonderful," I said, sighing. I missed her. I had called her a couple of times since coming to Chidambaram. She was glad I was staying with a new friend, was safe, and was enjoying the dance festival. But I could still hear the hint of sadness in her voice and couldn't let go of the feeling that it was the sound of someone left behind. "She owns a restaurant. She's a fabulous cook. She is kind, brave, and funny."

"She never got married?" Nalini asked, dipping her biscuit into the chai and nibbling it slowly.

"No." I shook my head.

"Wow," Nalini said. "That must have been difficult for her. Raising you by herself and managing her restaurant. She must be a very strong woman."

"She is," I said, wiping a tear from my cheek. I often wondered about Sasha being single when I was growing up. But it was only now, thousands of miles away, talking about her with my new friend, that I could really contemplate her in her loneliness. Sitting alone in Idaho, managing the restaurant, worrying about me, her only child, who had dropped out of school and decided to travel across the world alone. I couldn't speak for her, whether she had regrets about her life. But I imagined that all adults had regrets about their lives, as the years went on. And the thought of Sasha, who had always worked hard and put me first, having regrets—and possibly ongoing loneliness—made my heart break. I wanted to hug her.

"And you!" Nalini said, shaking me out of my sad reverie. "What do you do there? What are you studying?"

I felt the heat of shame in my cheeks. I knew I would be blushing if I could redden. I guess Nalini saw it anyway, as she looked at me intently, waiting for my answer.

"Well, I actually dropped out of high school." I avoided eye contact.

"What?"

It struck me that "dropping out" was a colloquialism in English that perhaps didn't make sense to her. I imagined that not going to school in India, if you had the opportunity, was probably the most shameful and wrong thing ever. A shame perhaps tantamount to not being married at an appropriate age, based on the conversations about marriage expectations I had with Nalini in prior days. She had told me, one evening, that her parents had had an arranged marriage, which was not at all uncommon in her family or among people she knew. As for herself, she hoped she would marry for love but was not opposed to her parents introducing her to suitable boys in a few years, if she had not found someone by her mid-twenties—age twenty-five, to be exact. That was the age at which her parents said she should get married.

She asked why I had stopped going to school, her tone free from judgment. She was simply curious.

"I don't know. I wasn't getting anything out of it anymore. I used to love school, but a few years ago, that changed. I was going through the motions, but I felt like nothing was going through my brain. I couldn't see my future."

I leaned back against the concrete-slab wall behind us. The stars in the sky were incredible. They reminded me of the view of our patch of night sky back home—there too they were numerous, endless, and bright. I had spent so many nights marveling at them while lying on the grass in my backyard, sometimes with Kale, sometimes with Sasha, sometimes alone. Yet they were spaced out differently here, and there was also a fogginess to the sky here, which gave the night a dreamlike quality.

"You just didn't like school anymore?"

I sighed. It had been more than not liking it. I *couldn't* go to school anymore; it was contrary to what my heart was telling me to do: leave school and find what mattered to me in life, where I belonged, and what my purpose was. And of course there was the whole part about years of unacknowledged anxiety about going to school that had built up inside me since I was a child. But how do you explain that to someone else?

"Yeah," I replied. "I guess I felt deeply in my heart like there was something else I should be doing. I wanted to move to a big city and learn dance, inspired by Shaila. But I didn't have the courage to leave Sasha or home right away. So, I started working at a bookstore, and, one day, I was motivated, somewhat impulsively, after reading a book on world dance, to come to India. To find my birth parents, understand my heritage, and learn about dance. And so, now I'm here." I shrugged my shoulders and mustered a smile.

"Wow!" she said, leaning into me with what appeared to be keen interest. "You know, Anokhi, I don't know why you are feeling ashamed—and don't tell me you're not ashamed, because I can see it in your eyes, okay? But really, what is there to feel bad about? Gosh, I know there were times during the last few years of school when I just wanted to stop going and go dance full-time. But you should be proud that you listened to your instincts. A lot of people can't do that. Or even if they wanted to, they just wouldn't," she said. "That takes a lot of courage."

The night breeze, though still warm, was refreshing. I reflected on what she said, having never thought of my decision as courageous. I'd been carrying so much guilt and shame with me over the last couple of years and questioning whether my logic was sound or my reasons legitimate. Now Nalini offered a new perspective, one that felt liberating.

"It must be such an interesting trip," she continued. "You being here in India for the first time as an adult. But not really your first time. You were born here." She crumpled the biscuit wrapper in her palm. "Did you know you are the first American I've ever met? But you seem like a mix of cultures. These days you have spent here with me, going to the festival, wearing my clothes, listening to these songs and watching these dances that are all so new to you . . . You seem to blend in here too. This is your home too, in a sense." Her eyes sparkled as she said this, and I knew she was being sincere.

"It's funny you say that. Sometimes I have wondered where I am from. After coming here, I'm not sure what to call home. The US or here. Though I only spent my first year of life here, and of course have no real memories from that time, this trip, especially the last few days . . . has awakened a part of me. In some ways, I feel more at home here with you and at the festival than I ever felt in Idaho, at school especially."

Nalini laughed. "You are complex, Anokhi, just like your past. Just like we all are. I am proud of you for making this journey, so far away from your home. I am confident there will only be more good adventures and fate in your near future."

I nodded in gratitude. Her wisdom, despite the fact that we were similar in age, continuously struck me as beyond her years.

"Okay, and also, shall we get back to this Kale fellow?"

Sitting so close to her, our knees touching, made me think

about what it might have been like to have a sister with whom I could have shared all my secrets. By now I believed I could tell her anything.

"Yes, Kale," I said, laughing. Saying his name made me miss him intensely, with a sudden pang that filled my core. I had built a wall within myself, preventing me from feeling the sadness that had enveloped me after that difficult walk in the woods together, and now the closeness I felt with Nalini somehow unleashed all the emotions I had been stifling, as if she had lovingly dragged me backward into a place with old memories I'd rather forget. "What about him?" I asked.

"Well, first off—is he seriously not your boyfriend?"

"No, no, it's not like that," I protested, though I hardly felt convincing and wasn't sure why I wouldn't allow him to have that title. "I've known Kale for over four years. He also stopped going to school, like me. A bit before me, actually."

"And what does he do now?" Nalini asked.

"He works at his father's store." Our lives back in Idaho, working at bookstores and convenience stores, sounded so incredibly drab on my lips, compared to Nalini's colorful life, that it almost hurt to say the words aloud. Even though she had been so kind-hearted, I feared that it would be hard for her to relate to two people her age who had dropped out of traditional schooling and worked day jobs in their hometown, with uncertainty about where their futures would go. Two young people with access to free education, turning away from it because of the wanderings of their hearts and minds? How faux romantic and indulgent did that sound to her ears? Kale and I long ago admitted to ourselves that we weren't normal. But when we spoke of this among ourselves, it was a source of unity and pride, not shame. She had said I shouldn't be ashamed. But I still was when I had to admit the truth to someone else.

It wasn't that other people didn't drop out at our school. There weren't many, but there were others. The problem was that Kale and I couldn't stop wondering what was on the other side after leaving the traditional path. I would occasionally catch him looking at a book in Dusty Pages with a certain longing, during the few times he would come by to keep me company when he wasn't working. I knew in those moments that he questioned his decision to drop out, if only for the uncertainty that the future held.

For me, working at the bookstore did not induce such feelings of regret. What did make my heart twist was wondering if Kale and I would forever be stuck, not knowing where we were supposed to be going, because we wouldn't leave our town and our jobs. Not that we had to physically leave, but it proverbially felt that our little town was too small for our big dreams, even if we didn't know exactly what they were.

How could I have left without Kale? Yes, this was *my* journey to find my parents. But the journey to find ourselves after falling out of high school, trying to find the education that better suited our lives and our goals, was something we had vowed to take together, without ever saying so explicitly. We were by no means done learning, and we both knew that. When I told him I was going to India, my plan symbolized a division between us, a split in the rope that had tied us together so closely for the past few years of our intense close friendship.

I felt very sorry suddenly. Sorry for hurting him and for not saying the words I wanted to say before leaving, though I hardly could bring myself to admit them now to myself. I loved him. I had for a while now. But I didn't have the courage to say it. Would it have changed his mind if I had told him? Would he have come with me to India?

I had been lost in my thoughts for a while. I looked at my watch. It was 10:00 p.m., and Nalini had dozed off leaning against the slab wall, so she hadn't seen the tears streaming silently down my face as I thought about Kale. As I wiped them from my cheek, I imagined that Kale might somehow intuit the essence of my tears, back in Idaho. I hoped that he knew I missed him so much, even though I never said that I would.

CHAPTER 17

The day after the festival ended, an eerie quiet descended over the city. Tourists had left in hordes, leaving noticeably higher piles of debris and silence. Stages were disassembled. Flower carts no longer covered the streets. No one needed to buy extra flowers anymore for murthis or hairstyles. Instead, white and orange petals were strewn across all the roads and paths, a reminder that the celebrators had just left.

I wondered if Shiva was still here, roaming the streets, his energy coursing up and down and around the huge temple that was erected in his honor over a thousand years ago. The Natyanjali Dance Festival was an annual tribute to him, Lord Nataraja, the god of dance. His enigma intrigued me. I wondered, How can Shiva dance or meditate constantly on Mount Kailash, and sit in the hearts of each of his devotees, *and* live in each and every black *lingam* that represents his eternal divine energy? It was silly for me to think of a god as divisible when clearly the idea was that Shiva existed everywhere, especially where his devotees wanted to see him.

Wasn't it also ironic that the Lord of Destruction was also the Lord of Dance, of endless power and procreation, symbolized by the phallic symbol, the lingam, through which he was worshipped in countless temples? Milk was poured over the lingam, poojas were performed around it, offerings made, flowers strewn. The devotional love for him was strong, boundless, and contagious.

I came away from the festival with a deep awe and respect for the culture and religion around dance. Dance was more than an art form; it was a vessel for spirituality and honoring sacredness. I understood now that such an intricate, complex history of dance could only be inspired by one of the most magnificent, omnipresent auras I now knew was his—Lord Shiva's.

I wasn't sure where I was going to go after the festival ended. Nalini was insistent that I could stay with her and her family as long as I wanted to, but I had already been with them for almost a week and didn't want to overstay my welcome. Deep down I could sense that that wasn't a possibility; they had already become like family to me, with the warmth of their love and hospitality dispelling any notion that I was a bother to them. Yet, I knew I would have to leave eventually. Chidambaram was a small town; aside from the temple and the festival, I didn't have much more to see. And Nalini had to get back to her college classes the following day. She was doing prerequisites to get a computer science degree.

"It's kind of the opposite of dance," she said, smiling, as she showed me her textbooks and course materials in her room. "But I don't mind it. Amma and Appa have always been very firm with us that education comes first. Priya and I can dance, but we also have to study. And Appa always said, preferably study something with good career prospects."

I nodded. It hurt a little to hear her talk about education

and her future with such security. I winced at the reminder that I had made choices that made my future more uncertain.

As if she were reading my thoughts, she patted my arm gently. "I know you don't know exactly where life is taking you right now, Anokhi. But you are on a true adventure. And I have faith in you finding your way. You already are," she said.

"Thanks," I said, mustering as good a smile as I could. "This has been the best. I'm so glad I ran into you at the train station here. I can't imagine how this trip would have been without meeting you."

"You mean when I saved your life!" she said, laughing.

I laughed too. I was going to miss her so much. It struck me that she was the first close girl friend I had ever had. I had never known the joy of having a strong female friendship before this. It was life changing—the feeling of sisterhood, of mutual understanding. I didn't want to lose it.

"I think your ideas about traveling more in India are good, Anokhi, but I don't think it is safe for you to go alone," Nalini said, taking on a more serious tone. I had told her that I wanted to visit other places, like the state of Kerala, famed for its backwaters and natural beauty, and then go to Mumbai or Bombay. "If I had holidays from college I would come with you, of course. I could take you places; we have some family both in Kerala and Bombay. But I can't leave my classes."

She was right. Sasha had said the same thing many times throughout my trip. "I guess I'll just take the train back to Chennai and then head back to Delhi to stay with my aunt," I said. "And maybe it's time for me to go home anyway. I've been here a little under two weeks. But it's been an incredible trip. And, of course, I can always come back."

We spent the rest of the day chatting, going to get lunch at one of her favorite restaurants, and enjoying the evening with her family. I researched train options and planned to take the train the following afternoon back to Chennai, and I caved and booked a flight back to Delhi for that same evening. I was tired. I didn't want to take the train all the way back to Delhi. And in my bones, I was feeling ready to go home.

The next day I slept in while Nalini went to college in the morning. In the early afternoon, her mother walked me to campus with my small suitcase and backpack because Nalini wanted to accompany me to the train station.

"Anokhi!" Nalini cried from several feet away, running toward me.

"Nalini!" I called back. Our names flew and rhymed in midair, meeting halfway between their respective arcs and fusing. Yes, she was the sister I never had, I thought, smiling as I ran toward her.

I hugged her tightly. "I don't want to leave," I murmured in her shoulder, hoping my words would be muffled into the cloth of her kurta, which had that distinct scent that I found all Indian clothes had from the various embraces I'd made. Something in between saffron, cumin seeds, and bliss.

"I wish you didn't have to. But you always have a home here; don't forget that," she said. "Come, let's walk. I don't want you to miss your train."

We headed toward the station together. I had gotten into the habit of just carrying my suitcase by the handle rather than dragging it along on the wheels after one of the wheels had come off when she and I had walked around the temple on that first day in Chidambaram. That felt like ages ago.

Nalini handed me my backpack when we reached the front steps, where just days ago she'd pulled me out of the way of a car. "I will miss you so much, Anokhi. You have no idea what a joy Natyanjali has been this year for me. I have seen it through the eyes of someone completely new and have come to appreciate it a thousandfold more in this way. I have you to thank for this new perspective. I don't think I will ever look at dance the same way again." Her deep exhale hinted at a suppressed sob.

I was flattered and embarrassed that she was crediting that level of new perspective to me, but I didn't say anything. I sipped her gratitude quietly and reflected on my own.

"I must thank *you*," I said in return. "You have made this visit to Chidambaram, this visit to India, the most amazing experience of my life. I will never forget it." Tears accumulated in my eyes.

"Take care. I hope you find your birth parents, and I hope you learn to dance. You will be a good dancer, I know."

"How can you know that?" I asked, honestly curious. After the past few days, I felt that I would never be even a thousandth of what these amazing dancers were. I lacked basic intuition, grace, and understanding. I could not shake my feelings of cultural imposter syndrome.

"Because you love it," she said. "It's that simple. Remember when we talked about Krishna and bhakti love? If you love Krishna purely, without holding back, he will love you back. I have always felt dance is the same: If you love dance with your whole heart, and hold nothing back, Lord Nataraja himself will shine through your dancing with all his unlimited love and grace."

I watched my friend walk away, her light blue kurta and white dupatta fluttering in the hot breeze as she followed the way we had come, back to her campus.

With the sweet aftertaste of Nalini's words in my ears, I walked inside the station and found the display board showing the incoming and outgoing train schedules. The next outbound train to Chennai was bolded in red; instead of reading 15:00, which was the originally scheduled departure time, it now read 17:00.

My heart sank. This meant I would miss my flight to Delhi,

which was supposed to leave Chennai at 21:00, and that was the last flight out for the evening.

I called Nalini.

"Anokhi!" she said, picking up the phone. "Are you all right?"

I told her my train had been delayed and I'd miss my flight to Delhi. She insisted I spend another night with her and take an early train in the morning. I agreed to wait for her at a nearby coffee shop until her classes were finished for the day and then we'd return to her house.

As I stood outside the station, gazing at the towering golden roof of the Nataraja Temple in the distance, I was tempted to go back to the temple one last time. I already missed it, after having spent most of the last five days there, wrapped up in the mystical world of gods, dance, and spiritual music. But instead I went to find the coffee shop, all the while reflecting on my fortuitous friendship with Nalini. I also thought about Kale, and wished he were here.

As I walked, lost in my thoughts, I tripped on the gnarled root of a tree growing on the side of the road. I caught myself before falling, but the suitcase handle slipped from my grasp and the suitcase fell to the ground. As I bent down to pick it up, two shadows were cast over me, coming from my right. I glanced up and saw two thin young men, who looked a little older than me, jeering at me with unfriendly smiles. One of them spit at the ground right next to my feet. As I stood up, the other one kicked my suitcase out of my reach, and it fell again on the dusty ground with a thud.

They started speaking to me in Tamil, the creepy grins not leaving their faces. Their teeth shone bright white in sharp contrast to their oily, slicked-back black hair.

My heart began to beat fast. I looked around in exasperation. Though it was the middle of the afternoon, and there were people walking on the other side of the road, there was no one immediately near where we were standing. They stood directly in front of me, their arms crossed over their chests. When they realized I didn't know what they were saying, their interest in me seemed to grow. They eyed my suitcase and my backpack, but more uncomfortably for me, they moved their eyes over my body. I pulled the dupatta that was slung around my neck down to cover my chest, using it like a shawl, as if somehow, more covering would protect me.

I was panicking now. One of the men reached his arm out to grab my dupatta, and I swerved to the side, but the other one was quick and pulled the other end of the cloth straight off me. Tears began to well in my eyes. I had been so stupid this trip, I thought. Walking around alone and traveling across the country. Now, even though I had a friend in the city, I didn't even know if I would be able to see her again.

Suddenly, I saw a short figure shrouded in white rapidly hobbling toward us. She was coming from behind the two men, and they didn't see her, though I did. As she drew closer, I locked eyes with her—an old woman with a myriad of wrinkles on her small face and dark brown eyes that were sharp and alert. In seconds, she lifted her wooden cane and began vigorously beating the two men from behind. The sound of the cane on their backs cracked like a whip, and they screamed in pain as they spun around to see the old woman, her eyes ablaze with anger. She was yelling at them in Tamil with such alacrity and thunder in her voice, even I was shaken hearing her. The men threw my dupatta on the ground and ran off down the street and around a corner. The woman continued to yell at them, waving her stick wildly in the air until they were out of sight.

At this point, several people on the road had stopped to watch the commotion, but once the two men had run away, they began dispersing, leaving behind only a barking stray dog to show any interest. By then, I was trembling and crying,

staring at the old woman in disbelief. *If it hadn't been for her
. . .* I shuddered to think what would have happened to me
next.

She was at least a foot shorter than me but held herself
with dignity, despite the apparent deformity in her back that
caused her to have a permanent hunch. She looked up at me
and let her intense gaze linger before forcefully spitting brick
red juice onto the ground next to her. This startled me and I
took a step backward.

"Don't worry," she said in a quiet, hoarse voice, in complete contrast to the shrill screaming she had displayed just
moments ago toward the men. "You will be all right now." She
reached out her hand and stroked my arm.

Something about this woman's face was haunting, and I
could not look away. Gazing into her deep brown eyes, like
dark pools in a cave, felt like I was looking at open pages in a
history book detailing a past full of secrets—but also immea-
surable wisdom.

"Come," she said, grasping my arm with her hand, her grip
strong and her fingers dry. I looked down and noticed she was
missing her pinky finger on that hand. Too shocked to reply,
I struggled to pick up my luggage, and then I let her lead me
down the road, past a cart heaped with ripe bananas. We
turned a corner onto a quieter side street. There was a building
with a large concrete wall built around it. She leaned against
the wall and pulled a water bottle out of a little cloth bag that
was slung around her shoulder.

"Drink," she said.

Something about the way she spoke, her speech so simple
yet commanding, made me listen. I did not have the power to
say no. I was also still too shaken from the incident with the
two men. I took it from her and drank. She watched me.

"Big eyes. Beautiful eyes. Shaila's eyes," she murmured.

I blinked. *I must have misheard her.* The stress of the event had gone to my head.

But she went on. "I had hoped I would meet you one day," she said, a faint smile coming to her lips as she continued to study me.

"What did you say?" I staggered, feeling faint and grasping the wall where we stood to steady myself. Something in the old woman's lined face tugged at my core. I could barely breathe.

She said nothing but kept her eyes fixated on me, and an eerie stillness hovered in the space between our two faces. A stillness, I came to believe, from which great moments in life are born.

"Shaila. You look just like my Shaila," she repeated. Her English had a thick accent, but her diction was very clear. I could not pretend that I had misheard her now, a second time. Disbelief took root in my shaking body, and I wondered who this strange old woman was who saved me from being attacked by two men, who now was saying these words that were dismantling the world around me.

She began to rock back and forth slowly, leaning on her cane, continuing to hold my eyes in her resolute gaze.

I drew in a deep breath now as I tried to find words in the mortified mess that was my mind. *Shaila?* How could this woman *possibly* know about Shaila?

Only four people in the world knew about Shaila: me, Sasha, Kale, and now Nalini.

Shaila. Dear expressive, terrifying Shaila, the ghostly dancer whose bells echoed from my dreams into my waking moments and back again into my dreams year after year. I found no words to speak back to this strange old woman.

My lips began to move soundlessly. I was shaking hard now, as if feverish. When the old woman placed her hands over mine, I found them to be rough but warm, and I closed my eyes, hoping to ground myself in the touch of her steadying hands. But instead I felt hollow and nauseous, like I was about to be turned inside out.

"My child," the woman said, "you look just like Shaila. Your mother."

CHAPTER 18

When I opened my eyes, I found myself staring up into the face of the old woman. My head was resting in the plushy white sari over her lap, as she stroked my hair gently and hummed a low tune. When she realized I was awake, she helped me sit up. She then picked up the water bottle with her hand and nudged it toward my lips. I gulped without resistance, completely robbed of the ability to refuse anything from this woman. Our conversation slowly drifted back into the forefront of my mind as I regained consciousness, sending another jolt of nausea through me.

"Are you all right, dear?" she asked, speaking slowly, as if she was afraid that I might collapse again if she spoke too fast and startled me. She touched my forehead with her hand.

I nodded, putting the bottle down on the ground to rub my eyes. I looked up at the sky; the relentless afternoon sun blinded me momentarily.

We were still on the side of the quiet road, sitting on the ground next to a concrete wall. My backpack and suitcase were beside me. I glanced at my watch, which read 3:00 p.m. I started to trace my way back to where I was before running into the men, then this woman. Chidambaram. My train was delayed. I had to stay another night here. Nalini was going to meet me after her class. Nalini . . .

"How long have I been . . ." I looked at the woman, whose eyes were fixed on me with a kind, motherly expression. I didn't know if the expression "passed out" made any sense to her, so I just hoped that she would understand.

"Don't worry, child. Everything is all right. You were just very shocked," she said, nodding her head.

I reconsidered what I had been thinking about before everything went black.

Shaila. My Shaila. This woman knew Shaila. She said I looked like her. She said Shaila was my mother.

Shaila is my mother.

The world no longer looked like the world. I didn't care where I was or what I was looking at, hearing, or smelling—it was all just white noise. I could only gape at this information that was still trying to take root and shape in my mind. There was no room. There was no ground. I had no words. I looked at her desperately. I needed guidance. I felt completely unmoored.

"We had better go inside and talk. It is very hot outside. You will fall sick because you are not used to this heat." This was not a request. She was firm about my next steps.

I nodded, slowly getting up and then taking my phone out of my bag. No missed call from Nalini. I didn't want to meet Nalini at that moment, but I knew she would be worried if she called and I didn't answer, so I made sure my phone was on so I could hear it ring. Somehow, though nothing else was making sense, remembering that I had a friend, who would be calling me soon, gave me at least one root to stay in touch with this reality, which seemed to be rapidly disappearing from my grasp.

I looked at the woman again. I felt weary, wondering if I should be following this strange person I'd just met somewhere. But something in my heart told me she was safe. She had saved me from the two men, after all. And now that she had mentioned Shaila, I didn't think there was anything inside me that could resist hearing what else she had to say.

"Where shall we go, Amma?" I didn't know what to call her, this woman who had been so motherly toward me in this short span of time, caring for me tenderly as I passed out on the side of the road. It only made sense to call her Mother. I had heard Nalini call her own mother Amma and loved the simplicity of the word. The term "mother" was such a complicated term in my life, as I stood here on the other side of the world from the mother who raised me, searching for the one who birthed me. And yet, it felt like the right thing to call this mysterious, ancient-looking woman beside me. And I felt a surge of both protectiveness and childishness as I towered over her.

"My home is behind this compound. Come," she said, gesturing toward an alley around the corner of the building. We walked slowly around the building's perimeter, with Amma holding her cane in her left hand and hunching forward. I hovered awkwardly at her side, wondering if I should offer a steady hand but resisting. Clearly she was perfectly used to walking alone.

Behind the compound, I found a very unexpected spectacle: rows of huts with corrugated metal roofs. I had seen only a few slums by now, and always from a distance. I saw a couple during my car rides in Delhi with Jasmine Aunty, and another when taking the train into Chennai, on the outskirts of the town before we arrived at the train station. From a distance, they looked like a cluster of metal, with plastic bottles and litter lining some of the dusty alleys. I could not fathom what it would be like to live there. And yet now here I was in a slum, walking toward this woman's home. This dumbfounded me, but then again, this old woman was clearly mystical, and

I might not have been any more shocked if she'd led me to a quiet, secluded magical forest.

The road was strewn with litter. More than once I stepped on a plastic bag or a piece of an old chip bag or a soda bottle. It was quiet here, with the sound of the main road a low hum in the distance, and I was surprised there were only a couple of people outside their huts. One small child with dusty and dry yellowish red hair, who was perhaps no more than three years old, played with a stick and a metal pot. Her eyes sparkled and she gave me a little toothy smile. Before I could react, Amma guided me into a hut. The entrance had no door and was much shorter than I was, so I had to crouch down. It was dark inside, though there was some light coming in from the front entrance and a small opening in the hut's wall in the back, which was covered with a plastic sheet with a few holes.

She told me to sit, pointing to the dusty ground that had a few tattered pieces of fabric set together in place of chairs. I sat cross-legged on one of the pieces of cloth and tried to stifle a gag; it was cooler inside, because we weren't directly in the sunlight, but the smell of the room was overpowering, primarily emanating from the stench of human waste in the alley outside, which did not diminish once inside. In fact, it seemed stronger, with walls now around us, keeping the air stagnant. I shuddered and gulped, trying to expel the nausea that was rising inside me.

The woman went to the corner of the hut, which was just a single room, put her cane aside, and brought back a bowl to me, placing it in front of me. It had some type of hard snack inside it. I had absolutely no inclination to eat, with the smell and the heat. And moreover, there were too many questions pounding inside my head. I sat quietly, waiting for her to speak.

"Where do I begin, my child?" she wondered out loud, staring out of the doorless opening to her home. Another small child ran past outside, screaming something playfully and waving an empty plastic bottle in his hand.

I was speechless. I didn't know what to ask her. There were too many questions. *Who is my mother? How do you know her? Where is she now? Who are you?*

It all felt like too much. There was nothing I *didn't* want to know. Rarely had I ever felt such true, uncontained willingness to just listen, as just then in that dim hut, scented with unimaginable smells, perched on the edge of society. I waited for Amma to speak.

"Your mother was a beautiful dancer. She . . ."

The look of horror on my face must have frozen the words in her mouth.

Was. Your mother *was* a beautiful dancer.

I felt the urge to get up and start running, far, far away. I felt sick to my core. I wanted to leave, to get to the airport, any airport, the closest one, and fly as far away as possible from here, all the way back home to Idaho. I wanted Sasha. My mother. My mother who was alive and who I left in search of my other mother, who now, this woman was telling me, was dead.

I felt a weight pulling me down. I wanted to melt through the dirt floor, somewhere underneath the surface of India, and never emerge.

She stopped speaking, leaned forward, and cupped my chin in her hand. "Dear child, what is your name?"

"Anokhi," I said quietly. Something about the shock I was experiencing now brought a feeling of emptiness to my mind—a good feeling, as if my mind had cleared like the air after a heavy rain. My judgments, my expectations, my hopes, all washed away in swirls, like oily rainbows swimming on tired asphalt roads. I had no idea what disastrous surprise would emanate next from her lips, though I hoped I had heard the worst of it. I felt totally suspended in uncertainty, with the heaviness of sorrow pulling on my insides.

"Anokhi, dear, your mother, Shaila, died many years ago. I am Devi—'Devi Amma,' as she would always call me. I was her friend, her very close friend. I loved your mother very much," she said. Her eyes were kind, but the darkness had never left them, since that first moment I met her. I realized, with a sinking heart, that the darkness must be there for a reason. She must have seen innumerable hardships during her long life, not limited to the death of my mother, her friend.

Devi Amma closed her eyes and took a deep breath. I did the same.

She was dead? Okay. Now I just had to know why. How. When. Where. Collecting details like flowers for a garland, weaving them with a needle onto the white thread and lining up facts in my mind to create something. I had to create meaning from all these horrible facts I was learning. What else was there to do?

And yet, right now, I had to detach myself somewhat from the present, because if I allowed myself to dwell too much on the details, the absurdity of this encounter, I would likely faint again, overwhelmed by the implications of it all.

"Shaila is my mother? You knew her?" I repeated, still awestruck. Years and years of visions of Shaila came to the forefront of my mind. Joyful dances, sad dances, angry dances. Foreboding ones and longing ones. But always, she was a phantom. Someone who appeared to me, spoke to me wordlessly, but never appeared to me in real life. I had never truly entertained that Shaila could be a real person, much less my mother.

"Do you know what a *devadasi* is?" Devi Amma asked, interrupting my reeling thoughts.

"Devadasi . . . 'Servant of God'?" I thought out loud, literally translating the word. I had learned from my days at the festival several words from the many dance performances and words that kept being repeated, like "*dev*," which meant "god," and "*daas*," which meant "servant."

"Once, yes. A long time ago. Now . . . not really. 'Servant of man' is more like it," she said, spitting on the ground beside us with disdain.

Her tone was dark and scared me a bit. Then I remembered my conversation with Nalini only days ago, when she was explaining to me the origins of Bharatanatyam over two thousand years ago.

"Weren't devadasis the first dancers to perform Bharatanatyam, since they were basically wedded to the temples?" I asked. Nalini had told me about the women who initially performed this art form and how they dedicated their lives to dance and music inside and outside of temples in service to god. But the tone of Devi Amma's voice and her eyes seemed to suggest a much more sinister counter or parallel history.

I wasn't sure if she heard me; Devi Amma was staring beyond where I sat as if into a window into the past. I waited for her to continue. It felt a bit like history class, hearing about someone else's life. Not my own mother. That was too personal and seemed so far away. So completely far away from me sitting here on the ground in this hut with Devi Amma, trying not to be baked by the hot air studded with flies that permeated her home. Several flies had already landed on my arms and buzzed close to my ears and continued to do so, though I kept swatting at them intermittently.

"Your mother was a devadasi. A servant of terrible men. In a temple not too far from here," she continued solemnly, ignoring my question.

I paused, absorbing her words. A servant of terrible men? I didn't want to believe it, but looking at Devi Amma with her eyes downcast, my mind began to piece together possibilities. It did not sound like my mother was treated well at all in that role. When Devi Amma lifted her eyes again to look at me, I noticed that, despite the darkness, the old woman had light gray clouds in the centers of them. Cataracts.

"Can you take me there?" I asked, suddenly itching to get out of the hut and back out into the heat. The dark hut, the concentration of flies, and the stench was beginning to overwhelm me. I felt dangerously close to vomiting or passing out again.

Devi Amma furrowed the saggy skin where a few gray hairs stood for eyebrows. "I'll take you there. We must take the train; it is a little away from the city. A village named Kotivalli. But we will not go inside the temple. There is nothing godly about that place."

We took an auto to the train station, which I paid for. Once we were there, I called Nalini, who had previously called—but I had silenced the call.

"Anokhi? Are you all right? Where are you?" she asked, when she picked up on the first ring.

"Nalini," I said, breathless and struggling to find words to explain anything about what had happened since I last saw her. "I'm fine. I . . . met someone. Who knows my mother. Knew my mother."

Silence on the other end. "What?" she asked finally. "Oh my god, Anokhi. Really?"

"Yes," I said. "I can't talk more right now—I'm still with her, but I'm okay. I am going to be with her for a bit. I will see you later tonight at your house, okay? I'll call you."

"Okay," she said, some hesitancy in her voice. "Take care. Call me if you need anything."

Devi Amma led me to the train station counter and asked for two tickets in Tamil. I took out my wallet to pay the fare, and after boarding the train in silence, I picked up where we had left off.

"How did she end up as a devadasi?" The train was relatively empty compared to the trains I had taken from Delhi to Chennai and Chennai to Chidambaram, so I felt comfortable asking such a difficult question.

"It was not her choice. Shaila was an intelligent woman. She would have gone to school, to university. She would have been something great. Maybe even a great dance teacher," she said, peering out the window. "Her parents sold her off when she was young. What else? What people will do for money, you will not even imagine." Her eyes flashed with anger.

My grandparents sold my mother? I could barely comprehend it. I leaned my head against the stained window and looked out at the flat fields outside. A fly buzzed near my ear. I shook my head; it seemed like we could not escape flies today. My mind wandered to history classes I had taken in school, when we learned about the slave trade. The thought of humans being sold for labor, or for their bodies, always sounded so bleak and unimaginable. It was hard to reconcile that something as horrific and inhumane as that could be so closely linked to my own family's past.

I felt dizzy with disgust as I imagined the people who contributed to one half of my genes doing something so unimaginable as selling their daughter. I tried to imagine what they looked like, and how they must have felt when they sold their little girl. My mind flashed back to the happy little girl sitting on the dirt road in the slums, playing with the metal pot. I tried to imagine what my mother looked like when she was younger. How old could she have been when they sold her? I shuddered.

"Were they poor? Is that why they did it?" I asked. I tried to rationalize the irrational, exercising defensive human instinct in the face of the unfathomable.

"I don't know," Devi Amma said, shaking her head. "I just know that your mother came to the temple when she was only nine or ten years old. She came alone, a small cloth bag in her hands. She was clutching that bag so tightly to her small body, her eyes big and wide. She had a beautiful face with eyes shaped like almonds, and she wore her hair in two braids that reached down her back. I remember her walking through the temple courtyard like it was yesterday.

"I used to clean the temple, and I was the first person who saw her. She had a small note in her hand, which I took from her, and all it said was *Here is Shaila. Ram Baba knows where to send the money.* I shuddered when I saw it. Ram Baba was the horrible priest at the temple who was running this underground business, stuffing his fat pockets with the money and keeping the girls, under the guise of dance and art.

"I wanted to tear the note into pieces and tell the poor girl to run far away. But I had nowhere to hide her, and I could not bear to tell her what lay ahead," she said sadly. "By that time, I had seen many girls come through the temple. They were always scared, their eyes big and bright, full of fear but also that pure hope that all children somehow have in the face of life's biggest dangers and sorrows. It would only take one or two days of their new life before their eyes would become dull and glazed over. How quickly a child can be robbed of their innocence and their childhood," she said, looking out the window sadly.

"Of course, the practice of selling girls and women in this way was illegal and had been for a long time. But that didn't stop evil men, like Ram Baba, from running these rings. They would often prey on poor villagers, promising money to the fathers instead of them having the burden of needing to marry off their daughters. Daughters who they could not afford to pay a dowry for. Or he would approach families who had a history of sending women and girls to the temple as devadasis. Of course, many years ago, this was considered a noble practice. But now, it is just what it sounds like."

She hadn't explicitly said what the selling was for, though I had a hunch.

"Selling girls in the name of religion and tradition," she said, shaking her head. Then, as if reading the confusion on my face, she added darkly, "Selling them to a life . . . that no child should live."

I winced at her words. My mind was scrambling fast to piece together her meaning from the dark way she was speaking and the way her words were somehow dancing around the actual horror of what the little girl—Shaila, my mother—and so many other innocent girls were forced into.

My throat hurt and my eyes began to tear. To my surprise, Devi Amma began weeping, her slim hunched torso shaking on the seat beside me. Age had softened her crying to the sound of gentle rain landing on rough pavement. I put my arm around her and allowed her to weep. She leaned her head on my shoulder. We both said nothing for a while.

"Your mother was different. Even after she had been there a few days, even though I could see the horror etched on her face, she still would smile at me every time she saw me. She would come talk to me when I was cleaning the courtyard and she had a break from her duties. More than anything, I wanted to help her body and soul escape that wretched place. But I could not tell your mother to go away." She paused for a deep breath. "If I sent her away, she would have been in danger. They would have found her and killed her, or worse. And Ram Baba would have found out that I sent her away—he knew how I felt about how he treated those girls. Then I would have stopped getting my rice and *daal* too. I had my own hungry children to feed." I detected guilt in her voice, but did not blame her for any of this, of course.

"And how far would she have gotten anyway? She would

have had no idea where to go, and he would have found her and beaten her and made her pay twice the price for trying to run away. They needed more devadasis at a young age, Ram Baba would say—'The younger they are when sacrificed to God, the more they can serve.' At such times in life, where there are different roads to take, when we see faces colored with hunger and pain and suffering on each road, how can we possibly know which is the best to take?" Her rheumy eyes conveyed decades of sorrow.

Devi Amma seemed to be trying to rationalize the decision she made that day, so many years ago, when my mother came to the threshold of the temple, a child encased in fear of the unknown. I probably clutched the straps of my backpack tightly to myself on my first day of school, but that was nothing like what Shaila had to face. I could not compare my experiences at that age to hers. How badly I wanted to draw parallels between us, to feel closer to her memory, yet doing so seemed utterly disrespectful and pointless. Our childhoods had been nothing alike, clearly.

My birth mother was sacrificed in the name of an ancient art form of temple dancing, but it had devolved, along with society, into an illegal and horrible practice of committing young, impoverished girls and women to a life of selling their bodies. And it was all under the guise of sacred art and holiness, so in some twisted way, it went on, behind the facade of the temples and the institution of religion. I wondered how much of my mother's childhood had been spent actually dancing, versus doing the other unspeakable tasks which were demanded of her. I tried to push my mind to its limits to imagine her as a child and to feel her suffering and pain, but I could only draw a blank void. It was black and bottomless, hungry for all the years that I could not go back and undo any of this, or even speak to her about what she had been through.

"It's okay, Amma," I said, not knowing what else to say.

She had largely stopped crying, but her head was still resting against my shoulder. I patted her gently. I wondered whether she could have kept my mother in her house with her other children, but I knew from the kind curved lines on her face that this was not a woman who would willingly reject an opportunity to help anyone, especially a young girl. There must have been a reason—an unwilling husband, too many mouths to feed already, threat of violence from Ram Baba—and I willed myself not to ask. "What ifs" were all I could think of, though.

"So essentially, to be sold as a devadasi was like being sold as a prostitute," I said quietly, trying to put together all the muddied, terrifying thoughts in my head into a sentence. It wasn't a question, yet I hoped that it was, and I also hoped that her answer would contain some glimmer of contradiction. I pieced this together, unwillingly, but the picture she painted was stark and unmistakable. My mother had been sold by her parents. As a young girl. My mind was running to places I desperately wanted it not to go to.

"It's complicated," Devi Amma said, bobbling her head. "In some situations, yes, that is what it was. The girls were dedicated to a goddess before they even matured properly, and they belonged to the temple after that. They were often dedicated to some local patron goddess, but generally the concept was that these girls were dedicated to serving God in the name of the female divine. Most of the girls came from very poor families; their parents could not afford to care for them and did not have any prospects of dowries to be able to get them married. Others had a family history of other women who took a similar path, so there was a precedent. Some even thought there was pride and honor in sacrificing one's daughter as a devadasi. Though we who worked in the temples where this took place, with the poor girls, knew it for what it was.

"Your mother lived in a hut with three other devadasi girls

her age from the temple. The temple priest gave nearby accommodations for these four girls because they were the most beautiful and therefore the most sought after. Their proximity to the temple made perfect sense. Many of the other girls would travel to neighboring villages to perform their services, but not Shaila and the other three girls. Prized devadasis, they were." She snickered, sarcasm rippling through rough words.

"You know," she continued, "many hundreds of years ago, devadasis were highly esteemed performers and masters of classical dance and music. They performed their divine dances in temples, took care of the temples, performed sacred rituals, and were very well-respected members in society, masters of the arts. Nothing at all like what it later devolved to. All of them knew dance and music very well.

"Your mother was the only one here, however, who took to Bharatanatyam with significant talent. I don't know where she learned it from; none of the other girls knew how to dance properly, and no one ever taught them, and that was not really what they were sold for. I think on a couple of occasions, when there were big rituals in the temple during holidays, your mother must have heard singing and the mridangam and flute, and her feet must have just found their place in the rhythm. She was born with that, I'm sure," she said, a wistful smile on her face.

"Thankfully, her shameful business was minimized because of her genuine talent for dance. As one of the most beautiful girls, there was always a high demand for her performances. Word of her gifted dancing spread far across many villages and towns. Many would come to the temple just to see her perform. Unfortunately, not all eyes were respectful; many were lustful," She shook her head.

"But you know, whenever I watched her, she reminded me of a much purer time, many years ago," Devi Amma said, a small smile coming to her thin, dry lips. "Through your mother's dance, I felt that a spot of holiness still existed in that horrible temple. God hadn't forsaken us completely yet, while she still danced."

CHAPTER 19

There are times when tears feel so unlimited that I think I will be able to sustain the crying forever. This felt like such a time. We got off the train and walked through the village of Kotivalli toward the temple, which was just a few minutes away. I texted Nalini, letting her know it would be another couple of hours at least before I was home, and that they didn't have to wait for me for dinner—I couldn't even fathom being hungry. When we stopped walking, Devi Amma let me cry indefinitely in the shade of a tree near the temple.

When my tears paused, she finally spoke. "You are not alone, Anokhi."

"This is worse than being alone, Devi Amma. Now that I know who my mother was, I feel so far away from everything and everyone I have ever known. I cannot even imagine how much she suffered," I said, wiping my face with the back of my hand.

"I know, my child," she said, nodding. "But you really are *not* alone."

"What do you mean?" I sensed her words held a potential hidden meaning and were not merely a standard expression of sympathy and acknowledgment about the general existence of other souls.

"I have not told you anything about your father, yet."

The air stilled. I caught my breath. *My father?*

Funnily, I had not thought at all about my father until now. I had been so consumed with Shaila, my mother—Shaila, the devadasi. I had just taken a harrowing, yet brief, look into her past, a past that I would never come close to seeing except in those apparitions in my head.

But now that Devi Amma mentioned my father, a nauseating thought tugged at me, though I couldn't bring myself to say it. Had my father been just another one of the horrible men who had used my mother? How did Devi Amma even know who my father was?

"Is he—"

"Alive, yes," she said, incorrectly anticipating my question but still surprising me. "As far as I know, yes."

"Who is he? Where is he?" I asked, desperation lining my voice. I didn't know if I would be scared, angry, or happy to hear more about him, based on everything she had just told me about Shaila.

"I will tell you, my child. But slowly. He does not even know that he has a daughter." She gestured down the road with a nod. "Let's go eat something. I will tell you then, while we sit."

My father was a doctor, Devi Amma told me over steaming hot *aloo parathas* at the only hotel we could find. There wasn't much in this little village, which was dominated by the temple. But there was this one hotel, where we sat at a fly-covered table on red plastic chairs. We were the only patrons.

"So where is he now?" I asked, pushing my plate aside. I

was not hungry but forced myself to eat a few bites, as I hadn't eaten in hours and it was almost six o'clock in the evening.

Wind rustled through a cluster of trees outside the restaurant as though anxious to hear what she had to say. "When your mother died, he left. He couldn't stand to be here anymore. He is a doctor—a great one, at that. He had been regularly coming to this village to take care of the girls and their children at the temple, but then he just stopped coming one day after she died. He only told me that he was leaving to return to his hometown. I was like a mother for him here," she said, sipping steaming chai from a steel tumbler.

My father, a doctor. It was so . . . different from what she had just told me about my mother. I felt my body relax a little bit. So far, though she hadn't said much, I wasn't getting the picture that he was just another horrible man who used women. "Where did he go?"

"To Hyderabad. His parents are from there, and he decided to go back and work there. The pain of this place, of this entire state, was too much for him to handle. He wanted to get far away."

Another city? I was surprised that my only reaction was exhaustion. This meant I would have to go to Hyderabad now, to seek out another potential ghost from my past: my father, if he was truly still alive. If he was even someone I wanted to know. I wasn't even sure yet that he was a good man in Shaila's past. I waited for her to go on.

"Dr. C. K. Narayan," Devi Amma said, enunciating his name slowly, rolling the *r* at the end of "doctor." "He was a good man. I always loved him like a son."

The dread in my heart settled a bit more upon hearing her say this. I leaned back in my chair, listening intently.

"He came here every week from Chennai to volunteer. Many of the children and the girls, the devadasis, were ill or became ill. It's not hard to imagine how, given the lifestyles they had to lead. He hated the system. He had tried numerous times to report it to the local police, but of course they did nothing. They received their bribes from the temple priest, so who were they to cause any problems when it served them to keep their mouths shut? It made him very angry.

"He gave them medicines, and he tried to teach them about safety and hygiene. He would sometimes teach the younger girls how to read and write, as he felt that the next best thing he could offer, after medical care, was education. He taught me too! That is how I learned English. You must see how many books he brought for me.

"'Amma,' he would say, 'you've got the brightest eyes I've ever seen. You have an incredible brain up there. You must learn to read; there is so much you would enjoy.'" She smiled with fondness as she remembered him.

"So how is it that he and my mother—how did they—I mean, wasn't she just one of the young girls he treated?" I felt disgusted with how all these thoughts were trying to come to-gether, and I didn't quite understand how I was born from all this, literally.

Devi Amma shook her head and clicked her tongue.

"No, no, no," she chided, as if it were the most obvious thing, "it was not at all like that. Your mother was twenty when they first met. She had already spent more than half her life in the temple. She was perhaps how old you are now. He must not have been much older, also in his twenties. He was a young doctor. And your mother was in the height of her danc-ing. She had become very good, and so busy with dance that they had allowed her to leave her . . . other work." Devi Amma grimaced. "Shaila showed a natural inclination toward dance, and Ram Baba let her travel to Chidambaram once a year for the dance festival to learn whatever she could from watching the famous dancers perform. But she always returned, because

Ram Baba had instilled such a sense of fear in her, right from a young age, that he would stop sending her parents money and they would all come after her. She never dreamed of running away." Now Devi Amma furrowed her brow with great conviction. Through her passionate tone, I could tell she really had loved my mother very much.

"She spent so much time dancing and practicing in the temple that she had less time to be given away to men. Ram Baba even discouraged it—she was the prized dancer, who brought flocks of devotees—and more lustful men—to the temple, and thus charity, and more business for the other girls, so he did not want your mother's health to suffer from being overfatigued. Ironically, her love for dancing, as pure as it was, saved her from the fates of many of the other girls.

"It was around then that your father started coming here to Kotivalli to volunteer his time as a doctor. I suppose he had heard about this village and the heavy concentration of devadasi girls here, and how many of them were falling sick and dying from infections. It was a constant problem." Devi Amma shook her head in disgust.

"Your mother was always bright. She would go talk to Doctorji—that's what everyone used to call your father— in her free time and ask him many, many questions. Your mother knew Tamil, of course, and had also picked up Hindi over the years. Doctorji taught her English too, and she learned so quickly that she helped him teach the younger girls as well."

I tried to imagine these two people from this impossible time falling in love. Then I tried to imagine myself somehow connected to those two characters. But there was too much distance and too much pain. It remained only a story to my ears. Yet my heart beat faster with each detail Devi Amma shared. I wanted to fill in all the gaps, my mind previously a blank canvas when it came to my birth parents, now suddenly filled with black-and-white outlines just begging to be colored in.

"They fell in love, beti. Do not think your father was a bad man and used Shaila—he did not. I watched them, like my own children, both. I watched them grow together. They were both very intelligent and kind. Two drops of gold in the sea of dirt that this place had become, as more and more girls were sent here by their families. Ram Baba became a bigger and more horrid crook every day. He would make his clients pay a lot for the girls. He was running a business, not a temple. And the strangest thing, beti, is that until he died, I think he sincerely thought he was doing something good in the name of God.

"I told your mother to leave this place with Doctorji, pleaded with her to go somewhere far away. But your mother, you see, never had a childhood, and so in some ways she never really grew up. She would say, 'No, Devi Amma, he is a good man, but if I stop dancing, if I stop being a devadasi, Ram Baba will tell my father, and Appa will come find us and kill us both. Appa is an angry man, and he will be furious if he comes to know that I have run away and robbed him of his income through me. Especially after he gave me away to this life—in his eyes, an act of honor. And I cannot put Chaitanya in the way of such danger as my father's wrath.'" Devi Amma paused. "Chaitanya Krishnamurthy Narayan. That is your father's name."

Ten syllables, I counted on my fingers, repeating the name slowly in my head as I bent each finger down in count. Seeing my hands clenched at the end of his name startled me a bit, and I quickly folded them in my lap.

"Why couldn't he do something about it? I mean, if he was a doctor—"

A rush of anger appeared, and then disappeared, from her face as quickly as a flash of lightning.

"Believe me, as I said before, he tried. He told us that

devadasi institutions were long since illegal, that they had been banned by the government decades ago. He told this to Ram Baba, who always laughed it off. 'Just do your job and take care of the girls' health, and leave the business to me, okay, Doctorji?' Ram Baba would tell him. He knew your father was a good man and would not stop doing his duty to take care of the girls, so he felt no real threat from him. Doctorji talked to the police back in the city so many times, but who will listen? No one wants to come into the villages and change anything. This is far away from eyes, a different world for the city people. And most of these girls come from poor families. Who wants to help them? Out of sight, out of mind. What do their laws mean here? Nothing." She shook her head and frowned.

"But Doctorji and Ram Baba had an interesting relationship. Ram Baba allowed him to come because he didn't want the girls to become sick and die. Sick girls, dying girls, meant worse business. But he knew that Doctorji would not stop coming to take care of the girls although he was disgusted by it all. So whenever Doctorji brought this up with Ram Baba, he would just sneer and wave the doctor's words away as if they were annoying flies. 'There is nothing wrong with this,' Ram Baba would say. 'These girls belong to God. They have been sacrificed in the name of Devi. If you have no respect for this, you can leave. No one is asking you to stay.' And so, in his own twisted way, he made your father a pawn in the very system that eventually destroyed your mother."

I had run out of questions. I stared at the road outside the restaurant. Beads of sweat were dropping down the nape of my neck. I had lost my dupatta back in Chidambaram and had nothing to wipe the sweat away with. I shifted uncomfortably in my seat. All this information, all these stories from the past, had given me a sharp headache. I couldn't drink the water here, and they didn't have bottled water. Devi Amma looked at me and seemed to sense my discomfort.

"Come, let's go," she said, getting up suddenly. "I cannot bear to stay here anymore. You have seen the temple. That's enough, isn't it?" she said.

We stepped outside the restaurant. The temple was just across the road. I looked at the building. It didn't look like anything extraordinary. Much smaller than the Nataraja Temple, and less gold. Stone, with some colorful statues intermittently punctuating the gray facade. Flowers and a bit of trash on the dusty road leading to it. A few groups of people milling about. I couldn't see memories and ghosts floating in the air, through the crevices, like Devi Amma could. But I stared, as hard as I could, trying to remember this place. For whatever bad had happened here, or around here, regarding my mother, I wanted to remember it, to honor her memory.

But I had no desire to go into the temple. My head was reeling from all the sadness and suffering Devi Amma had related to me. I was too disgusted, thinking about my mother's life attached to this temple, to want to go inside it. Devi Amma seemed similarly disinclined to pay the temple a visit. In unspoken agreement, we walked slowly to the station and boarded the evening train back to Chidambaram.

"Beti, when your mother found out she was pregnant, she hid the fact from your father as long as she could. And when she began to show, she made me promise I would tell him that she had returned to her own village to be with her parents because her mother was dying. To tell your father he could not come see her because her father would kill her if he discovered that she had a male friend such as him."

This seemed bitterly ironic to me that her parents—my grandparents—would be angry to know that she had 'a male friend.' Didn't they know that she would be dealing with male after male in her life as a devadasi? I shuddered.

"But she didn't actually go home, did she?" I asked. How could she go home, pregnant, unmarried, if she knew her father would kill her? I wasn't sure my heart could handle any more news about her tragic life.

"No," Devi Amma said, "she didn't. I don't know why she didn't want your father to know she was pregnant—he would have helped her; I am sure of it. He loved her. He would have taken her away. He should have done that before."

I also wondered why she didn't tell him, though I assumed whatever her reasons were, they were shrouded in pain and fear. "But then where did she go? Where was I born?"

Devi Amma was quiet as the train rumbled along.

"Where did she go, Devi Amma?" I repeated, unsure if she had heard me. Or maybe the truth was too horrible for her to say. Where could she have gone that had stunned Devi Amma, this fierce old woman who had seen it all, into silence?

"I don't know where you were born," she finally said. "I never found out. She left one day without saying goodbye. Months went by, and I had no word from her. I had no idea where she went, beti. Then in the middle of the night, during the monsoon season, on a night when the rain was particularly heavy, I heard the sound of a baby crying loudly outside my hut. I put on my shawl and walked to the door, frightened out of sleep. I barely slept anyway, after all that had happened and since your mother's disappearance. No one ever typically visited so late at night.

"I opened the door slowly, and there was your mother, drenched, holding a small bundle in her arms. She looked like a ghost. Her hair was a mess, her eyes were sunken and hollow. She thrust the bundle—you—into my arms. I think she was already mostly dead.

"'Take her,' she whispered to me." Devi Amma took my hand. "I was so upset by her appearance, yet relieved to see her, that I tried to pull her inside, but she pushed my hand away with such force. I was surprised she had any strength left; she looked so weak. 'Take her, and give her away.' It was not a request; she was not asking for a favor. It was a command.

"'But why? It's your daughter. Why should I?' I pleaded.

"Then she spoke to me with such clarity that it seemed like God was speaking through her. 'If you do not take her to an orphanage in Chennai and help her escape this place, this life, then these people who know me will make her life miserable. Then God will curse you, and me, and all of us, for not protecting this innocent child while we had the chance.'

"I could not argue back. I knew she was right. So, I took you to Chennai the next day. I left very early in the morning, around four o'clock, so that no one would see me, especially not horrid Ram Baba.

"I wished I could get in touch with your father, but I had no way of contacting him. He had come faithfully for a few months after your mother disappeared, but eventually, seeing that the chances of her returning were slim, he gave up—just one or two months before she showed up at my step, with you in her arms."

I gasped softly. Had he only come to the village for a couple of more months . . . would Shaila have given me to him, to take away to the city? Perhaps I never would have been given away at all. I could have grown up with my father. I swallowed the lump in my throat—the pain of confronting the possibility of a vastly different past was too tender to fully contemplate, but impossible to ignore.

Devi Amma continued, "But, without knowing how to find him, and the risk of you being discovered in the village, I resolved I had to take you to an orphanage myself. I wasn't going to just leave you somewhere unsafe or in the hands of a total stranger. Your mother wanted only the best for you, and I needed to make sure you got as far away as possible.

"I asked some people in the train station where the good orphanages were. Thank God, you know, I really think God was looking after you very carefully that day. A tall, smart-looking young woman saw me holding you and wandering about, looking lost, and she spoke to me in Tamil. 'Is everything okay, Amma?'

"I told her what happened, all of it—because her eyes were honest. I told her that if anyone from Kotivalli or Chidambaram found out about you, in relationship to your mother, they would make your life hell, and that you could not go back to either of these places. I told her about your mother being forced into becoming a devadasi, and how she did not want that future for you. She nodded and listened closely as it all came spilling out, and she agreed that you needed to get far away from that life. Finally, she told me she was a social worker and that she worked with children in Chennai who had been taken from abusive homes. She worked to find new homes for them, often working closely with adoption centers and shelters. God led me to her, I swear. She was exactly the person who I needed to help me help you. That is why I'm telling you really, Anokhi, that God was with you that day. And always has been.

"The woman told me to go to an orphanage called Rainbows of Hope in Janaki Colony. And she told me to give her name, Vidhya Subramaniam—see, I still remember her after all these years—when I went, and to tell them that Vidhya said this was a high-priority case. That Vidhya said it is a definite transfer case. I had no idea what this meant, but I knew that woman was Shakti herself—the divine feminine energy, the goddess of creation and ultimate wisdom. I could see the strength shining through her eyes and her determination to protect you. She was working for the welfare of children, like a mother for all of them."

The train was approaching the station, and I almost wished it wasn't. I had been trying to digest all this information in such a short span of time, and I still had a million questions for

Devi Amma. But we would be getting off soon, and I could see that she wasn't finished with this part of my story.

"And it was simple, really. Without meeting Vidhya, I don't know where you would be today. Of course, I was not as old as I am now, but I was still quite old, and I did not know how to navigate the big city that well. I took you to the orphanage and said exactly what she told me to tell them. They were very kind there and gave me water and food, and they gave you milk, because they saw we were both hungry and tired. They assured me that you would be fine, that they help many children all the time, and that they would send you to Delhi, so that no one could find you here. They also confirmed they would never tell anyone where you went, because it was against the law to do so. I kissed your forehead, reluctant to let go of you, but I did because that is what Shaila asked me to do. When I got home, I prayed to Shakti all night long. Isn't it ironic that the same power, the divine feminine energy in whose name your mother was dedicated to a life of servitude, manifested differently, delivered you into the hands of freedom?"

"Can you tell me more about my mother's dancing?" I asked Devi Amma. We were now sitting outside the train station in Chidambaram, waiting for Nalini to pick me up. I had initially intended to find my way back to her house by myself but felt too weak and unsure of myself after the eventful last few hours. I had called her as the train neared the station, asking her to meet me there and assuring her I'd fill her in on my day when she did. The sky was slowly morphing into a defiant shade of gray, and I felt a drop on my forehead, but nothing after.

I had been so consumed with the details of my mother's sad existence that I hadn't asked Devi Amma more about the one joy in Shaila's life: dance. Of course, I could not so quickly forget all the hardships she had suffered that I had just learned about. But was it not my duty to ask about the memories of her happiness as well, from Devi Amma, while I had the chance? But Devi Amma needed to go home; she was clearly exhausted. So my time with her stories was quickly waning. I begged her to tell me one more thing about Shaila's dance work before Nalini arrived.

"She was quite good friends with a man, Govinda, who came to the temple to play the mridangam for festivals, and later, for your mother's dances. She was amazingly gifted, and she sang in addition to dancing. After seeing a piece just once in Chidambaram, she would come back and sing the song to Govinda, and remembering all the steps, she would perform the dance too. He would watch her footwork and play the mridangam accordingly. That's how she would teach herself—just like that." Devi Amma paused. "I just wish your mother could have actually gone to a proper dance school and learned. She would have gone so far with her dancing, and under much more respectable circumstances. She would have had a beautiful, long life ahead of her . . . I know I keep saying this, and I'm sorry. There is no use in thinking about what could have been."

I shook my head. "It's okay. Lamenting is another way of remembering, sometimes."

"My favorites were the dances she did for Krishna. Of course, the temple in Kotivalli is a Shiva temple, and she danced beautifully for Shiva too. I can see her right now. How well she could do all the Nataraja poses." Devi Amma nearly beamed as she studied the sky and reminisced. "But her Krishna dances were always the loveliest. You could really tell that she loved Krishna above all. She was living this life, going through all the motions, experiencing sorrow and pain—but savoring whatever happiness and joy she had—and I think it was her love for Krishna that kept her anchored.

"Sometimes she would go dance by the river in the

evenings. She liked to dance alone and not always in front of people. I think she preferred that, dedicating her performance solely to Mother Earth and Krishna, watching her from the sky. No music, just her, singing and dancing. I often went to wash my clothes in the river, behind one big stone, so I could watch without her knowledge. People are so beautiful when they think they are alone. They are their truest selves."

I wished Devi Amma could transfer those visual memories of my mother's dances to me, so I could see them for myself. I now believed that Shaila *was* my birth mother—there was nothing not to believe; it was the truth. I had accepted this as soon as Devi Amma had told me that I looked like Shaila—there could be no other explanation for Shaila in my head. It was strange to me that I had still been thinking of her as Shaila and not as my birth mother. To me they were still two different people: Shaila, dancing in my head, whose origins and background remained, and always would remain, somewhat unknown to me, performing against a plain backdrop or a generic scene in nature—and now, my own birth mother, whose name was Shaila but first and foremost had become Amma to me. When I thought of her this way, I could not see her face when she danced. Trying to reconcile and merge the two characters just made them seem more distinct as two separate spirits—one whom I had known all my life, and one whom I was just beginning to know now. I figured it would take years to really figure out how to blend the two together in my mind; I certainly shouldn't expect to be able to do so in a single day.

And of course I still would need to reconcile the idea of having two mothers—Sasha and Shaila.

Shrill Tamil had been blasting through the loudspeakers outside the train station as we waited for Nalini, and now Devi Amma grasped my wrist with her fingers. I could tell from her posture that she was getting tired. She had not revealed her age, but I was certain she was in her late eighties, if not nineties.

"Anokhi, I must go home. I am feeling weak. But God has blessed me today by allowing me to meet you. Take care, my child. I hope you find him, your father. Please give him my respects. God bless you," she said, kissing my forehead softly as I bent down to hug her.

My heart wanted to break. It felt so full. I wanted to take her with me. And I wanted more time with her. I wanted to ask her more questions about my mother and father, and everything she had seen over the years during her incredible and long life.

"Devi Amma," I said, a lump in my throat threatening to hold back any more words. She took me in her arms, and I melted into the warm wisdom contained in the presence of her years and the depth of her embrace. "Please. I don't want to leave you now. I . . . have so many more questions for you. How will I find my father? What does he look like?" My questions came out panicked, though I realized it was mostly because I didn't want this woman, who felt like a grandmother, to leave me.

"It's all right, my child. I am with you always. Do not feel alone. Think of me, and think of your amma, Shaila, your beautiful, brave amma. Do you really think those who are dead do not still live within us and around us?"

I knew they did. I knew Shaila was always in my mind now, and now that I knew the truth, I knew she would never leave me. An unshakable vision. The fleeting images, her brief but frequent dances, all these years. It was like a television blurring and buzzing before focusing on the right picture. The full picture, for the first time.

Amma.

Without another word, Devi Amma hobbled away from me down the dusty road, where we had just walked together several hours ago. I watched her small hunched figure move farther and farther away from me, before she disappeared around the corner after the banana cart, like an apparition I had seen in a dream.

Nalini arrived outside the train station shortly afterward. She waved at me from the auto, and I hopped in next to her with my bags.

She searched my face. "Anokhi," she said. "Where have you been? Are you all right?"

I smiled, though tears immediately began to accumulate in my eyes. "I don't know how to answer that," I said truthfully. "I have learned so much about my past today, so unexpectedly, that I hardly know what to think of anything. But . . . I am so grateful my train to Chennai got delayed."

She wrapped an arm around one of my shoulders. "Everything happens for a reason." I think she could tell I wasn't ready to talk much yet about the day, so we rode home in silence despite my earlier promise to fill her in.

Later that evening, Nalini came to my room to check on me. That's when I unloaded all that had happened that day, starting with the two men who approached me, and the mysterious old woman who saved me, and everything from there on. She listened, wide eyed, silent.

"Wow, Anokhi," she said finally. "I am so sorry. That is . . . tragic about your mother." She wiped the corners of her eyes; we had both been crying as I told her about my mother being a devadasi. Then she smirked, and I knew she knew. "So you are going to go to Hyderabad to find your father now, aren't you?"

I grinned. She listened in as I called Jasmine Aunty to let her know that I wouldn't be coming back to Delhi just yet, and she helped me find a flight for the following morning to

Hyderabad. After we hugged each other good night, I made the call my heart had been waiting to make all day. The phone rang three times before she picked up.

"Anokhi, sweetheart! How are you?" Sasha said, her voice bright and energetic. I closed my eyes and imagined her going through her morning routine at home—coffee, newspaper, breakfast, heading into the diner. Imagining her doing her routine at home brought me comfort, just as calling her did, the few times I had been able to do so during this trip.

"Sasha," I said. "My birth mother is dead." I was not ready to call Shaila my mother, or my amma, in Sasha's presence.

"Oh, Anokhi . . ." She was silent for a few moments, and the static between us through the phone connection filled the void in place of words. "I am so sorry."

"It's okay," I said. "There is so much I need to catch you up on. Today was . . . crazy. But I wanted to let you know I am going to Hyderabad tomorrow. I found out my birth father is still alive. As far as I know anyway. I'm going to try to meet him."

I heard a small gasp from her. "Oh my gosh," she said. "That is . . . amazing. Wow." I could almost hear her thinking, but I could tell she didn't really know what to say. And I didn't mind, because I hardly did either. After the failed outcomes in Delhi and Chennai, we had not talked much about this part of my trip anymore; I had mostly been updating her about the dance festival, my friendship with Nalini, and overall impressions of India.

"I have so many questions for you," she said finally. "But I cannot imagine what kind of day you had. It sounds like you found out a lot of information. I am sure you need time to process." She sniffled softly. "Hyderabad. Another city, wow. How far is that from where you are now?"

Sensible Sasha. Always knowing what I needed emotionally, even when I didn't quite know it myself, and then switching over to practical matters. I closed my eyes. I missed her. My *mother*.

We talked about the next leg of my travel journey and then prepared to hang up. "I love you," I said. "I'll keep you updated. Good night."

"Good night, sweetheart."

My sleep that night was strange. I had a long dream that made the night stretch wide like a vast river, making me wonder if I would ever reach the other shore—morning. I was standing in a corridor on a train, leaning my head out an opening where there should have been a screen or door. Metallic sounds clanged, and fleeting breezes rushed past me at a high velocity. Stars migrated across the night sky overhead, never stopping to rest, because it's always nighttime somewhere.

I didn't know whether I was going home or leaving home. But it oddly didn't seem to matter. I felt like home might just be wherever I was in any given moment, if I always had the memories of my past and my present loved ones with me. The train became calming, and I had some intuition that the train would never stop. But as I stood in the corridor, gazing out at the trees and darkened landscape whirring by, I realized that even here, at the intersection of metal and air, I had companions—the stars in the night sky, swimming above me, accompanying me on my journey, wherever it took me.

Hyderabad, Andhra Pradesh

An incomplete shadow moved behind Shaila as she danced in front of a pale pink background, rich as a lotus. Although the two figures moved at the same time, they were not completely synced. The incongruities were distracting, such as when Shaila moved her right arm and the shadow raised its left arm, then dropped it quickly and lifted its right arm. A conscious correction.

Shaila may have been wholly unaware of the shadow's presence. At one point, she glanced back, but she exhibited no change in demeanor, no trace of fear. Perhaps she could not see it.

Then the shadow stilled as Shaila's footwork picked up in pace. She did a series of complex movements, squatting and standing, lunging right and left adeptly in quick succession. Not one misplaced step, not one jingle out of time, not one sign of fatigue. The costume's fan between her legs billowed and closed with each movement, like a peacock's feathers on beautiful display repeatedly.

When she finished, she beamed. She'd danced a varnam, *a long narrative dance, that depicted the story of Krishna's childhood. Her face glowed with both sweat and happiness. She soon disappeared, but the lotus pinkness and the shadow remained. The shadow walked up slowly to the foreground, as if on a stage. There were no bells on its feet. The figure now resembled a girl.*

Then a flash of light—perhaps a wink of the sun. The lotus pink faded into white. And the shadow filled in with color and details, and I was staring at myself.

CHAPTER 20

There were at least a hundred thousand Dr. C. K. Narayans in India, according to the internet. How many in Hyderabad? Before I had left her home that morning, Nalini had wisely encouraged me to look up my father's name on my laptop. It was a weird exercise. To narrow the results, I decided to type out the full name Devi Amma had given me—Chaitanya Krishnamurthy Narayan—followed by "doctor" and "Hyderabad."

The second search result seemed promising. It pulled up a web page titled "Charity Medical Hospitals." He was listed as a staff doctor there, but there was no picture. The hospital system had several branches throughout the city, but the main branch was in a historic area called Old City. Nalini didn't know anyone who lived in Hyderabad currently, but her mother had a cousin who used to live there, so they called her for the name of a decent, safe hotel near that part of the city. I called that morning to reserve a room, promising Nalini to call her once I landed and again when I reached the hotel.

After the train ride to Chennai, the flight was short, just about an hour. When I stepped out of the airport into the hot afternoon air, I headed straight toward the autos, now more comfortable taking an auto after having done so several times already. Though I had a specific hotel destination and my cell phone fully charged, and it was also broad daylight, I still felt shaken after my encounter with the two men that had happened just yesterday.

The streets were crowded with tons of cars, and large buildings and billboards lined the roads. Like Delhi and Chennai, Hyderabad was a big, teeming metropolis that was mostly foreign to me. Here, many signs were painted in Telugu, and the curlicues and circular letters that slid into one another reminded me of Tamil. There was a lot of English on the billboards, though. The city was noisy and dusty from all the traffic. I tried to find a differentiating factor, something to set Hyderabad apart from the other cities I'd seen, but struggled to do so. My mind was also distracted by the imminent possibility of meeting my actual father, alive and breathing, and I could not feel present enough to pay close attention to my surroundings.

As we pulled up to the hotel, I felt a sense of clarity for the first time since I'd stepped onto this side of the earth. I knew why I was here. I knew where I was staying. This was also now the fourth city I had traveled to by myself. Moreover, my stay with Nalini over the past week had emboldened me with some confidence and inner peace. And of course, the encounter with Devi Amma rekindled within me a sense of purpose—to find my birth father.

After I paid the auto driver the fare, I took my backpack and suitcase up the marbled steps to the hotel, which was built into a complex with a few restaurants and shops attached to it. As I approached the stairs, I passed an old man in white sitting on a small platform with wheels, scooting himself around with his thin arms. His white kurta emphasized that his body terminated at the bottom of his torso, legs nowhere to be seen.

After staring for a bit, I quickly averted my eyes. I did not want him to know that I was staring at him like everyone else. Or was it just me, gawking at everything and anything that was astonishing, surprising, or heartbreaking, since I was still so new to the unfiltered diversity and vastness of humanity in this country?

I thought back to one of the many wise things Nalini had said to me when I was so wistful about how I didn't feel as at home in India as I'd hoped I would, having been born here, and how I also never felt like I fully belonged back in Idaho. "Anokhi," she had said on one of the afternoons that we had been walking the temple grounds, "perhaps that is why you cannot feel fully yourself anywhere: because you have pieces of your soul in different places."

I checked into the hotel and took a shower, grateful for the shower head and running water. Nalini's home had only one bathroom, and the shower head was broken, which had not bothered her and her family because they were accustomed to taking bucket baths, filling a large bucket with water and using a smaller pail to douse their bodies with it. I hadn't minded, but it wasn't until this shower that I realized how much I had missed the luxury of water running over me, where I could just stand and allow dirt and fatigue to wash off me, drop by drop, mindlessly.

Afterward, I decided that I wanted to get a late lunch. Was I procrastinating—or avoiding the next steps toward finding my father? I just didn't feel quite ready yet, I told myself. I still had to emotionally process everything that Devi Amma had told me. I spotted a big restaurant near my hotel. It took me forever to cross the busy street, and even as I waited on the side of the road to cross, I was almost hit by three different motorcycles swerving dangerously close as they tried to bypass the slower traffic, the cars and clunky yellow trucks rolling by.

Then, I felt a rough hand on my wrist. I glanced at my hand

and then down to see a young girl, perhaps only eight years old. Her nails were short and yellow, and her hair stuck out wildly in uneven tufts of red, orange, and brown. She held a naked baby on her hip who had huge, beautiful dark eyes. The baby kept slipping from her grasp while also gnawing on the girl's ragged green dress at the shoulder. The girl kept jumping lightly as she tried to hoist the baby higher on her hip, to prevent her from falling, but nonetheless, the baby continued to slowly slip. The sight was so painful that I wanted to take the baby and hold her myself. Clearly the girl was too weak to hold her.

"*Akka, akka,*" the girl whined in a raspy voice, shaking my wrist. I made no attempt to push her away. It was the first time anyone had called me akka—"sister." I had heard Priya call Nalini this before.

The girl removed her hand from my wrist and pushed her fingers together and moved them near her mouth, indicating hunger. I stared, fixated, unable to move or say a thing. Cars and motorcycles continued to whir by us, where we stood at the edge of the road, with gusts of dust occasionally blowing into our faces from the adjacent traffic. I shielded my eyes from the dust, though the girl seemed entirely unphased. She kept looking at me, putting her fingers to her mouth, and rocking the baby on her hip with her other arm.

I felt incredibly selfish for spending so little time wondering more about all these children. I could have been one of them, had my mother not given me to Devi Amma to take me away. Had Devi Amma not delivered me safely to a good orphanage. Had something gone wrong. Or even, perhaps, had Sasha chosen another child. I imagined myself in this girl's position and could barely prevent myself from sinking to my knees right there on the dusty side of the road and burying my face at her feet. It wasn't fair. Why did some children have one fate, and others such a different one?

I took some rupee notes and all my coins from my purse and took her hand in mine, placing the money there. She almost dropped a few coins, but I held my hand under hers until she had a good grasp on them while still maintaining a relatively firm hold on the baby, who was oblivious to the transaction, innocently unaware of the importance that such paper and metal has in this world.

The girl looked at me, wide eyed, for a minute. Perhaps I had given her too much—I hadn't counted. And I didn't really know how much I was supposed to give anyway. Nothing seemed like enough. Suddenly she ran off, darting through traffic like a deer on a busy highway, the baby bouncing on her hip, but secure enough, it seemed, in the girl's surprisingly strong one-armed grip. As she ran fluidly across the chaotic street, I tried to keep my eyes on her, but I lost her as she dashed across the meridian to the other side of the road and disappeared.

Once I made my way to the restaurant, I ordered a cheese sandwich and a mango lassi. I then spotted a sign advertising Wi-Fi. I pulled my laptop from my backpack and powered it on to check my email, which I hadn't done for these last couple of chaotic days.

I was shocked to open my inbox and see a new email from Kale. He never emailed me. So why this? He could have called me instead—but then again, we hadn't spoken for a few days. Our last conversation, like our others throughout my whole trip, had been somewhat stilted. I knew he was excited for me and my new adventures, but the discomfort of that conversation before I left had lingered with us, it seemed. Our last conversation also fell rather flat, and I had hung up feeling a mixture of sadness and frustration toward him.

So of course his email, dated yesterday, surprised me, especially given the blank subject line.

Anokhs, I'm coming to India. I hope that's okay with you. I know it was important to you to take this trip alone.

The truth is: I've been miserable here without you. I should have come with you when you asked me. More on that later.

My flight leaves today. I tried calling you, but your phone went to voicemail. So I hope you get this soon! Sasha told me you are now moving on to Hyderabad. I had booked my initial flight from Delhi to Chennai, but I will get it changed. I'm pasting my flight information below. I'll call you when I get to Delhi.

I can't wait to see you.

Kale

I like to think the universe doesn't hand you bits and pieces of life until you are ready. When I read his email, I knew I had never needed Kale more in my life than in that instant when I saw his words. My heart felt like it was going to melt. His words were here, on a screen he had never touched. But no matter how pixelated and computer generated they were, he was unmistakably in them. I wanted to hug the screen.

I was so excited I began to tremble. Alone in this restaurant, with the air-conditioning whirring above me and the relative silence compared to outside, my emotions thudded in my head, like beats from a subwoofer based in my heart. I quickly paid for the meal and left. The street looked different now as I navigated the intersection to walk back to my hotel. I had been feeling confused about my relationship with Kale after our last few phone calls. I didn't know how to bridge the gap I was feeling between us, physically and emotionally. But now he was coming *here*! Maybe he felt it too. Maybe he felt like we needed to be closer. There was just no other way we could be.

It was late afternoon at this point, and although I had been excited to meet my birth father, that anticipation had now been replaced by the immediate excitement of seeing my dear friend. As soon as I got back to my hotel room, I called Sasha to share my excitement. Only after two rings did I realize it was not even five in the morning there. I hung up, worried that I had woken her up, hoping that I hadn't. But she called me back a minute later.

"Anokhi? Are you okay?" Her voice was sleepy but worried.

"Mom! Kale is coming to India?!" I exclaimed, half question, half excitement. Somewhere amid the adrenaline and heartbeats, "Mom" had come tumbling out like breath no longer worth holding in.

Everything screeched to a halt as a question bombarded me. What had I been trying to prove by not calling her Mom all these years? That term of endearment had never been fully lost or taken away from me. It had just been easier to let it slip away than to question why I was letting it go in the first place.

I knew she noticed, as there was a long pause on her end. I imagined her pressing her free hand to her forehead, smiling and soaking in something that only a mother can feel after being called Mom—after over a decade of that word's absence.

"Yes! He is!" she said, returning to the pragmatic part of our conversation, which was her second nature. "Where are you right now? Are you all right?" I could tell she was disoriented from the way her speech was faltering, sleep not yet fully having released her to consciousness.

"Yes, Mom, don't worry. I'm fine. I'm in Hyderabad." The word "mom" felt full of love—a love that should never be repressed or held back—and I vowed to myself to let it gush out of my mouth as much as I needed to, even to the point of excess. For there is no such thing as excess in love.

"Hyderabad! I'm glad you reached it!" she said.

"I'm sorry I woke you up. I was just excited, and I forgot what time it was at home. We can hang up and talk later," I said, though secretly I really wanted to talk to her. I hadn't told her all the details about my encounter with Devi Amma, only that my birth mother was dead and my birth father was still alive. And my plan had been to come here and meet him.

"No, it's okay." She yawned. "I'm just going to get up. I'd love to hear more about what happened."

"I don't even know where to start, or how to condense everything, but I'll try." I took a deep breath.

"Have you found him yet?" she asked. "Your father?"

"No. I haven't. I found the hospital where he works, at least per the internet. But I just got this email from Kale saying he's coming, so . . . now I'm all distracted." I was sure she heard me gushing. "But okay, back to the other news. It started when I met this old woman in Chidambaram who told me all this." I paused, wondering whether to tell her about the two men on the side of the road who tried to attack me and how Devi Amma had saved me. But I decided I didn't really want to focus on that right now, though I did want to tell her about it eventually. "She saw me on the side of the road, near the train station. My train to Chennai had been delayed, so I was planning to stay another night in Chidambaram and take a flight today to Delhi to go back to Jasmine Aunty's house." I paused here, remembering how homesick and full of resolve to go home I had felt before finding out all this information about Shaila and my still-living father. How quickly life can change in less than a day, in ways we could have never imagined.

"Anyway, you'll never believe this. This woman, this old woman on the road, she said I looked like Shaila," I said, pausing to allow Sasha to process.

"Shaila?" she whispered. Her voice echoed disbelief.

"Yes," I said. "She *knew* Shaila. She said I looked like her. She said Shaila . . . was my mother."

We were both silent a moment. I moved to the window and opened the sheer curtain, gazing down at the busy street, the noises faded but not completely silenced through the windowpane.

I took a deep breath and told her about the devadasi story, about my mother's horrific childhood. About my father, the doctor, and their beautiful love story that grew out of impossibly sad circumstances. As I spoke, I could hear her on the other end softly crying. I found myself crying too, as I recited this story out loud. This story from the past that connected to us both, here in the present—me, their daughter, and her, my mother who raised me, because Shaila could not. The circle of life felt complex, exhausting, but finally complete.

"Anokhi," Sasha finally said, when I was done speaking and we both had a few moments to wipe our tears. "Anokhi . . . I don't even know what to say. To think you were born to such an incredible woman like her . . . She must have loved you so much. I cannot imagine how painful it was for her to have to give you away. But she did it selflessly—to save you, to give you a better life."

I nodded. "Sasha . . . Mom," I corrected myself. "I am sorry. That I have not been able to call you Mom all these years. I know that must have hurt you so much. I don't have any excuse other than that I was growing. That I was confused. But, learning about this past, though I'm nowhere close to processing it all . . . I feel like I am already more at peace. And, no matter what happens with finding my birth father, just having these answers makes me so grateful for the life I have with you. And for the sacrifices that Shaila made so that I could have a different life, a better life," I said, wiping tears from my eyes. Now, in addition to feeling guilty that I hadn't allowed her to come with me, a new guilt was surfacing. I had been so selfish, all these years, to refuse to call her Mom. Of course it was not out of malice; it came from the hurt and confused heart of a child. Though now I could not call myself a child anymore.

"Oh, Anokhi, you don't have to apologize," she said. "This is so complicated. But you know I love you no matter what you call me, right?"

"I know. Thanks, Mom." I paused. "Okay, and what is this about Kale coming? Did you talk to him before he left?"

"Yes, he just left yesterday. I dropped him off at the airport, actually. He asked for your information. He's going to call me as soon as he gets to Delhi. That boy, he's been in twists ever since you left. He's been coming for dinner multiple times a week or spending time at the restaurant after working at the store, talking to me.

"A couple of days ago, he said he couldn't take it anymore. He had to go. I don't know what's gotten into him. His father was very surprised that he was ready to just leave the store like that. But I think he was secretly glad that he was finally leaving."

"Wow," I said. I was quite surprised to hear he had been so miserable since I left. He had sounded muted and quiet the last few times we spoke, which I had assumed was residual irritation toward me for leaving him and going on this big trip by myself. It never occurred to me that his heart could be broken, just as mine had been that day when we took that walk and he acted indifferent toward my leaving. "I literally am speechless."

"I believe it," she said. The sound of coffee pouring into a cup, on her end, brought a wave of homesickness into my chest. "How long will you be staying in Hyderabad?"

"I don't know. However long it takes to find my birth father, I suppose. But I am going to wait for Kale to get here first. So maybe a couple of days at least? I'll keep you updated," I said.

"It's okay, Anokhi. I miss you, but I want you to stay there as long as you need to. I just want you to be happy. I think you have grown too big for my arms. I can't carry you anymore. And I certainly don't want to hold you back." Her voice seemed quieter now, and I wasn't sure what to make of it.

I honestly didn't know if I could ever go back to living at home, pretending like this part of the world, of *my* world, didn't exist. Or did I feel like that just because I was here, every sense bombarded by color, smell, life, and new secrets? It was so omnipresent, I couldn't imagine *not* being here. I shuddered. In one sense, I felt I would never want to leave India, because I would never want to forget this unbelievable, strange past that my eyes had just been opened to by Devi Amma. But I also intensely missed Sasha. Perhaps I would be able to go home; maybe all it would take would be physical removal to forget.

The truth was that I still had no idea where home was, and this unsettled feeling was starting to feel more like a constant to me than a reason for panic or even immediate attention.

"I love you, Mom," was all I could say at that moment. And then we hung up.

Waiting was the strangest feeling. The rest of that evening I just spent resting in the hotel room, journaling about the last few days and particularly my encounter with Devi Amma. I wanted to write everything down; I didn't want to forget a single detail about what she had told me. My notebook for *The Chronicles* was almost running out of pages, but I felt too tired, bracing myself for what was to come—seeing Kale, and then meeting my birth father—to go search for a bookstore, so I took the pad of paper on the hotel room desk and continued writing there.

That night, I fell asleep physically and mentally exhausted, but then woke up at 4:00 a.m. to my phone ringing. It was Kale!

"Hello?"

"Anokhs!" he said, his voice bright. "I'm here! In Delhi!"

I smiled and pulled the covers around me, closing my eyes in thanks. I couldn't believe he was here, in this country. Kale. So close to me—even if still a thousand miles away.

"Sorry it's a bit early," he said. "I just wanted to tell you I'm here. And that I'm taking the earliest flight to Hyderabad. I'll land there around 11:00 a.m." His words were rushed in his excitement, and it delighted me to hear him talk this way.

"That's amazing!" I hoped my sleepy voice was able to convey my enthusiasm. "I'm so glad you made it safely. It's a long flight, huh?"

"So long! But I watched a lot of movies . . . Anyway, it's so early, you should go back to sleep. I'll call you when I land in Hyderabad. And just take a taxi to your hotel, I guess?" he said.

I offered to meet him at the airport, but he insisted I rest, after the crazy last few days I had had. I laughed when he said that—my entire trip had been sort of crazy overall. Besides, I thought about how different it would be for him, as a man, to be traveling solo here compared to how it had been for me. And then I didn't feel as bad about him taking a taxi to come to the hotel. "Yes, that works." I gave him the hotel's name and location.

"See you soon, Anokhs. Sweet dreams."

I couldn't go back to sleep after that, though I tried. I eventually got up and took a long hot shower. I then went down to the restaurant to have breakfast, ordering chai and a dosa, which had become my favorite food here. Afterward, I went back to my room to wait for Kale. I felt some guilt for not using the time to explore the city, but I felt no inclination to do that, with his arrival so imminent. Plus, I would much rather travel around this new city with his company than alone. The frightening encounter with the two men in Chidambaram was still weighing on me, and my sense of caution and alertness remained higher than it had previously.

The morning went by in a blur until Kale called a little after 11:00 a.m. He had landed. I paced the hotel room, tying my hair into buns and ponytails and then taking them out in waves of indecision. I rummaged through my small suitcase, which was crammed with the new Indian clothes I had acquired along the way, and found my favorite pair of jeans and a cotton shirt at the bottom. I wanted to look like old me, when Kale saw me, for some reason. I wanted to look like I was at home, though we were so far away. I had not worn my American clothes since the first couple of days of being in India, which was about two weeks ago.

I thought again about what "home" meant to me, and why it mattered so much. I had wanted India to feel like home—felt obligated to feel that way—because I was born here. But home, I realized, was where I had lived the majority of my life. Home was Idaho. And more than Idaho, home was Sasha and Kale. I had tried to keep in touch with them during the trip, but some of those conversations hadn't gone as I'd intended. Now that Kale, of his own volition, was coming here to see me, I finally saw that I could not take him, or Sasha, for granted ever again. They both were the brick pillars in my life who would be there unwaveringly for me when I needed them. I had neglected that part of home. I had hurt that home too, by leaving. And in Kale's case, I internalized his reaction as anger at me. But he was a complex person with his own thoughts. More likely, he was conflicted about me going because it made *him* feel at odds with his obligation to stay and help his family versus his heart's desire to travel the world. I could have asked him more about what he was feeling, rather than pushing him away with silence and my own wounded ego, not wanting to traverse uncomfortable subjects.

Home is not just an abstraction about a house, a city, or any place you can expect to always be there. Home is a living, breathing entity, a tapestry of souls connected together that must be cared for. Souls that in turn care for you and give you refuge.

Kale. Kale'a. Why was I suddenly feeling such a surge of longing for him? Memories of our last meeting flooded my mind. The unsaid words, the strange parting. I went reeling back, reminiscing, like the surging rush of a waterfall, vivid memories and bits of conversation swirling. I said I was going to India. He said it wasn't so easy for him to get up and leave. I noticed the painful space he wedged between us—mere inches that felt like miles. I proudly stifled the tears that threatened to fall. I wondered how someone you love could cause you so much pain, by leaving words unspoken.

And now, there he was. Kale. Standing at the bottom of the hotel entrance, beneath my balcony, with his unmistakable brown curls. Such moments mark life indelibly like heavy ink. No matter what would happen, and whether our fates would ultimately merge or diverge, the fullness of this moment would bleed into all that followed.

I love you. You just understand the universe and its beauty, and I want to see all of it with you. You understand me, and I understand you. How could I fall in love with anyone else?

I ran downstairs, past the small reception area, and pushed open the door.

"Anokhs," he said, stepping forward but not exactly running into my arms. Still, his face lit up with a smile. I couldn't help but notice his old black backpack slung over one shoulder, the zipper yawning open, and his white earbuds hanging out. Why did he never fully zip his backpack? His smile widened but still he stood at a comfortable distance at the edge of the street. Nervous, I knew, but happy.

An auto whirred by close behind him. He startled and moved in closer, under the awning of the hotel building.

I felt the need to tell him everything and nothing all at once.

Finally, we hugged. I pressed my face to his chest and took in the smell of him—his pine-scented cologne, his sweatshirt that smelled like all his other clothes at home. He still smelled like Kale after all those hours of travel. Like home. He was home. I was home.

After he put his bags in my room, we walked outside to get lunch. We could not stop talking the whole time. About everything—his impressions of the city, from the little he had seen while coming to the hotel, his flight, and my initial thoughts on Hyderabad, which were admittedly limited as I had spent most of it in the hotel so far. We did not talk about how he decided, in the span of just a few days, to fly across the world to meet me and leave his father's store for the first time. A task he had said just weeks ago was impossible to do because of life circumstances.

I waited until we got to the restaurant to update him on everything about Devi Amma and Shaila. After we ordered our food, I told him the story. He listened wide eyed, shocked, nodding occasionally, not saying much other than an occasional "wow" or "oh my god, Anokhs." I told him that my birth father was likely existing under this same patch of smoggy sky as we were at this very moment. Kale listened intently, staring at me in a way that made me feel seen and held, as if I needed nothing else from my life.

After lunch we decided to go back to the hotel; initially we had planned to do some sightseeing, but he was feeling understandably jetlagged and tired, so I said we might as well go back and take a nap. I was ready for one too—something about the thick heat made sleeping seem like a viable option at almost any time of the day.

My room had a full bed and a pullout sofa bed. Kale made

the sofa bed silently and slowly. I had the urge to have him sleep in my bed so I could cuddle and be close to him, but I was too paralyzed by him even being there in person at all to act on that. Later, I listened to the pauses between his deep inhales and exhales change in duration, knowing that sleep had set in.

I'd been thinking only of Kale since I read his email yesterday that said he was coming to India. I felt he was with me even before he physically arrived. But the air had a distinct quality now that he was here. Souls don't just float within bodies—they coat the inner linings, dribble, and diffuse through fingertips and cheeks and collarbones and into the fistfuls of air that we find between ourselves and others in the world. I felt his soul now, in the air around me.

He ended up napping for almost three hours that afternoon. I watched him sleeping peacefully on the sofa and didn't have the heart to wake him up. Plus, I was happy to just gaze at him asleep, looking at his handsome face, his features softened and relaxed. He was growing a little bit of stubble on his prominent, handsome jaw, though it wasn't quite a true beard. I could not lie to myself anymore about how attracted I was. Distance and time had made that attraction even stronger than I remembered. I smiled and laughed quietly to myself. Kale. Oh, Kale.

We went out to dinner that evening at another restaurant, though neither of us was very hungry—time seemed really warped for both of us. He had jet lag to blame, and I had nothing to blame other than his arrival, which had pulled the ground out from beneath me and made me feel like I was floating, in the best way possible.

When we got back to the hotel that evening, we both sat on his sofa and talked more. I hugged my knees to my chest, and he draped his arm around the back of the furniture.

"Anokhs," he said, after I finished telling him a long

rendition of the days at the festival with Nalini. "I just want you to know, I'm so happy to be here with you. And I'm sorry for how that conversation went before you left."

"Oh, Kale, it's okay . . ." I said, not sure why he was apologizing but glad that he was bringing this up. It had been on my mind too, often, though neither of us had spoken about it yet.

"I was jealous of you in that moment. Your confidence, your resolve to just up and leave. It was admirable. But also scared me. I wondered if I would ever have the courage you had, to take a real step toward such a big adventure. I was always talking about it, but you just . . . did it." His eyes revealed such bare honesty I was taken aback. It had only been a couple of weeks since I had last seen him, but he had changed. He had grown. He seemed wiser, more mature. And he never usually talked about feelings openly like this.

I smiled and put my hand on his arm. It felt electric, touching his skin, and I think it surprised us both a bit, but I didn't draw back. "Kale, I know it's not an easy decision. You have a lot going on at home. But I am so, so glad you came."

I didn't sleep much that night. There were too many emotions to process, and I was afraid I would not feel every drop if I slept, and I wanted to feel all of it. I had the urge to go curl up beside Kale, but I was scared, after how surprised we both had looked when I had touched his arm, which was just meant to be a friendly gesture. Or so I thought. Were we still friends anymore? What was happening to us? It was definitely morphing into something more, at least for me, but I didn't know what words to say to Kale to bridge this gap or encourage or confirm this change. I also thought he felt it too, but I couldn't be sure, and I felt insecure wondering if I was the only one who felt this way. I tossed and turned, wondering when I would have the courage to tell him about the love I felt for him.

I finally fell asleep deeply somewhere around 3:00 a.m. When I woke up, bright light was already flooding in through the opaque white curtains. I glanced at the sofa and saw Kale sitting up, his head in his hand. To my surprise, he was gazing at me, a serene look in his soft brown eyes. When he saw my eyes open and meet his, he quickly averted his gaze to the window, before looking back at me, his eyes more alert and less dreamlike.

"Good morning, Anokhs," he said, beaming. I just then noticed that he had his shirt off; it had been pretty hot in the hotel room, despite the air-conditioning being on. I had worn a tank top and shorts to sleep. Now I found myself staring at his chest and biceps, even more toned than I had remembered them being. Then again, it had been a while since I had seen him with his shirt off. Perhaps last summer when we had gone swimming sometime? I struggled to remember but struggled more to keep my eyes away from his frame.

As if my looking at him brought some modesty about him, he quickly fished a T-shirt from his bag and threw it on, to my silent dismay.

"Good morning," I said, smiling at him as I crawled out of bed. I had a strong urge to go up and kiss him. But I forced myself to walk to the window and pull the curtains back.

"Are you ready for the day?" he asked. My back was turned, but I was pretty sure he was gazing at me.

Last night at dinner, we had talked about going to the hospital this morning to try to find my father. I was glad Kale would be with me—I wasn't sure how this encounter would go and could definitely use the emotional support.

"I guess so." I turned to face him. "I'm also really glad you're here with me."

We took turns using the bathroom to change and get ready.

The air was thick with tension, but neither of us acknowledged it, so I forced myself to switch my focus to my birth father.

The hospital and clinic were about twenty minutes by auto from the hotel. We bought breakfast at a café next door first, and sat at a small table by the window.

"What kind of doctor is your dad?" Kale asked.

"General practitioner, I think. Maybe a pediatrician," I mused, remembering what Devi Amma had told me about his work with the girls. "The hospital's website just listed him as 'staff medical doctor.' There wasn't even a picture." I sighed and dropped my face in my hands. "This could be a wild-goose chase that never ends."

"And one of your parents is at the end of it, Anokhs!" he said with confidence. "The goose chase *will* end. You are so close. In this country of over a billion people, you've narrowed it down to the right city! It will be worth it. You got this." He patted my hand with his from across the table, and then let his hand rest on mine for a couple of moments longer before withdrawing it. I looked out the window casually, though I was burning inside, willing myself not to look at him so the moment would last as long as possible.

I swirled my chai around, gulping the last dregs. I tasted the crushed tea at the end, felt the black bits of brewed leaf ooze with bitter flavor on my tongue. The door to the café was open and hot air blew inside. Though the day was young, I knew I had mango-size sweat stains already under my arms and probably patterns down my back as well where the kurta stuck to my skin. I had opted to wear Indian clothes today. I felt that perhaps this would be better for when I met my birth father, who didn't even know about me, let alone that I was from the US. Dressed like a local, our initial greeting might go more smoothly than if I wore jeans, I thought, though the moment I opened my mouth it would be clear I wasn't from here.

"Thanks," I finally said, hardly able to contain my grin.

His optimism was, as it historically had been, infectious. "And you're here to help me find the end! Shall we go?"

Kale gulped the rest of his chai loudly and then cursed as he burnt his tongue. I giggled.

We stepped outside, and I flagged down an auto, emboldened and more comfortable with Kale at my side than I'd felt while traveling alone here. An older, bald man with a thick black mustache that was peppered with gray pulled up.

"Charity Medical Hospital," I said as I started to get in.

The man narrowed his eyes. "Old City?"

"Haan," I said. I remembered looking this place up with Nalini—they had a few branches around the urban area, but that was the main location on the website where my father's name had showed up. So we might as well start there.

It was Kale's first time riding in an auto—the novelty of sitting in this little miniature vehicle, the size of a golf cart, with a closed top and open on all four sides, was as amusing to him as it had been to me during my first time. It was like driving through the city with an open-air experience, where no sound was filtered, no smell was missed, and there was a full view of everything on the street. We pointed at sights on the road and talked about the roaming cows on the streets, the skinny old men biking with unimaginably large loads attached to the backs of their bicycles, and the daring motorcycles weaving in and out of disorganized traffic.

Sitting there, laughing and talking, it was like we had never been separated, even though our two weeks apart had changed everything for me. It confirmed for me that I loved him, a fact that I could no longer hide from myself. My love now only needed to be shared with him, once I had the courage to do so. What bigger change can there be to a friendship than that?

CHAPTER 21

"I can taste India, Kale," I said, my words scattering in the hot air that slapped our faces as we whirred through traffic on our way to the Old City.

"Yeah, breakfast was good." He nodded, looking out his side of the auto, the air tossing his curls about his face gently.

"No—" I started.

"What?"

Was it worth it? Would he understand? It wasn't that I thought him lesser or incapable of understanding. I knew he'd nod and listen quietly, but I wanted more than that. I wanted my words to be buried inside him; I wanted him to experience India as I felt it. Though I knew that was asking too much. We were different people with different experiences. And yet, I wanted him to share in everything I was feeling. I wanted us to feel things together, though I couldn't articulate exactly why it was that important to me.

"I can taste *India*," I repeated.

He swiveled his head toward me. "What do you mean?"

He knew I could get like this sometimes. I felt bad, unleashing upon him in the middle of the heat, only on his second day here. But I was sometimes prone to this inability to articulate exactly what I was feeling. Prone to turning myself inside out to have my insides stare at the world with me staring at the skin that lines this body, this life. Don't we all want to know why we are who we are? Don't we all just want to be understood exactly as we are?

When I felt myself spiraling, I usually didn't want to be pulled out. Instinctively, I wanted to resist anyone who wanted to pull me out of my own self-created vortex. But Kale always pulled me out. Perhaps that was the basis of our friendship. If he let me wallow, where would we go? I usually was glad, many laughs later. But I always felt a twinge of sadness when he didn't delve into my feelings completely with me and understand all my moods.

And then there was the fact that I could be very demanding. I demanded words from him. Reactions. At other times, I demanded long, drawn-out silences. I expected him to react this way or that way, and the only reason I knew I had expectations was that he invariably failed to abide by them. Yet it wasn't until sitting there in the auto, heat splashing like a wild wave against our skin, our sticky arms just shy of touching, that I realized I had expectations of him but had never bothered to define them. So how could he do anything but fail to meet them?

Recognizing how unreasonable I could be, I repulsed myself. I also felt more acutely aware of all these unspoken needs I wanted him to meet. More than friendship. Yet none of this could make it to my lips.

Now that I had turned inward with my moody thoughts, Kale shook me out of them.

"I wonder if this is Old City? Look at that cool building over there," he said, pointing.

I looked out his side of the auto and saw a beautiful off-white structure looming directly in front of us. Four minarets, thin and exact, towered into the blue sky, which displayed handfuls of light clouds sprinkled across it like powdered sugar.

"Oh, I think that's Charminar," I said by way of a reply. "I was reading about it yesterday when I was trying to find places for us to visit while here."

"Haan," the auto driver chimed in, to our mutual surprise. "Charminar," he said, also pointing at the building. His voice was rough and throaty, and it surprised me to hear him talk. I hadn't realized he had been listening to our conversation, but I didn't mind of course. I had assumed, perhaps incorrectly, that he wouldn't understand us, just as I could barely speak to him aside from telling him where we needed to go and saying "yes" in Hindi.

As we approached, I could see that the large structure was riddled with more yellows and grays than I had seen from afar. Still, the intricacies of the architecture became more apparent. It was clearly Islamic architecture, with dome-shaped archways positioned on each of the four symmetric sides of the building, revealing the air that lingered behind and inside the building itself. I was reminded of the Qutb Minar that Jasmine Aunty had taken me to see in Delhi.

"Undar bhi jaasakthe, madam," the driver said as we drove past it.

I nodded and looked at him through the tiny rearview mirror. Nalini had told me that both Hindi and Telugu were widely spoken in Hyderabad, which I felt a bit of relief at hearing. At least I felt slightly familiar with Hindi after my rudimentary Rosetta Stone studies.

"Translate, please," Kale said, nudging me with his shoulder.

"He just said we could go inside too."

"Oh! Well, we should. It looks beautiful. But maybe after

we go find out more about your birth father, right?" he said, raising one eyebrow.

I agreed it was a good idea, and as we drove away from Charminar, I continued to study the landscape. Old City had a different vibe compared to the other parts of Hyderabad. Here, there were more pedestrians and autos and fewer cars. In addition to all the billboards and telephone poles, buildings were tightly squeezed together. Within the impossibly small yet romantic alleyways tucked between them, there were crowded, colorful markets bustling with shoppers.

Our auto stopped in front of Charity Medical Hospital. We stood at the entrance to the building, tall, thin, and white with faded blue letters on the awning. Within a minute of the auto driving away, ten little children had already flocked to our sides, their small hands cupped, pushing into our ribs. "Akka, akka . . ." they shrieked throatily, their hair ragged, mumbling other words in pleading tones in a language I could not understand.

Kale and I looked at each other, exasperated and confused. In an unexpected moment of decisiveness, I pulled a fistful of coins from my bag and gave a few to as many children as I could, though there seemed to be too many to give enough to each one. I hoped they were all together and the older children would help the younger ones. Then I took Kale's arm, hurried him up the stairs, and pushed open the entrance door.

Inside, children and adults sat in a waiting area, and a woman in a rose pink sari was seated at the receptionist desk, clicking at a computer next to a vase of white flowers. I pushed them gently away from the edge of the desk, fearing they might be easily knocked over.

"Good morning," I said. "I'm looking for Dr. C. K. Narayan."

"Do you have an appointment?" she asked, not looking up from the screen.

"No, I don't." I took a deep breath, not willing to be shooed away by this woman after having come this far. "But I really do need to see him. I'm . . . family. It's urgent."

The woman frowned a bit, and looked behind her shoulder, where a curtain was drawn closed.

"One minute," she said, getting up carefully and walking over to the curtain. She pulled it slightly open and shouted something in Telugu.

A deep-voiced reply came from the other side. She drew the small gap shut again, and came back to stand at the desk.

"Dr. Rao said he will come out to speak with you in a few minutes. Please sit down," she said, pointing at the busy waiting area.

Dr. Rao? I looked at Kale in confusion. We looked around for a seat, but there were none, so we stood, waiting in the far-left corner of the room, near an empty magazine stand. I noticed several people staring at us. I looked at Kale—with his jeans, white T-shirt, curly hair, skin color, and features so clearly not Indian. I thought we must look like a funny pair walking in here where everyone else looked unmistakably local.

A small baby girl wailed in her mother's thin arms, her copper bangles clanging as she patted the baby's head determinedly, trying to lull her to sleep. The woman stood by the wall next to us, since there were no chairs available for her either. I wondered why no one gave up their seat for this poor woman with a little baby in her arms.

"Do you mind if I wait outside?" Kale whispered to me, though I wasn't sure why he was whispering.

"That's fine." He looked uncomfortable, but I wasn't sure how much more comfort he was going to find outside. I felt bad for him. This must be a lot to encounter a day after stepping off a plane in a foreign country that he had no connections to, other than me.

My memory of seeing him standing at the bottom of the hotel entrance, my heart filled with love and relief, felt like ages ago, though it was only yesterday. How was it that relatively short time durations could feel like an eternity? And how could I feel, or even think I feel, the span of eternity in my own short human life?

A small girl with a boyish haircut came up to me shyly, her fingers held in front of her mouth. She was wearing a tattered purple-and-white checkered dress and no shoes. Behind the gaps between her fingers, I saw little white teeth taking part in a shy smile.

"Hi," I said, squatting down so that I was just slightly below eye level with her.

She buried her face in her hands. I couldn't stop smiling—she was adorable. I looked up and saw a woman sitting at the other end of the room, in a sheer white-and-green sari. Her face was dark, perhaps from sun, and her eyes weary. She stared at me.

I played with the little girl, not eliciting any words from her and not speaking myself. I played peekaboo with her, covering my eyes and opening them with a shocked expression on my face every time—a dramatic, open mouth and wide-open eyes, followed by a smile. She smiled back at me with glee. We continued our joyful, silent game until I saw a pair of black shoes at ground level, moving toward us.

I looked up. A short, thin man peered down at us over his half-moon spectacles, smiling calmly.

I stood up. "Hello."

"Hello," he said, extending his hand. I shook it. "I am Dr. Rao. I heard you were asking about Chaitanya?"

He knows his first name. I nodded, relieved. I had been worried, tainted by the experiences at the orphanages in Delhi and Chennai, that despite having looked up my father and come to this clinic, I would hit another roadblock or dead end in my search. I thanked fate that this search seemed, so far, to actually be going in the right direction.

"Yes," I said. Then, I added, "He is my father. Do you know him?"

"Your father?" he repeated, with a slight raise of his brow. "Hmm, that's interesting. Well, yes—we have been colleagues for a very long time. We went to medical school together." He looked at me intently. I wondered if he was trying to match my face with my father's. This man standing in front of me knew my father more than I did. Had known him for longer, for years. I had known him for less than four days and in name only. I wouldn't even be able to recognize him if he were in this very room. It was a peculiar, distant thought.

"He never mentioned having a daughter," he said, keeping his voice down and turning away from the crowded room. His initial smile seemed to settle down and almost shift to a frown of sorts.

"I don't think he knows about me."

His eyes widened and he cleared his throat quietly. "Ah. Well, he's working currently in a village about two hours outside of the city, called Chityala," Dr. Rao continued, taking off his glasses and wiping them with a small handkerchief. "He is one of the doctors on staff here but does go to do rural work quite frequently. Things were getting busy there, so we had to deploy a few of our city doctors there to meet the needs."

"Does he live there?" I asked.

"Not usually, but since he started working there for this temporary period, he's staying to avoid commuting. Normally he lives here."

"I see. How can I find him? Is there a train that goes to Chityala?" I asked, slight desperation in my voice. I had really hoped I wouldn't have to travel more for a while now that I was in Hyderabad. I had spent a good portion of the last two weeks commuting all over this incredibly vast country.

"There is. It will take you at least two hours by train. But . . . are you planning to go alone?" he asked, widening his eyes. "I would not recommend that if you are not . . . familiar with traveling here."

"Well . . . no. I have a friend who'll go with me," I said, pointing out the window to Kale, who was standing outside, his back to us. I understood Dr. Rao was just expressing concern for my safety, and obviously he had surmised that I didn't live here, from my accent and way of speaking.

"Okay, then," he said. "When you get there, ask for the clinic. People will know. And if you're going—when are you going?"

"As soon as possible. Today, I guess." I shrugged. I saw no point in waiting.

"Would you mind taking some things to him? I think he needs some more medicines and supplies out there. He can barely keep up with all of the kids and their needs."

The train station in Hyderabad was loud and crowded beyond sensory processing, reminding me of how I had felt when I first stepped off the train from Delhi in Chennai. Bodies squished together, pouring in and out of trains, hanging off metal bars on the sides, running to catch trains. It was not a zoo— animals are caged in zoos, often alone. Zoos are hardly chaotic. Even the cries of the animals are restrained, echoing unanswered amid the ogling human onlookers.

In contrast, in this station, everyone was in one pen, not caged yet still pressed together, shoulder to shoulder. Sweat. Humanity. It makes you wonder just how much you really love your fellow human beings, or if you only love them from a comfortable, hygienic distance.

Kale and I tried to decipher the signs in the beautiful

endlessly curly Telugu, but it was impossible. At one point, we grabbed each other's hands, as if the interlacing of fingers was necessary for finding our train. It was too hot and chaotic to stop and react to this, but in my mind, I froze. This was the first time we had ever held hands. And we didn't let go. We couldn't. For survival's sake—we couldn't lose each other.

We finally found our train, and it was only after Kale assisted me up the metallic step and we found seats that he let go of my hand. Or did I let go of his? We sat next to each other, and I kept my hand, which he had just been holding, close to me on my lap. I could not get over how right it had felt to hold his hand, wondering how it had taken us this long to do something that felt so clearly, unmistakably good for us. I glanced at him and saw him looking out the window, a sweet smile on his lips, his opposite hand held close to his chest.

Wide, sprawling green grasses greeted us in Chityala. The hot sun was scorching, unobstructed by the lack of high-rise buildings. Only a couple dozen people milled about the station. I assumed that because it was three o'clock in the afternoon, people were inside taking their chai. I had become quite used to the ritual of sipping small cups of the sweet, hot liquid at various intervals throughout the day.

When I first had chai at Jasmine Aunty's house, I instantly discovered why there were chai stalls on nearly every roadside corner. It really was indispensable in helping the hot, humid hours roll together, smoothed with sugar, encouraged by cardamom. "Let's get some chai," I said to Kale, finding it unbearable to not have some after reflecting on its supernatural qualities.

Predictably, there was a small chai cart under a nearby tree. Several men in trouser-like white dhotis hung casually around the cart, chatting with the *chaiwallah*. Their chatter faded as they stared at us approaching. I wore a nondescript salwar kameez and Kale was wearing jeans and a T-shirt. I guess that was enough for us to look peculiar to them.

I'd been stared at throughout the days I'd been in India. In Delhi, Chennai, Chidambaram, and on the trains in between—even before I was walking with the noticeably foreign-looking Kale, with his brown curly hair and bronzed skin. I wondered if the air molecules hovering around my body as I walked the streets and sat on the trains were shrieking *America, foreign, look at me!* I couldn't fathom why, when I wasn't speaking, even though I wore Indian clothes and was Indian myself, I seemed to stick out so easily.

It had to be something other than my clothes—perhaps my skin itself, perhaps the way my nose twitched at unfamiliarity, or the way my eyes were looking at this part of the world that I'd stumbled into like an open page in a book that I hadn't read fully. I wanted *someone* to mistake me for a local. I wanted this also not to be a mistake, but the truth instead. I *was* Indian. I was born here! Why was I so glaringly foreign even before I opened my mouth to reveal my American accent?

We took two small steel tumblers of chai and sipped quickly, eager to get away and let the men resume their conversation without us. Then I remembered that we needed to find out where the clinic was.

"Umm . . . clinic *kahaan hai*?" I tried in Hindi, my voice shaking.

The men looked at one another. Then one of them looked at me and simply said, "Huh?"

"Clinic . . . doctor?" I tried again, enunciating the *r* as Devi Amma had.

"Ah, doctor," one of them said, snapping his fingers in realization and then saying something quickly to one of the other men. The other man nodded, and then they both pointed toward the right of us, down a dirt road.

"Doctor," he said pointing and flicking his wrist forward a few times, indicating that we had to go farther down a bit.

I figured those were the best directions we were going to get. There didn't seem to be too many options other than to go left or right, and I was beginning to doubt whether we had even come to the right place. The streets were empty. It was the most uninhabited place I had seen in India so far. How could there be enough children here to warrant an entire clinic?

Kale and I finished our chai, nodded our heads in thanks to the men for their directions, and walked down the road to the right.

"Oh, see that cluster of white in the distance?" He pointed.

I squinted. I did see something straight ahead of us. Half a mile away? It was so tough to gauge. Everything was flat, making the white mass stick out amid the green of the grass that surrounded us along with the speckles of color standing out in the fields—workers, farmers, all around us. Women, men, children working the fields of tall grasses. A small boy wearing no clothes ran past, screaming and nibbling on a green stick—sugarcane.

"Yeah, I think I see something up there. What is it?"

"I don't know. Maybe that's the village," he said.

We continued walking for about ten minutes. As we approached, it grew clearer and clearer. Kale was right—it was the village. It was huge. Plenty of mismatched roofs jutted out, some with corrugated metal, others with thatched straw. The village lay low, flat and sprawling like the land itself. A young woman carrying an extremely heavy-looking cloth bundle on her shoulder crossed the road in front of us.

"Excuse me . . . Doctor? Clinic?" I asked. I felt stupid fragmenting my speech on purpose, yet it seemed more efficient to speak fewer words than clutter my meaning with more.

She scrunched her face and looked at me quizzically. Then, with her spare hand she pointed down the road. I followed the tip of her finger and saw a short building a few hundred feet from where we stood. It was set apart from the rest, probably because it was made from concrete.

As we covered the remaining distance, my heart began beating wildly. I swallowed. We stood outside the clinic, an unassuming, pale yellow single-story structure. I stared at it in disbelief. I couldn't believe we were actually here.

"Are you going to go in?" Kale asked finally.

I nodded, though my feet were still firmly planted.

"I'll wait out here. I think you should be alone when you meet him." He patted my shoulder and gave it a squeeze. "It's going to be okay, Anokhs. He will love you. Who wouldn't?"

I walked toward the door. Inside, the decor of the clinic completely took me by surprise. Posters of unfamiliar cartoon characters. Nature scenes that were generic yet appealing. Cheerful colors. They all achieved the desired effect on me, even though I was not a small child, imparting a vague giddy sense that everything would be okay. Despite not knowing exactly what lay ahead.

It was hot inside, but not oppressively so. The compound was huge, with chairs, desks, beds, and cabinets. Children cried, nurses bustled about, and parents milled about the entrance area nervously. At the very end of the one-room clinic, I saw a man turned away from the rest of the activity. Even from such a distance, I knew by the peculiar hunch in his shoulders, and the way his head tilted as he spoke, that it was him. His hair shone like black liquid fire, illuminated by the sunlight that came in from one of the mesh-screen-covered window holes in the wall. The many windows in the compound created a well-lit space that made it feel like it was outdoors with the bliss of shade too.

When I had first opened the door, several of the adults gathered around to look curiously at me. Their faces were wrinkled, I supposed from working long hours in the sun, and their deep brown eyes revealed a sense of wonder. Now I moved slowly through the crowd toward the man at the back of the room. I passed several beds with thin, emaciated children lying on them, their eyes limply shut as if they were too weak to keep them open. I tried not to stare at all the people I walked by, a mixture of adults and children. The whole place seemed like part clinic and part hospital, the sort of place that people would come long distances to in order to get care for their children.

When I was no more than a few inches behind the man, the young woman he was talking to fell silent and stared over his shoulder at me. He finally turned around.

It was him.

Even though I hadn't seen a picture of him online when I'd looked him up, there was no doubt in my mind this was my birth father. In that first moment, I saw surprise come over his features—his eyes became a little wide, his mouth opened slightly, and he stared at me curiously, though not unkindly. I wondered if I looked like him. I wondered if my wish to see physical similarities in his face felt easier than the daunting task of digging through conversation and the past to find personal similarities, if we had any.

He blinked, and then, it seemed with minimal effort and maximal poise, he cleared the surprise from his face, and his soft features settled into a friendly, calm expression.

"Hello," he said, raising both of his eyebrows ever so slightly as he smiled at me. He smiled with his lips closed, and it was a calm smile—not effusive, but it seemed genuine and from the heart.

"Hi," I said. I couldn't believe it was really him.

"Can I help you with something?" The sound of his English stuck out conspicuously. The room grew quiet, seas of tongues parting for our foreign conversation to fill the spaces.

"I'm—I'm Anokhi," I said. *Your daughter. You don't know me but . . . No, too blunt.*

"Hello, Anokhi," he said. His eyes were kind. They gently searched my face. I didn't know how to break the news, but his expression calmed me and gave me strength. He waited patiently for me to continue.

"I don't want to interrupt you, if you're in the middle of something." I glanced around at the room full of children and adults, nurses administering medicines, patients waiting in lines to have their vitals taken, all of whom were stealing glances at us. Immediately I felt childish for what I had said. Of course he was in the middle of something!

"Let me just finish talking to this woman," he said, looking over at the young woman who was still standing behind him. "I need to explain to her what medications her daughter needs to take. Then we can talk."

I nodded, and stepped back near the window, looking outside at the few huts on that side of the clinic. The ground was slightly sloped, made entirely from dirt. I saw Kale outside, walking around the perimeter of the compound, looking out at the fields. I tried to wave and catch his attention, but he was walking away from the window where I stood, and I didn't want to call out to him loudly and make a scene. He was looking in the other direction.

The doctor tapped my shoulder, and as I had still been looking out the window, I was a little startled. When I turned, I felt like I was seeing him for the first time again. He was tall, not quite six feet. He was lean but looked quite fit. He had a full head of neatly trimmed black hair, just beginning to show signs of gray at the roots, and no facial hair. He wore silver-rimmed glasses with a few smudges on the lenses.

"Shall we go sit in my office?" he asked, leading me away toward a small opening in the back of the large main room that I hadn't seen before. There was no door, only an archway carved into the cement. Inside, there were two red plastic chairs and a small table covered with papers, boxes, and a laptop.

"Please sit," he said.

I sat silently, trying to absorb everything—the strangeness of this present moment on the cusp of the revelation I was about to share with him.

"So, how can I help you, Anokhi?" he asked, leaning forward and clasping his hands on the table.

"Well . . . before I forget, let me give you this," I said. I opened my backpack and pulled out the plastic bag of medicines and supplies that Dr. Rao had given me in Hyderabad to bring to my father. I placed it on his desk.

He opened the bag and looked inside. He removed a small paper note that was inside and scanned it quickly, smiling as he read. "Oh, wonderful. It seems you have come by way of Dr. Rao. Thank you for bringing these," he said, placing the paper on his desk before turning his attention back to me. He looked at me closely for a moment before he continued. "I assume you know Dr. Rao, then? Is this the reason you came all the way to Chityala to see me?"

I smiled. "No . . . Well, not the main reason. I guess . . . I just don't know where to start," I admitted.

"Perhaps start with yourself," he suggested, adjusting his glasses on his face. His eyes were dark brown, like mine; his expression curious but soft. "Why is it that you have come here?"

"I'm from the US," I said.

"I assumed so," he said, smiling. "Your accent is a bit of a giveaway."

I laughed. "Yeah. I can't seem to fool many people here. Or anyone, really."

"Have you been here in India for a while?"

"About two weeks."

"Ah," he said, leaning back into his chair, taking his stethoscope from around his neck and placing it on top of one of the stacks of paper. "I take it you aren't sightseeing. I mean, if you are, you've certainly chosen an interesting location. I don't know many tourists who come to Chityala."

"No," I said, laughing again. His humor was dry and magnetic. "I came to India to . . . find my birth parents. I was adopted from here when I was a baby."

"Oh, really?" He leaned forward again, now putting his elbows on the table and resting his chin on his clasped fingers. "That's quite remarkable. Have you found them?" His eyes shone, like he was fully invested in my quest, though he had just met me. It struck me that he really had no idea who I was.

"Well, sort of," I said, regarding him closely. I waited a few moments before answering, savoring the silence. I noticed now, sitting in front of him, how his face was lined by faint wrinkles near his eyes. He was still smiling but looked tired now that he was sitting down and more relaxed, away from the bustle and endless work of the clinic room.

I looked around the office room again. It was so minimalistic, so understated. I couldn't believe this man, this doctor, who had clearly spent most of his adult life in service to others, was my birth father. I was overcome by a feeling of respect. The little I had heard of him from Devi Amma—and what I could see of him now, here in this simple, busy clinic in the middle of nowhere—was overwhelming. I was amazed that such a humble, hardworking, and giving person was one of my parents. And yet the work he was doing here was absolutely consistent with the type of work he had done years ago when he'd met Shaila, from everything Devi Amma had told me.

He waited patiently for me to explain. I didn't know what exactly I was going to say but knew it would tumble out of me quickly.

"I'm . . . your daughter," I said with a sigh, closing my eyes.

"Devi Amma told me about you, about my mother . . . Shaila."
Her name sounded foreign in front of this stranger—who was
rapidly becoming a relative, with clumsy effort and abrupt
sharing of details on my part. It hung in the air, the link from
the past that connected us in this present. "I met Devi Amma.
She told me your name. So I looked you up and came here to
meet you. She said . . . you are my father."

I opened my eyes and found that his mouth had dropped
open. It didn't suit him, that look of complete shock. In the few
minutes that I had known him, he had struck me as the sort
of man who did not show surprise often, with his steady, calm
demeanor. He seemed like someone who inherently knew that
it was good to be prepared and levelheaded in the face of the
potentially difficult moments that lay ahead in life.

This moment was clearly too much, however.

He sank back into his chair, staring at me. He took off
his glasses, wiped his eyes, and studied me. "You are . . . my
daughter?" he whispered, his voice quivering.

I nodded. I knew he wasn't asking me because he didn't believe me; asking was just his way of pinching himself to make
sure he wasn't dreaming.

"Yes," I said, barely able to utter the word of confirmation.
I started to cry, seeing him react this way. There was nothing
wrong with his reaction, but now that the words had been said,
the news delivered, I felt suspended in the air. Would he like
me? Would he even want to have a relationship with me? What
would happen from here?

I dared to look at him through my tears and found him
smiling, his eyes wet with tears, like mine. He got up from his
chair and came around the table. I stood up and faced him.

"Anokhi, I am so glad that you have come here. I . . . I don't
have words," he said. And then he extended his arms and
hugged me.

I hugged him back, holding on tightly. He smelled like

incense, its smoke looking for a home as it travels through air, diffusing with distance but never losing its essence.

"Me too . . . Dad," I said tentatively, trying out the word. It didn't feel completely right, but I also wasn't sure what to call him. And to my surprise, it didn't quite feel wrong either.

He released me from his embrace and stepped back to take a full look at me. "You know, Anokhi, I have always wanted to have children. My whole life. All the children I take care of as a doctor, I consider them my own. But . . . of course it is different, you know," he said, wiping a final tear from his cheek. His eyes glistened, and he smiled at me, beaming. "Please, call me Appa."

CHAPTER 22

Kale and I spent the rest of the afternoon in Appa's cottage, where he stayed when working in Chityala. He had given me the key to wait for him until he was done working for the day. After we had gone there and rested, mostly to escape the heat, we went back to the clinic, and he was already waiting for us outside, leaning against the building. As we approached, a broad smile came to his face, and he came walking up to the road to meet us.

"Appa," I said, feeling a bit shy as I said the word. I was still getting used to calling this man, who had turned from stranger to family so quickly, Father. "This is Kale, my best friend."

Appa reached out his hand and shook Kale's hand. "Very nice to meet you, Kale."

"Nice to meet you too, sir," Kale said. I watched them silently, wondering what they would or could or should say to each other. It felt strange, having these two people, who were like two ends of a rope connected to my heart, here together in person, tying different pieces of my life together.

"Please, call me C. K.," Appa said. "Anokhi told me you also live in Idaho, and you both met in school?"

"Yes," Kale said, shoving his hands into his pockets. "My family is from Hawai'i, but we moved to Washington when I was young, and then to Idaho about four years ago. Which is when I met Anokhi," he said, looking at me with a quick grin.

"Wonderful," Appa said. "And how are you liking India so far?"

Kale laughed. "It's amazing. So much to see and take in. I have to admit, I didn't really know what to expect. My trip here was . . . a bit last minute. I came to see Anokhi." He looked at me again thoughtfully before continuing. "Coming on this trip was a huge deal for her. I wanted to be there for her. So I took time off from work and came," he said, speaking directly to Appa but glancing at me. When he did, our eyes locked for a moment, and I felt myself blush. Hearing him describe how he had come all the way here, just for me, was touching. Though I knew as much from his gestures, hearing him say it out loud hit differently.

Appa smiled. "That's wonderful of you to come be with her. And I hope you enjoy the trip. Well, what would you guys like to do? Are you hungry?"

"Why don't you and Anokhi spend some time together," Kale offered. "I'm sure you have a lot to catch up on. C. K., perhaps I can wait inside the clinic? Is there anything I can help with there?" he asked, his eyes eager.

"Yes, of course," Appa said. "You can wait inside, perhaps the staff will need help, otherwise please feel free to go sit in my office in the back. You can look at any of the books, if you're interested, though I'll admit they are mostly medically related."

Kale nodded and walked inside.

Appa turned to me. "He seems like a very nice boy."

"Yes," I said. "He is."

"Come, let's go on a walk," Appa said. "Before it gets too dark."

The sky became brilliantly calm once evening approached. As if all the heat and exhaustion of the day had never even occurred, as if there weren't sick children lying awake in the clinic that and every night, as if the women and men didn't have to wake before sunrise and start their long days again, life on repeat. For now, the sky was tranquil, and we could only follow by example for our own temporary sanity.

He said that walking through the fields of sugarcane was his favorite thing to do in the evenings in Chityala after seeing all the patients at the clinic during the day, finishing his paperwork, and updating the files of all the children who came for help. Some came back, some never again, but the clinic staff tried to keep everything organized. He had dreams of one day making the clinic into a proper hospital, where farmworkers in all the surrounding regions who couldn't afford or otherwise manage to travel to a bigger city could bring their children for both general and more-advanced medical care. For now, this existed as a local satellite clinic and short-term stay hospital affiliated with his hospital group back in Hyderabad.

"Your mother was a beautiful dancer," Appa said, changing the subject. We talked about my encounter with Devi Amma, and all the things she told me about him and my mother. I wanted to tell him about my visions of Shaila but wasn't sure how to bring up another new piece of big information. There was so much to process on this momentous day, for both of us, and I didn't want to rush it, though I felt, and I'm sure he did too, the pressure to fill in all the years we had missed, even though there was only so much we could do today. I also wanted to savor these moments. I still could not believe, as I looked at this tall, gentle, kind man, that I had a father. That *he* was my father.

"I see her dance in my head, Appa," I finally admitted quietly.

"Really?" He turned to me and scratched his ear, furrowing his brows. Another habit of mine, origin located.

"Ever since I was a child, I've seen a woman dancing in my head. I've heard her, felt her. For years. I knew her name was Shaila from the beginning, though no one told me. And it wasn't until Devi Amma told me that my mother's name was Shaila that I found out the connection, just a couple of days ago. Before that . . . well, I thought she was just some strange phantom of my mind. I knew I wasn't imagining her. But I had no idea who she was," I confessed.

Strangely enough, it felt like a distant memory, the time before I knew Shaila's origins. It felt like there would always be this division of time in my life from here onward: before and after I found out who Shaila was.

Appa stopped, closed his eyes, and put an arm around my shoulder. When he opened his eyes, they looked more serious. Two little girls chased each other in the field, their laughter rippling toward us over the sugarcane stalks.

"I've seen your mother dancing in my head too," he said, and we continued strolling along. "Ever since the last time I saw her. I remember the day—I always will. It was November, a quiet, cloudy day. We were walking around the village, enjoying the smell of the rain, and talking about how it lifted our hearts out of the season's stickiness and renewed our energy and love for life.

"At one point it started pouring hard. We were on the outskirts of the village. That evening she seemed very peaceful, and my heart was breaking because I wanted more than anything to just run away with her, far from that place. I wanted her to leave, but she said she wouldn't, she couldn't, because she was too worried about what her father would do if he found out. His income from Ram Baba would disappear, and she was worried he would come after her. And more than that, she never felt like she could ever disobey her father.

"It used to make me so angry, but she would always tell me to be quiet when I became angry. She told me that no matter what, her parents' wishes were her parents' wishes, and she could not do anything but obey them. That's the one thing I could never understand about your mother. Brilliant and strong, inside and out. Yet that undying loyalty to parents who so mercilessly gave her away to a life of—"

I finished the sentence for him in my head. It was painful for me to think, but I knew it was impossibly painful for him to say. He, who had known her and loved her before she left his life without explanation, forever. He had held her hand, seen her lips move when she spoke, watched her feet touch the earth when she danced. Even though she was only dancing by the time she met Appa, her days of forced prostitution were probably still with her. Those days likely haunted her body and mind until the day she died.

"I went to work in Kotivalli for months after she disappeared, and I asked Devi Amma about her every week," Appa said. "I went on Fridays and came back on Sundays. It took at least half a day to travel from Chennai. Each week that year, on the train rides there, I felt my heart swell with unimaginable hope that she would be back, that I would see her leaning against the pillars at the edge of the temple, waiting for me as she used to.

"Before she left, I had normally arrived at two in the afternoon, and her bright smile would be there to greet me, a shimmering oasis in the despair and sickness around her. During that time in my life, I lived for Fridays. After she left, my heart would sink to my stomach, a deep fall that strangled my breath, whenever I went back. The pain became worse each passing week that I did not see her. Eventually, I could not keep going back. When your mother left, my heart left that place, and while at first the only thing that kept me going back was hope, my hope eventually ran out, just as a flame cannot last forever."

I was silent, listening to him relate his pain at losing my mother. I also thought about how, incredibly, at that time when she disappeared, I was growing inside her. And he had no clue.

"Over a year later, I had an extraordinarily vivid dream about your mother. She was dancing but looked troubled, and it was like a nightmare that woke me. I couldn't sleep or stop thinking about her afterward. So just based on that dream, I decided to take the train back to Kotivalli one more time.

"As the train pulled into the station, Devi Amma was standing right there on the platform, waiting for me. I don't know how she knew I was coming. Perhaps it was coincidence, but knowing her, I am sure she could sense my arrival. And what a timely arrival it was, because when our eyes met, she looked down and tried to hide her tears. But I had already seen them.

"'Doctorji,' she whimpered as I walked slowly toward her.

"'Yes, Amma, what is it?' I had asked.

"'Shaila . . . She's dead,' she whispered.

"The station emptied, the village emptied, the world emptied itself of all noise. I didn't see anyone. I saw nothing but a sad blue sky and a hot dusty earth, pressing themselves so close to one another that there was no room for anything or anyone in between. We walked together to the temple. I kept asking her how Shaila had died, but Devi Amma would not tell me. 'Wait,' she said, and we changed course and headed for her hut. She hugged me and told me to go behind it.

"There I saw a bundle of white on the ground. I have never seen snow, but I imagined it would look like this: white and pure and cold. Then I came closer and saw Shaila's face, her eyes closed, and a huge red bruise spread across her forehead like misapplied *sindoor*, marking death instead of marriage.

"'The river,' Devi Amma said, standing in the shade of a tree behind me. 'I found her in the river when I went to wash my clothes. Floating like a lotus fallen too soon.'"

I rubbed my eyes. Tears hadn't stopped falling since Appa had started describing the nightmare about Shaila that had woken him up. I knew all too well that feeling, the foreboding that came with the visions and the dread that must have filled his heart, knowing something was wrong but not knowing exactly what. Until then.

That pain of finding out she was dead must have been unbearable. I tried to discern his expression, all these years later. It was getting dark, so it was harder to see his face, but I could see that tears had stained his cheeks too. I shifted my gaze upward. The stars blinked slowly like silvery eyes.

"So you left right after that?" I asked after a long silence. We had stopped in a barren patch of land in a sea of vegetation. I remembered Devi Amma mentioning that he had never returned to Kotivalli after he found out about her death.

"After what?" he asked.

"After Amma died," I said.

"Almost," he said, looking down and drawing imperfect circles with his toe on the ground. He had kicked off his brown shoes, battered and worn out at the heels, with stuffing squeezing out from the fake leather's seams.

"After I found out, I tried to convince myself that she would have wanted me to go on caring for the other girls like her own sisters or children. But I lasted barely another day in Kotivalli after I saw her covered in the white cloth, lying lifeless behind Devi Amma's hut. Perhaps I was just weak. But I knew I could not stay any longer."

I could not call that weakness. My mother's corpse, Shaila's body, could never be tangible to me as it had been for Appa. Even though she was Shaila, my Shaila, my connection to her would always be beyond true knowing—a leap of faith. But Appa leaving Kotivalli behind forever made perfect sense. It was clear how much he had loved her—and loved her still. I could never share this pain—only listen and imperfectly recreate my own narrative of their love story, secondhand.

"I wonder why . . . Did Devi Amma never tell you about me?" I asked, suddenly curious. She had given me away to the orphanage in Chennai months before Shaila died, months before my father went back to the village looking for her again after his nightmare.

He shook his head. "I don't know why she didn't. But I cannot blame that old woman. She only ever did what was best for your mother. I cannot criticize her." His expression was still sad but now a little perplexed. "Your mother . . . For her to be pregnant with you and not be able to tell me, and not be able to live a life away from servitude . . . I cannot imagine what pain *she* went through.

"And yet, now I wish Devi Amma *had* told me. Somehow. Perhaps it is my fault. If I had kept coming to Kotivalli even after your mother disappeared . . . then whenever Shaila gave you to Devi Amma, perhaps she would have given you to me instead." He wiped his eyes. "I don't know, Anokhi. This is all in the past. But the fact that you are standing here, next to me today? I thank every god. This is beyond anything I could have ever hoped for." He wrapped his strong arms around me once again.

We stood quietly at the edge of the road, looking at the night sky together.

"Do you know how much your mother loved to dance? She once told me something so beautiful about why she dances, and I never forgot it. 'When the flute cries, the mridangam raps a sense of belonging into me, the rhythm of life. That's why I dance. If I hear my ghungroos chiming, I know my feet are moving. And if my feet are moving, my heart has to be beating. From there it's not always a clear path, but knowing I'm alive is a start.'

"Shaila had a very difficult life. Then she disappeared. And then she was dead. And to think that despite all the pain she withstood, she still could create and channel joy somehow. And *you*," he said. "I don't even have sufficient words, Anokhi. I am just so blessed you have come into my life. Your mother was incredible. And we have just met, but I have no doubt you are too."

I leaned into his tall lanky frame. I hadn't had a father my whole life. Sasha had always fulfilled all parental roles for me as well as she could. But now that I had met Appa, a piece of my heart that I never knew was missing felt restored.

As we gazed out at the endless field in this small village, I felt grateful for my father. For the pain of our pasts bringing us to this beautiful, present moment together.

The three of us returned to Hyderabad on a train the next morning. Appa had been planning to stay another two days in the village for work, but instead he called one of his partners and asked him to take over for the rest of the week so he could spend more time with me. Besides, he was too distracted by my arrival to keep working as if nothing had happened, he said.

Shortly after we got on the train, Kale fell asleep, his head leaning against the window. Appa and I sat on the berth across from him.

Appa smiled. "Poor guy. He must be jet-lagged, having only landed here three days ago."

I nodded. "Yeah, and it was a very last-minute trip, as he mentioned."

"So, what about you? What are your plans? I know you mentioned you had left school two years ago . . ."

I had told him about my leaving high school, though that piece of news was overshadowed by us catching up on the past, particularly about Amma, Shaila. It felt difficult to broach the topic of the present and future without the blanks of the past being filled in.

"Do you still want to study dance? You can stay here in India with me," Appa said. I had mentioned to him yesterday that one of the other reasons I was drawn to India was my fascination with Indian classical dance, inspired by Shaila's mystical presence in my life as I grew up.

"I don't know, Appa. I don't know where I belong, what I should do." My ears stung with shame, admitting this to my father, the doctor, who had spent so much of his life giving to and helping others with what seemed to be such clarity of purpose. I felt bad for being so directionless in comparison, knowing that at my age he was already in medical school.

"It's okay," Appa said kindly. "You have been through a lot in your childhood. And coming all the way here to try to find me . . . and your mother," he added quietly. "That is a huge decision. You are very brave and clever, clearly."

"What about you?" I asked, wanting to change the subject from me and my lack of clarity about my future. The present seemed complicated enough to deal with; I could hardly know what the future was meant to look like. "After Amma . . . did you never get married?" He had mentioned that he had always wanted children, so I assumed he didn't have any other than me.

"No," he said, a sad smile on his lips. "Never. I just . . . was never the same after I met, and lost, your mother." He glanced out the window. Fields whirred past us in the opposite direction beneath the hazy gray late-morning sky.

I nodded. It made sense. He did seem like he had been, and still was, deeply in love with my mother. I couldn't imagine the emptiness and sadness that filled him when she disappeared and later when he found out she had died and would never return.

I thought again about his offer to stay with him here, if I wanted to pursue dance. But in that moment, I began to think about Sasha and felt my heart pull. This was the longest I had ever been apart from her. She was my mother. And she had raised me. It didn't feel right for me to come here and then stay indefinitely.

I looked at Kale too, sleeping peacefully against the window. If I chose to stay here, he would go back. He couldn't stay here. My heart felt like it was being stretched apart. How could I possibly choose between returning to the two people I loved most, and staying here and getting to know this father I miraculously now had after eighteen years of not knowing what having a father could feel like?

I wished I could live in the ocean, because choosing between going back to Idaho and staying here in India seemed too much. There was sacrifice on both shores. Obviously, I would have to decide about whether I stayed longer in India or went back to Idaho soon. I wished, in some way, that there would be signs to guide me. Or a story to tell me which was the right path.

I thought about the many mythological tales I had seen reenacted through dances at Natyanjali. Myths were often oversimplified truths and morals, but every human emotion was encapsulated in the characters and their fates. Our stories aren't always clear-cut, and we don't all have epic poems written about our fate to guide us. But still, I found that the stories I learned at Natyanjali offered so much insight into the human condition, and I found myself reflecting on them from time to time as my trip had continued.

I especially reflected on Krishna. I felt a flutter when I realized that he also grew up with adoring parents who were not biologically his own yet who loved him dearly, while his birth parents, Vasudev and Devaki, wilted away in a prison until he finally freed them years later. Krishna, living a life among mortals as a god, cried tears of both pain and joy, but always with a certain type of cosmic knowing. Why couldn't we mortals be detached, content with whatever fates rolled upon us like the plains rolling outside the train window?

Kale woke up from his nap and looked at me after rubbing his eyes.

"What about you, Kale?" Appa asked, looking at him. "What are your plans? Are you planning to stay in India for a while?"

Kale smiled at both of us, his eyes still sleepy. "Not really. I'll probably go back home," Kale said.

His answer shocked me, though it was perfectly reasonable. Now that I was with Appa, where did that leave Kale? I didn't blame him, but I felt panic set in. I felt a knocking at a door somewhere within me.

Don't let him go again.

Did this mean I had to go back to Idaho with him?

Appa and Kale continued to chat; Appa asked where Kale worked, what his parents did for a living, whether he had any siblings, and other questions that sounded typically fatherlike. I closed my eyes to reflect on—or maybe to avoid—Kale's answer to Appa's first question. Shaila appeared, this time dancing without music. I peeked at Appa to see if he also saw her, but he was completely engaged with Kale. Apparently, we did not see her at the same time, a theory which had been perco-lating in my mind and which I now considered disproven.

Through her dance, it was clear to me that she was tell-ing me not to let Kale go without telling him how I felt. Shaila portrayed a woman, then a man. She showed the man walking away and the woman standing on the edge, holding her hand out, looking at the man as he walked away. The man turned around, calling out to her, waiting, as she stood on the preci-pice, her face confused. Eventually, she twirled and twirled in the direction of the man and ultimately twirled out of sight, following the man in the direction he walked.

I knew she wasn't just telling me to follow him. Somehow, without words, she was telling me that more than the physical decision of leaving him or going back home with him, I had to make an emotional decision about being with him. I felt she was telling me that soon I would need to tell Kale what I felt for him.

It was incredible, now that I knew that Shaila was my birth mother, how her dances were like motherly advice from some celestial plane. She was gone, but she never *really* was gone, was she?

What would Sasha tell me? I'd never shared many of my feelings toward Kale with her. If I did, perhaps she would sur-prise me and give me the advice I needed. Perhaps she would encourage me to tell him how I felt too.

After integrating into my mind that Shaila was my birth mother, it seemed like having an amma and a mom—Sasha—was how it was always meant to be. Shaila had been with me throughout my childhood, like a mother too; I had just never seen her in that light. I wondered now if I had grown up with more love than I had realized. My amma and my mom had both filled different spaces in my heart and made my life richer.

I might never know why Shaila appeared to me, and in a way, I didn't want to fully understand. Shaila had always represented magic to me, and now that I knew she appeared to Appa as well, I was convinced there was some powerful element beyond my comprehension for how and why she came to us. Perhaps, as we were her family, she never wanted to fully leave us, although she could not physically be with us anymore. I imagined what Nalini would say and leaned into the notion of faith I had learned about through her, accepting that however Shaila appeared to me, it was for a reason, and that reason was rooted in love.

I contemplated what Sasha might say if I decided to extend my stay in India. I knew she would be sad but also would be understanding. I had known from the beginning that she supported my decision to come here and look for my birth parents, though it caused her pain, and my belief about that hadn't changed. Going forward, I knew she would continue to want what was best for me. She was so pure, always dictated by the simplest principles. *Dear Mom, why can't we all be well rounded and without jagged edges, like you?*

CHAPTER 23

When we arrived back in Hyderabad, Appa hailed an auto and we all went to his home, a simple two-bedroom apartment about twenty minutes from the station. Outside his complex, the main road was thriving in all its usual early-evening business. Appa let us inside, and we put our bags down in the living area.

"I need to run to the hospital for a bit to drop off some papers. I have a few patients to see too, since my other partner went to the village in my place, but I'll come home as soon as I can. Why don't you both go rest and then we'll have dinner and I can take you around the city when I get back?" Appa kissed me on the forehead as he picked up his things and headed for the door.

Kale and I went out to the balcony to take in the view beneath the foggy, pale blue sky. I wasn't wearing chappals, and the marble on the balcony was markedly different from the floor inside the flat. It was hot, and I jumped slightly when I first stepped on it.

"You all right?" Kale asked, leaning against the railing,

concern lining his handsome face. He looked well rested after his long nap on the train.

"Yeah." I propped my elbows on the railing and rested my chin in my hands.

"Anokhi . . . I need to ask you something," he said.

I waited, unsure whether I should turn to look at him. I finally did and found his expression earnest and open.

"Do you want me to stay or leave? I can do either." His question caught me off guard, and before I could think of a reply, he went on. "I mean it. Dad said whenever I get back the store will be there waiting for me with all the work. But he said no rush in coming back. He said he'd secretly been hoping I'd do something crazy like this and just up and leave . . . Said it wasn't healthy for me to just stick around obediently for so long. At least *he* wouldn't, if he were me." Kale laughed, rolling his eyes affectionately as he recalled his dad's words.

I laughed too as I pictured Mr. Kealoha saying this. It wasn't hard to imagine. But my laugh was a tentative one now that Kale was putting the proverbial ball in my court—it was a ball of nervous energy, with my stomach serving as the court. It had felt so natural, so effortless, to have him by my side during this part of the trip as I searched for my birth father. Being with Kale had made me feel at home. Though I didn't know where my *physical* home was anymore, I knew being with Kale made me feel emotionally at home. That much was clear.

But I felt so shy, so strange, trying to admit this to him. I didn't know why, because I never held anything back from Kale. Anything except my feelings for him, that is.

"What does your heart tell you to do?" I asked. *Don't let me be the reason that you stay or leave; I won't decide whether to stay or leave because of you either,* I wanted to say. But that didn't feel fair to him or feasible for me. After the last couple of days, I knew I didn't want to be apart from him.

Kale sighed. "Oh, Anokhs." He shook his head, and his curls bobbled gently around his face. He rested his hands on the railing. "Do you love me?"

My chin slipped from my hands. My cheeks burned. His were flushed too.

If I had thought of the dances from Natyanjali at that moment, I'd have remembered all the emotions, the expressiveness, the lack of inhibition. I'd have reflected on how the power, the beauty, and the strength from those dances could have lifted me out from my fear and vulnerability. But at a time like this, with someone I loved earnestly asking me if I loved them—which was a first for me—my mind felt too mushy to consider all that I had learned, all the wisdom I had gained on this journey. What eventually pushed me to respond was my memory of Nalini and her comforting words that she believed I had good things coming for me. But also that I would have to manifest that strength and goodness for myself. I took a deep breath.

"Yes, Kale. Of course I love you," I said, putting my hand on his. I felt the electricity and forced myself to look into his beautiful eyes and not take my hand away. His eyes were shining, gazing upon me. "I've always loved you—first as a friend, then as much more than that. I'm so happy you are here. This had been an unforgettable, life-changing trip in so many ways, but I had missed you so much. Coming this far away . . . made me realize how much I want to be with you. I feel so much better when we are together. I don't want to be separated again." Once I had said it all, I sighed out of relief. I felt stronger and lighter, having put the words out there.

He was grinning, a boyish, happy smile. He wrapped his arms around me, and I let myself lean into him without holding back. I pressed my cheek against his strong chest, folding into him. I stayed like that for a few moments, not wanting the feeling to pass.

"I don't know exactly where I'm going next," I said, looking up at him. "But all I know is I want to learn to dance." Another admission of truth. "But I still want to be with you. That's all I know."

He brushed a few wisps of hair from my face. "That's good enough for me, Anokhs. I don't know exactly where I'm going either. But being with you sounds perfect."

His embrace tightened, and as I looked up into his eyes, I could not contain my smile. Until he leaned down and kissed me.

It was a soft and quick kiss, and I think both of us were a little surprised that it had finally happened. We laughed a little and then pressed our foreheads together. I think we also both felt silly, now that we had said how we felt out loud, that we had waited so long for this.

We turned to face the railing, our fingers intertwined, and watched the city in silence together. An empty plot of land next to Appa's building, littered with bushes and a few huts held up by logs and spare plastic, reminded us that hardship is a part of life in whatever form it might take. But life offers its abundant joys as well. A few buildings away, I saw a woman stringing multicolored clothing on a drying line. The brilliant red, turmeric yellow, and saffron orange shone brightly against the pale white of her building. Down below, the honks and beeps of the city streets, punctuated by the occasional moo of a cow or the shout of a vendor, served as never-ending background music. The city was alive and beating, its dance of humanity carrying on, and farther in the distance, dozens of buildings formed a line against the hazy blue sky, with clouds gently passing by like waves in a sari rippling in the wind.

Time seemed to stop as Kale and I stood there, smiling, completely enthralled by the thrill and relief of sharing our love with one another for the first time out loud. For now,

Hyderabad it was. But we both knew I could dance here, or in Idaho, or somewhere entirely new. The stages and the performers might change, but the dance would always continue.

ACKNOWLEDGMENTS

I never thought I'd be writing an acknowledgments section for a novel that I wrote. I also never thought I'd be a surgeon, or a mother for that matter. Life truly is full of surprises. It's also full of relationships and interactions with people, from strangers to family, who influence and shape us in so many big and small ways. I'm thankful to everyone who helped, supported, and encouraged me to write and publish this story that is near and dear to my heart.

Almost fifteen years ago, while in college, I participated in National Novel Writing Month (NaNoWriMo), a challenge to write a 50,000-word novel over a month. Thank you to my old school friend and writing companion Amrita for inviting me to do NaNoWriMo with her, without which I would have never written the first draft of this story.

Indian classical music, dance, and Hindu mythology were important parts of my childhood. Mom, thank you for instilling in me from a young age a deep love and appreciation for these aspects of our Indian heritage and culture.

Anokhi's travels in India and her existential questions about cross-cultural belonging are in part inspired by my own childhood, growing up in the US but also spending time, including some schooling, in India, always wondering, Where do I belong? Thanks, Dad, for suggesting casually over dinner one night that I go to school in India—it was one of the most impactful experiences of my life.

To my dance teacher and guru, Smt. Veena Teli, thank you for the years you spent imparting your knowledge, love, and respect for Bharatanatyam with me as one of your lucky students. Your motivation and teaching inspired me to continually improve and eventually be ready for my arangetram. For that long lesson in hard work and perseverance I am so grateful.

To my high school English teacher, Dr. Minahan, thank you for encouraging me as an awkward, shy teenager to take myself seriously as a writer. You taught me that self-inquiry through writing is a fun and worthy way to employ one's time and mind.

To the team at Girl Friday Productions (GFP)—Kristin, Georgie, Reshma, and everyone else involved—thank you for your skill and expertise in helping me bring *Shaila's Dance* into the world to readers. To Gail Kretchmer, thank you for your insightful, thoughtful editing, which helped this story grow in so many important ways. Special thanks to my friend Preetma, who helped make this possible by introducing me to Reshma and GFP!

To all my loving family, friends, and coworkers, who I am so lucky to have in my life—thank you for asking me how my edits are going (so many edits!) and expressing interest and excitement in this book being published. Your support means more than you know, and I am proud and lucky to be able to share this with you.

To my daughter, Zara, for always asking me, "Mommy, what do you want to be when you grow up?" and before I can answer, saying, "A writer!"—thank you for reminding me that it's never really time to grow up, or give up.

Last but absolutely not least, to my husband, Tarek—any form of thank you is inadequate, because frankly, I would have never published this novel if it weren't for you. You read the first draft of this story and gave me unconditional love, support, and enthusiasm, even when (especially when) I doubted myself. You are the best husband and an even better friend. For all the countless walks, lunch dates, and conversations you've had with me (and more to come!) to ruminate on writing, life, and art—thank you and love you.

GLOSSARY

amma: term used in South India to mean "mother"

appa: term used in South India to mean "father"

arre: Hindi interjection similar to "Oh!" or "Hey!"

auto: abbreviation for "auto rickshaw," a short, three-wheeled motorized vehicle commonly used for public transportation (like a taxi) in India

beti: Hindi term for "daughter" or "young girl"

Bharatanatyam: classical dance form that is over two thousand years old, originating from the South Indian state of Tamil Nadu

chappals: flip-flops

churidar: style of pants in which the part below the knee tapers and is tight against the legs and ankles

dosa: popular savory pancake made in South India out of fermented rice and lentil batter

dupatta: long piece of versatile fabric that can be worn as a scarf, a shoulder wrap, or a veil

ghungroo: string of metallic bells sewn onto cloth and worn on the ankles of Indian classical dancers

guru: teacher—spiritual, educational, artistic, or otherwise

kurta: loose tunic worn by either men or women, which can be short (hip length) or longer; often used interchangeably with "kameez"

mudra: hand gesture symbolizing various meanings in dance

murthi: sacred image or statue of a god or deity; considered a physical embodiment of the divine

namaste: greeting with palms pressed together in "prayer hands" pose

Nataraja: another name for Shiva, meaning "Lord of Dance" or "King of Dance"

Nrithya Sabha: one of the main halls, or assemblies, at Nataraja Temple in Chidambaram, also called the Dance Hall, which is believed to be where Shiva danced his cosmic dance

pardesi: Hindi term for "foreigner"

pooja: Hindu ceremonial worship ritual

pradakshina: religious practice in which people circumambulate a sacred object or idol clockwise

pujari: Hindu temple priest

Pushpanjali: invocatory dance done at the beginning of a Bharatanatyam dance performance; it addresses God, the guru, the musicians, and the audience

raga: melodic mode or framework in Indian classical music

sabji: Indian dish made with vegetables

salwar kameez: two-part outfit commonly worn by men and women in India. "Salwar" refers to the pants, which are wide at the top and narrow at the bottom; "kameez" is a long, flowing tunic, usually knee length or longer

Shakti: the divine feminine energy or goddess

tabla: pair of hand drums from India; also a key percussion instrument in Hindustani classical music

ABOUT THE AUTHOR

Mohini Dasari is an Indian American writer and physician who grew up in New England but also spent two years as a teenager going to school in India. She trained in Bharatanatyam, the oldest Indian classical dance form, for almost a decade before performing her *arangetram*, or debut performance, at age nineteen. Mohini has always felt like she was straddling two cultures, growing up in America but identifying with a lot of the cultural and mythological aspects of India and Hinduism. Her study and love of Indian dance, and the stories that are heavily represented in it, inspired many aspects of *Shaila's Dance*. For more information, visit her website at www.mohinidasari.com or connect with her on Instagram @modawrites.